EDGED WEAPON

A GABRIEL WOLFE THRILLER
BOOK 16

ANDY MASLEN

TYTON PRESS

ALSO BY ANDY MASLEN

See the Dead Birds Fly

Playing the Devil's Music

Detective Ford

Shallow Ground

Land Rites

Plain Dead

DS Kat Ballantyne

The Seventh Girl

The Unseen Sister

The Silent Wife

The Lying Man

Other Fiction

Blood Loss – A Vampire Story

Purity Kills

You're Always With Me

Green-Eyed Mobster

In memory of Nick Youl, Denis Shore and Michael Stephenson, good men all.

'Life is neither good or evil, but only a place for good and evil.'

— Marcus Aurelius

1

He wrinkled his nose.

On this humid July morning, the stink swaddled the City of Love like a greasy padded jacket on the back of a street person.

The mayor of Paris, the city's inhabitants, and its striking refuse collectors pointed fingers at each other. But whoever was to blame, one thing was for certain. Given the stench of rotting rubbish, car fumes and dogshit, walking to work was for the poor, the stupid or *les écolos*, as the city's car-addicted inhabitants called environmentalists.

Gabriel Wolfe was none of these things. Yet still, he walked. Everywhere he could. He owned a car, but he didn't use it much in the city. Better for his blood pressure that way.

If it was too far to walk, he'd get a bus. If the bus didn't run where he wanted to go, maybe a Metro. But he found the tunnels and the noise and the crush brought forth unpleasant memories and emotions, and he tried to avoid them.

He turned into Rue des Poisonnieres. He was almost at the gym. He enjoyed his work there, helping older teenagers and young adults from the neighbourhood learn the disciplines of boxing, kung fu or karate, and not the fastest way to slit a handbag strap and mount a rolling moped driven by an accomplice.

Marc, the boss, was a former French para, so they had a background in common. After his military service Marc had joined the police for a while before going into business for himself. He'd hired Gabriel after he'd walked in off the street six months earlier and asked if he needed help.

Gabriel passed the Senegalese bakery where he bought his lunch most days. Looked in and waved to the proprietor, Amalie, who called out to him cheerfully, waving a chubby hand decked in gold rings.

'*Bonjour Gaby! Ça va?*'

He returned her greeting and spoke in the local dialect.

'I'll be in for a coffee and a pig beneath the sheets later.'

Amalie made her coffee strong, but it was the thickly sliced ham and brie sandwiches on crusty *pain rustique* that kept him, and Amalie's many other customers, coming back.

She laughed.

'Have a good morning. Don't get your arse handed you by one of those little—'

The salty term she used had no direct translation into English. But it referred to a habit of eating a particularly down-home Senegalese delicacy made from parts of a chicken you wouldn't find in a Michelin-starred restaurant. Or maybe you would: Gabriel didn't spend any time on the city's great preoccupation. *Le dîner gastronomique* was not for him.

Smiling, he broke into a jog as the gym's sign came into view around a slight bend in the road.

La Route Dur

The hard road. Appropriate. The gym's members walked it every day of their lives.

A high-pitched scream shattered the calm.

'*Au secours! Au secours! Elle a été poignardée!*'

A girl calling for help. Another had been stabbed.

Gabriel spun round. The cry had come from a narrow alley. He sprinted away from the shop front, down the metre-wide lane.

The girl's screams were louder now, more desperate. He jinked right and leapt a pile of burst-open rubbish bags whose noisome contents spilled right across the alley.

He emerged into a tiny patch of burnt grass, scattered with broken glass, sun-bleached soft drinks cans and used condoms.

In the centre of the chain-linked enclosure, a girl of maybe 16 or 17, her long hair coiled on top of her head in an intricate knot of blue and gold braids, crouched beside a younger girl. Her eyes were closed and she clutched a hand across her belly.

'Oh, thank God,' the kneeling girl said, in Senegalese-accented French. 'Help her. She's my little sister. These boys took her bag. It's got her phone, her money, her student ID, everything.'

Gabriel knelt beside the supine girl, who was breathing in shallow gasps. As gently as he could, he lifted her hand away from her abdomen.

Her white top was pristine. Gabriel frowned. She opened her eyes and grinned at him.

He felt a sharp prickle at the side of his neck. Froze.

From behind him, the older girl spoke in a mocking tone.

'Your money, asshole.'—*enculé*—'Now.'

Very slowly, he raised his hands. Whatever the weapon at his throat, he could tell it was razor-edged. Despite the absence of pain, he felt the telltale tickle as blood ran down his neck.

'You can have it. It's in my pocket. I'm going to stand up so I can get it for you, OK?'

'The fuck you will!'

Gabriel stopped mid-move. The girl before him got to her feet and stepped back a few metres, presumably to watch the fun.

He held his hands wide.

'If I can't stand up, I can't get it. These jeans are too tight.'

The knife point moved across the thin skin of his throat and into his left ear. He winced. A year earlier, an ex-CIA paramilitary officer named George Mason had used the same spot as an ashtray. The burn had healed fine, but he flashed on it all the same.

'Stand up then. But if you try anything, I'm gonna lobotomise your ass, hear?'

'Loud and clear.'

'She will, too,' the younger girl crowed. 'Sandrine be like a brain surgeon.'

Moving with infinite care, Gabriel got to his feet, taking his weight equally on both legs, using his outstretched arms for balance. All the time he was ascending from the ground to a standing position, the knife point stayed lodged in his ear canal. Never mind its owner's willingness to employ her surgical skills, he didn't want to stumble and earn himself an accidental craniotomy.

'Now hand it over,' the brain surgeon said. 'No funny business.'

Sadly for her, funny business was her latest mark's stock in trade.

He reached his left hand into his pocket, which meant he naturally leaned to his right. The knife point eased free of his ear.

Then he moved, rapidly and without conscious thought. Just as his old mentor Master Zhao had taught him when Gabriel had been a wayward teenager to the despair of his parents.

He spun away from the blade and ducked right at the same time before coming up again, now face-to-face with the older girl. Her eyes widened in shock and her right arm began to move. In Gabriel's hyperaware state of being, it looked like a slow motion action replay of a mugging.

He snapped out his left hand and clamped her right wrist. His right arm came across his body and he dug his thumb and forefinger deep and hard into the triangle of flesh at the base of her thumb. The girl yelped and tried to pull away. Her fingers opened reflexively, and the knife fell, handle-first, into Gabriel's waiting hand.

The younger girl leapt onto his back and started pummelling him. He dropped to the ground and dislodged her with a violent shake Master Zhao called Wet Monkey. She landed on her back with an 'oof!', her wind knocked clean out of her.

4

Gabriel stood, never relinquishing his grip on the older girl's wrist or the knife.

'Let me go!' she yelled in his face.

He looked at the knife. He recognised it. Not this blade specifically, but its type. In fact, its name, provenance and purpose.

The weapon he'd just relieved his would-be mugger of was standard issue for British special forces. He'd carried one himself often during his time in the SAS. A Fairbairn-Sykes fighting knife, the latest iteration of a design stretching back to World War Two. A stiletto blade with a spearpoint, a slender but robust cross-guard and a slim, grippy handle that terminated in a hemispherical pommel.

But what piqued Gabriel's interest was the knife's condition. It was entirely corrosion-free, polished to a dull sheen and possessed of a keen silvery edge. This was no rust-bucket collector's piece. This was a fighting man's personal weapon. And its last owner had even had his initials engraved on the blade, just above the guard. JB.

'Where did you get this?' he demanded.

'Fuck you!' Then she threw her head back and yelled 'Rape!'

Her sister added her own shrill voice to the chorus.

But nobody came. Maybe in this part of the Eighteenth, it took more than a woman being violated for a citizen to come running. Maybe they'd grown used to the ploy. Who knew.

He shook her wrist. Not wanting to hurt her unduly. More to get her attention.

'You want money?' he said. 'Stop shouting and I'll give you some.'

She drew in another breath.

'*Ta guele!*' he hissed—Shut up!—'Fifty euros each for the answer to one question.'

They clearly weren't used to their victims offering cash for information. Both girls went silent.

'Show me!' the older one said. 'And let go of my fucking wrist, man. You damn near broke it.'

He let go. She turned to run.

'Don't you want your wallet?' he asked, holding up a brightly coloured nylon ripstop wallet.

She glared at him, breathing heavily. 'The fuck you get that?'

'Never mind. Do we have a deal or do I call the cops?'

'Fine. Show me the cash first.'

'So you can take it? I don't think so.'

Just then two tall, skinny teenaged boys appeared in the rundown little corner, their dark complexions typical of the large African population in the Eighteenth, which some called *Petite Afrique*. This part of Little Africa was known locally as *Goutte D'Or* – Drop of Gold – home to Algerians, Senegalese, Côte d'Ivoireans, Malians, Moroccans, all of whom had brought their customs, their food, their distinct dialects and created a melting pot just five kilometres from the Eiffel Tower.

'Hey, Sandrine,' one called out. 'Trouble? You want us to fuck him up?'

She snapped her head round.

'It's nothing. Misunderstanding.'

'Sure?'

'Fuck off, Freddy,' she said with a toss of her head that set a few loose, beaded braids swinging.

So she was in. That was Gabriel's take.

Once they had the little patch to themselves again, he asked her, 'Where did you get this knife?'

She pulled her chin back.

'That's it?'

'All I want. Tell me and the hundred's yours.'

As a gesture of goodwill, he withdrew a folded wad of cash from his pocket.

Her eyes widened.

'You always carry that much folding? Guys like you, it's all Apple Pay these days. That or credit card. Me and Sophy be cleverer than them, though. Show him.'

The younger girl reached into a back pocket and produced her phone. She held it up so he could see the contactless payments app on the screen.

He shrugged. 'I'm old-school, I guess.'

She narrowed her eyes, kissed her teeth.

'Old school, huh? Maybe you're off-the-grid school. What's your deal, anyway? Pulling fancy moves like you just did. You like an undercover cop or something?'

'First I'm off-grid. Then I'm a cop? No. Truth is, I just like to mind my own business and I like other people to leave me alone, too. As you may have noticed,' he couldn't resist adding.

She smiled. It felt odd. They were almost flirting.

'I got it in a shop.'

'Which shop?'

'A shop sells knives and shit.'

'Called?'

'It's called,' she fluttered her long eyelashes, 'give me half the money.'

He peeled off two twenties and a ten. Held the notes out.

She plucked them from between his fingers, which then lanced out quick as a snake strike and clamped around her fist.

'Hey!'

'Maybe you think fifty's a good morning's work and you're going to run. I still want my answer.'

'OK, OK, Jesus! It's in Biron Market. The guy's name is Luc Torpichon. Got this stupid nickname: Torpedo. He sells all this army surplus stuff.'

'What's the name of his stall?'

'It's his name, OK? He's got this old-ass soldier dummy standing guard out front. You can't miss it. Now can I have my money?'

He released her hand and held out two more twenties and another ten. She added them to the other notes in her hand and stuffed the whole lot into a pocket.

She stepped away, her 'sister' close by, then turned.

'I see you again, I'll cut you for real.'

He smiled.

'You can try.'

She must have caught something behind the smile. Her predatory grin faltered.

'You the kind of guy enjoys hurting women? *Killing* women?'

'I don't enjoy hurting anyone. Like I said, I just want to be left alone.'

She kissed her teeth a final time. Nodded to her accomplice. They sauntered away from him, into the neck of the alley, where they disappeared.

Gabriel grabbed a sheet of newsprint fluttering against the chain-link fence at the edge of the patch of scrub. The headline read,

Même à dix, le PSG triomphe.

Paris Saint-Germain had beaten Manchester United the previous evening despite having their star striker sent off. From being completely uninterested in sport, Gabriel had acquired a taste for watching the local team and had spent the previous night in a sports bar cheering on PSG against their English opponents.

Now he wrapped the breathless account of their victory around the knife before stashing it in an inside jacket pocket. Unlike his darker-skinned neighbours, he had no worries about being stopped and searched by *les flics*. But he'd have a problem if one did decide to ask him a few questions.

This old thing? I use it for peeling les carottes, *officer*.

Yeah, because *that* would work.

He checked his watch. He was late. Cursing, he hurried on towards the gym.

He glanced at the time again and almost ran straight into a thirty-something woman coming towards him down the street, wringing her hands and crying.

2

Gabriel stopped at the woman's side, taking in her red-rimmed eyes and distraught expression.

'What's the matter, *Madame?*' he asked.

'It's my little girl, Odette. We argued last night and she ran off but she didn't come home. She's only twelve.'

She kept fingering the gold crucifix at her throat.

Gabriel looked around. Surely it couldn't be a second grift inside five minutes? He could see no obvious partner. Just a handful of elderly ladies with woven rush shopping bags and a couple of equally aged men playing dominoes at a rickety cafe table on the pavement.

'Have you spoken to the police?'

Her eyes widened.

'Of course! And what do you think they said as soon as they saw me?' She adopted a gruff voice presumably meant to be a cynical male cop. It was pretty much spot on. '"She's probably off screwing her boyfriend. Stop wasting police time. Get lost before I arrest you." I pay my taxes. I am legal. I live here ten years and he treats me like shit! Maybe if I was a rich lady from uptown he'd be more polite, but I am just a poor immigrant. A laundress. I can't even take the day off to look for her. I have to work. I owe money for my business.' She pointed up the street. 'Automat Cavally on Rue Hermel.'

'Maybe she's staying with a friend. Cooling off. Trying to worry you.'

'No! We called all her friends. My husband, Youssoo, he walked our whole neighbourhood, knocking on doors. She's gone.'

The woman clutched the front of his jacket. Her eyes beseeching.

'What am I going to do? Nobody will help me find Odette.'

As gently as he could, Gabriel took her hands and disengaged her clawing fingers from his jacket. He brought them down so they stood facing each other, hands clasped. He looked into her eyes, searching for the truth.

Since leaving Honduras he'd been striving to find his purpose. Some way to give his life meaning. He was done with grand missions involving politicians, secret military installations, billionaires and shady corporations. He simply wanted to help ordinary people. People like Pera Flores, the woman he'd left behind in Santa Rosa, with whom he could easily have set up home, adopted her teenaged son, Santiago – Santi. He could have carried on farming, been a father to the boy, grown old and died there without ever looking beyond the edge of the land he farmed for corn, chillies and mangos.

Not such a bad existence. But still, some spark ran through him like wayward electricity. A call to duty. Instilled him from childhood, first by his diplomat father and then his mentor, then his military commanders and finally, Don Webster, his boss at The Department.

He nodded. This was something he could do.

'What's your name, *Madame*?'

'Marianne Diallo.'

'My name is Gabriel,' he said. 'I will help you. I have to go to work but I mean it. Automat Cavally, like the river in Côte d'Ivoire?'

She nodded, wide-eyed.

'You know it?'

He smiled. 'I once spent some time in your country. I'll call in after work, OK?'

'OK. And thank you, Gabriel. You are a good man.'

As he left her, he wondered if she'd say that if she knew the things he'd done.

3

The gym echoed to the sound of gloves smacking against leather, grunts of those working the free weights or the resistance machines, the slap of skipping ropes on mats, calls of encouragement from the trainers and the scuff of boxing boots on the canvas ring.

Gabriel nodded to Marc and a couple of the kids he recognised, then went through to the men's locker room to change. Pungent with the smell of sweat, liniment and bodyspray, it was plastered with boxing posters and official information notices. Prominent was a laminated A4 sheet that declared in bold capitals:

Les drogues sont pour les trocards.

Gabriel doubted the kids who used the gym would agree that drugs were for losers. Half of them had side hustles, or even main employment, in the trade. But Marc had explained soon after Gabriel joined the team.

'If we want city money we have to follow the city line. Personally I think the odd joint makes life a bit more bearable, but hey, you know what they say.' He gave a Gallic shrug of his massive shoulders and switched to English. 'Money talks and bullshit walks.'

Marc's American accent was so bad Gabriel had burst out laughing. But the point was made. The gym ran on donations, funding from the city and grants from charities and philanthropists. Those kind of people wanted a clean message going out on anything with their name on the letterhead.

Gabriel emerged in his kit: a faded T-shirt with the gym's name across the chest, grey marl shorts and off-brand sneakers. The kids made fun of him for his lame choice of footwear, which was fine with him. On his first morning he'd put Marc on the ground inside ten seconds and the audience had cheered wildly and that was that. He was in.

'Hey, Gaby, not like you to be late,' Marc said, coming over to greet him with a fist-bump. 'Not a problem. Just you're always Mr Punctuality.'

Gabriel explained about the attempted mugging and his encounter with Marianne.

'I said I'd help her,' he finished.

Marc said nothing at first. He surveyed the gym with its aura of organised chaos, kinetic action and frowns of concentration from those running through martial arts sets. His eyes returned to Gabriel's.

'My experience? Kids round here don't stray far. They got this real strong sense of territory, you know? Maybe they take a trip to the Nineteenth or across the Périph to Saint-Denis, but that's it. Like there's an invisible electric fence keeping them inside their own little compound.'

Gabriel nodded. The 'Périph' was the *Boulevard Périphérique*, a motorway encircling the city and dividing it off from the suburbs. He'd learned quickly how that word had wildly different meanings depending on how it was used.

When the French talked about the suburbs the way the British or Americans did, they were thinking of nice bourgeois neighbourhoods like Neuilly-sur-Seine, with its Audis and Jaguars, its wealthy inhabitants sporting Chanel or Tom Ford, Michelin-starred restaurants and chic shopping streets. Neuilly was a *banlieue aisée* – a comfortable suburb.

But there was another kind of neighbourhood. The *banlieue défavorisée* – literally the disfavoured suburb. Poor areas like La Courneuve in Saint-Denis. Only seven kilometres from the centre of Paris but it could have been a hundred, or a thousand for all the resemblance they bore. Poverty was everywhere, the real, grinding kind that left its largely immigrant residents with few opportunities and even fewer prospects. Drugs were rife, as was casual violence. The police largely preferred to leave them alone provided they stayed within those invisible electric fences.

Some of the guys, and they were mostly male, who came to the gym made the short trip across the Périph from La Courneuve or its neighbours. Marc had very few rules, but one was unbreakable. You had a beef with someone inside its four walls, you settled it in the ring.

Occasionally a blade would come into the gym in a new user's pocket, or stuck down the back of his jeans. Marc would find it, or Gabriel would, and its owner would get a single warning. Never again. Break it, you were out.

Gabriel had asked Marc about it on his first day.

'Isn't that just putting them back out there with a blade, when we're about taking them off the streets?'

And Marc had shrugged philosophically.

'Maybe, but one thing we got no shortage of is young dudes with nothing to do. I kick him out, there are ten ready to take his place. *C'est la vie, non?*'

Someone tapped Gabriel on the shoulder. He turned. Looked down. Standing in front of him, her chest protector in place, gloves laced, was the gym's star, Assa Touré. At five feet six and 53 kilos, the diminutive 19-year-old had represented France at the previous year's Olympics in Paris, reaching the quarter-finals in her weight category.

She grinned, revealing a hot pink gumshield, which she slipped out.

'Spar with me, Gaby?'

'Sure. Give me a sec.'

She nodded, and headed towards the ring.

* * *

After helping Marc clear up at the end of the day, Gabriel showered and changed then strolled out into the soupy late afternoon air to find Marianne Diallo at her place of work.

He nodded to a couple of people he knew and turned into Rue Hermel.

He smelled the laundromat before he arrived. A sweetish, soapy aroma. Fifty or so metres down the street, clouds of steam hung at street-level, puffing from a vent above the window and rendering the air hotter and wetter, if a little better smelling.

Gabriel pushed through the door, setting a bell tinkling. A couple of older Black women looked up from their laundry, regarded him suspiciously.

'Good evening, ladies,' he said with a smile. 'Laundry day?'

The skinnier of the two rolled her eyes at his lame attempt at friendliness.

'*Every* day is laundry day!'

Her friend cackled.

'Maybe he thinks we like to come here for a rest!'

'I'm looking for Marianne. Is she here?'

Their eyes narrowed. The skinny one looked away. Her friend answered.

'Marianne? Who is that?'

He held his arms wide. 'I'm not a cop, if that's what you're thinking. I met her this morning. She told me Odette had gone missing. I'm here to help.'

She stared at him. Hard. He could feel his soul being weighed in the balance. Without taking her eyes off him, she called out in a voice that could have reached the Arc de Triomphe.

'Mari! There's a guy here says he's come to help you find Odette. A *white* guy,' she added, looking hard at Gabriel, as if his offer had to be a trick of some kind.

Shaking her head, she went back to her folding. A few moments later, Marianne herself emerged from a door at the back of the shop, clutching a small pink hand towel. Her face was glistening with sweat. She looked surprised.

'You came.'

'Did you think I wouldn't?'

She finished drying her hands.

'You're not from round here. You're white. You're educated, I can tell from your accent. I think maybe you're English anyway, not even French. You're nicely dressed. Why would you help a poor laundress?'

It was a good question. And, in truth, Gabriel wasn't entirely sure of the answer. In the past, he'd helped people out of a sense of fun or excitement, because he was being paid to, or – if he were totally honest with himself – because he just fancied a scrap. None of that applied now. He tried to frame an answer that might reassure her. And maybe explain his actions to himself.

'All of that is true, Marianne. And you're an excellent observer of people, by the way.' She smiled a little at the compliment. 'I … a few years ago, my wife died. I was lost. I felt adrift. I ran away and hid as far from my old life as I could get. But it still found me. I'm trying to live a good life. You said you needed help and nobody would step up. So I stepped up.'

She had started nodding as he spoke, giving him the confidence to finish this oddly intimate confession to a total stranger. When he finished, she looked him in the eye.

'Then thank you. And I am sorry for doubting you.'

'Has Odette called?'

'No. I tried the school, her friends' mums, nothing. She's gone.'

'And your husband. Youssoo, isn't it?' She nodded. 'Has he had any luck?'

'He's been calling too. Took a day off sick from his job. He's a carer at Bichat-Claude Bernard Hospital. Nothing.'

'What time do you close?'

'Seven.'

'Could I come to see you and Youssoo this evening? I need to know all about Odette. Her friends, where she hangs out. If she's ever talked about a place she's always wanted to visit, that type of thing. Would that be OK?'

'Of course. I just can't believe you are doing this.' Her forehead creased and her eyes flicked over to the other two women who, while continuing with their laundry, were clearly listening in. 'You have to know that I have no money to pay you,' she murmured.

He shook his head. 'I don't want your money. I just want to help you find your daughter.'

'Because you want to live a good life?'

'Yes, because of that.'

She nodded. He knew she was struggling to believe that a stranger who looked like him would want to help a woman like her out of the goodness of his heart. In truth, he thought he'd struggle too if the roles were reversed. All he could do was earn her trust by acting. And, hopefully, by finding Odette.

She took out her phone and transferred her address to his. They agreed he would come to their apartment at 8.00 p.m.

As he walked home, he could feel the weight of the Fairbairn-Sykes in his inside pocket. Another mystery he wanted to solve. Army surplus stores always had a selection of edged weapons, from US Marine Corps Ka-Bars to Nazi daggers.

But he felt sure nobody who'd been issued with an FS would part with it.

Not willingly.

4

Gabriel drove slowly down the narrow street, trying to avoid the worst of the potholes, though every now and then a wheel would drop sickeningly into a crater, shaking his bones and forcing him to clamp his jaws together to avoid losing a tooth.

He would have caught a bus, but none ran into this part of the banlieue and it would have been foolish to stroll around here alone. Not because he'd be putting himself in danger, but because dealing with it would draw attention, which he was keen to avoid.

Graffiti artists had plastered their work on every available vertical surface. Mostly elaborate tags, sometimes two or more metres long, shaded in harsh disco colours: neon green, bubblegum pink, fluorescent orange, electric blue.

Occasionally, like the one he was driving past now as he looked for the Diallos' apartment block, a stunning mural covered an entire end-wall. A woman's face in profile, exaggeratedly full lips, the upper, leaf-green, the lower, coral-pink, and a dramatically sloping forehead. Dreadlocks caught up in a braid at the top of her skull. Swirls of colour emanated from her. A white thought bubble floated above her head like a vast cumulus cloud.

It enclosed the words, '*Mama Afrique t'aime*'. Mama Africa loves you.

He found the Diallos' block and pulled up at the side of the road. Parking restrictions seemed not to apply in the banlieue. No meters, yellow lines or signs of any kind. He saw few vehicles. A couple of ageing panel vans, some small and dirty hatchbacks. A couple of knobbly-tyred motorbikes leaning on their kickstands.

Climbing out, he smelled decaying rubbish, spotting black refuse sacks lolling against overflowing green bins on the street corner. Sweat, kept at bay by the aircon, broke out on his face and arms.

He started walking and was immediately assailed by a rough, adolescent voice. A boy this time, rather than the female tones that led to his morning meeting with Sandrine and Sophy earlier that day.

Gabriel stopped and turned. Two skinny Black kids in their teens were slouching towards him across the street, hopping across the larger potholes, presumably to avoid sullying their pristine sneakers. Were they the owners of the trail bikes?

'Hey, bro, got the time?' the taller of the two asked, smiling.

Not a bad technique. Ask an innocent question, arrest your mark's progress, get them answering your questions. You took control of the situation before the mark had even realised. Gabriel realised. *Fool me once*, he thought.

'I'm looking for the Diallos,' he answered, refusing to play his allotted role. 'You know where they live?'

'The fuck are they?' the other responded with an aggressive chin-jut.

'Do you or don't you?'

'No. What you doing in our manor, city boy? You lost or something?'

In a synchronised move he assumed they must have spent long hours practising, the two boys produced blades. Not serious weapons made for fighting. One was a kitchen knife with a cheap-looking red plastic handle, the other a fisherman's blade with a wooden handle. An Opinel, probably, or one of the many knockoffs. Not serious, but deadly enough in the wrong hands.

He had no time for talking, so he spun, kicked out with his right leg, paralysing the taller boy's shoulder and sending his knife clattering into the roadway metres behind him. Still moving, Gabriel danced away then feinted low and, as the second boy lunged forwards, chopped him across the wrist and snatched the knife from his limp fingers.

'Stand still motherfuckers!' he roared, dropping into the lowest street slang he could muster and roughening his voice for good measure. 'You shitheads wanna see your mamas again, you stay the fuck there till I say you can move. I see your eye blink I'm gonna take it out and make you eat it. I hear you so much as fart you gonna learn to walk with this pigsticker up your ass. Hear me?'

Wide-eyed and trembling, they stood like statues.

'Chill man!' the taller said, nursing his injured shoulder. 'Don't hurt us no more. Fuck's sake, you be like a proper mental case. Where'd you escape from, Saint-Anne?'

Gabriel grinned wildly, inwardly thanking the boy for suggesting he'd come from the famous psychiatric hospital.

'Maybe I did. Maybe my meds ran out.'

Then he straightened, dropped the crazy man act and spoke perfectly normally, upgrading his speech to a citizen of the chic neighbourhood where he actually lived. Sowing more confusion.

'You don't want trouble, lads, and as you can see, neither do I. So, how about this? I'll pay you ten each to watch my car. I get back after visiting with the Diallos and it's still here, I'll double it. I come back and its gone, or the tyres are down, or the stereo's gone, I'll come and find you. Deal?'

'Deal,' they said in unison.

He handed them a ten-euro note each and walked off towards the Diallos' block. The tactic ought to work. It had many times before.

* * *

Gabriel peered into the stainless-steel lift. The interior was a mess of graffiti, discarded fast food containers and, in a corner, a soiled nappy. The stink made his eyes water. He took the stairs.

The Diallos lived on the fifth floor. He was still breathing easily when he reached their landing. Halfway along was their apartment. He stood before a red painted door behind a metal grille, its white paint flaking, and pressed the bell.

After a few seconds, the door opened inwards. A tall, slenderly built man stood there. His dark skin glowed in the evening sunlight skimming the face of the block. He had soft, almost feminine features, with slanted eyes.

'Gabriel?' he asked, his face taut with anxiety.

'Hello. You must be Youssoo. Did Marianne tell you about me?'

He nodded. 'Come in.'

He produced a key from his pocket and unlocked the grille. Gabriel stepped back so he could push it outwards and went inside, offering his hand, which Youssoo took in a warm, bony grip.

Youssoo spent a few seconds relocking the grille and then closing and locking the front door. He led Gabriel into a small sitting room.

'Please, sit down. Marianne is just with Julie. She will be in soon.'

Gabriel sat in a wooden-framed armchair upholstered in a woven throw patterned with zigzags in muted shades of brick red and sage green.

'Odette has a sister?' he asked.

'And a brother. Julie is six, Robert is nine.'

Gabriel nodded.

'How are they coping with their big sister being missing?'

'Roberts's not too bad. We told them she's gone to stay with her grandma. But Julie's been crying. She and Odette are normally joined at the hip. I think she knows something's wrong.'

'I hope I can help find her sister before too long, then.'

Youssoo leaned forwards, clasping his long fingers between his knees.

'Look, Gabriel, please don't take this the wrong way, because I really, really appreciate you helping us find our daughter. It's just …'

'You can't understand why I offered, when I don't know you and I have nothing in common with you?'

Youssoo smiled, just a little, though the expression was fleeting, as his features settled back into the drawn face of a distraught parent.

'Something like that, I guess.'

Gabriel sighed. He prepared himself emotionally to give Youssoo a more detailed version of the story he'd told Marianne.

'I was a soldier from the age of eighteen. I fought for Queen and country. I believed my commanders when they said we were doing good. But then I did a different kind of work, and one by one, every single person I loved or cared about was taken from me. And I started to think I must have been cursed, you know? Or maybe not cursed but I was the problem.' He thumped his chest, where a familiar heaviness was forming into a dark clump of sadness. 'I was going to be a father, like you. Our first. Then both my baby and my wife were taken from me. I ran away. I hid. And still I couldn't escape death. It followed me and more people got killed. I was on the point of giving up. I was in a plane. The pilot was dead. I let it dive down towards the sea. I was ready to die. To join my wife and child. My friends, family, loved ones, former comrades. But she spoke to me. I truly believe it was her and she saved me. She said I had to find my purpose. And I realised that if I was to make any sort of peace with myself, and those I had lost, I had to spend the rest of my life helping people. Not going to war, or working for the government, or fighting battles. Just living as best as I could and when I met people, like Marianne, who needed help, I would offer it. As simple as that.'

He stopped then, brushed his eyes with the backs of his fingers. Sucked oxygen into his lungs. Waited for the other man's response. Outside the door, he became aware of a third presence.

Turned his head. Beheld Marianne standing in the doorway, her own eyes wet with tears. She came in and sat on the arm of her husband's chair, laid a hand on his shoulder.

'I am sorry,' Youssoo said. 'For doubting you. You carry such a lot of pain. I can see it now, behind your eyes. It is like at the hospital where I work. I am a carer. A cancer ward. My patients, some of them, they have that look.' He looked up at Marianne, who nodded, then back at Gabriel. 'Please tell us what you need. And will you eat with us?'

'Of course. And thank you. I would love to.'

* * *

Marianne placed a glazed clay platter on the table in the Diallos' small kitchen, which was crowded with cooking implements, bottles of hot sauce, Tupperware containers of spices, and fresh vegetables and herbs piled higgledy-piggledy in baskets, tied in bunches and dangling from hooks, or grouped each side of the gas hob.

Arranged on a heap of fluffy yellow grains were browned rectangles of what looked like tuna, their seared surfaces glossy with oil and dusted with dry spices. Chopped onions, tomatoes and green peppers were scattered liberally over the top and the whole lot was drizzled with a dark tracery of brown cooking oil.

He bent his head and inhaled.

'It smells wonderful. What is it?'

'*Garba Attiéké*,' Marianne said, mounding the pale creamy grains onto Gabriel's plate before adding several pieces of the fried fish. 'We eat it all the time in Côte d'Ivoire. Garba is tuna. We deep-fry it then add it to the attiéké.'

'Is that a grain? Like couscous?'

'Similar but better. We think, anyway,' she said, glancing at Youssoo, who nodded. 'It is made from grated cassava.'

She served herself and Youssoo before sitting.

'Do you mind if I say grace?' she asked Gabriel.

'Of course not,' he said.

24

He lowered his head and closed his eyes. He started when Youssoo and Marianne each took one of his hands, their own warm and dry in his grip.

Marianne's dropped to a low, warm cadence as she began reciting the prayer.

'Lord Jesus, our brother, we praise you for saving us. Bless us in your love as we gather in your name, and bless this meal that we share. Jesus, we praise you for ever. And thank you, Lord Jesus, for sending Gabriel to us. Like your good and holy angel, we hope and pray he will soon return to us bearing good news of the safe return of our dear Odette. Amen.'

'Amen,' the two men at the table chorused.

Gabriel took a mouthful of the food, which was delicious. He swallowed. And then he raised the subject that had brought him to the Diallos' home.

'Tell me all about Odette. Has she been in any trouble at school? With bullies, maybe? Could that be why she ran off?'

'Odette is a good girl,' Youssoo said. 'Not the cleverest, but she is a hard worker. Only …'

Marianne took up the story.

'She has fallen in with a bad group of girls. She started cutting school. Her home-room teacher called me. But what can we do? With our jobs we do not have time to keep an eye on her every hour of the day,' she said. 'When Youssoo and I are at work, we rely on our neighbours to look after the kids. Everyone round here, on the block, I mean, we help each other when we can. Like a village you know, only up instead of spread out.'

Following an intuition he'd formed listening to Marianne describe him earlier, Gabriel asked the question that had been on his mind.

'In Côte d'Ivoire, did you run a laundry there, too? Or was your job different?'

She smiled sadly.

'I was a police officer. But we were all tired of waiting to get paid because the government ran out of money again and again. That's why we came to France. I applied to the gendarmerie and the police and they laughed in my face. Said they had enough applicants already without hiring a *bamboula*.' Gabriel flinched at the derogatory word for a black African, even though it seemed to cause her no problem. 'So now I run my laundry. But at least it is my business.'

Beside her, Youssoo tightened his lips.

'Does Odette have a phone?' Gabriel asked.

'Yes, but it's switched off. It goes straight to voicemail. She never does that. She lives on her phone,' Marianne said.

They finished their meal still talking and continued for another hour. By the time he left, just after 10.00 p.m., he felt he knew Odette as well as anyone could outside her family. He had a list of her friends, although he doubted he'd get anywhere with them if Odette's parents hadn't.

His car was where he had left it, his two temporary guards lounging on the bonnet passing a sweet-smelling joint between them.

'Bro! You're back. We been sitting here for hours, man. You need to upgrade the financial package,' the taller one said.

Gabriel nodded.

'Fair enough. Here's another twenty each. And thank you. Maybe if I'm back seeing the Diallos, I'll need your services again. What are your names?'

The second-in-command lifted his chin defiantly.

'Sure you're not a cop, bro?'

'Would I tell you if I was?'

He grinned.

'Double-bluff. Clever.'

'Otis,' the taller one said, thumping his chest with the side of his closed fist. 'My man here's Dylan.'

'I'm Gabriel. But you guys can call me Gaby.'

He nodded.

'Gaby. Cool.'

'All right, I'll see you around,' Gabriel said. 'Don't let the cops catch you with that.'

Otis kissed his teeth. 'They don't come round here. Too frightened. We got our own law here.'

Gabriel unlocked the car and climbed in. Fired up the ignition and pulled away, acknowledging their ironic salutes with a wave. As he drove back to the apartment he shared with Tara he realised she'd be back tonight. She'd been visiting friends in Italy, also fugitives from the Chinese security apparatus.

They had a lot to tell each other.

5

She'd pointed an Uzi at his belly, finger crooked round the trigger.

She'd held a sword to his back, ready to run him through.

She was the one person left in the world Gabriel trusted implicitly.

Yet as he waited in Arrivals at Orly Airport for Tara, flanked by taxi and limo drivers holding up electronic or hand-lettered welcome signs, he experienced a flash of anxiety. Would he recognise her? He shook it off with a shudder that had his neighbour casting a glance in his direction.

Of course he would! They'd been living together in her flat in Paris since he returned from Honduras, hadn't they? But every day, on seeing her for the first time over the breakfast table, it took him a moment to adjust to the fact that Tara no longer *looked* like Tara.

Yes, her new face kept her under the radar of the Chinese government's roving agents, but it had severed something important in the link that bound them.

No time to worry about that now. If nothing else, Tara would recognise *him*.

In ones and twos, then small clusters, then a steady stream, the arriving passengers from Rome filled the walkway that doglegged round a security screen before opening out into the concourse, separated by a single line of vinyl barriers from laughing, waving and in one case crying, greeters. Gabriel craned his neck, looking for the new Tara and seeing in his mind's eye only the old.

Then he saw her. And the anxiety vanished like steam wiped from a bathroom mirror, revealing the true identity of the person being observed. She wore a broad-brimmed straw hat that flopped over her forehead, but there was no mistaking her. She looked straight at him and beamed.

Yes. There was something *behind* the westernised eyes, the reprofiled cheeks, the plumper lips and new dentistry, the tweaked and uptilted nose. It was not so much a look as a *feeling* of a look. A bond between brother and sister that went so deep no amount of surgery could ever erase it. He cursed himself for a fool. How could he have worried?

She paused at the barrier to hug him fiercely then hurried around to the end of the walkway.

'How was Rome?' he asked.

'It was good!' But her eyes tightened, repelling the smile before it reached them.

'Tell me in the car,' he said, taking her suitcase and wheeling it along as they headed for the exit.

Gabriel swung the car onto the main road towards Paris. He waited until he'd settled into a steady 65 kph before asking Tara the question again. Briefer, this time.

'So?'

She sighed. Ran her fingers through her hair.

'Jin's fine. She and Gianni got married last year and she's got Italian citizenship. Plus she emigrated with the Party's blessing. It's quite happy to have Chinese engineers working in Europe.'

'But …'

'I met a few old contacts from the life. Word is, the Party's got this new drive to bring former triad members back to Beijing for trial.'

'Drive?'

'It's called the Office for Family Reunification. You'll love their mission statement,' she said in a bitter voice.

'Go on.'

'Their job is "bringing lost lambs back to the flock".'

'Where they'll be slaughtered,' he said grimly. 'Do we need to be worried?'

'Honestly, BB? I don't know. I hope not. I really like Paris. I've built a new life here. I have friends. I feel like I'm putting down roots.'

'Your cover's deeper than anything the Department ever would have constructed, Tar,' he said, testing his own belief in what he was saying, even as he said it. It felt solid enough. 'They could never find you.'

'You believe that? This is the Party we're talking about.'

'But you've got your tripwires, too, right?'

'Financial, social media, a couple of intelligence sources, the usual.'

'Right. So even if they did come sniffing around Paris for you, you'd know in plenty of time. And if you don't hear one of those little bells tinkling, you can carry on with your life, can't you?'

She twisted round in her seat. He could feel the heat of her gaze on him as he swung the car round a particularly tricky junction.

'But what kind of life is it, BB? You don't know what it's like! In every op you ran for Don you had a single target. Eliminate it and you were done. How can I eliminate *my* target when it runs a country with over a billion people? The Party could send a million people after me and if I killed them all? It could send another million.'

She sounded worryingly close to tears. This was so unlike

Tara. But she had a point. Even if some of his Department missions had veered way into geopolitical territory, his own identity had always been a secret. And the strikes he and his fellow operatives had conducted against rogue state actors, unfriendly powers and even, on rare occasions, friendly ones, had been seen by those on both sides of the equation as part of an ongoing war with rules by which everybody agreed, within reason, to abide. During the mission, Department operatives could expect to be terminated with extreme prejudice by the enemy. But once it was over, there was no campaign of personal retribution on the men and women behind the attacks or assassinations. Revenge happened at the state-level.

But the Chinese were different.

This wasn't about tit-for-tat attacks on military facilities or hostage-swaps. This was about ideological purity.

But as Gabriel knew, and Tara surely did after being trained as a child-assassin by the Party, purity could kill.

'So how about you?' Tara asked. 'What did you get up to while I was away?'

Gabriel told her about his brush with Sandrine and Sophy, and his encounter with Marianne Diallo.

When he finished the story, she turned to him and said, 'Well, they're lucky to be alive, and she is lucky to have you helping her. Let me know if there's anything I can do to help.'

He parked below street level in the secure garage excavated especially for the residents of the apartment block on Avenue Montaigne. Securing the permissions alone had reputedly cost the developer eighty million euros. Rumour had it a sizeable percentage went not into city coffers but directly into the newly created offshore accounts of a handful of senior officials.

Tara checked an app on her phone. She scrolled through a set of seven video feeds from inside the apartment. Nothing had been disturbed. No shadowy figures lurked in corners. She nodded.

'We're good.'

Had they not been good, they would have turned around and left. A brief stop at a ruined farmhouse twenty kilometres outside

Paris, whose cellar security would have surprised anyone curious enough to venture inside its ramshackle ground floor. Guns and go-bags collected, they would have driven south non-stop before flying out of France for ever.

But they were good. So they got out of the car and took the lift up to Tara's apartment.

Tara inserted the key in the lock and opened the door. Gabriel followed her inside, pulling her suitcase behind him. The rubber wheels hissed on the vestibule's parquet flooring.

As he slotted the telescopic handle down inside the case, something smashed in the kitchen. He froze. In front of him, Tara did likewise. She looked over her shoulder and signalled for Gabriel to head for the living room. She placed her palm against the door of a cupboard, grasped the brass knob with her other hand and slowly eased it open. From inside, she withdrew a Walther PDP fitted with a suppressor. No need to rack the slide, the pistol was kept permanently ready to fire.

Gabriel slipped through a door into the sitting room and crossed to a bookcase. Centred on the middle shelf was a blue, green and red blown-glass fish Tara had bought from the Murano factory in Venice. He moved it aside and pulled out a large leatherbound tome with a twelve-inch spine, letting its pages fall open. From the razor-cut cavity inside he extracted a Colt King Cobra revolver chambered for .38 Special rounds.

He rejoined Tara in the hallway and then, in a coordinated move, brother and sister burst into the kitchen, Gabriel standing, Tara crouching, guns up, fingers over triggers.

Tara laughed.

'Oh, Pom, you are shitting me!'

Shaking his head, Gabriel placed the revolver on a granite worktop. Tara put her pistol beside it then bent to scoop up a black and white cat, currently standing amid a wreckage of broken china, apples, blood oranges and pears. The cat mewed twice then commenced to purr deep in its chest.

'It would serve the damn cat right if she took a bullet,' he said as he fetched a dustpan and brush from a cupboard.

Tara pooched her lips out and rubbed her cheek against the cat's vibrating flank.

'Nooo! Poor little Pom-Pom. We wouldn't let horrible Uncle BB use us for target practice, would we?'

'You spoil that cat, Tar,' Gabriel grumbled as he bent to the task of clearing up the mess.

6

The next morning, Gabriel sat on the balcony, a cup of strong black coffee by his elbow. Below him, the shoppers and tourists thronging Avenue Montaigne passed by, oblivious to the man twenty metres above their expertly coiffed heads.

He called Marc at the gym.

'I need to take some leave.'

'Sure, bro. You haven't taken a single day off since you came to work with me. When?'

'Today.'

'Something came up, huh?'

It was one of the things Gabriel liked about Marc. Maybe their shared experience of combat. Marc asked only those questions he needed to.

'Something came up. I might need a few days, maybe longer.'

'Take what you need, bro. Just keep me posted, yes?'

'Of course. Thanks. I appreciate it.'

'Fuck off! You'll have me reaching for a Kleenex to dry my tears!' Mark said with a gruff laugh, before cutting the line.

Gabriel held the knife up so the razor edge caught the light. No traces of dried blood. So either Sandrine hadn't used it or she'd been meticulous in keeping it clean. Like a soldier. But whether or not she'd been the last owner, she certainly hadn't been the first. That would have been someone very much like Gabriel himself. A Royal Marine Commando, a Para or a guy from the SAS or their marine counterparts the Special Boat Service.

He smiled at a memory. Smudge Smith snorting and calling them 'frogs with guns, boss,' the derision in his south London tones tempered with grudging respect.

Gabriel flipped his grip on the hilt: point up, point down. Bloody memories swamped him.

Yes, burning through mags or even loosing off single shots from a sniper nest was fighting. And it took its toll. But when the ammunition ran out before the enemy did, you reached for the fighting man's oldest companions. Edged weapons. Knives, axes, daggers, tomahawks. Failing that, entrenching tools, chisels, whatever you could lay your hands on.

And there was something about a knife fight. A visceral quality. The fact you were no more than the length of your arm from your enemy made it personal. Almost intimate. You were looking them in the eye or breathing down their neck as you slid your blade between their ribs, or stabbed it into their neck, your hand clamped over their mouth, their scream, wet with humid breath, muffled against your palm.

He'd known men pinned down by insurgents resort to corkscrews and kitchen knives to fight their way out of an ambush. A battalion cook who, when her post had been overrun by Taliban fighters, despatched three with a meat cleaver she'd snatched from a rack. They called her the Butcher after that, a moniker she bore with pride even though she herself was a vegetarian.

And somewhere in this teeming city was the previous owner of this particular blade. Not a missing child, but someone Gabriel wanted to locate all the same. He pictured someone lost. He couldn't say why. Just so in need of cash they'd part with a surely treasured memento of their military service. It was like finding a row of Gulf War medals. You'd want to find the person who'd had no option but to sell them.

He checked his watch: 8.15 a.m. The market was open. He took his coffee cup inside and put it straight into the dishwasher. Tara was tyrannical about her kitchen. She scolded him if he left so much as a single teaspoon out on one of the pristine marble countertops. Pom trotted over and wound figure-eights around his calves. He reached down to stroke her silky fur then straightened.

Shod in lightweight approach shoes in well-worn olive drab suede and nylon, he strode down the street, heading due north. And an appointment with one Luc 'Torpedo' Torpichon. On the way he called Marianne.

'Has she come home?' he asked as he crossed the street, dodging onrushing cars apparently intent on pasting him into the tarmac.

'No. I am going crazy with worry, Gabriel.'

'Try and stay strong, Marianne. I'm going to find her for you.'

He wondered as he walked who the man behind the military nickname would be. A grizzled veteran of France's many foreign wars? Or a seedy chancer, dealing in militaria to wannabes and the odious kind of individual who had a hard-on for Nazi memorabilia.

He tried to be charitable. Pictured a kindly-faced old man in a moth-holed cardigan and half-moon specs buying and selling medals, uniforms, shell casings and the rest because, well, *Monsieur* – a Gallic shrug – one has to buy and sell something, *non*? But he already knew Biron Market, or, to give it its full title, Saint-Ouen Flea Market. Among its many stallholders you could find a great variety of types. But his twinkling eyed *grandpère* was not among them.

An hour later, his stomach rumbling and asking him why he'd skipped breakfast, he entered the market through the wide-open gates, beneath a battered yellow metal sign reading MARCHÉ BIRON ALÉE 2.

He realised he should have been more careful in asking Sandrine where to find Torpedo's stall. Hundreds of them were

37

crammed cheek-by-jowl along the market's narrow, crowd-choked alleys.

Here, antique chairs, battered metal trunks, scuffed plastic mannequins dressed in psychedelic sixties dresses, pink-tinted hippie glasses and fuzzy berets. There, stalls selling dull-looking hardback books over which bibliophiles pored with the feverish intensity of the true believer. Everything was on sale. Pornographic comic books with lurid covers, 1930s drinks adverts on rusted metal signs, dinner services of startling ugliness and breathtaking beauty side by side like Cinderella and her sisters.

Pervading the entire crowded arena of second-hand commerce, the smells of coffee and baking. Ham sandwiches rich in translucent fat and fragrant Dijon mustard. *Croque monsieur* drenched in pungent melted cheese. And, everywhere, street food from Francophone Africa, from jollof rice rich with the fruity, piquant, searing bite of Scotch Bonnet chillies, to the golden Senegalese fritters called *accara*, made from black-eyed peas and served with a tangy tomato sauce.

Gabriel stopped at a stall selling Moroccan snacks and bought a seafood *briwat*, a deep-fried triangular pastry stuffed with prawns and vegetables, then moved on to buy a *café crème* at a stall three doors down. While he waited for the barista to make his drink he leaned over the counter.

'Do you know a Luc Torpichon?' he asked her. 'He goes by Torpedo.'

She shook her head without breaking the routine of her coffee making.

'He deals in military stuff,' Gabriel added. 'Is there somewhere those guys hang out?'

She handed him his coffee.

'I don't know. But you could ask Manny,' she said, lifting her chin in the direction of an alley crossing the midway. 'He sells old guns and stuff. He might know this Torpedo character.'

'Thanks. I will.' He took a sip of the coffee and nodded his appreciation. 'That's good. Thank you.'

She smiled. 'Come back soon.'

He headed off in the direction she'd indicated. The junction was tight with the press of bodies. Shoppers, local and from other neighbourhoods, tourists following the instructions on apps or old-fashioned paper guidebooks. Youngsters taking pictures of everything then immediately stopping to upload it to their social media. Often standing with their back to the stall and getting themselves into shot. And those who had the mission-focused look of people searching for something specific. Not browsers, influencers or those with an hour to kill. People who wanted *that* copper cooking pot, first edition of Victor Hugo or 1920s beaded flapper dress and would return week after week, month after month until they landed the prize.

With a great many '*Pardon*'s and '*Excusez moi*'s, Gabriel penetrated and then freed himself from the press, finding himself in a less densely populated alley. He sighed a breath out then inhaled deeply, suddenly aware he had been feeling anxious in the throng.

He glanced down the alley and saw what he was looking for at once. Not a sign: these were all flush to the stall fronts. But a signal. A male dummy standing guard in front of a stall. Full Napoleonic uniform, from a plumed hat to spatted boots. And a musket with a two-foot bayonet plugged into its muzzle, resting at its right side in the order arms position.

Gabriel approached the stall, which was currently empty. He looked around but there was no sign of the proprietor. He patted the leather messenger bag slung across his body. Felt the hard shape of the knife in its newspaper wrapping beneath the flap. Torpichon had probably gone off for a piss, or a coffee. One tended to lead to the other in Gabriel's experience. What was it the Duke of Wellington had said? 'Never miss the opportunity to make water'. Something like that. And fine advice from a great military strategist. Routing the enemy was a lot easier with dry trousers. Defending yourself and your comrades equally aided by not having said articles of dress unzipped and your manhood hanging out.

He picked up a section of disintegrating belt holding five .50

BMG rounds. Each held enough propellant to blow a fist-sized hole through a brick wall, let alone send its 700-grain bullet hurtling supersonically over a mile or more before wrecking an engine block, smashing a hole in a radio transmitter or turning a target's head into a cloud of pink mist. He turned it in his hand so the primers were uppermost. No marks from a firing pin.

'Don't worry, they're deactivated. I invented a method of extracting the propellant and replacing the bullet without leaving tool marks on the brass.'

Gabriel turned, a ready smile on his face. The man facing him and clutching a takeaway cup from the same stall Gabriel had stopped at, held out his right hand.

'Luc Torpichon at your service.'

Gabriel shook. The owner of the hand had a hard grip, held for exactly the right amount of time. A handshake that said, in effect, 'I am a fair dealer, but not a pushover.' He warmed to him.

'Hi. I acquired a knife recently, and I hope you can tell me a little about it.'

'Of course. Let's have a look.'

Under Torpichon's hawkish gaze, Gabriel unsnapped the flap on his messenger bag and withdrew the thick tube of newsprint. He laid it on an olive-green steel ammunition box stencilled in yellow and unrolled the paper. He spread the final sheet wide and let Torpichon pick it up.

Was he face to face with the man who could help him find its owner?

7

———

Torpichon nodded his appreciation, turning the knife this way and that, hefting it and checking its balance, before bringing out a jeweller's loupe and screwing it into his eye.

'This, my friend, is a proper fighting man's weapon. Second one I've seen this month, funnily enough. You know what it is?'

Gabriel shrugged. 'Not really. It's why I came to you.'

'OK, cool. Well, it's a Fairbairn-Sykes fighting knife. British Special Forces use them. Although, I would call it a killing knife, rather than a proper combat knife for the *mano-a-mano* stuff, know what I mean? I could give you a good price for it. How does thirty-five euros sound?'

Gabriel thought it sounded derisory. But as he had no intention of selling he let that slide. He smiled and gave a little, regretful shake of the head.

'It's not for sale. But here's the thing. I'm very interested in where you got it from.'

Torpichon's eyes took on a shuttered look and he glanced to his left and right.

'Me? I think you must be mistaken.'

He might as well have held up a sign reading, '*I have a guilty conscience*'.

Breathing easily, keeping his hands loose by his side, Gabriel shook his head.

'No mistake. You see, yesterday a young lady held it to my throat. I think she wanted my wallet. She didn't get it, but before we parted company she told me she bought it from you.'

Torpichon backed up a pace. Was he going to rabbit?

'I think I'd know if I'd sold a knife to a young lady. It's mostly guys who buy from me. Older, usually, although I get the odd younger dude.' He used the slang word, *mec*. 'You know the type. They all watch that guy on YouTube, what's his name, Tate?'

As Torpichon gabbled on, adducing further evidence of his uprightness and good standing within the '*communauté de militaria*', Gabriel had to decide who to believe. Both characters had their flaws. Sandrine, a bloodthirsty street robber with a well-honed line in sassy patter. Torpichon, a seemingly respectable market trader lying about where he'd bought the knife.

Why would Sandrine lie about it when she could just have said she found it in the street, take the proffered cash and disappear with no blowback? On the other hand, if, as he suspected, Torpichon had acquired the knife from a desperate British veteran, he'd smell trouble coming if he admitted it.

While Torpichon had been talking, Gabriel had taken a series of small steps around him, effectively hemming him within the confines of his stall. He'd also maintained a very specific kind of eye-contact, while making small noises of agreement or encouragement. And, during this outwardly neutral set of movements, sounds and facial expressions, the knife had returned to Gabriel's hand. Now he held it between them, the small steel pommel facing him, the spearpoint gently pushing against Torpichon's belly.

'Let's take a breath here, Luc,' Gabriel said. 'May I call you Luc? Your nickname is an interesting one. I'm guessing it's a nod to your job. Or did you actually sell a torpedo one day? Anyway, you may not know this, but it's also a slang word in Russian. It means a contract killer. An assassin. A long time ago they used it about me.'

Torpichon gulped as he stared down at the seven inches of razor-edged steel currently connecting his unprotected abdomen to Gabriel's right hand.

'Look, man. This is totally unnecessary. I made a mistake, OK? An honest error.'

He looked up. Delivered a performance called 'a forgotten fact suddenly remembered' that would have shamed an amateur actor in a church hall pantomime and returned his gaze to Gabriel, actually snapping his fingers.

'Yeah, it's coming back to me now. I *did* buy it. Couple of weeks ago. This dude'—*mec*—'needed cash. I gave him a fair price—'

'Really? A fair price? How much?'

Torpichon held his arms wide, apparently forgetting the Fairbairn-Sykes prodding his guts.

'Look, the market's in the pits right now, times are tight. There's not so much interest in British stuff at the moment. It's—'

'How. Much.'

He swallowed nervously. 'Twenty euros.'

Gabriel shook his head. If he was in a more generous mood, he'd have shrugged. Commerce was commerce, after all. Buy low, sell high, wasn't that how it worked? Torpichon was a trader. It's what he did. But to stiff a vet? No. That would not stand.

'Describe him to me.'

Torpichon nodded, sensing he was moving onto firmer ground. The kind of ground that meant he wouldn't find himself connected to Gabriel by only *three* inches of steel.

'English, maybe forty, forty-five. Kind of scruffy.'

He smiled ingratiatingly, presumably thinking he'd earned a reprieve.

Gabriel wasn't satisfied.

'Go on.'

'Go on *what*, man? I just told you. He looked like a homeless, you know?'

'No, I don't know. I need you to try harder, Luc. A lot harder.'

For emphasis, he applied a little pressure to the hilt of the knife. The front of Torpichon's shirt dented in and he yelped.

'Stop! Jesus, just relax would you?' He inhaled quickly. 'Right. Let me think.'

He closed his eyes and beneath the lids, Gabriel could see the eyeballs moving about. Torpichon was consulting his memory properly this time. Visualising the seller.

Gabriel picked up a movement in his peripheral vision. He turned his head. A sixtyish guy, heavyset, moustache and beard, suspicion lingering behind his eyes, stepped closer.

'Everything OK here, Luc?' he asked in a smoke-roughened voice that spoke of a regular and prolific high-tar habit.

'We're fine,' Gabriel said, injecting a little steel into his voice, while simultaneously withdrawing the real thing from Torpichon's quivering belly. 'You can go about your business.'

The newcomer wasn't so easily put off, however.

'Luc?' he prompted.

'He's a customer. We're just chatting about knives and stuff.'

The guy shrugged and shambled off to his own stall. 'If you say so.'

'This guy,' Torpichon said. 'He was tall. Like, maybe one-eighty-five. Tough-looking but he'd let himself go, you know? Soft round here,' he gestured at his own loose jowls. 'Curling hair, your sort of colour, dark with silver in it. More than yours, though, like, mostly grey. Eyes deep, hooded. Bright blue. Drinker's nose. He was wearing a greatcoat, even in this heatwave we've been having. British. Brass buttons with crests. Gordon Highlanders. I recognised it but I checked out the regimental badge afterwards anyway. Just to be sure. It's an old habit.'

'This is good, Luc. You're doing well. Any distinguishing marks? Tattoos, scars, missing fingers, birthmarks? Anything like that?'

Torpichon shook his head.

'Nothing I could see. That coat, man, it was on the big side.' His eyes widened. 'Oh! He's got this walk. I think maybe he took a bullet some time, to his left leg. His knee's stiff. You can see how he has to, you know, lift over it every time he takes a step. Is that any good?'

'It's excellent. Do you know where he lives?'

'Lives?' Torpichon laughed, perhaps unwisely. 'That type? They live wherever.' He caught Gabriel's glare. 'Wait! Relax, man. He said something about pickings down at the Tower. Maybe he hustles tourists down there. That's all I have. Are we done?'

He looked down. The knife had gone. He stepped back hurriedly. Out of range.

'We're done. Thank you. You've been really helpful. One last thing, Luc.'

'Yes?'

'If another vet comes around offering to sell you some gear, I'd recommend giving them a really good price. I'll be checking up from time to time and I'd love to hear good things about your fairness.'

He left Torpichon nodding frantically, dragging a large red and white spotted handkerchief from the pocket of his cords and wiping his forehead.

Gabriel had a start. A decent description. And a potential location. The Tower was how Parisians referred to the Eiffel Tower.

Now he wanted to talk to the cops. Not about the English vet who'd been conned out of a fair price for his knife. That he would handle privately. But the missing girl: Odette Diallo. That was police business, whatever the racist cop Marianne had encountered had said.

He knew exactly how it would have gone down, even without Marianne's tearful recounting of her encounter with the desk cop. France loved to paint itself as a bastion of liberal values but on the streets, in copshops, in rural pubs, there was plenty of naked racism available for those who wanted to find it. And for those who most fervently did not.

And here was he, a white man, about to take up the cudgels on behalf of a poor immigrant from Africa. He'd get more of a hearing, he knew that, but he wanted to use every weapon in his arsenal.

And that meant a trip to the kind of shop he hadn't set foot in for half a lifetime.

8

Gabriel strode between ambling tourists and wealthy Parisians who didn't have to clock in, or hit the cubicle, or log into the Zoom call at 8.30 a.m., looking for a very particular kind of emporium.

Known as the best shopping street in Paris, Rue du Commerce ran southwest between the traffic-clogged dual-carriageway Boulevard de Grenelle to Rue des Entrepreneurs, and the triple-arched frontage and spire of Église Saint-Jean-Baptiste de Grennel. The sun had brought out even more passersby than usual and it was slow going. He resorted to using the middle of the road, stepping back onto the pavement smartly as delivery vans, moped riders and taxis made known their displeasure at his antics.

He found the business he was looking for sandwiched between a pungent cheese shop, *Les Fromages du Paradis*, and a lingerie boutique, *Elodie + Belle*, whose wares seemed to be priced in inverse proportion to their coverage.

Gabriel placed his palm on the wrought iron handle, already warm from the sun slanting across the street, and pushed into the store. The interior smelled of leather and tobacco. A masculine aroma. The sun entered with him, catching swirling dust motes in mid-flight so they flashed and twinkled like distant gunfire.

A man in his mid-sixties, immaculately dressed in tailored trousers and a buttoned-up waistcoat, and sporting a ginger moustache and beard, came out from behind the glass-topped wooden counter.

'Good morning, sir. How may I help you?' He glanced surreptitiously, although Gabriel noticed, at Gabriel's street clothes before resuming eye contact. 'I'm afraid we have a very limited supply of casual wear.'

Gabriel smiled and shook his head.

'I'm looking for a suit. A shirt, tie, cufflinks, shoes, socks, belt. The best you have.'

The proprietor of *Miller Hommes* beamed. He pulled a pair of glasses from his waistcoat pocket, and perched them on the end of his nose.

'Let's get started then. Do you know your measurements?'

'It's been a while since I wore anything formal.'

'Not to worry.' The shopkeeper produced a tightly rolled tape measure. 'Let's start with your chest.'

Ten minutes later, the shopkeeper had added Gabriel's measurements to an old-fashioned leatherbound ledger on the counter, and appended Gabriel's name.

'May I take an address? Your email?'

'Let's not. If I need anything else I can just pop back.'

The man dipped his head.

'Of course. So, a suit. For a special occasion? A sporting event. Work?'

'Something that means business. Perhaps the type the president enjoys wearing.'

The man grinned.

'Ah. Something, how shall we say, *Jupiterian*.'

'Exactly. I want to make an impression.'

* * *

The sharply dressed man with the military bearing who stepped out of *Miller Hommes* into the swelling crowds, was unrecognisable from the casually dressed *flâneur* who'd entered two hours earlier. Eyes hidden behind green-lensed tortoiseshell sunglasses.

His suit, of a lightweight wool, was French navy. Appropriate, Gabriel thought. A burnt-orange silk handkerchief stuck its head above the parapet of the breast pocket. The cut, though simple and unflashy, bore the unmistakeable signature of a firm that had invested generations of talent in its style. As it should have done, given the four-figure sum it had cost Gabriel. His shirt, ironed personally by the proprietor, was snowy white Egyptian cotton, buttoned at the collar, around which was tied, in a precise, medium knot, a knitted silk tie in forest green.

Charcoal grey Falke socks in a cashmere blend cushioned his feet inside a pair of black Loake brogues, the shop's concession to what its owner self-deprecatingly called, '*Le look Anglais*'. The shoes, though not uncomfortable, were stiff and Gabriel felt every crease as the leather began the slow but enjoyable process of fitting itself to the new owner's feet.

Had he really gone around London dressed like this back in the day? He felt like an impostor, although the approving looks bestowed upon him by a trio of ladies out for a morning *café au lait* made up for his discomfort.

Seven doors down, he entered a watch shop, *Temps Trouvé* – time found – having passed the scrutiny of the black-clad security guy at the door. Amazing what some decent duds would do for your standing in the community. He doubted the curly-earpiece-wearing gorilla with the tight suit and mean stare would have admitted him if he'd tried *before* buying his new rig.

Inside, all was bright, hyper-white light. Nothing overtly masculine in this shop's aroma. More the stink of money. Glass display cases arranged like tanks in an aquarium lined the walls, the timepieces within lit as if they were exotic sea creatures. Which, for the diving models, he supposed they were.

A slender twentysomething with the figure and hauteur of a catwalk model approached.

'Are you looking for something in particular, sir? Our pilot watches are particularly popular at the moment among men ...' Gabriel tensed. Oh, Christ, was she going to say, 'of your age'? Had he reached that time of life where attractive redheads saw him as middle-aged? '... with your classic style.'

'Yes. A pilot would be good.'

In the end, despite the sales lady's attempts to steer him towards French and Swiss brands, Gabriel settled on a Bremont Fury, its navy face a perfect match for the suit and its English origins a pleasing twin with the Loakes.

His final purchase, from a luggage store, was a slender aluminium attaché case.

As he strolled back down Rue du Commerce he found people made way for him. He picked up his pace. The gaps grew wider, and opened up faster.

Offering a great many, '*Merci*'s, he made his way back to his car. Here was where his newly curated image fell apart. The battered little Renault had mojo for days, but it didn't exactly shout 'sophisticated'.

No matter. He'd park it round the corner from the copshop.

9

Gabriel left the rusty little yellow Renault in a side street. If some *mec* wanted to key it or even steal it, he guessed he could live with that. Something told him his old life was slipping away anyway, with or without his consent. As he mounted the steps of the police station he paused before opening the door.

Which was it? With his consent or without it? He nodded. With.

He'd had enough of other people deciding on the shape of his life. From now on, he was going to take charge, seize life by the scruff of the neck and push, shove and if necessary drag it where he wanted it to go.

Starting with the front desk of this rundown copshop in an unlovely corner of the Eighteenth. It was the nearest station to the Diallos' apartment so it seemed the best bet. He'd checked in with Marianne and she'd confirmed this was the same one where she'd first reported Odette's disappearance.

Inside, the heat of a Parisian summer day lessened a little. Although the building – old, shabby, a product of the 1930s by the look of it – had no air conditioning. A pedestal fan in a corner creaked arthritically from left to right and back again, moving the stale-smelling air around and creating swirls in the sunlit dust clouds.

Gabriel strode up to the front desk, drawing the attention not only of the officer behind it, but also a trio of skinheads handcuffed to a row of chairs on the far wall, their faces bruised, scabbed and, in one case, emblazoned with a spectacular black eye.

'Fuck me, someone's got Macron for a lawyer,' the black eye crowed, to sniggers from his friends.

Figuring he'd achieved his aim if the three brawlers had clocked him as a ringer for the president, Gabriel nodded, unsmiling, to the overweight bearded cop behind the desk. They'd called him a lawyer. He'd trade on that without having to use the deception he'd planned.

'My client's daughter is missing. She has already reported Odette's disappearance and received, I am disappointed to hear, particularly dismissive treatment from either you or one of your colleagues. I want to know what's being done, and by whom, to find her,' Gabriel said, pitching both his tone, sentence structure and accent at the very top of the Parisian social register.

The cop sat straighter. Stretched his neck and ran a finger round the inside of his grimy shirt collar, which was several shades closer to grey than the immaculate number Gabriel was wearing.

'Odette, you say?'

'That's correct.'

'Surname?'

'Diallo.'

Something changed in the cop's demeanour. It flicked from subservient and respectful to suspicious, bordering on hostile. He tried, and failed, to suppress a scowl.

'Diallo.'

'You're not hard of hearing, officer? I see no hearing aids, so I'll assume not. Diallo is what I said. Is there a problem?'

'No. It's just, you know, those people ...'

Gabriel regarded the man dispassionately, projecting the coldest, most official stare he could summon. He channelled a major he'd once met, a barrister working for the Service Prosecuting Authority based at RAF Northolt in London. Major Barratt's co-workers claimed he'd once literally frozen a defendant to the dock at a court martial, merely with a look.

'I'd advise you to think most carefully before you complete that sentence, constable. Odette Diallo is a French citizen. She is, as I have said, missing. I'd like to speak to the detective investigating her disappearance.'

A bead of sweat trickled down the cop's face, from his hairline, across his temple and into his beard. He sighed.

'Hold on. Let me check the computer.' His lips moved noiselessly as he thumped away at the keyboard. He frowned, tapped, scrolled around with the mouse, then looked back up at Gabriel, half a smirk on his face. 'We have no record of a missing girl by that name.'

Gabriel had been half expecting it. Why wasn't he surprised? Whoever Marianne had spoken to probably hadn't even made a pretence of starting a missing person report.

'I see.'

The cop spread his hands.

'Sorry I can't be of more help, *Maître,*' he said.

Perhaps he thought that would be it. And the lawyer, whose correct form of address he'd just used, would simply walk away as his client had done. One more brushoff, one more victory for the cop over sharp lawyers and their waste-of-space clients.

In that, he was to be disappointed.

'I want to speak to a detective.'

The cop frowned.

'But I just told you—'

'Yes. Like you, I also do not require hearing aids,' Gabriel said, cutting across him. 'But the fact remains, my client's daughter is missing. Has been missing now for over 24 hours. And despite her coming here to make a formal report, you appear to have done nothing. Not even making a record. Am I to assume citizens with African surnames do not receive the full attention and help from officers in the Eighteenth Arrondissement that others do?'

The cop sighed.

'No, *Maître*. Not at all.'

'Excellent. A detective, then. I'll wait over there.'

He spun on his heel, ensuring the new leather squeaked loudly on the scuffed linoleum flooring and took a seat a couple down from the trio who'd been enjoying his interaction with the desk cop.

The nearest thug leaned over, revealing a swastika tattoo on the inside of his right forearm as he did so.

'I could do with some legal advice, too, *Maître*,' he murmured with an evil leer. 'More than some fucking nigger does.'

Gabriel stared back at him, controlling his voice, and his temper. Dropped his French down through the social scale like a stone plummeting into a well.

'You want some advice? Get the fuck away from me and don't say that word again unless you want me to break something.'

The thug sneered, baring small, widely spaced brown teeth. He lunged at Gabriel, forcing his neighbour to cant over as their shared handcuffs snapped taut.

'I'd like to see you try, nigger-lover.'

Gabriel shot his arm out and seized the thug's left index finger in his fist. A sharp jerk backwards and the digit broke across the knuckle between the middle and proximal phalanges with a sound like a twig snapping. He reared away from Gabriel, screaming.

'What the fuck? This cunt just broke my finger!'

The cop looked up, rolling his eyes at Gabriel. He levered himself out of his chair and, while the thug filled the odorous waiting room with his yells of pain and anguish, left the confines of his glass-fronted cubicle.

Gabriel stood and met the cop halfway between the screaming thug and the front desk.

'He went for me. I think he caught his finger between the chairs.'

The cop leaned towards the skinhead, who was clutching his injured finger to his chest.

'Shut the fuck up and let me see,' he shouted.

The skinhead gingerly released his finger and held it out. It was already swelling and turning red.

'Aren't you going to arrest him? That nigger-loving lawyer just broke my fucking hand!'

By way of answer, the cop slapped him.

'Shut the fuck up!' He turned. 'Sorry, *Maître.*'

'Forget it.'

The cop pulled out his phone and murmured into it for a few seconds. Then he addressed the wounded thug.

'Station doctor'll be down in a few minutes. Until then keep your trap shut.'

'What about him?' the thug complained, eyes wide. 'He broke my fucking finger.'

The cop straightened, hands on hips.

'Right. A lawyer, and not some minimum-wage public defender either, comes in here to discuss a client's missing daughter and by way of entertainment he, what, instead of reading the paper or checking his emails, attacks you and snaps your finger? Give me a break.' He looked at Gabriel and winked. 'No pun intended.'

At that moment, a door at the rear of the reception opened and a young woman in a pale blue blouse showing dark circles of sweat under the arms, came out.

'Are you the lawyer enquiring about a missing girl?' she asked Gabriel.

'My client's daughter has disappeared,' Gabriel said. 'And I'm here to ask what's being done about it.'

She nodded, holding the door open behind her.

'Come with me, please.'

Gabriel followed her through the door, leaving the thug hurling abuse at him. Before the door swung fully shut on its pneumatic closer, a final threat sneaked round the jamb.

'I see you again, I'll fucking kill you.'

And from somewhere deep down, Gabriel's inner voice spoke up.

'*Not if I kill you first.*'

The door closed behind him.

The cop led him to a small room off a large open-plan area where plainclothes officers clustered around whiteboards, sat in huddles or hunched over computers pecking out reports with two fingers.

'So, what can I do for you, *Maître?*' she asked, closing the door behind her. 'My colleague said you are searching for a missing girl?'

'Her name is Odette Diallo. She disappeared yesterday morning, first thing. Her mother, who has retained me, reported her missing at the desk downstairs. She runs a laundromat in Goutte D'Or. Apart from treating her very rudely, it now transpires the desk officer didn't even register the child missing.'

'Yeah, well she hadn't been gone long enough. Not much we can do before 48 hours have elapsed.'

Gabriel suspected this was a convenient fiction. He had no doubt if Marianne had looked like him, been dressed like him, spoke like him, and turned up with a report of a missing girl, the police would have been a lot more interested.

'Not even enter a few basic details, captain?'

She shrugged. 'She's probably off somewhere having fun with her boyfriend. She'll come home when the drugs or the condoms run out.'

'Odette Diallo is twelve years old.'

'Look, despite your excellent French, I can tell you're English, right?'

'Yes, but I don't see what that has to do with anything.'

The detective flicked a glance at the door behind Gabriel, as if concerned nobody should overhear her. She leaned towards him.

'These people, they aren't like us. Officially, yes, the races don't exist. Nobody sees skin colour. *Officially,*' she repeated. 'Sadly that's a fiction the politicians like to swing around along with their dicks. The truth is, these people? They start early. It's 'cause they have no dad at home, you know?'

Gabriel was tiring of the casual racism infesting the station like mould.

'Her father's name is Youssoo. He's a carer at Bichat-Claude Bernard. He is there for Odette every day, when he's not wiping French arses or serving French meals. Now, what are you going to do about Odette?'

The cop looked at him inquiringly.

'Which firm did you say you represented?'

'I didn't. Is that relevant?'

The cop pulled out a notebook, finally.

'You tell me. Only according to you, the mum runs a laundromat and the dad's an arse-wiper at BCB.' She looked him up and down. 'You probably paid more for your pocket handkerchief than either of them earns in a day, no? Now I'm starting to wonder how a couple of immigrants can afford your fees. You sure you're a lawyer, *Maître?*' she finished, adding a nasty edge to the honorary title.

'I'm working pro bono,' he replied, which was true, at least.

She nodded, making a note.

'Pro bono,' she repeated, drawling the Latin phrase 'for nothing' until it started to sound ridiculous. 'Very … public-spirited of you. So, which firm?'

Gabriel fixed her with a look. Switched his focus from her left to her right pupil, back and forth, left to right, in a specific set of movements, with its own precise timings. Matched his breathing to hers. Tipped his head to one side then the other. He'd been practising with Tara since returning to Paris with her and while he had nowhere near his old command of the technique, part of *Yinshen fangshi* – 'the Way of Stealth' – its rudiments were coming back to him. He answered in two intertwined voices, one at conversational volume, one a lilting murmur of exact, almost musical tones.

'My law firm … *you* … has a dedicated fund to help those … *want me to* … without the funds to pay … *go back to my clients* … for legal advice ... *and tell them not to worry* ... it's called Fox, Lang and Abarbanel.'

He coughed, a sharp sound that refocused the cop's eyes, which had gone glassy. She sat straighter in her chair and looked around for a couple of seconds, a fleeting look of puzzlement on her face.

'So we're done here?' he asked her with a smile.

'We're done,' she said, blinking rapidly. 'Go back to your clients and tell them not to worry. I'll show you out.'

Gabriel left her in the reception area, now free of neo-Nazi thugs, and headed out into the sunshine.

How could the cops be so uninterested in a missing twelve-year-old girl? Surely she would be a high-risk individual, prey to all kinds of unsavoury characters from paedophiles to people traffickers? However long she'd been missing?

Something shifted in his mind. An unwelcome thought.

Unless they were being paid to be uninterested.

10

Gabriel had almost reached his battered little Renault when he saw a familiar face. Correction, two familiar faces. His would-be muggers from the day before. Sandrine and Sophy.

Today, Sandrine sported puffy-looking white sneakers with thick, comically oversized soles. Sophy rocked heels and a shimmering dress covered in gold sequins. The girls' heads were turned in towards each other and they didn't see Gabriel until he was standing right in front of them.

'Hey, dickwad, move your ass,' Sophy said with a jut of her pointy chin. Then she clocked the sharp-dressed man in front of her. Adopted a servile attitude Gabriel saw as just another disguise. 'Sorry, boss. Don't mind me. You haven't got a ciggy have you?'

Beside her, Sandrine was staring open-mouthed at Gabriel. He nodded, offered a smile.

'Hi again, Sandrine.'

'What the fuck, man?' She turned to Sophy. 'It's him. The English dude who fucked with us yesterday.'

Now he had both girls' full attention, Gabriel cast out the bait he suspected they'd find irresistible.

'How do you fancy some well-paid, honest employment?'

'We're not whores,' Sophy said smartly, her eyes blazing. 'We're entrepreneurs.'

'I know. Which is why I have a business proposition for you.'

'Pretty fancy phrase,' Sandrine said, 'and what's with the threads? Bit of a change from yesterday.'

'Can I buy you both a coffee? Maybe something to eat?'

They looked at each other. Communicating wordlessly for a few seconds. Gabriel couldn't read their expressions, not exactly. But he could figure out the gist.

— *Should we?*

— *It's probably a trap. Maybe he's a cop.*

— *He didn't act like a cop yesterday.*

— *Let's listen to this "proposition".*

Sandrine turned to face him.

'Fine. And we're hungry. Like, steak-frites hungry not croissant-hungry.'

Gabriel nodded his assent.

'Good. You know any OK places for a grill round here?'

The steaks were thin, seared on their outside to seal in the juices, and served with a mountain of skinny fries sifted generously with salt. As they ate, the girls wolfing down mouthful after mouthful, washing the food down with gulps of the house red, Gabriel waited for Sandrine to speak. She was the boss of their little outfit, after all.

She dabbed at her lips with the paper napkin then eyeballed him.

'Talk, white boy.'

'First of all, if we're going to work together, I think we should drop all this "white-boy" bullshit. I do you the courtesy of using your first names, you should repay that respect to me. I'm Gabriel.' He held out his right hand. 'Gaby.'

She extended a slender hand adorned with multiple gold rings. They shook. Her grip was hard and she squeezed tight. From a man it would have come across as a weak power play. From her it suggested a resilience and strength born of a life bending to her will a world not designed to favour girls such as her. He liked her for it.

'Gaby,' she said. 'OK. You better call me Drine, then. My sister's Feeso.'

Sophy looked up from her plate and gave Gabriel a fist bump.

'Don't fuck with us,' she growled, then returned to her fries.

'My sister's a tough little cookie,' Sandrine said. 'Any funny business and she'll do you. Properly this time.'

Gabriel had to smile, but he disguised it with a cough.

'I don't doubt that. Let's get down to it.'

'You want to talk business?'

'Don't you?'

'Sure. Lay it out then. This "business proposition".'

'I'm looking for a lost girl. Or maybe she ran away, I don't know yet. Her name's Odette Diallo. Her mum runs Automat Cavally on—'

'—Rue Hermel. I know it. The lady there's cool. She'll lend you money for the machines if you're short.'

'OK, good. I tried the police earlier.' He gestured at his suit. 'Hence the new look. They were worse than useless.' Sophy snorted. Her disdain so obvious it was like a neon sign just flickered on over her head. 'So I need some help I can trust. You girls know the streets, you know who runs things in the Eighteenth, I bet. What's going on where the police can't see or hear. I want you to be my eyes and ears. Ask around, and if you hear anything, let me know.'

'That's it?' Sandrine asked.

'That's it. Just intelligence gathering.'

'How much you gonna pay us for this "intelligence gathering"?'

'How about a hundred a day?'

'Between us?'

'Each.'

She focused deep brown eyes on him like twin gunsights.

'Yesterday you paid us fifty each just for one answer.'

'Yeah, but now I want to put you on a retainer. Steady work, lower hourly rate.'

She glanced left, at Sophy. Back at Gabriel.

'Two hundred. Each.'

Gabriel returned her gimlet stare.

'Three hundred between you.'

'Three-fifty. We got overheads.'

'Three or I find a couple of other kids with lower overheads.'

She stared at him for a few seconds.

'Three, then.' A beat. 'Plus expenses.'

Gabriel laughed loudly, causing the proprietor, an elderly guy in a grease-stained black apron over white shirt and black trousers to look over, frowning.

'Fine. Three hundred between you, plus expenses.' He held up a finger as she and Sophy high-fived. 'With a fifty-euro cap on daily expenses. And I want receipts.'

He waited, allowing her to fix him with her most considering stare yet. Then he dropped his eyes to let her take the victory. He wasn't in the business of playing hardball with a couple of street kids, even ones who'd tried to roll him the day before.

'Deal,' Sandrine said. She spat daintily into her palm and offered her hand for the second time.

Gabriel spat in his own palm and they slapped their hands together. No theatrics this time. A quick shake, a wipe on a napkin, and it was done.

'How we gonna find your ass?' Sophy asked, dabbing her grease-slicked lips with a paper napkin. 'I'm guessing you're not going to DM us on TikTok.'

Gabriel smiled.

'I wouldn't know how. How about I meet you opposite the laundry tomorrow evening, say seven?'

He settled the bill, after asking the *chef-patron* to take extra for desserts and coffee, then left his two new investigators at the table tucking into strawberry ice cream and waffles with chocolate sauce.

He had a British Special Forces veteran to find.

11

Gabriel settled behind the Renault's wheel, twisted the key and listened as the overstressed, underpowered engine roused itself and coughed into life like a war pensioner on a sixty-Gauloises-a-day habit.

He drove reasonably carefully, palm resting on the steering wheel boss, through Paris's honking, fume-belching traffic from Chateau Rouge to the Eiffel Tower.

The route initially took him roughly southwest through Montmartre on Doudeauville, Custine and Caulainecourt, past the cemetery, then onto Clichy, Batignolles, Courcelles, Alfred de Vigny and Hoche to the Arc de Triomphe. Round Place Charles de Gaulle formerly known as Place de L'Etoile, the hand on the horn button now pressed into action. Then down Marceau, over the Seine at Pont de l'Alma, west along the Rive Gauche on Quai Jacques Chirac before parking on a side street and walking the last hundred metres to the Eiffel Tower.

The heat had built during the forty-minute drive and he was sweating inside his fine new clothes by the time he reached the tower. He sat on a stone bench, the seat mercifully cool, and scanned the crowds.

Despite an orange dot-matrix display warning people, in English, not to engage with street vendors, rangy, dark-skinned men in linen trousers and loose tops, leather sandals slapping the pavement, threaded their way among the tourists, hawking silver and gold models of the tower, leather bracelets, handbags, bead necklaces and sunglasses. Presumably the rewards outweighed the risks of a caution or arrest from the cops.

Where would a homeless alcoholic vet hang out? Assuming he was working a hustle or grift of some kind, even if it only amounted to begging, he'd need to be somewhere he could appeal to tourists. And without attracting too much attention from *les flics*, although they seemed mostly interested in moving on the African street vendors.

Gabriel rose from the bench and headed in a spiral towards the centre of the square, head swinging left to right as he searched for someone who might, conceivably have once owned a Fairbairn-Sykes.

How had Torpichon described him?

He was 185 centimetres, so dead on six foot. Maybe a bit heavier than he ought to be if his face was soft. Curly hair, mostly grey. Hooded eyes of bright-blue. A drinker's nose. And a Gordon Highlanders greatcoat. The walk was promising, too. A limp favouring a busted-up left knee. If he was here, Gabriel reckoned he'd find him.

He talked to anyone he found who looked like the street was their home, drifting through the crowds like flotsam on the Seine's green-brown surface. The first two, a man and a woman who looked seventy but were probably twenty years away from that milestone, were too strung-out to make sense.

An obese man in a peasant smock and battered straw hat coughed a cloud of fierce-smelling cigarette smoke in Gabriel's face and demanded ten euros before admitting he'd only arrived from Rouen the day before and knew nobody in Paris.

Then Gabriel spotted a thin, tattooed woman in a floaty, tie-dyed maxi-dress talking to a well-dressed couple he guessed were Dutch, or maybe German. When they'd transacted their business, which involved money going into the woman's hand and a small baggie into the tourist guy's, Gabriel went over to her.

Close up, he saw that she was beautiful, or had been, once. Her cheekbones were too prominent now, the result of a poor diet and the rigours of street life. But her eyes, starred with crows' feet, were a piercing blue and filled with intelligence and, as she looked him up and down, her mouth widened into a smile.

'Hey, handsome. You looking for something to help you forget your business woes? You're a Gemini, right? Geminis can get too focused on work to relax properly.'

'Capricorn.'

She crinkled her eyes, deepening the stars of creases at their outer corners.

'The goat. Playful. Driven. Maybe you need something for a party, sweetie?'

'Actually, I need to find someone.'

He described the veteran as best as he could, using Torpichon's description as a basis and interpolating details he thought would probably be true.

Her eyes flickered into life when Gabriel mentioned the greatcoat.

'Ah, yes! I know him. English guy, right?'

'That's right.'

'Yeah, yeah. I know him. He's …'

Her bloodshot eyes shuttered. Gabriel saw what was coming. She might as well have had her thoughts programmed into the dot-matrix sign behind her. *What's it worth?*

Gabriel ignored the actual wording – *Please do not buy anything on the street* – and waited her out.

'He's a friend of mine,' she said. 'I don't want to get him into trouble.'

'You won't be. The opposite. I want to help him. He's a veteran, I think. So am I.'

She pursed her lips.

'I just helped a very charming Dutch couple out. Only thirty euros.'

Gabriel tilted his head on one side as if considering. But it was a low price to pay if it would lead to the knife's previous owner.

He handed her the money. There was no real risk. If she tried to run, a call of 'Stop thief!' from a man dressed as he was would shake the cops out of their heat- or apathy-induced torpor. Gabriel could easily outrun her, but the cops would ensure any counter-claims fell on deaf ears.

'Thank you, sweetie,' she said, tucking the cash away inside her dress. 'The man you're looking for is Jacko. Blake, like the poet, you know?'

Gabriel nodded, recalling a couple of lines that he felt described his life.

'He who binds to himself a joy, does the winged life destroy.'

She smiled and completed the quotation, in English.

'He who kisses the joy as it flies, lives in eternity's sunrise.'

'You know his work?'

'I used to teach English, way back when.' She looked up into his eyes. 'You're not playful, are you? Not even a little. But you *are* driven. I see it now. Give me your hand.'

As if under the influence of whatever she'd sold her previous customers, or maybe her own brand of Yinshen fangshi, Gabriel let his right hand float out in front of him where she took it in a cool, firm grasp and turned it palm uppermost.

She ran the tip of her right index finger along a line traversing his palm like a track through the desert. Pursing her lips, she tapped a couple of spots where other lines crossed it.

'Two loves. Two lives lost. You've known great sadness, *Cheri*, haven't you?'

'Look, I—'

She raised her hand and touched his lips to silence him.

'*You* look, *Cheri*,' she said softly, but urgently. 'Here.' She tapped the long curving desert track. 'A third crossing. There is yet another great love in your life.'

Gabriel shook his head, suddenly angry with her. Deep down in his belly, a worm of anxiety had uncoiled and was slithering, cold and prickly, through his gut.

'No! Look, I'm sorry, but this is all bullshit, OK? Maybe it works on the tourists, but not me. I asked you a question and I paid you for your answer. Now let me go. I need to be going.'

She released his hand, which felt frostbitten.

'He was over by the ice-cream truck earlier. Try there. He often hangs out near the end of the queue.'

Smiling sadly, she turned to go, already heading for a group of young, obviously well-heeled tourists.

'One more great love, Gabriel,' she called over her shoulder.

He frowned. How had she known his name? He must have told her.

It didn't matter. He needed to find Jacko Blake. And he had a location.

12

Gabriel looked up at the board and then addressed the girl looking down at him enquiringly from the counter.

'Pineapple sorbet please, and a scoop of vanilla on top.'

She smiled. 'Coming right up. Card or cash?'

'Cash.'

She grinned again. 'Old school. Nice clothes, by the way. You're not hot?'

'Why do you think I'm buying a ten-euro ice cream cone?'

She laughed, then shrugged. 'Hey. I just work here.'

Ice cream in hand he turned away from the counter and came face to face with a six-foot tall man in an army greatcoat. This had to be Jacko Blake. He matched Torpichon's description, right down to the hooded blue eyes and softening jawline, which was hidden by a half-decent beard in a fiery shade of ginger. He needed a shower. Possibly, two. And a shave. Gabriel didn't flinch, though the man's stink made his eyes water.

'Nice-looking ice cream,' he said in perfect French. 'Got a few euros to spare an old soldier?'

Gabriel smiled warmly.

'Of course. Do you want something to eat as well as some

money? Maybe a coffee as well? Or a beer? There's a nice sandwich place over there,' he said, gesturing to another overpriced joint catering to the tourist trade.

As he'd been speaking in English, Blake's eyes had widened, revealing the entirety of those startling blue eyes, the colour of sapphires, despite the broken capillaries criss-crossing the yellowed sclera.

'Is this a joke?' he asked, switching to English.

'No joke.'

'You think they'll let me in looking like this?'

'We can sit outside.'

'Why?'

'Why what?'

'Why are you being so … nice? You don't look the type to take pity on someone like me.'

Gabriel needed to ask, but he didn't want to frighten Blake off, if it really was him. Nothing for it but to try.

'Are you Jacko Blake?'

Those sapphires disappeared into the shadows again.

'Blake?' A Gallic shrug to rival that of his new countrymen. 'Never heard of him.'

'Look. I'm not a cop. But if you are Jacko, then I have something of yours.' Gabriel leaned closer. This close, the acrid smell of stale sweat and urine was overpowering. 'Your knife.'

Blake took a step back. Eyes narrowed, he scrutinised Gabriel. Not for the first time that day, Gabriel felt himself being measured up.

'You served, didn't you?'

Gabriel nodded.

'Paras, then SAS, D Squadron. A girl held your Fairbairn Sykes to my neck yesterday. I asked her where she got it and I traced it via a trader at the flea market back to you. I just want to return it. And to talk.' He held out his hand. 'My name's Gabriel.'

Blake's grip was hard, the skin of his palm greasy and hot. Gabriel felt calluses.

'Jacko. Gordon Highlanders, then SAS. Pleased to meet you.'

13

They made an odd couple.

The one, suited-and-booted, dressed for a business meeting, or possibly a political rally. The other, filthy, unkempt, dressed for the street or possibly, the gutter. They had a table to themselves, despite its being large enough to accommodate six. Tourists would approach then catch something in the eyes of the two men, or possibly Jacko's stink, and swerve at the last moment.

Gabriel had ordered a Coke to go with his ice cream, Jacko was working his way through a croissant filled with ham and cheese. By his elbow a tall glass of lager, its foamy head making steady progress towards the bottom.

Now he'd found his man, Gabriel was in no hurry. Jacko was clearly starving. While he concentrated on his lunch, Gabriel ate his delicious if overpriced ice cream and surveyed the crowds. An incongruous movement caught his eye twenty metres away, in the criss-crossed shadow of the tower's southern leg.

A child, maybe twelve or thirteen, laughing and calling over her shoulder to a friend nearby, bumped into a Chinese tourist. She held her hands up in apology and darted away. The tourist smiled and shook his head, then a few seconds later, frowned and patted his hip pocket. He looked around, face creased with concern. Then shouted in English.

'Thief! She stole from me. Police!'

Gabriel tracked the pickpocket. She slipped deeper into the shadows then jinked right and emerged into a patch of sunshine. A man was leaning against a signboard, reading the paper. Without breaking stride, she passed a wallet to him. It disappeared into a shoulder bag and, after a quick look left and right, he folded the paper and walked off.

A latter-day Fagin and his crew had set up shop beneath the most famous landmark in France. A cop had arrived and was questioning the tourist. A waste of time. Gabriel could easily imagine the tenor of their conversation. He'd be offering reassuring words about a crime report number for the insurance company. But realistically, *Monsieur*, what can we do? They are everywhere. Little street rats.

Like your two private investigators, Gabriel's inner voice chipped in.

The trouble was, the longer he lived, the more he found his sympathies lay with the street rats and less with the kind of people who despised them. Racist cops, corrupt politicians, obscenely rich industrialists or tech entrepreneurs who thought their money entitled them to a free pass on any moral issue. How did you weigh the theft of a tourist's wallet against a plan to unleash a Doomsday weapon?

Other memories crowded in. A charity founder selling the children in her care as guinea pigs for a bioweapon test. A French cult leader who'd poisoned his 600-strong flock because he could. A prime minister who'd arranged the assassination of a princess to further his plans to install himself as a dictator.

Cold liquid dribbled down his wrist, startling him. He looked down. His ice cream was melting fast, sending a pineapple-scented stream of liquid towards his shirt cuff. Swearing, he dumped the cone in a nearby bin and grabbed a handful of paper napkins from a chromed dispenser on the table.

'Should have had a sandwich,' Jacko said, finishing his beer. 'So, my knife?'

Gabriel nodded and leaned over to retrieve his briefcase. He placed it on the table and popped the catches. Inside, the knife in its newspaper wrapping, waited for its owner to reclaim it.

'Careful,' Gabriel said, as Jacko began unpeeling the sheets of newsprint. 'There are cops everywhere. We wouldn't want you to be arrested for possession of a deadly weapon.'

Jacko leaned over the briefcase and quickly spread the final layer of paper. 'Like the world's worst game of pass the parcel,' he said with an off-kilter grin. He glanced at the knife and nodded. Covered it over again. Lifted it out and slid it into an inside pocket.

'Thanks, Gabriel. I know it looks bad, selling it, I mean, but desperate times, you know? How'd you get it back, anyway. You kill the girl?'

'Let's just say I negotiated.'

'Negotiated,' Jacko repeated flatly. 'You mean you fucked her.'

'No! I took it off her fair and square, and then I paid her to tell me where she got it. That led me to the market trader, Torpichon, and he led me to you.'

'Fair enough.'

'So, what's the story, Jacko?'

'You mean, how come I went from the Regiment to begging in Paris?'

'I want to help you. If I can.'

Jacko shrugged as if he would simply accept Gabriel's help as something the fates had sent him.

'I got an honourable discharge in 2017. But like a lot of blokes, I couldn't cope with civvy street. It was so boring, you know? I didn't have PTSD or anything, but it was like, I don't know,' he rubbed his bristly cheek, 'like being underwater. Just this sluggish way of life with zero excitement, zero thrills. I actually missed the danger.'

'Your marriage didn't survive.'

Jacko frowned. 'What?'

'Your finger still has the dent from your wedding ring.'

'Oh, right. No. Cherry left me a year after I got out. I was hitting the booze pretty hard. Getting into fights. Just to feel something. I can't say I blame her. She got the kids. I mean, Christ, Gabriel, if I was the judge *I* would have awarded her custody. So I sold everything, cashed in what I could, gave it all to her and took off. I bummed around Southeast Asia for a while. Thailand, Vietnam, Cambodia. You ever been?'

'Once or twice.'

'Anyway, I'd been in Laos for a month and I met a guy in Vientiane. He was ex-French Foreign Legion. It sounded cool and I liked how you could join just like in a story. No names, no pack drill.'

'You signed up?'

'Bought a ticket to Paris that day. Jumped through a few hoops, nothing too hard, although I had to clean myself up a bit, cut back on the beer. I was assigned to the *Deuxieme Régiment Étranger de Parachutistes*. We were based out of Calvi in Corsica. I saw a ton of action, made some good friends. Then I got shot in Gabon. Some shit-for-brains NATO commander got us into the mother and father of clusterfucks. The Rupert disappeared and us lot got left in a firefight with this gang of insurgents or terrorists or drug dealers. They all blend into one after a while, don't they?'

'Was it serious? I saw you limping.'

Jacko nodded, rubbed his left knee.

'My knee was well and truly fucked. Got invalided out. There's a bit of a pension but Cherry gets most of that. The only bright side was I got automatic French citizenship on account of getting wounded fighting for *La Belle France*.'

'Then what happened?'

'Ah, well, Gabriel, mate, there's the rub. Not much money, foreign country, no qualifications. I took a couple of ill-advised jobs for some shady characters, and somewhere along the way I got this new habit. The rush was just beautiful – I forgot everything. Like the first time you fire live rounds after basic training. It quieted the flashbacks, the screams in the night. It all just,' he waved a hand languidly, 'went away.'

'What was it?' Gabriel asked, wondering whether he truly

believed Jacko's claim not to be suffering from PTSD. He wouldn't be the first man to deny the obvious, even when it was staring him in the face, screaming like a banshee.

'Heroin, what else? I've never been one to do the old dip-a-toe-in-the-water shit. They used to call me "Orla" back in the day. Like, "All or Nothing". And it was never nothing. Booze, women, fighting, sports. If I did it, I went all in. Every time. Sadly for me, the heroin's a bit of an Orla too. It takes everything till all you've got is nothing. So how about you? What's your story?'

Gabriel sighed. Prepared to relive every awful, blood-soaked moment. They said that it got easier, the more times you told it.

What bullshit.

14

Ali Soltani closed his eyes and leaned back in the wicker armchair he'd pulled into the shade of the tall cedar tree. He allowed a smile of satisfaction to steal across his broad face. Ran a palm over his shiny, newly shaved scalp.

Somewhere overhead a woodpecker was *tok-tok-tok*-ing out a new hole. A place to raise its kids, or chicks, or whatever the hell they called them. His own children, Thérèse and Andromache, were in Switzerland. Boarding schools. Costing him an arm and a leg, but it was all worth it. It was why they'd started the business in the first place. To better themselves.

Maybe these damned French would never accept him and Bashar, but the new generation? With their classic French names? Their perfect manners? Their skills at tennis, chess and soccer? Their upper-class drawls and their eye-wateringly expensive education? Oh, yes. Those, they bloody well *would* accept.

Ali inhaled deeply through his nose. His smile widened. Time was, you did that, all you got up your nostrils was the stink of diesel fumes, camel shit and army cooking. But that was a long time ago. *Syria* was a long time ago. He and Bashar had sensed which way the wind was blowing long before it all came crashing down. They got out while the going was good. Cashed in their assets, sold the business they'd run from the base – drugs, weapons and girls out, dollars, euros and other hard currencies in – and got the hell out.

Now all he could smell was … he didn't have a word for it. It was just … green. Fresh. He ought to try harder. Bashar was great with words. Read poetry, everything. OK, so he could detect the earthy background of the leaf mould under the cedar tree. Above that, like his wife's perfume, a sort of fresh, floral scent. That 'green' smell. Dammit! What was it? He sniffed again. A few short ones, then a long breath he drew in through pinched nostrils. It smelled like … like … their father's place. Up in the foothills of Mount Qasion north of Damascus. The pine trees. When they got hot they emitted a resiny smell. This wasn't exactly that, but it was in the right ballpark.

He felt the sun warming his eyelids. Orange and yellow behind the thin membrane of skin. Skin so delicate it only took the slightest pressure with a sharpened pencil or a corkscrew or a paperknife to puncture it and let the light in. And the screams out.

So many screams.

They were undesirables. Subversives. Terrorists. More to the point, they were sent to him for interrogation. A job he felt he'd been born to do. All the shit he got at school for his behaviour – his 'choices' as his teachers hand-wringingly described it to him, and then his father in after-school meetings – it turned out the Government actually valued what he could do. What he didn't mind doing.

No, be honest, Ali, what he *enjoyed* doing.

His superiors in the regular army had noticed his aptitude for causing pain. Instead of being disciplined, as he'd been expecting after a summons to his CO's office, he was drafted into the State Security Bureau. An outfit so secret even those whining Western agencies always bleating on about human rights had no idea it existed.

And there, he was allowed, was *encouraged*, to flourish. He developed new methods. New tools. He was promoted. He was given larger and better living quarters. An expense account. Foreign travel to train with the CIA. Then he trained others in the region. And, shit, that's the way it should have gone on. But Bashar, the older one, the clever one, had invited him round for dinner one night and laid it on the line.

'Five years from now, brother, this,' he spread an expansive hand around, to encompass not just his 3,000 square foot apartment but also the capital city, 'will be gone. People like us? We'll be lower than street dogs. They'll come for us when it all goes to shit and it won't be pretty. We need to leave.'

Ali had argued. Forcefully, then ferociously, then physically. Bashar had allowed him to expend all his energy and then, calmly restated his case. And, at 3.31 a.m. that morning, February 15th 2020, his eyes gritty with fatigue, his head pounding, Ali had simply nodded.

'OK,' he'd said.

And that was that. It turned out Bashar had been busy long before calling his brother and inviting him over for lamb kofte. Plans were in place. Currency. New identity documents. New supply lines. Even places to stay in Paris. The only hitch, Ali getting caught up in the periphery of a terrorist truck bomb attack. Cuts and bruises would heal, but his left eye was ruined. The remains extracted at a military hospital. They'd offered him a prosthetic but he'd spurned it. Opted for a simple black patch instead. It had worked for the Israeli general, Dayan. It would work for him.

They'd uprooted their families, and Ali's only surprise was how willingly Rania had agreed. He suspected at the time she'd been talking to her sister-in-law, Nisreen. But it turned out she was just happy to leave Syria for, as she put it, 'somewhere more civilised'. He thought she probably meant somewhere you could go shopping for a new Chanel handbag without a bodyguard, but he let it go. They were on their way, that was what counted.

The crackle of dry leaves was faint. A less sharp-eared man might have missed it.

Ali's one good eye snapped open and his hand was halfway to the Glock at his side before Bashar laughed.

'Whoa, little bro. Chill. You shoot me I won't be able to tell you the good news.'

Ali turned in his chair, accepted the glass of mint tea his brother was holding out.

'It's on?'

Bashar smiled.

'It's on. She goes under the hammer in six days.'

15

Gabriel checked the time on his new watch: it was just after six. The sun was still blazing down out of a clear blue sky but the daytime heat had softened and a cool breeze had sprung up.

'I can't talk here. Are you still hungry?' he asked Jacko.

'Always. Smack's supposed to kill your appetite but mine's just like always. My mum used to say I could out-eat a horse. Maybe because I don't inject.'

'You smoke it, then?'

'Yep. Chasing the old dragon round and round. The high's not so intense but I never was much good with needles. They'd laugh if they knew, wouldn't they? The Walter Mittys, the wannabes, the public. Big scary SAS guy frightened of a flu jab.'

Gabriel smiled and nodded.

'Maybe. With me it's spiders.'

'Really?'

'Can't stand the bastards.' He shuddered involuntarily. 'I got myself out of a tight spot last year by chucking one at a bloke's face. But I tell you, Jacko, having that little fucker in my hand battering against my fingers to get out, I was almost ready to take the guy's bullet instead.'

Jacko laughed. A rough sound that had a few nearby tourists looking round, their mouths already turning up in empathetic good humour until they saw the source of the laughter and hurriedly turned away.

Gabriel consulted his phone and found a little bistro close by the restaurant. The former special forces soldiers walked there, side by side, the crowds parting before them, this time not so much because of Gabriel's presidential attire but because of Jacko's fearsome appearance.

Gabriel spotted the young girl he'd last seen filching the Chinese tourist's wallet fifteen metres in front of him and to the right. She was approaching at an oblique angle. Smart move. Either well-trained or experienced enough in her trade to know people tended not to pay much attention to things in their peripheral vision. Correction, *civilians* tended not to.

Gabriel turned his head a little to his left and murmured to Jacko.

'My three.'

He tightened his grip on his attaché case, even though it was empty. He'd had an idea.

She was ten metres away now. Tracking Gabriel in the shadow of an immense man in pastel shorts and a billowing Hawaiian shirt. He was filming his progress past the tower on an iPad, which he was holding aloft, staring intently at its massive screen. '*Why not just look at the bloody thing with your eyes?*' Gabriel wanted to shout. But he kept his mouth shut. He didn't want to frighten off the girl. Who, even now, was dipping practised fingers into the shorts and lifting another trophy. A phone, this time.

Five metres.

Tagging along with a small group of children laughing and giggling some distance behind their parents. A couple of them looked at her with puzzled frowns, but she smiled at them and began chatting and soon it was as if they'd known each other their whole lives.

She was good, this mini-grifter. She'd learned how to blend in, to win people's confidence.

Three metres.

She'd fallen off the tail of the gaggle of kids and was readying herself for the swerve, bump, apology and run.

One.

As she stumbled into him and slipped her fingers around the handle of his briefcase, Gabriel turned and clamped down on her wrist with his free hand.

'Not this time, *Cheri*,' he said.

She yanked her hand back but he held firm.

'Let me go, asshole!' she hissed. 'Or I'll drop you in shit up to your armpits.'

She turned her head away. Drew in an enormous breath. The ploy was obvious even without hearing it.

'You shout "paedo" and I'll shout "thief",' Gabriel said, 'and let's see who the cops believe, eh?'

The '*p—*' he could see forming on her pursed lips never escaped. Beside him, Jacko was scanning the crowds.

'Give me the phone you just took.'

'Fuck you!'

He gave her slender wrist the gentlest of twists.

'I can break it if you want, but I'd feel really bad about that. Now hand it over. I saw you pinch a wallet earlier so I know you're having a good day.'

'Fine.'

She reached into a pocket and pulled out the phone. Handed it over. Gabriel passed it to Jacko and indicated the fat tourist, still walking along with his iPad held high, oblivious to the events transpiring not ten metres away from him.

'Tell him he dropped it.'

While Jacko approached the tourist with the recovered phone, Gabriel knelt in front of the girl.

'Who was the guy you handed the wallet over to?'

She lifted her chin in an arrogant gesture of defiance.

'I don't know what you're talking about.'

'I think you do. And I have twenty euros to back up my hunch.'

'Fuck you.'

'Thirty.'

'He'll kill me.'

'So there *is* a guy.'

Her eyes flicked left and right. She was worried. Maybe the gangmaster kept his pocket-sized grifters under surveillance.

'Let me go, man,' she said, her voice panicky now. 'I gotta go.'

Gabriel pulled out a hundred-euro note.

'I'm looking for a girl named Odette. Odette Diallo. She's missing and her mum and dad are really worried. Does the guy you work for recruit other kids?'

She reached for the note. He kept a tight grip on his end but let her pinch the edge nearest her between thumb and forefinger.

She nodded.

'Does he have a name?'

'Rafi.'

'Does he run things?'

'Here.'

'There are other patches.'

'Mm-hmm.'

'Who's the big boss, then? Of all the patches?'

She wouldn't meet his eye. But in his grip, her arm was trembling. She was frightened. No, she was terrified. Time to stop this. Let her go, back into the shadows.

He released his grip on the banknote.

She turned and snaked her way into the crowds, still thick even at the tail-end of the day. In moments, she'd vanished.

Jacko reappeared at his side. He was grinning broadly and held up a hundred-euro note. For a moment, Gabriel thought he'd pinched it back from the little street robber.

'Look who got a reward for being, "*un bon citoyen et un gentilhomme*".'

Gabriel smiled. 'Excellent work. We'll have you getting a certificate from the mayor before long.'

With the good citizen and gentleman secreting his reward

money deep in one of the pockets of his greatcoat, Gabriel led him across the street towards the bistro.

Where they met a solid wall of resistance.

16

The *chef-patron* of Bistro André met them just inside the door, the name of his establishment embroidered in burgundy on his black apron, his own name on his immaculate chef's whites.

He folded muscular arms across his chest. Glanced at Jacko and then stared at Gabriel, inviting him to speak.

'A table for two please. By the window would be nice,' Gabriel added, indicating a vacant table beside a window, half-covered by a net curtain threaded onto a brass pole.

'We're full.'

'That table's empty, though.'

'Reserved.'

Gabriel smiled. 'I don't see a sign.'

'I don't use signs. It's reserved. For a regular.'

Gabriel looked around the restaurant. Several tables were unoccupied.

'Well, perhaps, just for today, you could seat your regular at another table.'

The chef shook his head.

'Try the McDonald's down the street.'

'Let's go, Gabriel,' Jacko murmured. 'You know what the problem is.'

'Let's stay, Jacko,' Gabriel said brightly. 'I fancy some fish. Maybe a nice bottle of white wine.'

The chef, unwisely, halved the distance between him and Gabriel.

'Look, friend. I already told you. I have no spare tables.' And then he committed his final error of protocol. 'If you were on your own, well, of course, that would be different. You are …'—he used the French term *un homme urbain*, loosely translated as 'a man about town'—'but your … friend? No. Impossible. We do not serve dossers here.'

Gabriel fixed the chef with a stare that had transfixed far bigger, far more dangerous men.

'My friend once served his country in battle. Now, that may not mean anything to you, but here's the thing. He also served yours. You've heard of the Foreign Legion, I assume?'

The man's eyes flicked over to Jacko and back at Gabriel. No need for hypnosis this time. The truth was far more powerful.

'Of course. But—'

'My friend was a member of the Second Foreign Parachute Regiment. Not only that, but he was wounded in action. Gabon. And his bravery in service of France, as I am sure you, a proud patriot, would know, earned him French citizenship "for blood shed". So, André,' Gabriel straightened the chef's apron straps over his collar bones, 'it ought to be your *honour* to serve my friend. Now, how about that table?'

The chef was blushing a deep crimson as he nodded and showed Gabriel and Jacko to the window table. As he seated them, he snapped his fingers. An elderly, black-aproned waiter – stooped, skinny, with tufts of white hair sprouting from his ears – appeared.

'Yes, Chef?'

'Bring a bottle of the eighty-five Marsanne.'

The old man's eyes widened and his wiry grey brows lifted halfway to his forehead.

'But, Chef. Those bottles are for special customers. You said so yourself.'

'Paul! The eighty-five. Now!'

The chef turned to address Jacko directly. He held his hand over his heart, obscuring his embroidered name badge.

'Sir, I apologise for my rudeness. Thank you for your service. You are a true Frenchman. Dinner is on the house. Order whatever you wish.'

Soon, the table was laden with stainless steel platters containing cream-and-brown- striped snail shells drenched in vivid green garlic and parsley butter, a basket of thick slices of crusty *pain de campagne* – 'tastes of the country but baked right here, monsieurs' as the waiter explained with pride – pots of egg-yolk-yellow butter spiked with crystals of sea salt, and glasses of the best white burgundy Gabriel had ever tasted. Creamy, apricot and peach flavours, and a delicate yet heady aroma of fresh-cut garden flowers.

Jacko prised another brown curl of snail meat from its shell with a pronged implement like an undersized lobster pick and popped it into his mouth before wiping the melted butter from his beard.

'God, these are good,' he said. 'So, you were going to tell me your story.'

Gabriel nodded, and for the third time in as many days, recounted the sad history that had taken him from a military man who believed in concepts of honour and duty to whatever the hell he was now, 'some sort of freelance problem solver, I suppose,' he concluded, 'although I'm done with taking orders.'

Jacko nodded, ate his last snail and washed it down with a considerable gulp of wine.

'And now you're looking for a lost girl.'

'I was wondering whether she might be caught up in some sort of gang like the teen who tried to relieve me of my case just now.'

'You get anything out of her?'

'A name. Rafi. Runs the pack by the tower. There's some sort of organised crime gang behind it but when I asked her who the big boss was she looked like she was going to wet herself.'

Jacko nodded thoughtfully. He opened his mouth then closed it as the waiter materialised at his side to clear the table of the remnants of the two dozen unfortunate molluscs.

He returned and began scraping breadcrumbs from the thick white tablecloth into a miniature dustpan with a little silver blade like half a straight razor.

Gabriel pointed to the bottle.

'We'll have another, please.'

The waiter stiffened, and paused in his barbering of the table linen.

'I'll bring the wine list.'

'No need,' Gabriel said, winking at Jacko. 'This is perfectly acceptable.'

Their main courses arrived along with a second bottle of wine. A whole sea bass for Gabriel and a veal cutlet the size of a barn door for Jacko.

'After I left the Legion, I told you I made some unwise career choices,' Jacko said. 'I ended up as an enforcer for this charming pair of brothers. Syrians. Ex-cops or secret police or whatever. Evil, basically. Ali and Bashar Soltani. They control the drugs trade in the Eighteenth, Nineteenth and Twentieth. But they've got their fingers in all kinds of pies. Extortion, arms dealing, people trafficking. I wouldn't be surprised if that lass who went for your case worked in one of their little side hustles. Or if they don't control it, they'll be paid rent.'

Gabriel leaned forwards. Was this worse than he'd assumed? Maybe Odette's fate was darker than being recruited to a street-crime gang rolling tourists.

'You said people trafficking. Illegal immigration? Boats to the UK, that sort of thing?'

Jacko shook his head.

'They steer clear of that. Too much political heat means too much police interest. Plus, the gangs who do that? They're big and very well resourced. The Soltanis are violent and they're devious and they're greedy. But it's basically just the two of them. If they tried muscling in on the small boat trade they'd end up in pieces in the Seine.'

'So what then?'

Jacko shrugged and cut off another chunk of the veal. Chewed and spoke round the meat.

'Domestic servants. Well, they call them that but in reality they're little more than slaves. Nail bars, although that's mainly the Vietnamese triads in Paris. And sex, obviously. They bring girls in from Africa, mainly the French speaking bits. Mali, Senegal, Cote d'Ivoire, Congo, Chad Burkina Faso. Christ, I fought in half those places.'

'Me, too,' Gabriel said thoughtfully. 'Do you think it's possible they might have taken the girl I'm looking for? She already lived here but her parents are from Cote d'Ivoire and Senegal.'

'Those guys? They'd do anything. How old did you say she was?'

'Twelve.'

Jacko winced.

'Nonce territory, for sure. Plenty of those evil bastards in Paris would pay top dollar for a chance to,' he looked down at his plate, then dropped his cutlery and pushed it away from him, 'you know. The first time.'

Something dark and cold and greasy uncoiled in Gabriel's gut. Jacko was right: they'd fought in some of the same places. And against the kind of enemies who, when they weren't leaving knackered Landcruisers filled with sugar and fertilizer outside embassies, or emptying the mags of their AK-47s at anyone straying into their territory, would cheerfully kidnap and gang-rape schoolgirls.

He clenched his jaw, the wine suddenly tasting metallic. He needed to find the Soltanis, without them knowing about him. But first, looking across the table at his fellow SAS veteran, he needed to help Jacko get himself straightened out.

17

Tara looked down at her immaculate manicure. French tips might be fashionable elsewhere, but in Paris, the trend was for natural right now.

The boy – for he couldn't have been more than eighteen – who'd performed the service for her, drawing his brushes down her nails with painstaking care, was Vietnamese.

She'd asked him where he came from and he'd immediately become cagey. Finally, murmuring 'Hanoi', he'd looked towards a door at the back of the room and then glanced meaningfully at her as if begging her not to ask any more questions. She'd tipped him twice the cost of the manicure, in cash.

And now, she sat at an outside table of a chic little cafe on Boulevard Saint-Germain, haughty waiters bustling between the cane and bamboo chairs and glass-topped tables. The bag hanging from a hook beneath the table was Hermès. The foot bobbing beneath it was shod in a Ferragamo loafer. She'd come a long way.

She pictured her eight-year-old self, hooking grotesquely toothed fish out of the river that ran through their little village on the mainland. They'd all called it the Little Mekong. A joke: the real thing was thousands of miles to the west, running through the country where her manicurist had grown up.

What would little Wei Mei and her best friend Xi Ping think of this elegant creature dressed head to toe in designer clothes, a fifteen-thousand euro handbag by her knee containing enough cash to flee to any country in the world? Tara smiled to herself. She'd probably admire it and then snatch it up and have it away on her toes, ducking down an alley before disappearing forever with her spoils.

And what a life that precocious little street rat had led! Kidnapped as a baby in a triad ransom scheme gone wrong. Spirited from Hong Kong to a rural backwater in Guangdong Province. A runaway who ended up in Shenzhen Mega City before being talent-spotted by a woman who turned kids into state assassins at a secret facility deep in the interior. Finally, snatching freedom before they could execute her, and finding herself back in Hong Kong, now working for the very same man who'd kidnapped her. First as a bodyguard, then as a roving troubleshooter, and, finally, his assassin and successor.

'Earth calling Tara! Earth calling Tara!'

She smiled, and shoved the memories down.

'Sorry, Alice, miles away.'

Like Tara, Alice had ditched as much of her former identity as possible. Like Tara, she now had a western name. Like Tara, she'd had eyelid surgery to westernise her appearance. Although she hadn't gone to the extremes Tara had. No excruciating leg-lengthening procedures. No ear re-siting, jaw breaking or hairline alteration.

'I said, did you hear that they've got agents in Paris now?'

Tara frowned. Or at least she thought she did. The Botox meant the expression was a largely internal construct. There was no need to ask who 'they' were.

'Do you know how many people they've got here?' Tara asked Alice, wondering whether Paris would prove to be as temporary as Berlin, Singapore and London.

'No. And to be honest, it might only be a rumour.'

'Rumours don't come from nowhere, though, do they?'

Tara glanced up and down the street. Parisians, tourists, office workers, food delivery guys on those fat-tyred electric bikes the mayor was kicking up such a stink about. Nobody scanning the crowds as she was. No dull suits and sharp eyes. She moved her left foot until her toe was touching the Hermès bag. It didn't matter. She'd be ready. She was always ready. A street shoot-out would be ugly, but if necessary, she'd have the Taurus compact nine millimetre pistol out and in her hand in seconds.

It was a risk, carrying a firearm. Arrest, charges, a trial. Prison time. Yes, a risk. But realistically, it was minor. Dressed the way she was dressed? Speaking French the way she did? With the accent she'd worked so hard to cultivate? Behaving the way she did, from body language to her confident worldly manner? A cop would be more likely to warn a beggar to stop bothering her than to ask what was making that beautiful handbag bulge so.

Alice smiled, revealing newly straightened and whitened teeth.

'We'll be fine, though, won't we? I mean, there's nothing to connect us to our old lives.'

'I wish that were true, Alice, I really do. But there's always a connection.' She laid a hand on her chest. 'Us. My brother thought he could disappear and even with all his training, his old boss still found him.'

'How is Gaby? Still teaching street kids how to be better at fighting?'

Tara wagged a finger at her friend, who was grinning mischievously.

'You are a naughty girl. You know that's not what they do up there. And, to answer your question, he's fine. He's got a new project, as a matter of fact.'

Alice raised an enquiring eyebrow.

'Sounds mysterious.'

'Not really. He's helping this couple find their missing daughter.'

'Isn't that what the police are for?'

'Maybe if you're white and well-heeled and you don't live in a *banlieue.* But the girl's parents are African. Apparently the cops just gave the mother the brushoff. Gabriel, too, even though he was better dressed than the president.'

'Well, if Gaby's on the case, they won't have to wait long.' Alice inspected a fingernail, a perfect oval of metallic red. 'How's his girlfriend coping with him spending all his time playing at private detectives?'

Tara arched an eyebrow.

'You might want to work on your casual questioning technique, Alice, because that landed like an Airbus in a high wind.'

Alice grinned.

'Fine,' she said, pouting. 'Is Gabriel seeing anyone at the moment?'

'No. He isn't. But as I think I told you before, my darling girl, he's not in the market.' Tara sighed. 'In fact I don't think he'll ever be in the market again.'

Alice blew a delicate raspberry. 'Don't be ridiculous. He's a man. They always come around.'

'And ninety-nine times out of a hundred I'd agree with you. But BB? He nearly killed himself over her. She was the love of his life.'

Alice looked at Tara from beneath lowered lids, so she was peering through the long false eyelashes she habitually wore.

'Love? Who said anything about love?'

Tara let her mouth drop open in mock-outrage. 'You're incorrigible! Anyway, let's not spend our evening talking about my brother. What have you been up to since I last saw you?'

'Oh, you know,' Alice said, tucking a stray curl behind her ear, 'still running the CIA's drugs-for-guns programme in Turkmenistan. You?'

'I play a lot of tennis. I go to lectures at the Sorbonne. Oh, and I've started killing people again. Not a lot. But it was what I was trained for and it seemed a shame to let it go to waste. All that "legitimate businesswoman" act was getting too boring.'

'Targets?'

'Organised crime, mostly. Like Murder, Inc. used to do in the US.'

Alice signalled a passing waiter and ordered two more coffees. '"Mostly"?'

Tara shrugged. 'I did a tech executive last year. He was skimming profits to support this conspiracy theory website. And a serial killer in Spain. The cops knew who it was but his lawyer got him off on a technicality.'

'You should have done the lawyer as well as a gesture of goodwill.'

Tara smiled.

'The client wanted me to. But she couldn't afford it. There's an *abogado* living in a nice house on the outskirts of Madrid who has no idea how lucky he is.'

Their coffees arrived.

18

From across Boulevard Saint-Germain, a woman in black trousers and a blue shirt watched the two women chatting and sipping their *cafés au lait*.

She recorded a short voice note on her phone.

19

Gabriel made coffee while Jacko stood in the centre of the apartment's vast open-plan living room and slowly turned a full circle.

'Did you win the EuroMillions or something?'

'It's my sister's place.'

'OK, well, did *she* win, then? Because I'm telling you, mate, you couldn't afford this on an army pension.'

Gabriel's lips formed around the beginning of a lie. Then he stopped himself before the falsehood found air enough to grow. He'd chosen to hide who he was from most people he'd met since moving to Paris. And it was a wearying existence. In Jacko Blake, he felt he might have met someone with whom he could be completely honest.

He looked over at him, now standing with his hands in the pockets of that vast, stinking greatcoat.

'She used to run a triad in Hong Kong. Got out while the going was good. Went legit. Then sold up and quit the country altogether before the Chinese authorities made a move.'

Jacko rubbed his beard. Took another spin, his eyes roving

over the artworks, the antique Chinese porcelain, the Bechstein grand piano.

He looked back at Gabriel. Nodded.

'Nice.'

Then he guffawed, a laughter so natural and unforced that soon Gabriel had to join in.

The inner front door opened and in walked Tara. A smile on her face. It slipped as she took in the hirsute tramp standing in the centre of her antique Turkish rug, then she hoisted it back in place.

She went to Gabriel and hugged him.

'Hey, BB. Are you going to introduce me to your friend?'

He loved her all the more for it. The way she took in situations at a glance and always, *always*, made the right call.

'Tara, this is Jacko Blake. I met him at the tower today. He's ex-SAS and French Foreign Legion.' Gabriel turned to Jacko. 'Jacko, this is my kid sister, Tara.'

Jacko crossed the expanse of wine-red carpet with its intricate geometric patterns and extended his hand.

'*Enchanté*,' he said, in a horrible French accent that had Tara smiling.

He drew her hand up and kissed the half-inch of air he left between her skin and his lips.

Jacko stood back.

'I'm sorry about my somewhat louche appearance, Tara. And the smell. I have been living an indigent life these past months and sadly my membership of polite society lapsed some time ago.'

'But not your way with words. What a pretty speech, Jacko,' she said, still smiling. 'But you're right. You stink like a market butcher on an August day, so I'll show you the guest bathroom and you can have a shower. No, wait. Better have a shower and a bath. And a shave.' She stood back and looked him up and down. 'I'll get BB to set out some clothes for you. You're a bit taller than him but I'm sure we can find something that will work. Come with me.'

She held her hand out and, with a half-grin at Gabriel over his shoulder, he allowed himself to be led away by Tara.

A few minutes later, Tara returned, accepting the glass of cold white wine Gabriel had poured for her. She took a sip and then raised her eyebrows: an unspoken question. *Well?*

'Those girls who mugged me? It was his knife,' Gabriel said. 'I found him by the tower. He really needs help.'

'Then let's help him.'

'That's it? You're OK with it?'

'Of course I am! You brought him here. That's good enough for me, BB.'

'Thanks, Tara. So, how was your coffee with Alice?'

Tara rolled her eyes.

'Fine. But you should know, she's got you in her gunsights. The mere mention of your name has her going all breathless like a nympho in a room full of rugby players.'

'Quite the visual image. Did you tell her I'm not the dating kind?'

'I think she saw that more as a challenge than a stop sign.'

'She still running guns for the CIA?'

Tara's eyes widened.

'How did you …?'

'She "bumped into me" a few times while you were away. We had a coffee. She's quite the girl, isn't she?'

Tara drank some more wine.

'She's not looking for a relationship, BB,' she said quietly. 'And she's a lot of fun. You could just go on a date with her. Even just dinner? It would do you good.'

Gabriel felt the anger he kept clamped down inside him threatening to break free of the restraints he shackled it in.

'No! It really wouldn't.' Guilt rushed upon him. 'I'm sorry, Tara. Really sorry. But please, let's just leave it. I'm not your project. I don't want you to "fix" me.'

'No, *I'm* sorry. I know you're still grieving for Eli. I'll tell Alice to back off.'

He shook his head.

'It's fine. If the worst I have to deal with is a sex-crazed Chinese, ex-pat, black ops gun runner, I'll probably cope.'

That earned him a laugh.

'So what's the plan?'

'For Jacko?'

'For Jacko, and for finding Odette.'

'Not sure. Maybe they're part of the same plan.'

'What do you know so far? Tell me.'

Tara listened with all her attention as Gabriel sketched out the intelligence he'd gathered, as sketchy as it was. A missing girl. Not the type to get into trouble. Diligent with her schoolwork. Strong same-sex friendships and membership of a couple of after-school clubs. Religious, but undecided which way to follow God: so church with her mum on Sunday, mosque with her dad on Friday. All in all, not the type to, as the cops had suggested, go off with a boyfriend to party until the drugs or the condoms ran out. The inescapable conclusion: she'd either met with an accident, been kidnapped or been murdered.

Tara dismissed the first option out of hand.

'A girl like that, she'll have a routine. Home, school, club, home again. Well-trodden paths, main streets. Friends she's in contact with. If she'd been run over or fallen somewhere, someone would have found her by now.'

'Agreed. So either she's been taken or she's been murdered.'

'Who'd murder a twelve-year-old schoolgirl?'

Sadly, Gabriel thought, the answer was all too many people.

'If this was Rwanda or Cambodia or Colombia or Afghanistan, I'd say militia, secret police, IS, the Tali, gangbangers spraying rounds from a passing car, all kinds.'

'Yeah, BB, but this is Paris. Sometimes the binmen go on strike, or the farmers dump cowshit outside the Elysée Palace, but it's hardly Cali cartel country.'

'No. So that only leaves us with paedophiles and serial killers.'

Tara shook her head.

'Not serial killers. If there was one operating in Paris we'd know about it. The media would be full of it.'

'Not if Odette was his first,' he countered.

She pursed her lips, her habit when she was thinking. He found it strange that they should be calmly discussing the likelihood of there being a serial killer operating in Paris as if they were deciding where to eat dinner.

'But statistically, the odds are against it. I reckon the mostly likely explanation is she's been snatched off the street.'

'I agree. Next question, by whom? And why?'

'Ransom?'

'Her parents work hard but they're poor. Marianne runs a laundry and Youssoo is a carer at Bichat-Claude Bernard Hospital.'

'But gangs can work all kinds of rackets. Maybe they don't ask for millions of euros, just help hiding drugs or even couriering them.'

'Nobody's contacted Marianne and Youssoo, though.'

Tara poured more wine into her glass. Tipped the bottle towards Gabriel. He shook his head.

'I hate to say this, BB, but back in Hong Kong? Some triads, not the White Koi, by the way, but some, the Coral Snakes, the Four-Point Star, they used to run the sex trade. Hookers, yes, but other stuff. Dark stuff. You know those …'—she used a piece of untranslatable Chinese street slang whose nearest English approximation would be *rotting dog-gut fucker*—'who get off on doing kids. Animals.'

'I know. I met a few in Phnom Penh.'

'Oh, yeah? How did that go?'

'I had sore knuckles for a week. They got arrested and, I hope, brutally treated by the cops, the courts and then their fellow inmates. The Cambodians don't take kindly to Western paedophiles.'

'Look, maybe she just had enough of being nagged to do her homework. Or she took a pill at a friend's house and is too ashamed to go home, but my opinion? Someone's got her. And they're going to stick her in a flat somewhere and let the …'—the Chinese phrase again—'have her, until the poor little thing's no good to them.'

'We need to find her. Fast. Jacko said there are these two Syrians. Brothers. Soltani's the name. They're involved in sex trafficking. I think maybe Jacko can help me.'

Footsteps on the wooden floor of the hallway.

'Help you do what?'

Gabriel and Tara turned together. Her mouth dropped open. Gabriel's smiled.

'And you are?' he asked.

Jacko stood facing them, his hands in the pockets of a pair of navy linen trousers. On Gabriel they were ankle length. On their new wearer they were more like Capri pants. The shirt, a Cuban guayabera in white cotton, was snug across Jacko's massive chest and biceps, but it was a decent fit. Just.

But it was his face that had the Wolfe siblings captivated. The piratical red beard was gone, revealing gleaming pink cheeks, albeit spotted with shaving nicks here and there. He'd combed his hair back from his forehead and some of the hooded look had disappeared along with the grime, so his startlingly blue eyes twinkled from beneath newly trimmed eyebrows.

'I borrowed some of your aftershave, too, Gabriel. I hope that's all right.'

'Of course, that's why it's in there. My God, Jacko, that's quite the transformation.'

'Turn around, handsome,' Tara said.

Jacko executed a balletic pirouette, apparently unfazed by her interest.

'Well,' he said, coming to rest facing her again. 'Do I pass muster?'

She went over to him, leaned closer and inhaled deeply, eyes closed.

'Mm. Nice.' She opened her eyes again. 'Very nice. If only all our house guests smelled like you.'

'If only all my hosts were so charming,' he replied.

'Are you hungry?'

'We ate earlier. But a drink would be nice.'

'Come on, then. Let's find you some shoes. There's a lovely bar just across the street. I know the owner.'

Gabriel winked at Jacko.

'She *is* the owner.'

20

The sign over the door had no words, just a semi-abstract painting of two creatures apparently fighting. A bull, its horned head lowered in a charge. And a crane, wings outspread, dagger-beak spearing down towards the bull's exposed neck like a matador's sword.

On the window to the right, gold script gave the bar's name. *Le Taureau et la Grue.*

Tara led the trio inside and nodded a greeting to the girl behind the bar.

'*Bonsoir,* Evelyne,' she called. '*Ça va?*'

'*Ça va,* Tara.'

A sharply dressed waiter in black trousers and shirt led them to a corner table. Tara ordered champagne. He returned a few minutes later with a bottle in an ice bucket, which he placed in a floor-stand, and three glasses. Once the business with the wine was concluded, vapour curling from the neck as he extracted the cork with a hiss of escaping gas, he withdrew.

Tara poured then held her glass aloft. Gabriel and Jacko followed suit.

'To our mission,' she said.

The two men exchanged glances, and Gabriel looked at Tara as they clinked rims, then drank.

'*Our* mission?'

'You didn't think I was going to sit this one out, did you, BB? A young girl is missing. For a start, I wouldn't let you do this alone and besides, you might need a woman's touch.'

Jacko turned to Tara.

'Why do I get the feeling when you say that, you're not talking about soft words and emotional intelligence?'

She grinned and took a healthy swig of the champagne.

'Oh, I can do those, too. But I was thinking more like getting a man to let his guard down before slitting his belly open.'

He nodded. Drained his glass and reached for the bottle to refill it. The waiter appeared at his elbow, causing him to rear back.

'*Pardon, monsieur*, allow me,' he said tilting the bottle and pouring more champagne.

Jacko took a sip this time, before replacing his glass on the table. Gabriel watched his new friend closely. There was something behind his eyes. A watchfulness. Anxiety. Was it PTSD? Despite Jacko's earlier denial? The way he'd started when the waiter had materialised. Hypervigilance. Although his lifestyle might have taken the edge off it. Or was that why he chased the dragon? To find some peace and escape his demons? Even if that meant swapping those wielding AKs and machetes for a different species, just as deadly and with claws that would lodge in your flesh and never come out.

'I've fought alongside some pretty feisty women,' Jacko said. 'Not army, more like insurgents, freedom fighters, that type of thing. Forgive me, Tara, but you don't give off that sort of vibe. Where did you learn your trade, if it wasn't in uniform?'

She smiled. 'Oh, I had a uniform. For a while, at least. BB saw me in it, didn't you?'

Gabriel nodded.

'A very fetching white-leather number.'

'Must have been hell getting the blood out,' Jacko said dryly.

'My boss owned laundries,' Tara said, making Jacko's remark seem as wet as the Seine. 'Tell him how we met, BB. Last time, I mean.'

Gabriel rubbed his nose and looked away from the table. At the wall, where a very talented artist had painted a bigger version of the image above the front door. Trust Tara to include an depiction of combat in her interior decor. Another vision floated past his eyes. He described it to Jacko as he watched the internal movie playing as an overlay on the mural.

He'd just slaughtered the boss of a Russian *mafya* gang, along with his two lieutenants, his cook and a tame Siberian wolf the size of a heifer. He left the blood-spattered dining room, and three corpses dismembered by machine-gun fire and a ceremonial Cossack sword, to be confronted by a young woman in black aiming a submachine gun at his belly. Flinching as the bullets tore into his abdomen he fell to the ground, only to find the flinching was caused by plaster dust raining down after she emptied her magazine into the ceiling.

'And she turned out to be my long-lost sister,' he concluded. 'Although we didn't really connect until she saved me from being killed by her boss.'

Jacko nodded his appreciation.

'My sister lives in Manchester,' he said. 'She's an accountant. Her husband's in insurance. I haven't seen her for five years.'

'Maybe you could go back to England, when this is over,' Tara said. 'Visit her. Family is important, right?'

He wrinkled his nose. 'Maybe. But I'd have to get myself clean first. She's got kids. Two boys, two girls. I've got nephews and nieces I've never seen.'

'We could help you, couldn't we?' Tara said, turning to Gabriel. 'Get you some help. A doctor, a psychiatrist, a clinic, whatever you need.'

'Why are you doing this, Tara?' Jacko asked, leaning towards her. 'I mean you only met me an hour or so ago.'

'Do you think I should wait for a few years and then decide to help you?'

'No. But I could be anybody. Look at me.' He glanced down at his fresh, clean clothes and smiled guiltily. 'OK, look at me how I was this afternoon. Like the chef where we ate said, I'm just a dosser. A homeless, druggie dosser. I was begging on the street, for Christ's sake.'

She leaned forwards, mirroring his body language and gently lifted his hand so she could envelop it in hers.

'You're not "just" anything, Jacko. I already told you, Gabriel believes in you or he would never have brought you home,' she said fiercely. 'You think I started off like this? Owning a bar, rich beyond most people's dreams? I grew up in a tiny little village in the middle of nowhere. Caught fish out of the river to eat, scrounged clothes, cut school to play in the forest. Then I lived on the streets in Shenzhen. I ran with a pack of street rats, that's what the cops called us. I wasn't just a "street rat" then, I was me. I still am. And you're still you. You joined up to serve your country. You fought alongside your friends and I bet you saw them die too, and it cut you down to the bone. I don't care what happened before to bring you to our door. You're here now, you're helping Gabriel find a missing girl, and if I decide I'm going to help you then that's what's going to happen.' She paused, breathing heavily, and swigged some champagne. 'Or I could bat my eyelashes at you and slit your belly like a fish, if you'd prefer?'

Jacko laughed loudly, but this time nobody turned a disapproving glare in his direction.

'No, no, it's fine. I'll take option one, please. So look, if we're in this together, we need a plan. What are we going to do?'

'You mentioned these Syrian brothers. The Soltanis,' Gabriel said. 'Odette disappeared in the Eighteenth. You said they control the drugs trade there. So they probably control everything else too. You remember what it was like in the sandbox, and in Africa. Local warlords run the drugs trade in their area, but whatever other criminal activity is going on, even if they don't control it, they know about it and either license it or shut it down.'

'Same with the triads,' Tara said.

'Exactly. So if she's been kidnapped, for ransom or the sex trade, the Soltanis will either have done it themselves or know who did.'

'So how do you want to handle it, Gabriel? Because I honestly don't think a frontal assault would be any good. I told you they're only two, but they've got plenty of muscle,' Jacko said. 'All ex-legionnaires like me. There's a revolving door between the Legion and the Soltanis. It's an open secret. If you want a job after you leave, there's a fat monthly paycheque waiting. Well, a carrier bag full of cash, anyway.'

Gabriel nodded thoughtfully. He had an idea. It had worked for him once before, in Estonia. It would work for him again.

'I'm going to apply for a job.'

'That sounds like an excellent plan, mate, but you're going to have to excuse me. Somewhere I need to be.'

Before either Wolfe sibling could say anything, Jacko pushed his chair back, stood and left the bar.

Tara shot Gabriel a look.

'What was that about?' she asked.

'He told me he smoked heroin. I think he's jonesing for a fix.'

She frowned.

'Can we trust him, do you think?'

'Without the drugs, I'd say a hundred percent. Once a trooper, always a trooper. But if push came to shove and he needed a fix and he had an order to follow, well, you must know what junkies are like?'

'Then we need to have each other's backs, BB. No way can we get him clean in time. Odette needs us now.'

He nodded. 'In the meantime, while I'm going in through the front door, can you go in through the back? Find out all you can about the Soltanis.'

'Leave it to me. I have a couple of very reliable tech guys I can call on. They helped me when I turned the White Koi into Lang Holdings.'

She got to her feet. No need to signal for the bill when she owned the place.

He stood, too. Needing sleep. Tomorrow was going to be a big day.

21

The following morning, Gabriel turned up at the gym for work at 9.00 a.m.

Marc nodded a greeting.

'Thought you were taking leave of absence.'

'I am. But what I need to do doesn't start until after lunch. Thought I'd come in and lend a hand.'

Marc lifted his chin towards the corner.

'Assa's in. Just changing.'

Gabriel waited by the ring. He'd thought about hitting the streets first thing, but reasoned the kind of men working for the Soltanis probably kept musicians' hours, waking late and working through the night.

'Hey, Gaby, you're back. Spar with me?'

He turned, smiling. Assa Touré stood waiting for him.

'Come on then, and don't hold back this time. I need to see what you're really capable of.'

Her grin widened, then she slipped in her gumshield, electric blue this time. She tilted her head at the ring. *After you.*

Gabriel slipped on a pair of black and red Metal Boxe hook and jab pads. Turned to face Assa, who was already bobbing and weaving, ready for the workout. Her first flurry of blows had Gabriel smiling and shaking his head. Her speed was breathtaking. He resettled his stance and shouted, 'Come on, Assa! That all you got?'

She flashed that bright blue grin and attacked. Harder. Punches crashing in against the pads' surfaces hard enough for Gabriel to feel the shocks in his fingers and wrists.

As they manoeuvred around each other, Gabriel changing his hand positions to force Assa to recalibrate her strikes, he found himself splitting in two. One half present in the ring, pushing Assa into harder and faster combinations, retreating then turning, pressing her back. The other, the analytic part, wondering where Odette Diallo was, and whether she'd be free one day to practice whatever hobbies occupied a 12-year-old girl. He banished the doubt. No 'ifs', no 'buts'. Between them, he, Tara and Jacko would find her, and free her. And visit appropriate punishment on whoever had kidnapped her.

The next moment, his vision of delivering justice to Odette's persecutors vanished in a white-out, accompanied by flashing sparks and a ringing between his ears. His head snapped sideways and he stumbled backwards before taking a knee in front of the diminutive female boxer who'd cried out as her right glove connected with the side of Gabriel's jaw.

Assa crouched in front of him, lifting his chin with her gloved hand.

'Gaby! Gaby! Are you OK? You just dropped your guard in the middle of my last combination. I'm sorry. I tried to pull it but it still felt pretty hard to me.'

Gabriel sat down, shook his head to dispel both the ringing and the unreal sense that someone had unscrewed his jaw and wired it back on a couple of inches to the left.

'I'm OK,' he said, rubbing the tender spot where her punch had connected. He got to his feet, grinning ruefully. 'That'll teach me to lose my concentration when I'm sparring with an Olympic champion, eh?'

They resumed the routine, this time with Gabriel fully present.

He felt it was a necessity unless he wanted to begin his search for Odette with his jaw wired. After another fifteen minutes, Assa signed for a break.

'I want to do some weights, Gaby. Thanks.'

She held her gloves up and they double fist-bumped.

'Hey, Assa, before you go? Look, don't take this the wrong way, because I know you avoid those places, but do you know where kids go to score weed or pills or whatever?'

She took out her gumshield. A mixture of amusement and puzzlement flickered across her face.

'Don't tell me you're looking to score? I mean, no offence but you look like more of a wine guy.'

He smiled, shaking his head. 'You're right, I am. No, it's nothing like that. But I'm looking for these guys. Really bad guys. They control the drugs trade round here so I figured this might be an easy way to track them down.'

Assa glanced around then nodded towards a corner where posters of the body's major muscle groups flanked a fire door. Gabriel followed her.

She took off her right glove. Then looked away from him, at the poster and pointed to the figure's back, and the triangular, red swathe of its *latissimus dorsi* muscle.

'Those guys are seriously bad news, Gaby,' she murmured, describing the edge of the muscle with her fingertip. 'They're called the Soltanis. They're like these ex-Syrian torturers or whatever. Everybody round here knows about them and everybody stays well clear. It's not just the drugs they control. It's the cops, the judges, even the traffic wardens. They are seriously bad news. The fuck you want to get into it with them for, anyway?'

He didn't look at her. Instead, he tapped the figure's left deltoid muscle and spoke to the back of its head.

'Someone's taken the daughter of a friend of mine. Her name's Odette Diallo and she's twelve. Either the Soltanis did it, or they gave somebody else the OK to do it. Either way, I need to find her and rescue her.'

Assa's eyes widened, then glistened. A tear rolled down her cheek and she dashed it away with her still-gloved left hand.

'Shit, man. Not Odette.'

'You know her?'

'Not *know* know. I mean, she's just a kid. We don't hang out or nothing. But I see her after school at her mum's shop. The laundrette?'

'Yeah. I know it.'

'She's a really sweet girl. Clever, too. Much cleverer than I was at her age. God, much cleverer than I am *now*!'

'Do you think she'd just run away? If she'd had a row with her mum and dad? Go to a friend's house?'

Assa shook her head. Thumped the illustrated figure's spine with her gloved hand.

'Never. No way. That kid loves school too much. She told me she'd never missed a single day.'

'I just had to check. So where should I start looking?'

Assa glanced around the gym, but everyone was concentrating on their work. Beneath the rumbling slap-slap of a nearby speed ball being beaten into submission, she spoke.

'You know Passage Ruelle?'

'I'll find it.'

'It runs by the train tracks. Where it joins Cité de la Chapelle there's this playground. Guy deals nearby. The moped park.'

'Thanks, Assa.'

She laid a hand on his forearm.

'Wait! You need the code word. Otherwise he'll blank you,' she said. 'Say, "Franco told me you sell the best burgers in town".'

Gabriel nodded. It was a rudimentary precaution, but then he guessed those who sold drugs to kids outside playgrounds were rudimentary kinds of people.

He stayed until midday, then left for one of the poorer parts of one of the city's poorer neighbourhoods.

Sure enough, beyond the chain-link fence at the far end of a row of mopeds, a dodgy looking guy was standing with his back to a wall, looking at his phone, eyes coming up periodically to check on his surroundings. A few youths were shooting hoops on the playground, laughing good-naturedly.

Gabriel observed him for twenty minutes: in that time, a few people came up to him and in a brief handshake, money and drugs traded places. An unsophisticated routine. In other cities, on other lurks, Gabriel had watched as a money-man, a spotter and the dealer himself operated in a triangle of deniability. Nobody caught would have more than one element of the crime. But here, the dealer was apparently happy enough to handle business alone. Maybe the police didn't come down here. Or maybe they were paid not to.

Gabriel slouched over, hands bunched in his pockets, eyes flicking left and right. Five metres out, the guy looked up. Gabriel hadn't bothered to silence his steps, but it was an impressive feat of situational awareness all the same.

Gabriel glanced into his eyes, then looked over his shoulder. Back at the dealer.

'Franco told me you sell the best burgers in town.'

This close Gabriel could see the dealer was no older than twenty-five. Wispy blonde beard that barely covered his chin. Pale-blue eyes that were filled with suspicion. Clearly, Gabriel didn't fit his usual client profile.

'I don't know no Franco, man. But if you're hungry there's a Burger King on Rue Marx Dormoy.'

Gabriel closed the distance between them to half a metre.

'My friend's reliable. He told me you sell the best burgers in town. And I'm hungry.'

The guy looked left and right down the row of mopeds, across the playground. Back at Gabriel.

He shrugged. 'What's your pleasure, my friend?'

'Pleasure can wait. I'm looking for work.'

'The fuck you think I am, a job centre? Fuck off man, before I call some people who'll do some work on *you*.'

Gabriel smiled.

'Now, you see, that's the kind of people I want to work for. Listen, Mister Drugs 'R' Us, I'm guessing you know people who could use an ex-Special Forces guy who's looking for cash and isn't too particular how he makes it.'

The dealer rolled his eyes.

'"Special Forces"? Right.' He turned away. 'Blow me.'

Gabriel stepped in, lanced out a foot, and threw his man to the ground. His left cheekbone hit the pavement with an audible crack. Gabriel stepped back and waited while the half-stunned drug dealer clambered unsteadily to his feet.

'What the fuck, man, you just chipped a tooth.'

'Give me any more lip and I'll pull it out between my fingers,' Gabriel snapped, leaning into the role of aggrieved and impatient ex-Foreign Legionnaire.

Hands held up to ward off this hair-trigger nutcase in front of him, the dealer backed away.

'OK, OK. Chill, man. Yeah, I know someone. He's connected to the dudes who run things round here. You ever hear of the Soltanis?'

'No, but I like a few sultanas on my porridge in the morning.'

The dealer crinkled his forehead.

'Whatever. Come back in half an hour. I need to make a couple of calls.'

'Don't fuck me around.'

'I won't! Jesus, you really need to chill the fuck out, man.' He rubbed his cheekbone. 'I think you broke something in there.'

'Stop being such a pussy and phone your friend. I'll be back. Maybe I'll get a Whopper while I wait.'

* * *

Thirty minutes later, when Gabriel approached the dealer for the second time, he had a second man with him. Dressed all in black. Leather jacket, jeans, scuffed boots, through which steel toecaps gleamed. His head was shaved, revealing nicks and scars. His face looked as though someone had scrunched it in a giant fist, chin, nose and lowering brow striving to meet in the centre. All in all, the picture of openness and trust.

The muscle lifted his stubbled chin at Gabriel.

'Name?'

'Gabriel.'

'Gabrielle? The fuck? Your parents gave you a chick's name, man.'

He bellowed with laughter and the dealer joined in, happy now he had protection to have some fun at Gabriel's expense.

It was such an obvious provocation, Gabriel wondered at its purpose. Was he supposed to launch himself at the muscle, to show he had what it took?

Over the years, Gabriel had met a number of men, and the occasional woman, who he considered to be psychopaths. Maybe not the ravening, sexually depraved, torturing monsters of popular imagination, but psychopaths just the same. An assassin named Sasha Beck. A cult leader named Christophe Jardin. Something missing from their psyche, all trace of remorse or empathy burned away by trauma, or just bad genes. He channelled them now. Looked the muscle in the eye, smiled a little, let all his muscles relax, and spoke in a calm, emotionless voice.

'My parents are dead. If you mention them again I will come to your home in the middle of the night and kill you.'

The muscle took a few seconds to think about this. Then he took half a step back. His own muscles were flexing and releasing beneath the leather jacket. Particularly the right arm. It wanted to dive inside the jacket. Which bulged just beneath the armpit. Reading him was child's play. Should I counter-attack? Or would that lead to the kind of trouble I can't afford? Gabriel saved him the trouble of deciding. He grinned ferociously.

'Joke! I was the one who killed them. So, your man here says you can hook me up with these Soltani guys. What are they, brothers? Cousins? Doesn't matter. What does matter is I'm looking for a job.'

Gabriel waited for the play. When it came he remained calm,

relaxed. Further psychology to unsettle the muscle-slash-go-between.

Muscle brought out a battered Browning 1911 .45 automatic and stuck it in Gabriel's face.

'One reason I shouldn't blow your fucking head off?'

'You mean apart from the fact that piece of shit'll probably jam or explode and blow your hand off? OK, you see that tall building over there?'

Gabriel held his left arm out, finger pointing, and held it at a thirty-degree angle.

Muscle turned to look. Gabriel struck fast, grabbing the Browning's slide with his right hand and immobilising it with his thumb in front of the hammer. A sharp clockwise twist and the guy had no option but to let go or have his wrist broken.

Casually, Gabriel waggled the pistol to and fro in front of Muscle's now pale face.

'Could we just stop all the dick-swinging now?' He dropped out the magazine and racked the slide to eject the round in the chamber. 'I want to meet the Soltanis. One of them, anyway, to discuss my future employment. I'll come back tomorrow. Same time, same place. Meet me here and take me to them.'

'My gun.'

Gabriel smacked him in the face with it.

'You can have it back tomorrow.'

22

Bashar Soltani pointed to the livid purple bruise that had spread from William Boulanger's cheekbone down to his jawline.

'The fuck happened to your face?'

Boulanger shrugged. He was embarrassed. Not a good look for a hired thug like him to have been bested in a street brawl. Although there was something seriously off about that Englishman.

'Lucky punch. This British dude wants a job. Things got kinetic while we were talking.'

'Lucky punch, eh?' Bashar prodded the centre of the bruise, two centimetres below William's left eye. He flinched and bit back an oath. Bashar always had this knack for pinpointing the exact spot on a body that would cause the most pain. Went with the territory, he supposed. 'Sure about that, William? Or did he give you a beat-down and your shame prevents you from telling me the truth?'

Damn, he was good! People said Bashar was the smart one of the two. Ali One-Eye? Well, he had the same look as the Englishman. Gabriel. Psychopath, no doubt.

William offered up a rueful grin, a dog caught out by its

master in the act of filching cold chicken from the fridge. Hoped it would work.

'What do you think, boss? You want me to bring him in? He claimed he was Special Forces.'

Bashar shook his head.

'Too cocky. I don't like men who think they can swagger their way into my organisation. Plus,' he patted William on the shoulder, though not before allowing his hand to take a detour perilously close to his cheekbone, making him flinch again, 'he beat up one of my staff. My loyal staff. You are loyal, aren't you, William?'

'Of course. Hundred percent.'

'Well, then, we can't have that, can we?'

'What do you want me to do?'

'He say how he knew about us?'

'No. Just that he guessed Micky might know someone who knew someone. That kind of thing.'

Bashar nodded decisively.

'I don't like it when people I don't know start making guesses about my business. Fuck him up.'

William went to leave.

'No, wait. I don't want him coming back for a second bite. Kill him.'

'Use our guys?'

'No. Outsource it. Give it to someone on the shortlist for a job.'

'How about those skinheads keep pestering me for work?'

'Fine. Try them out. Tell them if they do it right there's a thousand euros each and a month's tryout.'

'And if they do it wrong?'

Bashar smiled that crocodile's grin of his. William's guts clenched. That was the trouble with working for the Soltanis. It was like being a tick bird in the croc's mouth. Plenty of food, a certain amount of protection, but always, that maw of evil yellow teeth just waiting to slam shut and reduce you to so much smashed flesh and crushed bone.

'If they fail, they'll need to leave town before Ali finds them.'

William nodded. Recognised a dismissal without needing to actually hear it.

He had a call to make. Nasty little neo-Nazi by the name of Sven Robicheaux was about to get his wish.

23

What would he do if it was *his* organisation?

Gabriel considered this question as he shuffled down Passage Ruelle wearing Jacko's greatcoat and a once-white ballcap, greasy with someone else's sweat and sloughed skin cells, pulled down low over his face.

Clearly, the one thing he *wouldn't* do was simply agree to a stranger's proposal. Especially a stranger who'd just bested one of his men and relieved him of his weapon.

Best case? A hooded excursion in a car boot to some unit on an industrial estate or dock. A brutal interrogation. And maybe a job at the end of it.

Worst case? An invitation to try synchronised swimming in the Seine with the added fun of a kettlebell strapped to the ankles.

He shifted his grip on the shopping cart, which he'd filled with a dozen or so Carrefour carrier bags bulging with newspapers, discarded coffee cups, charity shop clothes and even the carcass of a dead crow he'd found behind a dumpster outside a restaurant.

Just before the junction with Cité de la Chapelle, he stopped and bent his head to light a spaghetti-thin roll up. He placed it between his lips and squinted ahead towards the playground. It was empty. In fact, the whole street was deserted. He nodded to himself. Someone had established a cordon sanitaire. Nobody in or out. Except, presumably, for the ex-Special Forces guy looking for work.

No sign of the dealer. Nor of the muscle. And no one who might conceivably go by the name of Soltani. He pictured the kind of gangsters he'd met in the Middle East. Tough, battle-hardened men in black leather jackets. Beards and moustaches. Bristling with concealed weapons and the potential for explosive violence.

He lounged against the wall, blending into the water-stained concrete, a figure safe to ignore. Part of the street furniture along with the overflowing litter bins, graffiti, discarded needles and broken bottles.

He was an hour early. Forty minutes passed. Beyond the confines of the playground, the backs of the rundown office blocks and the two streets forming an enclosing L, traffic noise reached Gabriel. Sirens blared, dopplered and faded. Horns tooted. A dog barked three times.

The skinheads arrived in a knot from the northeast corner. And he recognised them. They'd been in the copshop when he'd gone to enquire after Odette.

Gabriel experienced a pang of disappointment. His search for Odette had just encountered another delay. In their white T-shirts, red braces and tight stone-washed jeans over tall, cherry-red Dr. Martens, they looked like throwbacks to a different era. One carried a length of pipe, another a baseball bat, the third a length of rope. Did they intend to lynch him?

So, no introduction to the Soltanis was to be forthcoming. That left him with very little option. He needed to reach them. If they wouldn't hire him based on his self-proclaimed credentials – for which, in all honesty, he couldn't blame them – then he'd have to do it the way he once had in Tallinn, the capital of Estonia. A practical demonstration. Some street theatre, if you will.

He christened the skinheads Rope, Bat and Pipe. They were looking around. Hands on hips, weapons dangling at their sides. Easy-to-read body language. *The fuck is he?*

'I'm right here, boys,' he murmured, pushing himself from the wall, and grasping the handle of his supermarket trolley. 'Which makes today your unlucky day.'

He pushed the trolley towards the moped park, its front nearside wheel rattling loudly. Rope looked up, his sharp features pinched into an angry scowl.

'Hey! Shithead! Get the fuck out of here!'

Bat and Pipe followed his lead, glaring across the short distance that separated them from Gabriel. Bat's nose had been broken at some point; the bridge was flat and the end canted to the right. Pipe had large yellow teeth like a horse. And Rope's features were sharp and narrow, like a collection of stiletto blades. It gave him a starved look. The index and middle fingers on his left hand were strapped together with dirty white adhesive tape.

They sneered as they took in his appearance.

'I can smell you from here, you piece of shit!'

Unlikely, Gabriel thought, as he'd showered not an hour earlier.

'Fuck off before we fuck you up!'

'Get lost, loser!'

In reply, Gabriel just tottered forwards a few more steps, weaving left to right, a disarming manoeuvre made easier by the trolley's off-centre front left wheel.

'Can you help me out, boys?' he croaked. 'Ten euros for a meal and something to drink?'

He was ten metres out now. Close enough to see the double lightning bolt tattoo on Pipe's bulging right bicep. The slogan on Bat's left forearm: *Immigrants dehors!* And the swastika on the inside of Rope's right forearm. Gabriel wouldn't have shied away from what was to come. There was too much at stake. But now he recognised them, he felt completely justified.

Five metres.

The abuse grew in volume, though not imagination. Bat hefted his club. Pipe swung his steel. Rope held his coil of polypropylene in his left hand and clenched his scabbed knuckles into a fist.

Two metres.

'Come on, boys,' Gabriel wheedled. 'Five then. Gimme five euros and I'll be on my way.'

One metre.

The baseball bat came whistling in towards Gabriel's head. He ducked and simultaneously shoved the shopping trolley into Bat's groin. He doubled over with a grunt. Gabriel shucked off the coat and danced back a step, so Pipe's length of what turned out to be scaffolding tube arced harmlessly a few centimetres in front of his nose.

Gabriel lashed out a foot, catching Rope on the side of the right knee. It was a brutally effective move, banned in rules-based combat sports for just that reason. Gabriel had used it more than once during his illegal cage fights in Honduras. Ligaments sheared with a disgusting cracking sound.

It's hard to fight when someone has just kicked your anterior cruciate ligament into the middle of the next arrondissement. Rope shrieked in agony, staggered sideways, put more weight on his ruined knee and screamed some more as he smacked down onto his broken fingers on the glass-strewn concrete.

One against two. OK, against one-and-a-half, since Bat was still trying to locate his testicles. It was hardly fair. But Pipe still had some fire in his belly.

'Mother*fucker!*' he yelled, raising the heavy length of steel over his shoulder and bringing it down onto Gabriel's skull. Which had left the target zone a split-second earlier.

The end of the pole struck the concrete with a hollow metallic clonk. Pipe's mouth contorted as tooth-loosening vibrations worse than a mains electric shock shot from the tip of the pole through every sinew, muscle and bone in his arms from fingertips to shoulder joint. Foolishly, not that his shutdown muscles offered him a choice, he dropped the pole, which rolled away before coming to rest beneath a moped's back tyre. He looked up at Gabriel with terror in his eyes. So far, the fight had taken less than twenty seconds and he was still trying to process the fact that he and his mates were having their arses handed to them by a wino.

Gabriel felt no pity. *Don't start what you can't finish. And three thugs against a poor defenceless tramp? Hardly sporting, boys, now was it?*

He hit him, hard, on the tip of his nose, breaking it with a noise like bubble wrap snapping.

There! Now you've got one to match Bat's.

Blood fountained out, the two streams of scarlet washing down over his T-shirt. He screamed and clamped a hand over his squashed-sideways nose, screamed again as sharp ended bones rubbed over each other.

Gabriel thought a period of anaesthesia might be a mercy and cold-cocked him with an uppercut to the point of his jaw. Pipe toppled backwards, knees and hips locked by an adrenaline-driven muscular response so that he rotated about his heels.

Gabriel flashed on a cricket match his father had taken him to see once at Kowloon Cricket Club. The pitch at 10 Cox's Road had been so green the eight-year-old Gabriel hadn't believed it could be real. The batsman had taken the very first ball of the match on the rise and lofted it over the boundary for a six. The crack of seasoned willow against polished leather was not dissimilar to the sound of Pipe's occipital bone meeting the playground's unforgiving, and decidedly grey, surface.

Despite his ruined knee, Rope had one more trick up his sleeve. He pulled a flick-knife from the top of his boot, the blade emerging with a *snick*. It came curving in, aiming for the back of Gabriel's left leg. Not a bad target if you could find the popliteal artery behind the knee, or, if your arm was tiring from prolonged pain, the peroneal, or the anterior or posterior tibial artery in the calf muscle. Yes, any one of the three would do significant damage. Easily a life-ending injury if you couldn't get a tourniquet on it fast enough.

No, not a bad target. But by the time Rope's vicious, slender blade arrived, the arteries were out of range as Gabriel dodged the incoming strike. Rope swept the knife around in a last desperate attack, slicing open Gabriel's shirt so the material fell away from his ribcage. But it was too late, and he hadn't even touched the skin.

Gabriel crouched over him, grabbed his wrist with both hands and dropped all his weight through his knee onto his right arm. Both bones of his lower arm snapped with the noise of dry branches cracking. Or—*Be honest, Old Sport,* a spectral voice intoned, *you've heard it many times before*—the sound of a human radius and ulna parting under force. He screamed and curled into a foetal position, cradling his broken arm.

That just left Bat, who was levering himself to his feet using his Louisville Slugger as a prop, both hands gripping the business end. He was staggering away from Gabriel, but Gabriel was in no mood to allow combatants off the Field of Mars without a post-fight debrief.

Gabriel walked after him, drew back his right foot, took a check-step then kicked the improvised crutch away. It sailed up into the air, rotated twice then bonked down, bouncing from knob to end cap before rolling up against the chain-link. Bat wobbled, stumbled then pitched forward onto his face, aided by a kick in the small of his back.

Behind Gabriel, a scrape told him Rope was on the move. Without breaking stride he barked, 'Stay there!'—*Restez là!*—in his best parade-ground tone, infused with just a hint of Master Zhao. It ought to work, but these weren't soldiers, used to obeying orders. Even in mid-mutiny, a well-trained soldier still had that instinctive reaction to the tone of command. It was why officers could still quell a rebellion without resorting to shooting. Sometimes. Of course, there was also the possibility you'd be bawling your orders as your men fragged you with a grenade. But, then, maybe if it had got to that point, you deserved it. *C'est la guerre.*

It worked.

Gabriel turned away from Bat, who looked visibly relieved, and bent to grab Pipe under the armpits. He was still out cold. Gabriel dragged him over to the row of parked mopeds and laid him at its rightmost end. Carefully, he arranged his unconscious form on its front, in the recovery position: right leg straight, left knee raised, right arm by his side, left an L-shape in front of his face, head turned to the left. And then he kicked the last moped over across his prone form. Better than handcuffs.

He looked up. Eli was watching. He wasn't surprised. She hadn't appeared to him much since leaving Honduras. But then, since rocking up in Paris he'd drowned himself in work, in routine, avoiding the kind of high-stress interactions with other human beings that his ghosts took as their signal to appear. Eli smiled. He heard her voice between his ears though she was way across the playground.

— *Will you kill them, my honey?*

— *I want to.*

— *So kill them. They were going to kill you.*

— *It'll bring the police.*

— *Not if there're no bodies.*

He shook his head. Ghost-Eli was his emotional core, what was left of it. The part of him that wanted to dispense righteous justice against killers and torturers and child abductors and every species of evil human beings could conjure when morality took a furlough. But since reconnecting with Tara, Gabriel had begun to find strength from another side of his character. The one that said there was more than one way to get what you wanted.

He shook his head like a horse trying to dislodge a fly, bent to the ground and picked up Rope's discarded flick-knife. Yes, there was always another way. Eli nodded, at his shoulder now. *Good boy.*

Gabriel pocketed the knife then went over to Rope, snagging his length of blue polypropylene from the ground as he went. He dropped it into his lap.

'Get over to the fence and tie yourself to it. Tight. If I think you've left any slack I'll loop it round your neck and garotte you with it. Understood?'

'Y-yeah,' Rope said, eyes wide with fear, teeth chattering.

He dragged himself over to the chain-link and began looping the rope through the mesh before winding it five or six times around his ankles and cinching it so tightly Gabriel heard the creak of the fibres as they meshed in a knot.

That only left Bat. And the flick knife.

24

Gabriel sat heavily astride Bat's chest, driving the wind from him with an *oof*. He leaned over the skinhead, making him go cross-eyed as he attempted to focus.

'Who sent you?'

'Fuck you.'

Gabriel leaned back and reached behind him. He pulled the flick knife from his pocket and opened it. Tested the edge against his thumb, drawing a little blood. He nodded, then smiled down at Bat.

'I'll ask you again. Who sent you? I think I know, so you're not giving much up.'

Bat tried to buck Gabriel off his chest. It was a brave if foolhardy move for a man who'd watched his crew dismantled by a wino who'd turned out to be anything but.

So Gabriel stabbed him. A hard, fast strike, into the top edge of the left trapezius muscle. Lots of nerves, lots of pain; no major blood vessels, although the subclavian artery ran a handful of centimetres south of it, so there was always a bit of a risk.

He pulled the wicked, thin little blade free with a sucking

sound. The white T-shirt, already grey and scuffed from its wearer's contact with the ground, blossomed crimson.

Bat groaned and his right arm flapped uselessly against Gabriel's hip as he instinctively went to shield the wound.

'I was trained in warfare,' Gabriel said in a conversational tone of voice, as Bat writhed beneath him. 'There's a Latin phrase. "*Ius ad bellum*." Do you know it? No? It means, and I'm translating loosely here, the law of war. Take torture, for example. That's a real no-no. As is mistreating prisoners.'

'Then you got to obey that rule, man,' Bat stammered. 'I'm your prisoner. You got to let me go.'

It appeared all trace of his earlier bravado had deserted him. Too bad.

'Yes, but the thing is, I'm not a soldier any longer. And I've seen too much, done too much, to be governed by the laws the military instilled in me. Now I follow my own code. And right up near the top is a simple rule. Don't hurt children.'

'But you're not a kid, are you?' Bat whined, as blood continued to surge out from the knife wound in his shoulder. 'You're a fucking grown man! I'm bleeding out here! I need the ER.'

'That's true. But if you'll let me finish, I think the men who sent you to kill me are called Soltani. And I also think they've kidnapped a 12-year-old girl. So now my rule number one comes into play, and for that, I'm afraid I may well have to mistreat you, up to, including, and quite possibly past the point of torture.'

'No! OK, fine. Look, it was them.'

'Say it.'

'The Soltanis! Fuck, what do you want to hear? I'm already a dead man.'

'Names?'

'I just told you.'

'First names. And descriptions.'

Gabriel pushed the top of the flick knife against Rope's other trapezius muscle. It loosened his tongue admirably.

'Ali's the younger one. Bashar is the older. They're brothers.

Bashar's the boss. He's like scary-big. One-ninety tall, easily, maybe a hundred and ten kilos. Big beard and tache combo. Ali's got this eye-patch like a fucking pirate. He's short. Clean shaven. That's all I got.'

'That's very good. Well done. Where's their base?'

'Oh, man, don't make me tell you. They'll kill me.'

Gabriel pushed the tip of the blade harder so it broke the skin beneath the white cotton of the T-shirt. A red rose bloomed around the steel.

Rope squealed.

'They got this fuckoff house out in the country. The Versailles Forest. Tiny village called Saint Martin on the Paris Road.'

'Good. Now, we have to decide what to do with you. I mean, you've been really helpful, and even put your own life on the line for me. I guess you've earned your freedom.'

'Yeah? I mean, yes! Yes, I have, haven't I? Cool. So, look, man, let me up, OK? I'm sorry we tried to fuck you up. But it was the Soltanis. They told us to. We were just following orders.'

It was a poor choice of phrase, but Gabriel let him up all the same. They stood facing each other.

Then the skinhead looked down at Gabriel's torso, the skin exposed through the gaping rent in his shirt where Rope had slashed at it.

Something in his expression changed. His previous sneering demeanour flooded into his eyes.

'The fuck's that?' he asked, pointing at a tattoo visible on Gabriel's chest. 'Is that fucking Hebrew?'

Gabriel looked down. He'd had Eli's name inked onto his body in Honduras shortly after his first successful cage fight.

He looked calmly into the skinhead's eyes, now alight with hatred again and apparently impervious to the danger signals radiating from Gabriel's.

'It's my wife's name. Why?'

'You married a fucking Jew? That's fucking—'

The rest of the skinhead's toxic thought escaped his body not through his mouth, as words, but through the wide, bloody smile

139

in his throat – a scarlet spray carried on a long descending whistle. He fell sideways, arterial blood jetting two metres into the air and spattering the playground in looping overlapping arcs.

Rope screamed from his position where he'd lashed himself to the fence. The sound reminded Gabriel he ought to set him free.

He walked back to the fence, crouched in front of Rope and stabbed him cleanly through the heart. He died without making a sound. Then again, and again, ten times in all, at various points on his chest and neck. Pipe, still unconscious beneath the toppled-over moped, was last. Gabriel righted the moped and dragged him out. It took some effort, Pipe was a big lad, but eventually he had him positioned beside Bat's blood-soaked form. Gabriel looped the rope tight around his throat, yanking it tight until the pulse disappeared from the carotid artery above it. He held it there until he was sure the man was dead, then wrapped the free ends in and around Bat's right fist. He wiped the bloody knife down and then clamped Bat's dead fingers around it.

As a narrative it worked, just. Three skinheads had got into a brutal, bloody, murderous fight. Bat had tied Rope to the fence and stabbed him to death. Pipe had argued with Bat, only to get himself strangled with the rope. With his dying breath he'd slit Bat's throat. Yes, the story had more holes than Pipe's chest. But then again, the cops in this part of Paris seemed unable or unwilling to do their jobs properly and were presumably in the pay of the Soltanis anyway.

Would the Soltanis realise what had happened when their tame squad of wannabe SS shock troops didn't come back? Maybe there was another way out of the impasse. Gabriel called Marc.

'Didn't you tell me you had a mate who owns a scrapyard?'

25

Gabriel stood twenty feet back from the battered yellow machine. It measured eight metres from end to end.

Marc's friend pushed a green silicon button and the powerful hydraulics hissed into action. Slowly, the massive block of steel descended, making contact with the old Citroën's roof with a *crump*. The machinery's hum deepened, then rose in pitch as the press continued. The windows popped out with a shower of glass fragments that caught the sun, like exploding diamonds falling to the greasy black ground. Two horizontal rams moved towards each other from left and right, driving the flattened car into a cube. Animal-like squeals erupted from the disintegrating car as steel scraped against steel, and everything not cast from iron or milled from solid blocks of metal crumpled, shuddered, splintered, collapsed and died.

Somewhere inside that tortured block of metal, the three human corpses took on new forms as well. The beautiful symmetry beloved of everyone from Ancient Greek sculptors to French painters disappeared as the huge forces transformed flesh and bone, muscle, nerve and sinew into a messy, formless stew. As the rams juddered to a halt and went into reverse, a thick stream of blackish-red liquid flowed from the bottom of the cube.

'Where'll you put it?' Gabriel asked.

'Way out back. Next pickup's end of the month. By the time it's been shredded, de-tinned in caustic soda and melted down, anything organic is just water vapour.'

Gabriel thanked him and left with Marc.

'Who were those guys?' Marc asked.

'They were working for the Soltanis.'

Marc whistled.

'You just made two very powerful enemies, my friend.'

'Not being rude, but that's a line I've heard before.'

'Oh, yeah?' Marc grinned. 'Let me guess. You knew your way around a scrapyard before you met Henk?'

'Actually, not for body disposal, although I did once engage three Chechen kidnappers in a firefight in one.'

'So what now?'

'Can you drop me outside the gym? I'm seeing a couple of … well, I guess at this point they're my employees. Subcontractors at the very least.'

* * *

Gabriel walked from the gym to Rue Hermel. He was pleasantly surprised to see that Sandrine and Sophy were waiting for him outside Automat Cavally. He checked his watch: 6.55 p.m. They were five minutes early. He liked them all the more for that.

'Hey Drine, Feeso,' he said.

'Hey yourself,' Sandrine said. Sophy kissed her teeth. Attitude for days, that one.

'What news from the Eighteenth?'

'We been asking all around the block. Nobody seen Odette for a couple of days,' Sandrine said. 'But Feeso, she talked to this dude, name of Peewee. Tell him, Feeso.'

Sophy pushed herself upright off the laundromat's plate glass window.

'Peewee said he saw some young chick getting into a black Hummer on Rue Duc, near the skatepark. I asked him to describe her and I reckon it was Odette.'

'Did he get the licence plate?'

'Man's a crackhead or some shit,' she said with a toss of her head. 'Think he goes around memorising licence plates?'

Sandrine's eyes flashed.

'Yo! Have some respect, Feeso! Gaby's paying us now, OK? We're professionals.' She turned to Gabriel. 'Don't matter what Peewee did or didn't see. Only people round here drive a motherfucking Hummer are the Soltanis. They got your girl, Gaby. I'm sorry.'

He shook his head.

'Don't be. That's good work. It means we have a target now.' He got out his wallet and took out three hundred-euro notes and handed them over to Sandrine. 'Any expense receipts?'

She shook her head.

'Covered. Just get her back, OK, Gaby? And fuck up the Soltanis for taking her too.'

He nodded.

'That's the plan.'

26

Tara smacked a fist into her palm.

'Those fucks, BB! We have to find them.'

'I know. Now I've put them on notice this goes one of two ways. Either they send in more knuckleheads to try and take me out, or they hire me.'

'Which do you think they'll do?' Jacko asked.

Cleaned up, the SAS vet was presentable, but there was still a lost look behind the eyes Gabriel knew all too well. A man who'd stood on the precipice, stared over and contemplated leaving all his troubles behind, then stepped back. Only now every waking minute, and quite a few sleeping ones, he was wondering whether he'd stepped in the wrong direction.

'Those skinheads weren't ex-Foreign Legion. They were chancers,' Gabriel said. 'Probably spent their time beating up immigrants and jerking off to *Mein Kampf*. Maybe the Soltanis sent them after me as a test.'

'Looks like they failed it, then,' Jacko said with an off-kilter grin.

'I think the test wasn't for them,' Tara said. 'It was for Gabriel. They wanted to see what he could do.'

'Then you passed, mate,' Jacko said, spreading his arms and simultaneously swiping up a can of lager from the arm of the sofa. 'With flying colours.'

Gabriel rubbed his chin.

'We'll see. But I'm worried about Odette. Whatever they've got planned for her it has to be happening soon. Did you find anything out?'

Jacko shook his head.

'I've been down among the dead men, what you might call Paris's dark underbelly. Nobody's heard anything, or if they have they're too scared to talk.'

'How about you, Tara?'

She furrowed her brow.

'I've been on the dark web all morning. Fuck, the people there, BB, they're unbelievable. The shit they're into. Makes me wish for the good old days when I ran the White Koi.' She shuddered, and Gabriel wondered what could be so bad it would make his sister, a former triad assassin, react like that. 'I think I found something. But it's bad, BB, really bad.'

'What is it?' Gabriel asked, though he had a shrewd idea.

It could only be one of a few things. He'd heard about them when he'd been living in Honduras, though he'd never got close. Live, on-air executions. Rooms where people were tortured to death. And, somehow worse than both, auctions where kids were sold off to whichever subhuman slimeball had the cash to exchange for the poor soul's body.

'A user calling himself AliX is advertising a "retreat for lovers of tender chicken" in Martinique. Three days from now.'

'Show me.'

Tara opened her laptop and turned it round to show Gabriel the screen. He leaned over and read the opening post. His flesh crawled and he had a strong and violent urge to hit something. AliX, who surely had to be Ali Soltani, had written:

. . .

146

At 12 years old, this chick is just coming into her prime. A young bird rich in dark meat. Bred from the finest stock: Senegal and Cote d'Ivoire strains. Whoever plucks this chick will not be disappointed. Sale ends at 23.59 Central European Standard Time, 1 July 2025. Auction winner acquires title of goods and use of our exclusive, private beachfront lodge for 14 days. Location disclosed on payment of non-refundable deposit of 50,000 euros. After that time, title reverts to AliX. Odette will remain in Martinique but be available on short-term lets subject to secondary arrangements. Winner responsible for own travel expenses. Sale is final. No-show = no refund.

Gabriel clenched his fist so hard the knuckles cracked.

'They're selling off her virginity. She's just a piece of meat to them.'

'It happens everywhere, BB,' Tara said softly. 'You must have seen it. I know I have. And once whichever pervert has finished with her, she'll be put in a brothel and worked until she dies of some fucking awful disease or the drugs they hook her on.'

'Or some bastard strangles her,' Jacko grated out. 'I wish I could find them. I'd fucking slaughter them all.'

'You'll get your chance, Jacko,' Gabriel said, grimly, 'but we have to find her first.'

The next morning, Gabriel, Tara and Jacko split up. One of them had to find a way to break the wall of fear the Soltanis had built round themselves. Time was running out for Odette.

Gabriel headed deep into the backstreets of the Eighteenth. Looking for, hoping for, a contact with someone on the inside of the Soltanis' operation.

He was about to cross the street when the roar of a stressed motorcycle engine made him prick his ears up. Round the corner, boot out and sliding along the tarmac, a black-clad biker screamed up towards him. Gabriel instinctively reached for his sidearm, but he wasn't carrying.

The biker slid to a halt. The helmet was black, the visor, too. So when he looked into the expanse of curved plastic all he saw was a distorted Gabriel Wolfe staring back at him. The rider was female, obvious from the figure encased in skin-tight leather.

He didn't drop his guard: Tara was female and had once favoured a similar outfit, albeit in snow-white. His sister hadn't been shy about separating men from their lives, slicing through the thread that bound them to the world of the living with a Samurai sword, a kitchen knife or her bare hands if need be.

His pulse raced and he let it: the more oxygen for the fight the better. Somehow the Soltanis had identified him and presumably had their spotters out looking for him.

But instead of attacking, the biker slid a hand inside her jacket and pulled out a slim white envelope and held it towards him. Hand steady as a rock. No nerves. Something told him she felt the enclosing hand of protection the Soltanis offered its employees.

He did nothing. Impatiently, she jerked the envelope towards it, the meaning clear. *Take it!*

He took it. It was too thin to contain any kind of IED and somehow he didn't think ricin or anthrax was the Soltanis' style. A soon as his fingers touched the leading edge, she let go, forcing him to grab it or let it flutter to the cobbles. She dropped the clutch and wheelied away down the street, earning a few appreciative whoops from a group of school-age kids clustered outside a sweetshop.

Left in a cloud of blue-grey exhaust smoke, Gabriel watched her go, all the way down Rue Polonceau until she slid the bike round the corner into Rue des Gardes and disappeared from view.

He took the envelope to a cafe, ordered a coffee and then opened it. The message was typed. Short.

You want a job?
Old Citroën factory. Rosny. Noon. Today.

A.S.

Ali Soltani. Reaching out to his potential new enforcer. Gabriel texted Jacko and Tara to tell them he had a lead. Tara responded immediately.

I'm coming too.

Gabriel punched in his reply.

No. Just me. They'll be watching.

Then take a weapon.

Don't worry.

I DO worry!

Gabriel frowned. It was odd, having his sister worry about him. For so long he'd thought himself alone. Then he'd discovered he had a sister and for a few brilliant, bloody, rambunctious years, they'd run ops together. But after Eli had been murdered, he'd wanted to sever all connections between him and his old life. But his old life had other ideas and came back to claim him.

One thing Tara was right about was his need for a weapon. No doubt the Soltanis would search him when he arrived, but he didn't intend to go in naked. If it was a setup, he'd be ready, and from then on it would be all-out war. No more pretence at wanting a job. He'd simply hunt them down and kill them.

Gabriel detoured back to the apartment. The sitting room windows gave onto Avenue Montaigne, elegant, tall rectangles of slightly rippled glass that made the pedestrians ambling down the chic shopping street undulate as they shopped.

Beneath the panes of eighteenth-century glass, a former occupant had installed a window seat, a beautifully made wooden bench with tailormade cushions that fit the angled embrasure perfectly. Like something off a yacht, Gabriel mused, as he slid the cushion aside to reveal the smooth, varnished top of the bench.

He pushed a spot in one corner, and, at the other end, a small panel popped up by a few millimetres. He inserted his thumbnail and lifted the little hatch up. It clicked against the glass on smoothly milled brass hinges.

Beneath was a keypad. He punched in a number only he and Tara knew: 6424235 – their brother Michael's name on a phone keypad.

With a barely discernible hum, the front of the bench slid out. When it had completed its forty centimetres of travel, Gabriel reached into the wide, deep drawer it revealed and lifted out a rugged black nylon holdall with black-and-yellow striped handles.

He placed it beside the coffee table, an antique Indian piece imported by Tara. He gripped the brass tab of the zip that ran along the centre of its uppermost side. The two sides of the zip parted with a rasp as the sharp-edged teeth disengaged from each other.

Gabriel spread the opening wider and, one by one, lifted the items inside onto the coffee table, their metal parts occasionally clinking on the iron nails driven almost flush with the surface of the stained and weatherbeaten wood, now darkened to black in places.

When he was done, he sat back on his haunches and surveyed the arsenal. It hadn't been particularly difficult to acquire. Unlike the UK, gun laws in France, while not lax, were remarkably permissive. If you stuck to straightforward handguns, rifles and shotguns, you could pretty much buy whatever you wanted. They'd had to join a registered gun club and undertake three supervised sessions with an instructor before getting *la carte verte* – the green card – that would allow the holder to purchase their own firearms.

As it was, the Wolfe siblings had built a small but flexible armoury that would have shocked their well-to-do neighbours. Some of them undoubtedly kept a shotgun or two, maybe a rifle, at their country places or hunting cabins. But Glock 19s equipped with laser sights? Subcompact Taurus GX4s? A Sig Sauer P226 with a suppressor? A Benelli semi-automatic shotgun with a pistol grip? An all-black FAMAS bullpup assault rifle with a telescopic sight? No. Those would be met with a frown and a disbelieving, 'For hunting? Really, mademoiselle?'

Hard to explain that when you were running from the Chinese government there was definitely a hunt, but one in which you were the hunted.

Gabriel picked up the P226, his favoured sidearm since his days in the Regiment. Dropped out the magazine and checked the ammunition. Slid it back in again and seated it with a solid click from the latch. He also took out a credit-card-sized piece of black plastic, thicker than the standard Visa or Mastercard by a factor of three. And a thick barrelled, satin-grey ballpoint pen.

Showtime.

27

Gabriel parked a kilometre away from the abandoned Citroën factory in Rosny.

He left his car in a dusty lane inhabited by a dozen stray cats. He looked all around. An abandoned railway line ran north-south along one side of the lane. The other was bordered by a half-built housing estate. Tall, unlovely concrete towers still had the plastic wrapping on sections of cladding. Spikes of rebar poked out from the tops like a porcupine's quills.

A gap in the chain-link fencing allowed him access to an even narrower track littered with broken bottles, sun-faded Coke cans and used condoms. Needles were scattered like fallen leaves. He made his way due west, glad he'd put on ankle-high walking boots as the Vibram soles crunched through the debris of hundreds of going-nowhere lives.

Ahead, the factory's chimneys loomed. This was no modern manufacturing plant, closed in one of the endless waves of corporate reorganisations as production shifted to Hungary, or Belarus or China. It dated from the Twenties and was obsolescent before the Second World War.

Gabriel checked the time. He had thirty minutes before the

meeting with Ali. He advanced to the factory and made an entire circuit of the site. No cars, trucks or vehicles of any kind, not even a pushbike. He doubted Ali had walked, which meant he had the place to himself, just as he'd planned.

He found the perfect area to watch and wait: a trio of vast wooden cable reels. He hunkered down in the space between them and watched the road that brought vehicular traffic to the factory. Anyone appearing who didn't fit the mental profile Gabriel had constructed for a former Syrian torturer would meet with a swift and uncompromising interrogation that would yield the Soltanis' location.

He rechecked his pistol. Racked the slide. And waited.

Five to twelve.

The site was eerily quiet. He remembered a mission in Afghanistan. A small, dusty town in Helmand province. One minute the air was alive with the angry sounding but actually friendly banter between market traders and their customers, the cough and roar of venerable diesel engines and the laughter and squeals of playing children. Then the sound was replaced with a silence so absolute Gabriel picked out the keening of an eagle high overhead, circling the town on a thermal.

Gabriel looked at his second-in-command and they'd nodded. A short, decisive signal. Trouble. They sprinted for the cover of a pockmarked building that functioned as a rudimentary town hall. With twenty yards to go the first RPG arrowed down from a rooftop, sailing over their heads and hitting the front door of the town hall. The detonation blew them off their feet. Amid shouts, another RPG streaked down, hitting a fruit truck and blowing it off its axles. The troopers returned fire as they scrambled inside the town hall and through to the back, where they knocked out the flimsy back door and ran into the next street over.

It took them an hour of street-by-street fighting, during which time they were joined by a squad of US Marines, before the last of the enemy fighters was despatched with a burst from Smudge Smith's rifle.

Gabriel felt a fluttering in his throat, an echo of the crippling

PTSD that had afflicted him after Smudge had died in Mozambique, his lower jaw torn off by a .50 calibre round from a Russian-made "Dushka" heavy machinegun before being caught in the chest and dying in a welter of his own arterial blood.

He shook his head. Squeezed his eyes shut and opened them again.

Gabriel looked at his watch. The face doubled, and the numbers blurred. He blinked again and the two resolved into one. Noon. Where the hell was Ali Soltani?

Maybe it was another test. Fine, let him play games. Gabriel checked the immediate environs. No other place to lurk. The factory then. It was where Ali wanted to meet him after all.

At the back of the factory a loading bay offered a way in. Gabriel clambered onto the raised floor of the bay where lorries would reverse up to drop off parts. The huge wooden sliding doors stood half open and he simply walked through. As he crossed the threshold, the light dimmed to a gloom so profound Gabriel had to wait for a minute until his eyes adjusted.

Whatever machinery the workers had used in the Twenties to manufacture the Citroën cars that had gone on to grace the streets of Jazz Age Paris was long gone. The floor was strewn with rubble and broken glass. The steel girders and columns that supported the roof were streaked with rust. And, as in most parts of Paris, graffiti artists had left their signatures.

Amid the tags, the crude statements of youthful defiance against '*le régime tyrannique*', and the pornographic scrawls, 'Julie sucks cock', 'Armande fucks good' was a single beautiful mural. A woman's face in profile, weeping. A thought bubble rising from her head enclosing the words, '*Mère, où êtes-vous?*' Mother, where are you?

The loss and longing in that brief, four-word question, and the formal use of the *vous* rather than *tu*, touched Gabriel in a place he'd thought calcified by grief.

He thought of Eli. A mother-to-be when she was gunned down on that Godforsaken island in the Outer Hebrides. Where was she now? In Heaven? He didn't believe in such places. Eli had once told him Jews did believe in the afterlife. 'We'll all be together in the Garden of Eden eventually.' 'How about Hell?' he'd asked her. 'I've done so many bad things.' And she'd smiled and reassured him that for her, hell meant a cleansing.

'Think of it as a spiritual washing machine,' she said with a smile as she adopted what he playfully called her 'rabbi voice'. 'If your soul isn't cleansed before you die, then you will undergo a period of cleansing afterwards. You'll feel the hot water but it's necessary before you move to the afterlife.'

Sighing as the grief-beast he mostly kept at bay sank its teeth into his heart, Gabriel walked the length of the factory and found an intact iron staircase that led to a mezzanine floor that had once, to judge from the remains of partitioned cubicles, held managers' offices.

At the far end, he lay down among the decades-old debris, smashed-up desks, crushed cardboard, even a primitive office stapler, and waited. Looking down at the factory floor from this vantage point gave him a measure of security. He'd see Ali, and any muscle he'd brought with him, before they saw him.

He checked the time again.

12.15.

Outside, a high-performance engine revved, exhausts blatting. Not a Porsche. That characteristic six-cylinder rasp was absent here. This was a V8. A tuned Range Rover, or some sort of American muscle car. Maybe an AMG Mercedes, although the music this one was playing sounded too uncivilised to have come from Stuttgart.

Gabriel closed his eyes for a second. Steadied his breathing, and his pulse. Was he about to get his first glimpse of Odette Diallo's kidnapper?

28

A lone figure entered the factory at the far end.

From this distance, Gabriel couldn't make out any features. Just a general build. Short, stocky, thick through the shoulders and chest, arms hanging out from his sides. Overdeveloped lats preventing them from hanging straight. Gabriel had seen the same look among the jarheads he'd fought alongside in the desert.

Was this Ali Soltani? Or a stooge sent to bring in this troubling wannabe muscle who'd disposed of three hyperactive skinheads as if they were mosquitoes?

The figure walked the length of the factory floor, skirting the larger puddles of stinking water, kicking bits of debris aside. The gait was confident. Not a swagger, not quite, more of an assertive stride that suggested he was unused to feeling fear, or even anxiety.

As he got closer, his features resolved and the eyepatch confirmed his identity. No gun in sight, although there was plenty of room amongst those overdeveloped muscles for a pistol in a shoulder holster. Or the old standby, the back of the waistband.

He stopped thirty metres back from the mezzanine floor

where Gabriel was watching him. Turned a full circle, hands on hips.

'Are you here, my friend? You want a job, you need to come out and talk.' He spoke English.

Gabriel stood, slowly.

'Who are you?' he called down from the edge of the parapet.

'My name is Ali Soltani. Why don't you come down from there and introduce yourself?'

He was smiling. A five-year-old would not have been fooled. Ali's expression held as much warmth as a Parisian street in midwinter.

Nonetheless.

Gabriel sauntered along the rubbish-strewn floor and descended the staircase, making sure his bootheels rang out on each step. The pistol dug reassuringly into the small of his back.

He crossed the thirty metres of bare concrete and stood facing Ali Soltani for the first time.

'My name is Gabriel.'

'Gabriel what?'

'Just Gabriel.'

Ali's smile sharpened like a blade being stroked along a whetstone.

'Well, Gabriel-Just-Gabriel, it's a pleasure to meet you.'

He held out his hand. Gabriel grasped it. The shake was warm, dry and brief, a model of the executive greeting. No macho power-plays, knuckles ground inside one another's grip to establish a petty kind of dominance.

Soltani drew his power from somewhere deeper than simple physical dominance. Gabriel had met his kind before. Warlords, arms company CEOs, generals, crime bosses, triggermen. You were facing the man, or occasionally a woman, but they were merely the outer part of something larger. Something submerged, lying in wait for the unwary with row upon row of dagger-teeth and an urge to rip and rend, tear, shred, destroy.

'Likewise. Although I didn't appreciate that little welcome party you sent to … kill me.'

Ali's smile faltered, just for a split-second, and Gabriel glimpsed the monster within. Then the micro-expression was gone. Affability returned.

'Oh, Gabriel, they would not have killed you. But we can't accept just anyone into our organisation, however outwardly impressive their credentials might be. Let's just say my brother and I wanted to conduct a little pre-interview test.' He scratched beneath the eyepatch. 'Where are they now?'

'I put them in a car.'

'To where?'

Gabriel tipped his head to one side.

'I'm not exactly sure. It was a big scrapyard.'

Ali shrugged.

'Ah, well. No great loss. If I may ask, why did you kill them?'

'One of them insulted my wife.'

'You're married?'

'I was.'

'I myself am married. I have two children who I love more than life itself. If anyone insulted my family, I would kill them too. Tell me something, Gabriel-Just-Gabriel, are you carrying?'

Gabriel nodded.

'Are you?'

Ali grinned.

'Of course! Paris is a dangerous city. Especially dumps like this where the tourists and *les bons gens* don't go. One has to be careful, no?'

'Exactly. You never know who you're going to run into.'

'I mean, look at us. An ex-British Special Forces member and, well, I suppose honesty is appropriate at this point. A former member of the Syrian security police. Anyway, I'm going to need your gun.'

Ali held out his hand.

Gabriel looked down at it, then back into his eyes.

'I'm going to hang onto it, if you don't mind.'

'If you're going to work for me you need to get used to obeying my orders, Gabriel-Just-Gabriel.'

'Am I working for you now?'

'Nothing's been agreed. For now.'

'Then I'll keep my gun. And you can keep your orders.' A beat. 'For now.'

Gabriel's pulse ticked up from sixty to sixty five. They were playing a more subtle version of the dominance game lesser players fought with their bone-crusher handshakes. Outwardly, you had to appear calm, unruffled, amused, even. Inwardly, you were readying yourself. To strike, to counterstrike, to dodge an incoming blade or slip a punch.

Ali nodded. Gave a brief smile, this time tinged with respect.

'If you knew more about me, Gabriel-Just-Gabriel, the things I have done, the things of which I am capable, you would be a little less arrogant.' He twitched the fingers of his extended left hand upwards. At the same time, he completed the move he'd begun a few seconds earlier as they'd been trading verbal bullets. His right hand had reached his hip and snaked inside his jacket. 'Give me your gun.'

Time to raise the stakes. Gabriel didn't want to push Ali into a flat-out walk-away refusal, or to actually pulling the gun he was clearly itching to. He would be hired, but it would be on his terms. Men like Ali Soltani only respected one thing. Strength. Gabriel was about to give him an object lesson.

'There was a man, a little like you,' he said in a conversational tone of voice. 'He worked for the Iranian Ministry of Intelligence and Security on Delgosha Alley in Tehran. His name was General Bakhshi. I was careless and he captured me. Took me down to the basement of his building and there he tortured me.' Gabriel held out his left hand, palm-down. 'You see that scar? The round one between the two tendons?' He wiggled his fingers so the tendons raised and lowered beneath the skin on the back of his hand. 'That's where he hammered a six-inch nail through my hand and fixed it to the table we were sitting at.'

It was interesting. For all his obvious power and barely suppressed capacity for violence, Ali Soltani was in the grip of the oldest human form of culture: the well-told story. That it was being told with a seasoning of the voice control techniques of Yinshen fangshi only added to its hypnotic quality. And as Ali was a former torturer himself, Gabriel could see he was drinking in the details, comparing them to his own methods. Wondering where the story was going to end.

'Yet, you are here, Gabriel-Just-Gabriel. I am wondering, where is General Bakhshi? In a crushed car in a Tehran scrapyard?'

'I doubt it. He would have received a formal funeral of some kind, though maybe not with full military honours. You see, I used that nail to kill him. And then I took his clothes, cut off his top lip, moustache – a bit like yours actually – and all, applied it to my face and walked out of there.'

'Very impressive. But—'

Gabriel held up a hand.

'There is a dacha in the Russian countryside outside Moscow. At one time it was the home of a man who ran a Mafya gang. He kept a pet wolf called Piotr. I killed the wolf with my bare hands, donned its pelt then returned to the dacha and cut that gangster's head off with his own Cossack sword. I tell you this, Ali, not to boast, but to illustrate that you are not alone in having stories to tell about what you are capable of. And I will only add one more thing.'

'What's that?' Ali asked, now totally in thrall to Gabriel's judicious use of pause and teaser.

'Your victims were brought to you chained and shackled. Hooded. Already beaten, terrorised, starved. The people I have brought down were either fully trained combat soldiers armed to the back teeth and intent on killing me, or their civilian equivalents. Cartel bosses, professional assassins, Hell's Angels … it's a long list. And the one thing they all have in common is that they're dead by my hand.'

Al inhaled slowly through his nose. Then let the air out in a controlled sigh.

'All of which is very impressive. And I think we can find a place for you, despite the fact you did not fight for France in the

Legion. After all, one must not be chauvinistic, eh? But if you are to come to work for me, you need to show respect. I see that issuing orders will not work, so we must try a different approach.'

He scratched beneath the eyepatch again.

The bullet whined past Gabriel's left ear so close he felt it disturb his hair. It smashed into the wall twenty metres behind him. The crack-thump of the report suggested a high-calibre battle rifle, fired from outside the building.

'Stand very still,' Ali said. 'Or the next one will make you squint.'

He came to stand just a few centimetres from Gabriel, so close Gabriel could smell mint on his breath. In an almost intimate gesture, he reached around to the small of Gabriel's back and lifted the P226 from his waistband. He stood back.

Footsteps crunched over the broken glass. Gabriel looked over Ali's shoulder. A taller figure, dressed in urban camouflage, grey, black and faded beige geometric patterns, strode across the factory floor towards them. Across his body he held a long-barrelled rifle. As he came closer Gabriel ran it against his mental database of firearms. An FN C1 self-loading rifle. No telescopic sight. So the guy was a natural sharpshooter. The kind of backwoods skill that could shoot a squirrel in the left eye from five hundred yards.

'Allow me to introduce my brother, Bashar.' Ali turned to the other man, tall, where he was short, angular, where he was bullish, and clean-shaven, where he was bearded. 'Nice shooting, Bashar. Meet our newest recruit, Gabriel-Just-Gabriel.'

Bashar Soltani stopped when he stood shoulder to shoulder with Ali. At this range, he must have known the rifle would be ineffective. All Gabriel had to do was take a single step forward and he'd render it as nothing more than an over-engineered club.

'The fuck kind of name is that?' he growled.

'Gabriel-Just-Gabriel is, I sense, a private man.' Ali turned to Gabriel. 'No names, no pack drill, that's what you Brits say, isn't it?'

Gabriel shrugged. 'I assume you don't have an HR

department that wants my details for the payroll, so where's the need? So, do I have the job, or what?'

'Yes,' said Ali.

'No,' said Bashar.

Ali turned to his brother.

'No?'

'I don't trust him. We use Legionnaires for a reason. The system works. I don't want to change it.'

'I know we have a system, brother. But we have to be flexible. Like the tech bros say, what kept you alive yesterday will kill you tomorrow. He could be useful.' Ali spoke to Gabriel without breaking eye contact with Bashar. 'What else can you do apart from kill people?'

'I speak eight languages. I can drive anything on two or four wheels. Fix most of them, too. Martial arts. I can pass for an English Milord or a Parisian street person. Basic combat medicine. Proficient marksman although not as good as your brother, and I'm familiar with the operation of small arms, and heavy weapons. I can make IEDs, rig booby traps and—'

'That's enough!' Bashar barked, levelling the rifle and pointing its muzzle directly at Gabriel's heart. 'You turn up out of fucking nowhere and you know about us, our operation. You have money, education, yet you want to work as an enforcer. If it wasn't for the fact you're English, I'd have pegged you for an undercover cop. And then, believe me, *Gabriel-Just-Gabriel*, they'd be fishing you out of the Seine in pieces.'

He took a step back, then another. Giving Gabriel no chance to rush him and disarm him. He brought the butt stock up to his right shoulder and pushed it against his right cheek.

'The fuck, Bashar!' Ali said, stepping between Bashar, Bashar's gun and Gabriel, and holding his hands out. 'He's an asset. OK, not from our traditional source, but I think he could be useful to the organisation.'

'Like I said,' Bashar gritted out, the words sliding between his distorted cheek and the polished wood of the stock, 'I don't trust him. Whatever he wants, it isn't a job.'

Bashar was obviously the smarter one of the two Soltani brothers, Gabriel gave him that. He'd seen through his cover story, which, Gabriel admitted without any need for torture, wasn't the strongest legend he'd ever operated under. It looked like a job with the Soltanis was out of the question. He'd have to find another way to get to Odette.

But first, there was the small matter of the imminent arrival in his body of a 7.62 x 51mm copper-jacketed NATO round.

Ali Soltani had Gabriel's pistol, so felt comfortable turning his back on him. A mistake he was about to regret.

Gabriel slid his hand into a pocket and retrieved the chunky rectangle of plastic that a casual observer might take for one of those high-tech wallets. But a thumb slid across its corner released a blade that pivoted outwards and locked into place.

Nothing dramatic. This was no foot-long zombie knife or machete favoured by gangs from Bogota to Brazzaville. Just a triangular blade with a curved edge, no more than four centimetres to a side. But it was sharp. Gabriel had shaved with it that morning. He thought Gillette might want to take a stake in the company that manufactured it.

Bashar was yelling at his brother to get out of the way, but Ali, clearly, was feeling the need to assert himself. Maybe he'd always been the underdog, bullied by his older brother, despite their respective builds apparently favouring Ali.

'But Bashar, think of the upsides. He could really help us to—'

Gabriel stepped close behind Ali, their second interpersonal encounter of the morning, and whipped the blade around and up until it rested, firmly, against the carotid artery on the left side of his neck. Gabriel relieved him of his pistol. One-handed, he dropped out the magazine. It clattered to the floor and he kicked it away into the shadows. He spun the pistol in the other direction, waiting for the metallic clonk as it bounced off the wall and fell into a heap of smashed-up wooden packing cases. He retrieved his Sig and stuck it into his waistband.

Killing the Soltanis was never an option. He needed them alive to find out where they were keeping Odette. But now the covert option was blown, he had to leave them alive while still getting away cleanly. Hopefully, Tara and Jacko would have played their part by now.

'Not another word,' Gabriel murmured into Ali's left ear, crouching so that his captive's body shielded him. 'You so much as twitch and you'll be bleeding out before you even feel the pain.'

In front of him, Bashar kept his rifle levelled, though there was no way he could hit Gabriel without sending the round tunnelling through his brother's body. And whatever the power imbalance in their relationship, he was relying on family ties being strong enough to keep Bashar's finger off the trigger.

'Now what, Englishman?' Bashar sneered. 'You going to stand there all day? You're going to get tired and expose a part of your body and that's when I will shoot. Or Ali will tire and slump. Maybe you'll slit his throat, maybe you won't. Either way, you'll die before he does.'

He had a point. Gabriel could try wheeling round, maintaining position behind Ali, but at this range Bashar would spot the tiniest opportunity to shoot him through a shin or a shoulder as he manoeuvred Ali back towards the door.

So he drew the blade across Ali's throat, all the way from the soft point below his left ear, in a deep curving smile all the way to the other ear.

Bright scarlet blood sprayed out in a fine mist of droplets that filled the air between the two Soltani brothers. Ali screamed as the incision gaped, releasing a scrim of blood from the subcutaneous blood vessels that sheeted down over his neck and into his shirt collar. He clamped a hand over the wound and screamed again.

'Bashar! Help me!'

As the words left his lips, Gabriel shoved him, hard, between the shoulder blades. He took a half-step, then pitched forwards as Gabriel hooked a foot around his leading ankle, straight into Bashar.

The rifle got tangled between them as Ali reflexively put out both hands and threw his arms around his brother.

'Get the fuck off me, you fool, it's not deep!' Bashar snarled.

But Ali had lost his wits and was screaming still. In truth there was a lot of blood. But had he been able to calm down he'd have realised, perhaps from the way the air in front of him was not currently criss-crossed by great curving spurts of hot, arterial blood, that the wound was superficial.

Bashar threw him aside and brought the rifle up again but by then Gabriel was within striking distance. He drew the satin-grey ballpoint from his inside pocket.

The implement would function perfectly well for writing, but was oddly heavy for the task. Without depressing the switch on the barrel that would release the writing tip, he clenched it in his fist like a dagger, thumb over the top and rammed it down onto Bashar's right shoulder.

He'd never used a tactical pen in combat before, although he'd met a couple of US troops who swore by them for self-defence in non-carry states, but it had one important advantage over every other weapon.

It looked normal.

Until its hardened steel point was penetrating your soft tissue or breaking a bone. That's where 'normal' ended and the screaming began.

As Bashar did now.

The rifle fell from his hands and he staggered back, dark eyes wide with shock and the agony now radiating from his wrecked shoulder joint.

Gabriel stepped in and punched him in the left temple. He dropped to the ground in an untidy heap.

He spun round. Ali was lying on the ground, face up, the blood already congealing at the wound site and on the surface of the pool spreading out from his neck.

'Where's Odette?' Gabriel shouted.

'What?'

Gabriel kicked him hard in the middle of his thigh, drawing forth a howl of agony.

'Don't fuck with me, Ali. The girl you kidnapped. Her name's Odette Diallo. Where is she?'

'I don't know what you're talking about.' A sly look entered his eyes. 'You're not going to kill us. If you were we'd be dead by now. So you need to leave. I've got a crew coming in a little while. They were going to pick you up or dispose of your body depending on how the meeting went.'

Gabriel knelt astride him and flicked out the credit-card knife again. Pushed it into the soft flesh under Ali's unpatched eye.

'I could give you a matching pair.'

'Do what you like. I have no idea who this Odette girl is. But unless you kill us both you're going to have a shit-ton of trouble coming your way in the next ten minutes. I promise you, even if you get away today, we will hunt you down. And then we will take our time with you. You will wish you could go back to your basement at the Ministry of Intelligence and Security on Delgosha Alley in Tehran. What General Bakhshi did to you? It will feel like a Thai massage compared to what we will visit upon you. My brother and me? We do not simply know how to cause pain. That is child's play. We know how to *prolong* it. That is the real skill. And believe me, we have had many, many years of practice.'

For a moment or two, Gabriel contemplated simply killing them both right now. But Ali had called his bluff. And he had nothing else. Or not right now.

Gabriel slid the wicked little blade back into its black plastic sheath, pocketed it and stood.

He picked up the rifle and slung it over his back. Turned to Ali Soltani.

'If you have Odette Diallo? I will take her back from you. And then I will kill you both. And if you're telling the truth? Then I will simply kill you.'

Ali stared up at him, defiance radiating from his smile, despite the horrifying mask of blood through which his teeth shone whitely.

'Until we meet again.'

He turned his head to the side and spat pink saliva onto the concrete.

Gabriel left him there, scrambling to find something to bind his neck wound.

Penetrating the Soltanis' organisation as a new hire had failed as a strategy, so he'd have to try something more like his old way of working in the Regiment. And one of the skinheads had given him an address outside Paris.

A big house on the Paris Road in Saint-Martin in the Versailles Forest.

Shouldn't be too hard to find.

29

Just as he'd done many times before, when on a lurk, Gabriel used a change of outfit to blend in to his surroundings.

A set of thick cotton overalls in deep, dusty blue you could see on millions of working men all over France. Serviceable, shapeless and so ubiquitous as to render the wearer invisible. The battered grey hat helped. As did the scruffy grey wig and straggly moustache. A shambling gait and a roll-up dangling from his lower lip completed his transformation from man-about-Paris to slouching rural odd job man.

He parked down a lane and walked back up to the Paris Road at the outskirts of the village. Checking over his shoulder, he started walking towards the church tower peeping above a line of trees.

At each private drive he stopped and checked the name on the mailbox. Were the Soltanis so confident of their power they'd advertise the fact to *La Poste*, the French postal service? Thirty minutes later he had his answer. No. They were not. Perhaps confidence was the wrong quality. But they were certainly discreet. Probably just as well given their line of business.

Ahead, a woman on a sturdy looking bicycle was pedalling

towards him. The wicker basket ahead of the handlebars was overflowing with fresh green vegetables and a couple of baguettes. As she neared him he raised a hand in greeting.

'Good morning! I don't suppose you can help me?'

She slowed to a stop, the rod-brakes emitting a piercing squeal.

She smiled an apology.

'Sorry, my dad says I should buy a new one but I love Coco too much. Anyway, how can I help you?'

'I'm supposed to be doing some work on a house along here somewhere but I lost the address. I had it written on a piece of paper but I left it in my other overalls and the wife washed it.'

She smiled. Adjusted her weight so she could flatten her foot on the road.

'Do you know the name of the people who own it?'

No point in telling her the Soltanis' real name.

'It's a foreign name. Arab, I think. Syrian, maybe? Brothers. One's short and stocky with an eyepatch, the other's more tall and thin. Like Laurel and Hardy.'

She blanked on the reference. Wrinkled her nose.

'Could it be the Khalifas? I mean out here there aren't that many foreigners, you know? I wish there were but you don't have to go very far out of Paris to see an older version of France, if you know what I mean. My kids are prone to point and stare when they see anyone who doesn't look like them.'

She didn't look old enough to be married, let alone have started a family. Gabriel's natural curiosity got the better of him.

'You have children?'

She must have detected the note of surprise. She laughed.

'Not of my own. I'm a teacher. At the primary school in the village.'

'Oh, sorry. But anyway, yes, the Khalifas. That's them.'

She turned and pointed over her shoulder.

'You see that tall tree with the broken-off branch?'

'Yes.'

Just beyond it there's a little track. You'd never see it unless you were looking. Follow the track for about three hundred metres and the house is at the end.'

He nodded. Cracked a wry smile.

'Those Khalifas like their privacy, no?'

She laughed. 'Oh, yes. I only found it by accident. I was walking my dog and she ran off down the track. I had the devil's own job getting her to come back.'

Gabriel nodded, and smiled affably.

'Well, thank you, miss, you've been really helpful. But I should let you get on.'

She smiled again. 'What kind of work are you doing anyway?'

'Pardon?'

She frowned.

'You said you were doing some work for them. I wondered what kind? Only you have no tools with you.' She looked around. 'Or a van.'

'Oh, right. It's landscaping. They have all the tools there, in a shed. And I like to get my steps in every day.'

She shot him a look, clearly not believing his improvisation. A workman needing to get his steps in? Really? No wonder she looked sceptical.

'It's the wife,' he added, then rolled his eyes. 'She likes to compare at the end of the day. Got herself a Fitbit for Christmas.'

'Well, good luck with your competition.' She readied herself to push off. The venerable bicycle looked like it weighed several times what she did. 'Bye.'

He held a hand up.

'Bye, and thanks again.'

He watched her go, not moving until she disappeared around a curve in the road. Then he walked back towards the village. Sure enough, there was a tree leaning out into the road with a freshly broken branch – it looked like a truck had clipped it trying to make the tight turn down the overgrown track into the forest.

After fifty metres, he turned and checked the line of sight. The road had disappeared, screened by a dense mass of vegetation. The track widened out. Twin ruts filled with gravel showed signs here and there of fat, rugged off-road tyres. Some kind of four-by-four to judge from the depth and width.

He pictured a blacked-out Hummer, Odette, terrified, cowering inside, and strode on.

After a hundred metres, Gabriel left the track and pushed deeper into the woods. The trees were a mixture of oaks and ash, with a few sycamores and yews thrown in. A proper old-growth forest, with no sign of the commercial pine-monoculture that had changed so much of the English countryside. He shook his head. When was the last time he'd even seen the English countryside? Apart from a brief visit to Liverpool the previous year on a recruitment drive, he'd not set foot in England for over a year. Maybe two, his memory was fuzzy on the point.

Around him, birds kept up a constant symphony. He stopped and closed his eyes, just to listen. Somewhere to his left he heard a pattern of regular rustles, followed by a few seconds of quiet. A few more, plus a faint snap. Then silence once more. He turned his head slightly, following the sound. Keeping completely still, he opened his eyes.

Seven metres away, peering at him through a gap between some slender downcurved branches, was a deer. The buck regarded him not with fear, but with something akin to curiosity. Its glistening black nose twitched and it snuffed at the air between them.

Then, miraculously, perhaps because it either sensed he was not there to hunt it, or because it knew what long guns looked like, it raised a long, spindly foreleg, and delicately lifted it over a fallen branch. The other foreleg followed and then both hind legs. It took a couple more hesitant steps. Now they were only five metres apart.

This close, Gabriel could see the delicate eyelashes fringing its huge dark eyes. Its coat was a dark cinnamon colour, dappled with spots of pale sand. He kept his breathing light and steady, relaxing from his core outwards, achieving a state of stillness Master Zhao used to call, 'active passivity'. You were alert, and ready to spring into action, but also so still that an enemy would barely notice you, as you gave off none of the usual signals that indicated the presence of a human being.

Street thieves, especially pickpockets, employed versions of the same technique, though Gabriel doubted they gave it a name as poetic as Master Zhao's.

His active passivity was working on the deer. It was now a mere two metres away and regarding him with a look of frank interest. To speak would be to break the spell. Gabriel let his eyes communicate for him, beaming a message into the deer's brain that said, '*I am not here to hurt you*'.

The deer's left ear twitched. A miniature radar dish turning towards a signal Gabriel couldn't detect.

Every muscle tensed and it turned away and bounded back the way it had come, white tail flashing through the lush greenery before disappearing.

Gabriel pushed on, spotting first the slate roof, then the upper windows and finally the brick front of a largish farmhouse tucked away deep in this little corner of the forest.

The shutters, deep-blue and in need of a fresh coat of paint, were closed and bolted. He circled round to the back of the house. No vehicles parked on the concrete apron at the rear. Or in the three-bay carport of brick and corrugated iron. More windows, also shuttered. The third side offered the same picture. He completed his circuit of the house, arriving at the front. Five windows on the upper floor, two each side of the front door, also deep-blue, also in need of a touch-up.

A dog barked behind him. He turned to see a liver-and-white springer spaniel bounding towards him. Ears flapping, mouth lolling open in a goofy grin. It wore a collar, so unless it was a runaway, a human wouldn't be far behind.

Could it belong to the Soltanis? It was possible, but the house looked closed up, and somehow he struggled to imagine either of the men he'd encountered earlier being the dog-walking type. If they did, it would be something on the aggressive, terrifying side. A Doberman, a Rottweiler or some kind of Pitbull. Not this decidedly soppy spaniel currently rolling onto its back in the hopes of a belly-rub.

He knelt to welcome it, rubbing its bare tummy and earning a grunt of pleasure.

'Hey! Who are you?'

'Help you?'

Gabriel looked up. The dog's owner had arrived. Dressed, as Gabriel was, in dusty blue overalls. But whereas Gabriel had turned up without whatever implements a landscaper might need, this man, who had to be pushing eighty, with a magnificent beer belly straining the front of his overalls, was pushing a wheelbarrow laden with gardening tools.

'She's a lovely dog. What's her name?' Gabriel asked with a smile as he straightened.

'Layla. Who are you?'

'Jeff. My boss sent me out here. Apparently the Khalifas want some rubbish clearing.'

'Where's your truck then?' the gardener asked, looking around.

Gabriel laughed easily.

'The job's more like clearing some deadwood and burning it after. And I felt like a walk, anyway. So where's *your* truck?'

'Needs a new clutch.' He lifted the handles of his wheelbarrow. 'Why I'm pushing this sonofabitch.'

Gabriel nodded, let his smile slide towards the wry end of the spectrum.

'Tell me about it.' He fished out a packet of cigarettes, part of the disguise. 'Smoke?'

The gardener smiled. 'Nice one! Thanks.'

Gabriel shook a couple free and lit them. Handed one to the gardener who inhaled on it so hard the tobacco crackled.

Gabriel turned and pointed up at the house.

'What's going on anyway? They even here, these Karimas?'

'It's Khalifas, and no. I heard them talking the other day. They're going down to Corsica. Got a place in Bonifacio, right on the coast. They took their *niece*.'

He injected a certain amount of scepticism, mixed with distaste, into that final word. Gabriel felt the end of a thread just within reach, a thread whose other end was attached to Odette Diallo. He'd seen the brothers that morning so they'd clearly only just left this house.

'Niece?' Gabriel prompted.

'Pretty little thing. Doesn't look like them at all. Dark, you know. Like those Africans you see in the city. They're more like Arabic, if you know what I mean.'

'How old is she?'

The gardener shrugged. 'Eleven, twelve, maybe thirteen. It's hard to tell. And by the way, that's not me being a racist or anything. I mean young girls these days, they all look about twenty by the time they're thirteen, don't they? Makeup, their hair all done-up, tits out to here.' He made a cupping gesture in front of his own chest. 'In my day, girls looked like girls. Modest, you know? They played with dolls, not bloody phones. Fucking state of this country.' He hawked, spat.

'I have a niece of my own,' Gabriel said. 'Her name's Lisette.'

'Hmm, pretty. They call her Odette so I'm thinking she's from one of the old colonies, you know? Gabon, Chad, Mali, one of those?'

'Côte d'Ivoire?'

A shrug.

'Maybe.'

'How did she look? Happy? Well-fed?'

'You know, average, I guess. She was wearing nice clothes.'

And then, as if remembering he might owe his employers some sort of duty of care, or at least confidentiality, the gardener narrowed his eyes.

'You ask a lot of questions for an odd-job man, you know that? Sure you're not a cop?'

Gabriel smiled. Shrugged.

'Just nosy. The wife says it'll get so long she'll cut it off.'

'Long as that's all she cuts off, eh?' He laughed around his cigarette, sending a cloud of pungent blue smoke Gabriel's way.

'Anyway, look, we better get to work, no? Your deadwood won't clear itself and I got a couple of beds to redo.'

'Trouble is, how'm I going to do my work without tools? Far as I can see they locked the shed up, too. I was told there'd be chainsaws, the works. I better call my boss.'

'Good luck with that. Signal round here's pretty patchy.'

Gabriel made a show of placing a call, nodding, shaking his head, uttering the odd, 'uh-huh'. He pocketed his phone.

'Says I've got to go back and pick up one of his trucks. Got all the gear in for another job just got cancelled. I guess I'll be an hour or so. You still be here?'

'Sure. I've got a whole day's work planned out.'

'All right then, I guess I'll see you later.' He bent to scratch the spaniel behind the ear. 'You too, little Layla.'

He gave a laconic wave and started back up the track.

It was time to rally the troops. A trip south beckoned.

30

Before leaving for Corsica, Gabriel paid a visit to Marianne Diallo's laundromat in Petite Afrique.

The tautness of her smile as she greeted him in the soap-scented shop betrayed the anxiety she was feeling. His heart went out to her. How could anyone carry on a semblance of a normal life when their child was missing? A spectral voice he knew oh-so-well murmured in his left ear.

'We never got the chance to find out, did we, my honey, my soul?'

He tried to shut it out.

'Hi, Gabriel. Do you have news of Odette?'

She was folding a pair of trousers as she spoke, and her fingers twisted and scrunched the denim.

'She's alive, I'm sure of it. But it looks like the Soltanis have taken her to Corsica. We're flying down there in a couple of hours. I just wanted to come and see you first.'

Her eyes, reddened from crying, widened.

'Corsica? But why? What are they going to do to her there?'

'I don't know. But I spoke to a man who saw her just a couple of days ago. He said she looked fine.' It wasn't precisely what the gardener had told him. But Gabriel felt he was on reasonably safe ground extrapolating from what he *had* said. 'Look, I know you're worried, and I wish there was more I could tell you, but I promise you, Marianne. We will go down there and we will find her.'

She must have picked up on the unspoken, 'one way or another', because she burst into sobs. He gathered her into his arms and hugged her. She was shorter than he was and as she buried her head into his shoulder he could smell the oil she used in her hair. A sweetish perfume, peaches, maybe.

Once the racking hitches in her chest had subsided, she released him from her grip.

'I am so sorry. Forgive me. I mean, you are doing so much for me and you don't need my tears staining your clothes.'

He smiled.

'To have a mother's tears wetting my clothes? I'll take that, Marianne, really. And I swear to you, and to Youssoo, I'll find her for you. And I'll bring her back.'

31

Gabriel, Jacko and Tara stepped onto the burning hot tarmac at Figari-Sud Corse Airport amidst a small contingent of French tourists.

The air was infused with the heady aroma of aviation fuel as a tanker swung round their plane on its way to refuel another.

They headed inside and collected their baggage. Tara hired a Jeep and soon they were driving towards Bonifacio. The T40 was a two-lane road, surfaced in pink tarmac. Fragrant, low-growing scrub to both sides: mint, myrtle, laurel and lavender. The smell was like driving through a Frenchwoman's kitchen.

They arrived in Bonifacio at 3.55 p.m. The small coastal town occupied the southern side of a one-and-a-half-kilometre natural harbour formed by an inlet. To the south, Sardinia, the two islands forming a barrier between the Med and the Tyrrhenian Sea.

After checking in at their hotel and changing into the outfits Tara had selected, they met up in the lobby. Next stop, the sea front.

* * *

Tara parked the Jeep in a free space at the end of the harbour. Yachts and pleasure cruisers were moored on the northern bank. Among them, a huge super yacht that took up at least a quarter of the available space, a gleaming white behemoth that towered over the smaller craft.

Tourists milled on the paved and pedestrianised area at the water's edge. Tara's intuition about the outfits they should wear was on point. Among the men, a good three quarters wore some combination of white and navy. Brown deck shoes were the preferred footwear, and straw hats with colourful bands shaded their wearers' heads from the sun, which blazed down out of a cloudless azure sky.

Tara pointed to the vast white boat.

'Think that's theirs?'

'Could be. But maybe it's too showy,' Gabriel replied, adjusting his Ray-Bans a little. 'Could just as easily be one of the smaller boats.'

Jacko climbed out. 'I'm going to have a look, be right back.'

He wandered off towards the superyacht.

Tara looked at Gabriel.

'Think he's OK?'

'Yeah, why?'

'I don't know. Yesterday, while you were out, he disappeared for an hour or so. Came back looking much happier. None of that twitching he does. I'm worried he's using.'

Gabriel shrugged. 'He's hooked, Tara. It's not going to be easy for him to get himself off it.'

'You think we can trust him if things get sticky down here?'

'In a way, more if he's got something to take the edge off than otherwise.'

She wrinkled her nose. 'Just … keep an eye on him. I like him, but there's a young girl's life at stake here. We can't afford for him to go AWOL when things get kinetic because he needs a fix.'

'He'll be fine. But yes, I'll watch him.' He nodded in the yacht's direction. 'Look. He's there and he's doing a pretty good impression of a mindless tourist.'

Jacko was standing with his back to the prow of the superyacht. He was holding his phone aloft and moving it around to get the best angle for his selfie. Apparently satisfied, he pocketed the phone and sauntered back around the harbour wall to the Jeep.

He climbed in and turned his phone round so Gabriel and Tara could look.

'Check out the name.'

Gabriel zoomed in on the script emblazoned on the bow.

'*Simoom.*'

'Which means?' Tara asked.

'It's the desert wind in Syria,' Jacko said. 'All the others are called things like *Wave Rider* or *Not Tide Down*. You know, typical boaties' idea of a witty name for their pride and joy.'

'It's not conclusive,' Tara said.

'No, but it's something,' Gabriel said. 'We know the Soltanis have a place here. And there's a big boat moored in the harbour named after their local wind.'

'So what do we do now?' Jacko asked.

'Split up. Ask around. Tara, remember when you played that film star in Serbia? When we rented the slime-green Lamborghini?'

She grinned. 'That was such fun, having you as my assistant to boss around.'

'So, get into character. Go and chat up the deck hand or whoever's on board *Simoom*. Say you're thinking of buying one. Get them talking and see if you can find out who owns it.'

She snapped off a salute. 'Aye, aye, Captain!'

'Funny. Jacko, you and I are going to go for a little pub crawl. The Soltanis know I'm on their trail, but they don't know about you, so two of us won't raise any suspicions.'

Jacko pointed to Gabriel's all-over grey dye-job, courtesy of Tara.

'Especially since you look like you're about sixty.'

Gabriel pointed to a crowded seafood place whose umbrella-shaded terrace was crowded with diners, black-aproned waiters bustling among them like worker bees tending to their queen.

'We'll meet in that restaurant at six.'

* * *

Tara smoothed the turquoise sundress down over her thighs. Whereas Gabriel and Jacko looked like every other man on the harbour in their white and navy outfits, she'd opted for an altogether higher-toned look.

Every item bore a discreet designer label. Chanel, Balenciaga, Gucci, Versace. She'd topped the outfit off with a broad-brimmed straw hat wound around with a hand-painted silk scarf. Audrey Hepburn would have approved, she felt. The heels she'd selected added three inches to her height and she felt omnipotent as she clicked among the ambling tourists towards *Simoom*.

Behind her oversized Chanel sunglasses she could scrutinise everyone she passed. It gratified her to note that most of the men and a goodly proportion of the women were checking her out. The former with undisguised sexual interest – ugh, French men! – the latter with emotions ranging from frank appreciation to curiosity. Who was this woman striding among them dressed for the Cannes Film Festival? And what was she doing on the southern tip of Corsica?

On the spur of the moment, Tara added another line to her legend. She was thinking of buying not just a yacht, but a property. *Yes, darling! Right here on Corsica. So discreet! So private! One simply has to get away from the paparazzi, non?*

She'd already decided on her name. Kelly Chung.

'Bonjour, Mademoiselle.'

She looked to her left, where a man in his forties or early fifties was tipping his straw hat to her.

'Bonjour, Monsieur,' she said, affecting an atrocious, American-inflected French accent: *Mon-sewer.*

She flicked her eyes over his body. A tight, white, V-neck T-shirt tucked into tan chinos. Terrible fashion choice, but no place to conceal a pistol unless he had one in the waistband in the small of his back, but that would be visible, so not there either. Navy sweater slung casually over his shoulders and knotted at his breastbone. There was a soft place just below that twist of merino where a fist strike would send your opponent to the ground, the nerves of their diaphragm paralysed, leaving them terrified they'd never breathe again. Or an upthrust with a blade would enter the heart and stop them breathing for ever.

'A beautiful day,' he said, in English. 'You are American.'

'And in a hurry. Excuse me.'

She moved to walk away, but he fell into step beside her.

'Excuse my persistence, but you look familiar. A model perhaps? An actress?'

With his tousled grey-and-black curls and knowing smile that he probably imagined was irresistible to women, he looked every centimetre the typical bourgeois French male she'd encountered since moving to Paris. She needed to get rid of him. She glanced at his left hand.

'Won't your wife be missing you?'

He followed her gaze. Offered a sly smile.

'Off shopping with our daughters. My Gold Amex card will be wilting at the corners by the time they've finished. So, which is it? Model or actress?'

She stopped dead, turned to face him.

'I'm sorry. You must have me confused with somebody else. Now, if you'll excuse me, I'm just enjoying a little walk. On my own,' she added, stiffening her tone just a touch. She didn't have BB's skill in all that mystical shit Master Zhao had taught him. But she had spent a decade carrying out the orders of a triad boss called Fang Jian and she knew a thing or two about warning people off.

He smiled.

'Don't be like that,' he said, a hint of – what? A predatory glint? – behind those lazy eyes. 'A beautiful woman like you should be used to male admirers. How about a drink? I know a lovely little bar round the corner. None of these,' he waved a dismissive hand to encompass their fellow strollers, 'tourists.'

Suddenly, she wondered whether the wedding ring was merely a prop. No room on him for a gun, but a little glass bottle of a date-rape drug? Oh, that she *could* imagine. Was he one of those so-called pickup-artists? Men who saw women as nothing more than sexual targets, to be identified, pursued, fucked and forgotten? Where consent was a null concept, and any method of persuasion, up to and including drugging, was acceptable. A recent, horrifying rape case had done nothing to improve the image of Frenchmen in Tara's mind. Time to be rid of this one.

She offered him a demure smile, dipping her head.

'Why not?'

She threaded her arm through his and wheeled around, moving him to her outside. And then her heel caught in a crack in the paving. She squealed in alarm and pitched sideways, clutching his elbow tightly for support. A shove, her other ankle hooked, briefly, around his. A tug on his other hand and he was falling, arms windmilling, over the parapet. He barely had time to cry out before he hit the water. Alone among the dozen or so people who rushed to the edge, some already pulling phones out to capture the accident, Tara moved away from the commotion. As a lifebuoy was thrown down to him, narrowly missing his head, she wove through the incoming crowd and made her way along the north side of the harbour towards *Simoom*.

A couple of young men in matching burgundy polo-shirts were standing at the bow, watching the rescue. Tara approached and stopped at the curving iron bollard to which the bow rope was tied.

She summoned her American accent, a Los Angeles version she'd picked up on a trip with Fang Jian and called out.

'Ahoy, there!'

A third man, a little older than the two boys at the bow, appeared.

'Ahoy yourself! Can I help you?'

'I was just admiring your boat. She's a beauty.'

'She'd be saying the same about her admirer,' he said gallantly. 'Is there anything I can do for you, Miss …'

'Chung. But you can call me Kelly. I don't know. Maybe? I'm thinking of buying a yacht and I saw this and just,' she flapped a hand, 'I mean, OMG she's just so perfect. I don't suppose …?'

'You want to come aboard? Sure, why not? We're just resupplying at the moment. Nothing planned until the day after tomorrow. Hold on.'

A couple of minutes later, Tara was standing on the prow beside the man who'd helped her aboard. He'd introduced himself as Max, the second officer.

'Forgive me, Kelly,' he said, 'but these babies start at five hundred thousand euros. What are you, an entrepreneur or something?'

A point to Max for not insinuating she'd got to wherever she'd got on her looks rather than her brains. She warmed to him.

'I'm an actor.'

'Oh? Anything I'd have seen?'

She rattled off a list of invented films, drawing the expected blank.

'How about *Simoom*'s owners?' she added. 'Are *they* entrepreneurs?'

'Businessmen,' he said.

'Ohh,' she said, smiling as she drew out the word into a conspiratorial shared joke. 'You mean, like, *legitimate* businessmen. I played a gangster's girlfriend in my last film-but-one. *Sicilian Kiss*, it was called. The critics hated it!'

He smiled, but there was an uncertainty in it.

'They're from Paris,' he said, as if gangsters couldn't possibly come from there. 'And Syrian, not Sicilian.'

She shrugged. Why would it matter to her where they were from? She trailed a finger along the chrome rail.

'Half a million?' she asked.

'Where they start, yes. But there are so many upgrades. For example, the Soltanis went for custom upholstery. It actually added another one-fifty to the price. A firm in Italy who do work for Ferrari,' he said, the pride evident in his confiding tone.

Now she had direct confirmation of the ownership of the boat, Tara wanted to be off it as soon as possible.

'Well, this has been fascinating, Max, but you probably have a million and one things to take care of and I have a cocktail party to change for. Thanks again, though.'

He smiled easily. 'But I haven't even shown you below decks. The state rooms have to be seen to be believed. Real double beds. Silk sheets.'

'Oh, I'm sure they're delightful. Another time, perhaps.'

He pooched his lips out in that characteristic French expression called a *moue*.

'Sure. Don't let me keep you.'

He escorted her to the companionway and watched as she negotiated its swaying boards to the harbour. She turned and blew him a kiss.

'Ciao!' she called up.

He touched an index finger to his forehead and turned away.

This was fantastic. They'd only been here for a couple of hours and she had hard intelligence on the Soltanis. And, she suspected, the route they'd use to get Odette off the island.

32

Maximilian 'Max' Audet was fully aware of his employers' line of business.

As a former gun runner in the Caribbean, he'd no qualms about their trade in drugs, weapons or people. As long as they paid him well and left him to his own devices on his days off, he was content.

And Max was loyal to the Soltanis. Once the woman claiming to be an actress had stepped onto dry land, he watched her cross the plaza fronting the harbour, heading for a crowded restaurant terrace. He brought the binoculars he'd grabbed from the bridge to his eyes and focused on her back as she sat down at a table shaded by one of the restaurant's massive blue-and-white umbrellas.

Max knew the owner. They played cards together, shared a bottle of something cold from the restaurant's cellar. And, occasionally, snorted a little of the coke Max brought in from a contact in Algeria. Sammy ran a small distribution operation from his kitchen, selling to the well-heeled visitors who patronised *Le Petit Homard*.

He called him now.

'Hey, Sammy, you got this super-glamorous chick just took a table backing onto the windows. Big straw hat, designer labels from heels to hooters. Keep an eye on her for me, would you? Tell me if she meets anyone?'

'Sure, Max. Hey, when are you next making a run to the fish market? I need some more swimmer crabs.'

Their code for bringing in more blow.

'Next week. How much you need?'

'A half-barrel.' Half a kilo.

'Sure. I can get you that. Talk soon.'

'Laters.'

Max hung up and called Bashar Soltani.

'Hey, boss. Listen, it wasn't a guy, but we had a visitor this afternoon. A chick. Good looking, maybe mid-thirties. Vaguely Chinese-looking. She said she was thinking of buying a boat. Said she was an actress, but I never heard of a single one of the films she listed. I checked IMDB too. She was lying.'

'What else did she say?'

'Asked about who owned the boat.'

'And you told her?'

'Like you said. Made it look all casual, like.'

'Good work, Max. You did well.'

The line went dead.

Max wouldn't exactly have said he *enjoyed* his conversations with Bashar. There was always that edge to them. In the flesh, he was even more imposing. A calm, quiet presence that had the cockier individuals they'd encountered, from cops to business rivals, regretting their words.

Ali was louder. Lairier. Always ready to impose himself physically. Max guessed it was because he was short. Or was it the eye-patch? Whatever. The guy had a real Napoleon complex, for sure. The thought of the stocky Syrian in a tricorn hat, grey greatcoat and tight white riding britches had him smiling. The thought of what he'd do to Max if he knew what he was thinking wiped it straight off again.

Max went below decks to continue prepping for the voyage.

The distance from Bonifacio to Casablanca was a shade under 1,000 nautical miles. Bashar had said they'd be sailing non-stop, so according to Max's calculations they'd arrive in roughly 30 hours given no strong headwinds.

Refuel in Casablanca, conduct some side-business of his own, and then they'd be heading west.

He smiled at the thought. Began coiling another rope.

33

While Tara was investigating the yacht, Gabriel and Jacko wandered the streets just back from the harbour. Jacko was twitchy, sniffing and rubbing his hands together compulsively.

'I need to take a leak,' he said, ducking into an alley.

'I'll wait.'

'No! I mean, you go on ahead. It's better if we split up anyway, we'll attract less attention.'

Gabriel glanced at Jacko, but he'd already turned away. He shook his head. He wanted to help his fellow veteran, but Jacko didn't make it easy. Could he be relied on if things got hairy?

He needed a legend. Something simple that would give him an excuse to talk to well-heeled strangers. The film business had worked for him and Tara before. Maybe it would again.

Ahead, fronted by a huge, tree-shaded courtyard, a restaurant was doing healthy business. Among the many varieties of the French accent, Gabriel picked out a quartet, two men, two women, speaking Russian.

Gold glinted on hairy wrists and stubby fingers, diamonds sparkled at ears and throats. Cigars the size of nuclear torpedoes waved, sending blue smoke curling into the sun-baked air. A

Range Rover, apparently covered in gold foil, sat at the curb like a motorised ingot. All in all, quite the display of ostentatious wealth.

He took a table at a cafe across the small square and ordered a sparkling *citron pressé*, a refreshing drink made from freshly squeezed lemons and soda water, sweetened with sugar by the customer at their table.

Gabriel winced at the first sip. They grew extra-tart lemons this far south. Must be the climate. Added more sugar with the long-handled spoon and stirred it vigorously in the tall glass in its metal cage.

Odd snatches of conversation escaped the foursome's table and floated across the square to him. They spoke Russian with St Petersburg accents.

'... *crypto's still the way to go, Sergei ...*'

'... *the Gucci show was a massive disappointment ...* '

'... *she said Vladimir was a hoot but his wife was as cold as a Siberian winter ...*'

The foursome lingered for twenty minutes. Gabriel looked around from time to time, hoping to see Jacko, but he didn't appear. Charitably, Gabriel assumed he was pursuing leads of his own, maybe in less salubrious parts of Bonifacio than this chi-chi square.

Finally, the Russians asked for the bill and paid. Gabriel caught a glimpse of a twinkling credit card. Diamond-encrusted? Surely not. Swarovski crystals, then. It seemed a possibility. Must be scratchy in the wallet, he mused, a half-smile playing on his lips.

He finished his pressé, left a few euros on the table and sauntered across the square, catching the Russians as they were gathering bags and preparing to leave.

'Hi,' he said, loud, confident, as if he expected to get a hearing from anyone he decided to engage in conversation. 'Sorry to interrupt, but I noticed your fantastic wheels over there. It is yours, right, the Range Rover?'

The two women were eyeing him up with unabashed curiosity.

The men were more guarded. Faces impassive, shading into suspicion.

'It's very pretty, isn't it,' the older of the two women said.

'It should be in the Hermitage,' Gabriel replied, grinning.

She laughed loudly, a little drunkenly, too. He caught the sweetish smell of good white wine on her breath.

'Among the Fabergé eggs? Why not?'

'Can we help you?' one of the two men said, moving closer to the woman and encircling her slender waist in an arm built from four-by-twos.

Gabriel stuck out his right hand. It hung, unshook, in the air between them for a few seconds. He smiled artlessly and let it drop.

'Jonny Adams. I'm a location scout. For the movies?' he added in a tone meant to suggest ordinary people might not know what that was. 'I'm working with Steven Spielberg on a new war movie. Think *Saving Private Ryan* meets *The Boy in the Striped Pyjamas*. We need a villa overlooking the sea. I don't want to make assumptions, but I heard your voices and I figured you might be the kind of discerning people who'd know if anyone owned a pad like that on this little island?'

The second woman flashed her eyes at him.

'The movies! Hear that, Denis? Our place could be perfect.' She turned to Gabriel. 'Would we get to meet Steven Spielberg?'

'Absolutely! Steven likes to approve every location personally. Kind of an article of faith with him.'

The man imprisoning his wife in a bear's grip, shook his head.

'No. We are private people, Mr Adams. Now, if you'll excuse us.'

'Oh, right, of course. I get it. I mean you come down to this beautiful little town for peace and quiet, am I right? Not for some movie guy to start throwing money at you for the temporary use of your home.'

It was an obvious move. But then, in Gabriel's experience, the super-rich were usually obvious people. And the most obvious thing about them was their hunger for money. No matter how much they'd managed to accumulate, by fair means or foul, they always seemed to want more. More than one had gone to their grave chasing it, only to find their last sight was Gabriel Wolfe wielding an edged weapon, or a firearm.

'How much?' the first woman asked, wrestling herself free of her husband's controlling embrace.

'Oh, it varies. But the starting rate is a hundred grand a day plus a grand *per diem* for each occupant. You know,' he spread his hands wide, 'on account of the inconvenience and the fact they have to find alternative accommodation.'

'How many days' shooting would this be for?' she asked, lowering her eyelashes and regarding him coquettishly from beneath their spidery canopy.

'It's hard to be specific at this early stage, but it's a major setting. Could be a month. I appreciate it's a lot of disruption, so …'

'Three million euros,' she breathed.

Gabriel smiled easily, allowed himself a little laugh.

'Dollars, ma'am. We're a US studio.'

He caught the signal that flashed between the two men. Stepped back to minimise the threat they clearly felt he posed. They closed ranks in front of him.

'Maybe you are a little hard of hearing, my friend,' the big man said. 'I said, we are private people. And we have plenty of money already without,' he made air quotes, '*Steven's* three million.'

Gabriel pooched out his lips. He looked down at the ground, let his shoulders drop.

'Oh, sure, no, I get it. It's just I'm under the cosh here. Running out of time, you know? You wouldn't know of anyone else with this type of property, would you? I could offer you an introduction fee? I'm authorised to make an ex gratia payment of ten thousand.' A beat. 'Dollars.' Another beat. 'Cash.'

Why was he doing this? Goading the two oligarchs with bribes as if they were street informants or low-level gang members who'd flip for a brown envelope stuffed with bills? Because he needed to find Odette? Of course. And for that he desperately needed to locate the Soltanis. But there was something else, too. Something that predated his promise to Marianne Diallo.

He just hated people like the four in front of him. He knew without a shadow of a doubt that they hadn't come by their wealth honestly. One way or another, Russian oligarchs had built their vast fortunes on stolen state assets when the Soviet Union collapsed. The financial repercussions of that massive, sudden and catastrophic change of economic system had enriched a few thousand people including the current president, and left tens of millions of ordinary people even worse off.

The bigger man flexed his shoulders inside his jacket. His large, hairy fingers bunched.

'How about those Arabs up the road from us,' the younger woman asked, her eyes searching Gabriel's person as if she could x-ray him and locate the ten grand.

'Arabs?' Gabriel repeated, keeping his smile open and enquiring, rather than triumphant.

'Two brothers. Ali and … I forget the other one's name. Basil? Bashy? One of those weird ones anyway. Their place is enormous, *and* it looks out over the sea.'

'It sounds perfect,' Gabriel enthused. 'Which road is it?'

'The one that runs past the old fort. Right at the end by the lighthouse. You can't miss it. It's got lions on the gate posts.'

'Amazing! Thank you so much …?'

'Natalya,' she supplied. Then looked at his breast pocket and raised her eyebrows, which, like her companions, were immaculately shaped and an oddly even shade of brown that looked painted on.

'Your finder's fee! Of course.'

Gabriel reached for his pocket, but the younger of the two men snapped out a hand and clamped it around his wrist.

Feigning shock, and wincing with what he hoped was a convincing look of a man unused to violence, Gabriel gasped. In other places, other times, the fingers encircling his wrist like a handcuff would be broken by now, dangling uselessly at their owner's side as he shrieked in agony. But today he was Jonny Adams, and Jonny was hurting.

'Jesus, man, what are you doing?'

'Are you deaf? My friend already told you, we don't want your money. Now, you've got your location and we need to be going.'

He dropped Gabriel's wrist, which he massaged while looking pained.

The younger woman shot Gabriel a look of disappointment mixed with apology as she was led back to the ingot-on-wheels. He shrugged and offered a half-hearted wave.

Gabriel waited until the billionaire quartet had entered the confines of the Range Rover and slammed the doors, and for the driver, the older man, to execute a showy doughnut in the centre of the square before roaring away, leaving the remaining diners and tourists flapping hands at the dust or clamping tissues over their faces.

He left the square, heading back to the harbour and the meet with Jacko and Tara.

A good start. They had a location. Not for a Hollywood blockbuster, but there would assuredly be a certain amount of kinetic action before the final scene.

34

Jacko closed his eyes and took a long ecstatic breath.

As the junk flooded his system, the pain that was his daily – and nightly – companion left him, replaced by the euphoria he could count on lasting for a few sweet, sweet hours.

He unwound the belt from his upper arm and threaded it back through his trousers. The needle, poked into a takeaway cup, went into a waste bin. He felt bad, leaving his shit in a public place but what option did he have? Gabriel and Tara were well-meaning, and he appreciated being brought along on their little vigilante jaunt, but what he needed more than their money or companionship was the drug currently taking up residence in his brain and smoothing off all those spikes and burrs that his troubled psyche kept catching on like sheep's wool on a barbed-wire fence. He felt bad, lying to the boss about chasing the dragon when he'd been injecting for a while. First skin-popping, then mainlining for the ultimate high. But what could he do when the drug had its hooks into him? *All* the way into him.

The sun warming his back, he stepped out of the alley and into the main drag, quieter now as more and more people headed for bars and restaurants.

He rubbed the side of his nose. It hadn't always been this way. He'd been a fine soldier. First in the green army and then in the SAS. Until that fateful day when everything had gone from righteous to rotten and his slide towards a medical discharge had begun.

The heroin was demanding he found somewhere to curl up for a bit. He knew he ought to be checking out possible leads on the Soltanis, but that would have to wait. In the end he found a bench under a pine tree. It was crusted with dried, white birdshit and, consequently, vacant. He sat down folded his arms across his chest, and let his head droop.

The screams of the children jerked him awake. Christ! How could he have fallen asleep in the middle of a fucking firefight? The kids were crouching behind a bunkbed. The walls of the bedroom, which had once been painted with a mural of flowers and horses were now pockmarked with bullet holes from assault rifles.

Jacko stuck his M4 out of the shattered window and fired a couple of three-round bursts. Didn't hit anything. Hadn't expected to. The insurgents were everywhere. Talk about faulty intel.

Donkey appeared the doorway, face dust-smeared, those pale-blue eyes standing out starkly.

'Orla! We have to go. Extraction in ten minutes from the oil depot across town. Mick's got a motor.'

Jacko turned back to the kids, their terrified faces streaked with tears.

'I can't leave them, man. Look.'

Donkey nodded. He got his moniker because he was the stubbornest bastard in the patrol, but he had a heart as big as a whale.

'Come on, then. We'll get them out with us.'

Jacko crouched, ducking as a burst from an AK smacked into the far wall, showing plaster over the smallest child, a girl of no more than four, who screamed pitifully.

'Come on, kids,' he said holding out his free hand. 'Time to go. Who wants an adventure, eh?'

The oldest girl shook her head, gathered her brother and sister tighter into her arms. Jacko reached for her and tried to hold her hand but she snatched it away. She mumbled something in Pashto, but Jacko wasn't the linguist. That was Sushi, and he was currently slumped against a white-painted wall, his rifle in his lap, in a pool of his own blood, half his head missing.

'Please, darling, you have to come with us,' he pleaded, extending his open hand and aiming for a reassuring smile.

It didn't land. She huddled further from his grasp, right in the corner.

'Orla, we've got to go,' Donkey urged, pulling him up by his shoulder strap. 'The fuckers have overrun the town. We're gonna get slaughtered like pigs if we stay.'

'But the kids, Donkey. What about the kids?'

'They're locals. They'll be fine. They don't kill kids. It's us they'll fucking cut into pieces. Now *shift* yourself!'

Jacko cast one final, despairing, begging look at the children, but they'd all scuttled into the corner of the bedroom and were out of reach. So he left with Donkey.

As they emerged into the street, they were greeted by a hail of gunfire. They sprinted down the street, firing bursts on the turn, bullets spanging off ruined vehicles, ricocheting off walls and generally turning the experience into something akin to running through a giant wasps' nest. Their air reeked of burning diesel, red hot brass and the acrid stink of burnt propellant.

At the corner, a swirl of rubbish blew out and then ascended in a spiralling cloud.

Donkey pointed.

'The chopper! Come on!'

They redoubled their efforts to reach the corner before a bullet found its home, and skidded into the narrow side street as lumps of brick and plaster sprayed out in a hail of sharp-edged fragments that gashed Jacko's cheek.

As they ran towards the extraction point Jacko had time to observe a nine-inch splinter of timber detach from a window frame, whicker through the air and embed itself in Donkey's back. He didn't even break stride. Adrenaline: nature's answer to morphine.

The chopper's skids were kissing the dusty surface of the square. As soon as Donkey and Jacko had been hauled on board, the pilot lurched the bird up and banked immediately into a stomach-dropping climb. Jacko screamed as he slid towards the open door before hooking his clawed fingers through the netting bolted to the interior of the loadspace.

His head hanging out of the doorway, he had a birds' eye view of the house where he'd been trapped with the children.

He wasn't much of a one for religion, more of a close-the-eyes-and-think-of-home guy while the padre was talking about Jesus. But he prayed then. *Dear Lord, if you exist, save those kids. Don't let them—*

The RPG streaked in ahead of a white trail of smoke, through the window where only a few minutes before Jacko had been firing. The explosion was shatteringly loud, and the shockwave threw the chopper aside like a bird caught in a sudden crosswind.

His mouth dropped open, as the entire upper storey of the building, and its neighbours either side, were vaporised. A sheet of orange flame and black smoke blew out in a circle, before swirling upwards in a conical cloud as the chopper's downdraft caught it and then dispersed it.

Jacko screamed.

'Excuse me? Are you all right, sir?'

He opened his eyes.

A woman was looking down at him, her forehead furrowed, her eyes so full of concern he had to look away or risk crying in front of her.

'Yeah, yeah, thanks. I'm fine. Just a bad dream.'

'But you screamed,' she said.

'I'm fine!' he snapped. 'Leave me alone.'

She backed away hurriedly, recrossing the street and joining a man and two children, a boy and a girl.

Jacko felt bad for shouting at her. He raised a hand in some kind of half-arsed apology but the man was glaring at him and the woman was leading him and their children away. He squeezed his eyes shut, shaking his head and pounding his fists against the sides of his skull, trying not to see that nightmarish image, trying, as he had so many thousands of times since, not to imagine those poor kids' last seconds before their flesh was burned from their bones and their tiny, fragile bodies were turned into so much pink mist.

He lurched towards a flower bed and vomited, spitting acidic bile into the dry soil.

Wrinkling his nose at the stench of his own stomach contents, he turned away, only to see a cop coming towards him. Great. Trouble.

The cop put his hands on his hips, the right actually resting on his gun butt. Time was, Jacko could have disarmed him and shot him with his own weapon before he'd had time to say, '*Bonjour, bonjour, bonjour, and what do we 'ave 'ere then?*'

But that was then. When he was whole. When his veins weren't collapsing from the shit he kept sticking into them. He went for the most unthreatening body language he could manage. Right now, that didn't feel like much of a stretch.

'You are … unwell, *monsieur?* Too much wine at lunchtime?' the cop asked in English, albeit with a strong Corsican accent.

The cop seemed decent enough, though, and was presumably giving Jacko the benefit of the doubt as a tourist.

'Something like that,' Jacko replied, sticking to English. If he spoke French he thought he'd be more likely to be pegged as a local indigent and shown, with rather less courtesy, to the inside of a cell.

'Maybe return to your hotel, then. We do not permit sleeping on public benches.'

Jacko smiled and nodded enthusiastically, as if this was the wisest and most instructive advice he'd ever been given.

'Of course, officer. You're absolutely right. Forgive my lapse in manners. It won't happen again.'

The cop smiled indulgently.

'No harm, no foul, as you British say.'

'Actually, officer,' Jacko said, suddenly having a brainwave, 'maybe you could help me out. I'm looking for two friends of mine. They're Syrian. Ali and Bashar Soltani. I'm supposed to be staying with them but foolishly I lost the address.' He rolled his eyes. 'Probably somewhere halfway down that second bottle of wine.'

The cop shook his head.

'I'm sorry, I do not know the gentlemen.'

'Not to worry. I'll be off to my hotel. Maybe get a shower and a nap.'

'Very good sir,' the cop said, turning to go. Then he stopped. Smiled. 'Which hotel?'

'Pardon?'

'Your hotel? Where is it? Perhaps I can escort you?'

Jack felt close to panic. He had no idea where they were staying. He chest felt tight and whatever pleasant effects of the heroin he'd been experiencing had dissipated.

'It's fine, thank you. I'll make my own way.'

The cop offered a magnificent example of that archetypal Gallic shrug, involving his entire upper body.

'As you wish. Good day, sir.'

'Yeah, cheers.'

Jacko let the cop get twenty metres away and then turned and headed back towards the harbour. He'd struck out, but maybe Gabriel or Tara had had better luck.

35

The plate spun past Ali's head, narrowly missing his right ear. It hit the wall behind him, splashing the rich, tomatoey fish stew up the whitewashed plaster. It looked exactly like what happened when you stuck a pistol barrel in a prisoner's mouth and pulled the trigger.

'Eat, you little bitch!' he shouted at her.

She glared back at him.

'I want my mum!' she screamed, her lips drawn back from her teeth.

He didn't know what to do with her. She was hardly going to fetch a decent price if she was all skin and bone. The men who'd be bidding didn't like any hint of a womanly body, but they didn't want to fuck a skeleton, either.

Maybe Bashar would know.

He left the little room, double-locking the door behind him and twisting the knob, just to be sure.

His phone rang just as he was descending the stairs.

'Yes?'

'Mr Soltani, Sir, it's Constable Buonaventura.'

'What is it?'

'Well, it might be nothing, sir, but I just had words with an English tourist. He was asleep on a bench but when I rousted him he started asking about you.'

Ali's ears sharpened instantly. This was the second incident in as many hours. No way was this a coincidence.

'What did he say, and I mean word for word.'

'Oh, r-right. He, er, well, he said something like—'

'I don't pay you for "something like". Tell me exactly what he said or you're off the payroll and onto a different list altogether.'

The tremor in the cop's voice gave Ali a *soupçon* of pleasure. Pain was a powerful tool, but the fear of it was sometimes better. People in pain would say anything to get it to stop. People *frightened* of pain were strongly motivated to tell the truth.

An audible swallow on the line.

'He said, "I'm looking for two friends of mine. They're Syrian. Ali and Bashar Soltani. I'm supposed to be staying with them but foolishly I lost the address." That's it. Exactly.'

Ali killed the call. Fuck. So Wolfe had recruited help. A man, and a woman pretending to be an actress in order to get information. He sneered. An ex-soldier who thought killing three losers with Nazi tattoos was some kind of achievement, a drunk and a woman. Hardly a revolutionary militia, was it? He and Bashar could take them with their bare hands.

Could.

But they had men to take care of the wet work these days. And maybe it was time to move the girl to their final destination. A rather beautiful beachfront property where the photographer was waiting to take the product shots.

He made a couple of calls. Then went to find Bashar.

36

Gabriel lay prone on the cliff above the Soltanis' house.

Natalya's description had been perfect. They'd driven the Jeep out of town on a gravel road that led to the old fort. Once the lighthouse had come into view, they left it in a lay-by and climbed the low hill that rose to the north of the house.

Through the binos, he could make out the scowls on the faces of the gold-painted lions sitting atop two concrete pillars flanking wrought iron gates. A squawk box was mounted on the left-hand post. They wouldn't be using it.

Beside him, Jacko shuffled forwards a couple of inches. Up close, he smelled of vomit and his eyes looked pink. No alcohol on his breath, though.

The conclusion was inescapable: he'd been using right here on the island. Gabriel worried that he'd picked the wrong man for the job, letting pity for a fellow PTSD sufferer cloud his judgement. Too late now. And for all his flaws, Jacko was still ex-Regiment. He'd promised Gabriel he'd be fine when the moment came.

Tara unzipped her rucksack and took out a cardboard box.

'What's in there?' Jacko asked.

'Our weapons.'

'How did you get guns through airport security?'

She shook her head. 'Knives. I bought them right here. If we need guns, we'll take them off the Soltanis. Or their muscle.'

Jacko nodded. Held out his hand.

Tara placed an Opinel hunters' knife in his palm. Shiny, varnished wooden handle, steel collar that you twisted to secure the opened blade. Ten-centimetre blade. Two more followed, one for Gabriel, one for Tara.

Gabriel locked eyes with his sister, then Jacko.

'These men are killers. Torturers. And they've kidnapped a twelve-year-old girl to auction off to a paedophile. We go in, we find Odette and we get her out of there. Anyone gets between you and her, kill them. Anyone *not* between you and her, ignore them.'

Jacko and Tara nodded.

* * *

They slithered down the gritty slope of the cliff. Gabriel had pinpointed a couple of security cameras on the side of the house facing the road. There were none at the rear. He supposed the Soltanis felt protected by the cliff. Or maybe their own anonymity down here on the southern tip of Corsica.

He, Jacko and Tara arrived at the bottom and crept up to the rear of the property, which was enclosed by a two-metre, whitewashed stucco wall topped with barrel tiles that matched those cladding the roof.

He and Jacko boosted Tara over, Jacko went next, stepping up into Gabriel's interlocked fingers. Finally, Tara and Jacko stretched down their hands for Gabriel to haul himself up and over. They dropped soundlessly inside the Soltanis' compound. And waited.

No barking Dobermans. Gabriel hadn't seen any through the binos, but you never knew. Guard dogs needed sleep like any other fighting unit, and he guessed out here they didn't have a great deal to do.

He timed a minute on his watch, even chucking a couple of

pebbles across the rear of the property to bounce and skitter across the yard. Still no fevered yelping and skittering of claws.

Good. No dogs, then. He'd dealt with dogs before – a memory of a blood-soaked Estonian scrapyard came to mind – but he preferred not to.

Gabriel nodded. They split up. Left, right and up to the rear door. Gabriel tried the handle. It moved down silently and he pushed. The door opened. Definitely over-confidence on the Soltanis' part.

Inside, he stood still. Let his hearing dominate. Sight was always the default sense. But it tended to drown out other, more pertinent information. Everything you could see clamoured for attention. A splashy painting on the wall, a vase of cobalt-blue agapanthus flowers, a door that looked as though it might lead to a utility room. The view of a kitchen through another open door.

He reached out with his hearing, straining to detect the smallest of sounds – a radio playing music, a washing machine going, male voices speaking in murmurs, the clack and ratchet of small arms being readied. But what he heard was nothing. The house was entirely silent.

He checked the time. Bit late for a siesta. And would a couple of former Syrian security service agents do anything so risky? With a prisoner? And, as they surely knew by now, a former special forces soldier on their tail? He thought not.

A sense of foreboding settled over him like a heavy, grey cloak. They weren't here. Gripping the knife in his right fist, he mounted the stairs: terracotta tiles edged in blue and white mosaic. As he'd done so many times on covert operations, he wore crêpe-soled desert boots, protective but light and, more importantly, silent. A small click from the ground floor had him whipping his head round.

Jacko had entered via the door that led to the kitchen. He looked up at Gabriel and raised his eyebrows. 'Anything?' he mouthed.

Gabriel shook his head.

Tara appeared from the opposite side of the hallway to Jacko. She glanced at them both and shook her head.

Gabriel pointed left and right. They hurried away, searching the ground floor and for a basement. In his turn, he reached the upper storey landing and turned left. Four doors led off the long corridor, which terminated in a sun-filled window. He reached the first, flipped the knife around in his hand so it was point uppermost, took a quick breath, twisted the knob and then burst in, his hand raised.

The room was empty. But he could smell aftershave. The bedlinen was rumpled and, when he checked the wardrobe, it was full of men's clothes.

He checked the next two rooms. Both were empty. The second clearly recently vacated by whichever brother hadn't been sleeping in the first room. That left one last room, right at the end of the corridor.

Odette *had* to be in here. Somehow he knew they wouldn't be keeping her on the ground floor. He readied himself, took a steadying breath, then swung the door open and launched himself through, knife in front of him, ready to plunge into the belly of whoever was waiting on the other side.

The window was barred.

The single bed was unmade. A pink teddy bear lay on the floor. His chest clenched as he took in the splash of gore on one wall before he saw the plate on the floor. And smelled garlic, tomatoes and fish. He nodded. *Brave girl. You threw the food at him. I hope your spirit can hold out just a little longer.*

He went to find the others.

Gunshots shattered the silence.

37

Gabriel dropped to a crouch and slid back round the corner of the wall.

From his vantage point he had a one-eighty-degree view of the ground floor. Two black-jacketed men had come in through the front door, pistols in hand and were firing indiscriminately. The rounds smashed through furniture and wall hangings, leaving gaping, splintered holes, pale wooden edges showing starkly against the dark varnish. Hollowpoints.

Within a second of each other, they burned through the last round in their magazines. Acting in synchrony so precise it looked rehearsed, they dropped the empty mags out of their pistols and began reloading.

A scream rent the air. Gabriel recognised it. But the two men whirled round, eyes wide.

Tara came at them at a sprint, knife up. Gabriel raced for the stairs and reached the ground floor seconds later, his feet flying over the tiles.

The first guy was still figuring what to do when Tara stabbed him in the side and kept on punching her blade home into his torso.

To a shocked bystander, her strikes would have looked frenzied, but Gabriel knew his sister had studied human anatomy as diligently as he and his former comrades had.

Tara hit his liver, his left kidney, then his right, and then, closing in for the kill, she drove the point of the knife into his belly on a steeply upcurving trajectory that took it straight into his heart. Blood fountained from his gaping mouth and he toppled backwards, dead from massive blood loss before the back of his skull smacked into the floor tiles with a hollow clonk.

Gabriel was still two metres away from the second goon, when he slapped the new mag home into his pistol. He brought it up and pointed it at the back of Tara's head. In that weird, slowed-down combat time that descended on him when things got kinetic, Gabriel watched the blood leave the gunman's knuckle as he squeezed the trigger.

'Tara!' Gabriel screamed, simultaneously slashing at the shooter's arm with his own knife.

Tara spun round, her face a mask of red from the dead heavy's breath-borne blood spatter. The gun went off, a thirty-centimetre jet of flame speared towards her face, smoke and particles of gunshot residue spraying sideways and forwards.

Somewhere in that red-hot, toxic cloud of burning gas, gunpowder and smoke, a hollow-point bullet was travelling at subsonic speed towards her brain.

The devastation was instantaneous, enormous, and fatal. The pressure as the bullet's kinetic energy strove to conserve itself exploded her skull like an eggshell hit with a hammer. The few kilos of greyish-cream jelly inside were vaporised and hit the wall like the fish stew Gabriel had seen upstairs. And blood. So much blood. The arteries in the brain were at full pressure supplying that miracle of biology. Hitting one with a bullet was like smashing an axe through a firehose. Crimson jets spurted upwards in two-metre arcs, painting the ceiling in great looping curves that dripped back down onto Gabriel's upturned face before spattering the floor like a tropical rainstorm.

Gabriel's scream died in his throat as the horrific image snapped off like a dead TV set. Tara was alive. The bullet had missed her by millimetres, scorching her temple before burying itself harmlessly in the wall.

He'd been absent for a fraction of a second, but his arm had continued its downwards path and the blade of his Opinel hunters' knife had cut through the gunman's elbow down to the bone, where the edge now grated and screeched as he yanked it free.

Over the gunman's screams, Gabriel brought the knife round again and jammed it straight through the soft place under his chin. The knife travelled upwards, slowed a little by the root of the tongue, then the soft palate, then the base of the brain pan, before ending its murderous journey buried halfway through the man's frontal cortex. His eyes rolled upwards in their sockets and he fell sideways, blood running out of his nostrils, mouth and underside of his jaw in dark-red streams that splashed onto the floor, releasing a metallic stench of copper and iron.

Gabriel turned to Tara.

'You all right?'

'Yes. No Odette?'

'No. Not there, and nor are the Soltanis.' He pointed down. 'Get the guns. We need to find them before they leave the island.'

Jacko appeared at the open front door.

'I searched the garden. No shed. No outbuildings. No—' His eyes widened. 'Fuck me! What happened here? It looks like a slaughterhouse.'

'The Soltanis left a welcoming committee. We need to find them.'

Jacko nodded.

'Tyre tracks on the inland side of the property. There's a gate in the fence. Looks like a 4x4. They might have gone cross-country.'

'Or they're heading back to the airport,' Tara said.

'Or the boat,' Gabriel added.

* * *

It took them ten minutes at a run to reach the Jeep. Gabriel climbed behind the wheel and fired up the engine. It caught with a loud, rattly protest and belched a cloud of thick blue diesel smoke from the exhaust.

He shoved the gearbox into first and took off, all four wheels scrabbling for grip on the coarse pink grit before digging in and sending the trio hurtling after the Soltanis.

Gabriel rounded a bend, not braking but feathering the throttle just a touch. The Jeep shimmied into a slide as the loose gravel beneath the wheels failed to offer any purchase despite the four-wheel drive, but Gabriel kept the grille pointing into the direction of the skid and drifted round the bend.

'Shit! Take cover!'

Ahead of them, standing in the centre of the road, a man stood with an RPG launcher already on his shoulder.

'No!' Jacko screamed as he dived out of the rear seat, hitting the ground and rolling away and down into a ditch.

Gabriel and Tara left the Jeep on opposite sides, diving in unison left and right, tucking and rolling as they raced to put distance between themselves and the incoming rocket.

Even as he sought shelter behind a triangular pink boulder, Gabriel picked up the click-pop-hiss as the RPG blew free of the launcher on its preliminary charge. The main motor ignited with a whoosh and three seconds later the Jeep leapt upwards as if a giant had stamped down on the other end of a see-saw. Amid the smoke and flame of the shatteringly loud explosion, the burning 4x4 turned somersaulted in the air before crashing down at the side of the road. It rocked there for a few seconds, as if undecided on whether to stay or roll down the hill.

The fuel tank went up with a huge bang, sending a yellow and scarlet fireball edged in turquoise and emerald-green rolling around itself. A secondary explosion sent fragments of glass whickering outwards in a razor-sharp sphere. Shards tinkled everywhere as they hit rock or pattered to the ground.

The Jeep made its decision, aided by the inescapable force of gravity. It tilted, metal shrieking in protest, then turned over, once, twice, then, gathering speed, a whole series of bouncing rolls, eventually leaving the ground with each rotation, shedding metal parts, bits of seating and whatever remained of the windows before smashing into a stand of gnarled-looking trees and coming to rest upside down, its blazing wheels scorching the dry branches of the trees.

Gabriel was up first, Tara a few metres behind him, sprinting after the man who'd fired the RPG. He'd dropped the launcher and was racing away up the road towards a trailbike heeled over on its kickstand.

Gabriel dropped to one knee, steadied his right hand with his left and started shooting. The man ducked, then zig-zagged left and right, but he needn't have bothered. Gabriel wasn't trying to hit him. A moving target at that range with a pistol? Even in the preparedness of a range exercise, that would be a tall order. But out here, with adrenaline making every muscle shake? No. Not possible.

The bike, on the other hand, presented a more realistic target. It was stationary. It was side on. And it was at least two metres from front tyre to rear.

Gabriel shouted for Tara to shoot and she too dropped to one knee and started pumping rounds into the bike.

Bullets spanged off the bright work, one hit an indicator and exploded it in a glittering spray of orange plastic as the sun backlit them like fragments of orange peel. Tara hit the engine block. Then Gabriel put a round through the fuel tank. It went up with a sharp bang. The bike skittered sideways before crashing onto the road and bursting into flames as the petrol hosed out and turned it into a two-wheeled Molotov Cocktail.

Deprived of his escape route, the Soltanis' rearguard turned, drew two pistols from his belt and walked towards them, firing alternate weapons and sending 9mm rounds towards them at quarter-second intervals.

'I'm out!' Tara shouted.

From his prone position, Gabriel aimed at the guy's midsection. Centre-mass was the percentage shot.

He missed. Squeezed the trigger. The slide locked back. Empty.

The guy wielding the twin automatics grinned and stopped walking. Levelled his pistols to keep Tara and Gabriel pinned down.

Gabriel looked across the road at Tara. Their eyes met. Was this it? After all the missions, all the ops, all the countries of the world they'd travelled in, singly and together, they were going to end up being gunned down by a hired hand on the arse-end of Corsica?

Gabriel thought of Eli. Maybe it wouldn't be so bad. Even if he didn't believe in the afterlife, he could take some comfort from the thought that if he was wrong, they'd soon be reunited.

A bloodcurdling bellow rent the air. Half-human, half-animal. It sounded like an enraged bear.

The gunman flew sideways as Jacko's fourteen stone cannoned into him from the ditch he'd been crawling along. Without a pistol of his own he'd fallen back on the SAS's oldest weapon. Stealth.

One pistol flew from the gunman's grasp and disappeared into a patch of thorny scrub on the other side of the road. He brought the other round and jammed it into Jacko's face.

Then his own face twisted and his mouth dropped open in a wide, round, 'O'. Blood poured out, tumbling over his bottom teeth and running all over his chin and down his neck. His whole body jerked and the pistol fell from his hand as Jacko plunged his Opinel knife into his belly over and over again.

He clambered to his knees and threw a leg over the prostrate heavy's chest, raised the knife over his head and screamed a death-cry:

'Die, you cowardly bastard!'

The knife hit his sternum with such force Gabriel heard the ping as the blade snapped clean in two against the sheet of bone. Jacko had his berserker's blood up now, though. He pulled the stubby square blade back up and this time plunged it down through the right eye with a wet crunch. He got to his feet and stamped on the hilt, driving all but a few centimetres of varnished and now bloody handle into the man's brain.

He turned to Gabriel and Tara.

'You can get up now.'

38

Under a baking sun that cast deep-black shadows in front of them, it took Gabriel, Tara and Jacko two hours to walk back into Bonifacio.

They entered the town and headed straight to the harbour.

The berth where the Soltanis' yacht had been moored was empty.

All that remained was a rainbow-hued scum of diesel oil on the mirror-smooth surface of the water.

Simoom was gone.

And so was Odette Diallo.

Gabriel exchanged looks with Tara and Jacko.

'We've lost her,' Jacko said dejectedly.

'No! We haven't. I won't allow it,' Gabriel shot back. He grabbed Jacko by the front of his shirt and shoved his face in close. 'Don't you ever say that. She's alive and we're going to find her. We're going to save her, you hear me! We are *not* giving up.'

A big man like Jacko could have put Gabriel on the ground with a single swipe of one massive forearm, but he sagged back, eyes wide and pleading.

Tara intervened, threading her arm between them and disengaging Gabriel's grip on Jacko's shirt.

'Stop it, BB! Stop it! If it wasn't for Jacko we'd both be lying in the ditch full of bullet holes. Nobody's talking about giving up. But we have to regroup. Figure out a new plan.'

'To be honest, we also need to get back out to their villa. Clean up a bit,' Jacko said. 'And the guy with the RPG. We don't want the cops sniffing round us. I've got a strong feeling at least one of Bonifacio's finest is in their pockets.'

* * *

It took them an hour to find a car rental place and buy some supplies from an edge-of-town hardware store. They drove back up the old fort road, stopping first at the scene of their near-fatal encounter with RPG guy. They dumped his body in the boot, wrapped in plastic decorators' sheets. Gabriel and Jacko manhandled the wrecked trail bike over to the edge of the road and sent it wobbling, then tumbling, then finally somersaulting through the air, down the hill to smash into pieces at the bottom, fifty metres from the stand of scorched trees where the Jeep lay on its roof.

They drove on to the Soltanis' house. Gabriel popped the boot, and he and Jacko carried the corpse inside and laid it near the two dead gunmen the Soltanis had left in wait for them.

'We need to blow it,' Gabriel said.

Tara nodded.

'I've got this. I noticed something when we arrived.'

She led the others into the kitchen. In a curtained-off corner stood four tall blue propane tanks, one connected to the cooker via a rubber tube. She detached the tube, coiled and pocketed it. Lifted a wine bottle from a rack in a disused fireplace and uncorked it.

'We having a celebratory drink or something?' Jacko asked, his mouth quirking into a puzzled smile.

Tara shook her head, flicking the cork away and then

emptying the pungent, dark-plum-red wine down the sink. She grabbed a tea towel, tore off a strip, then headed for the door.

'Come with me. Oh, and BB? Open all the valves on the gas tanks, yes?'

Gabriel nodded, releasing the first valve with a loud hiss, his nose wrinkling at the stink of the propane. Tara had a talent for improvising explosives. He could see that what she had planned would do a fine job of obliterating every trace of their presence inside the house.

Back at the car, Tara uncapped the petrol tank and threaded the orange rubber hose down the filler tube. She held the empty wine bottle ready with her left hand, then brought the free end of the tube to her lips and sucked, her cheeks shadowed as they hollowed from the suction. She turned away and spat out a mouthful of petrol and stuck the end, now delivering a stream of petrol, into the wine bottle.

Jacko nodded.

'Nice,' he said, with feeling.

The bottle full, Tara let a little more of the petrol splash onto the strip of tea towel, then pulled the pipe free and set it aside. She screwed in the fuel cap and closed the filler door.

She worked one end of the petrol-soaked tea towel strip down into the neck of the bottle. Looked at Gabriel. Then Jacko. Retrieved a lighter from her pocket.

'Ready?'

'Ready,' the two men said in unison.

She flicked the wheel on the lighter. The yellow flame was invisible in the bright sunlight, but it was there all the same. She held it to the free end of the fuse and set it burning merrily.

Tara took a couple of steps, brought her arm back and launched the petrol bomb in a graceful arc towards the house. Gabriel had once destroyed an illegal munitions factory the same way, but his fuel-air bomb had been constructed from TICs and TIMs – toxic industrial chemicals and toxic industrial minerals. And rather than a petrol bomb, his detonator had been an RPG.

He'd been with Eli. Her face, blood-spattered after killing the factory owner, an extreme-right wannabe politician, had been beautiful. The rage in her eyes like a banked-up internal fire.

Tara's aim was true. The wine bottle, trailing its flaming, ragged ribbon of a fuse, smashed through the kitchen window.

The free gas filling the room ignited with a roar, blowing out the other windows. But that was merely the overture. One by one, taking no more than five seconds in all, the four propane tanks, each holding 47 KG of liquefied gas under pressure, detonated. The sound was like a bank of howitzers firing in unison. Huge percussive wallops of sound so loud it was a physical sensation that hurt the ears.

'Down!' Gabriel yelled and they threw themselves to the ground.

Shit, we're out of practice, he thought as chunks of masonry and razor-edged pieces of shrapnel from the gas tanks spun through the air.

He uncovered his head, and got to his feet.

The house was ablaze. Flames leapt twenty, thirty metres into the air then died back down as they consumed everything in a vast, accelerating rush of heat, light and smoke.

With nobody to raise the alarm, how long would it take before whatever passed for a fire department in Bonifacio turned up? He had no idea but couldn't imagine the little tourist town having much beyond a basic outfit, probably staffed with volunteers.

It was time to go.

39

PARIS

Their plane landed in Paris at 11.57 a.m. the following day.

Back at Tara's apartment, Gabriel made coffee. Jacko declined a cup, saying he had business to attend to. As the front door clicked shut behind him, Gabriel and Tara shared a look.

'He's using,' Tara stated. 'Can we rely on him?'

'You said yourself, we'd have been rotting in some Corsican morgue if it hadn't been for Jacko.'

'I know, BB, but now Odette's in the wind, I just don't know if we can trust him. What if he blacks out or something just when we need him?'

Gabriel shrugged.

'We'll just have to manage. We've done it before. Have you checked the auction site?'

She nodded. 'It's like some twisted eBay site for perverts. I wish we could get to the men who'll be bidding for her as well as the Soltanis.'

'When I was in Cambodia once, I fell in with a group of guys, they called themselves paedo hunters. I helped them break into a ... ' he frowned, 'I was going to say brothel but that almost sounds innocent compared to this place. Anyway, it was full of children. And all these nonces, mostly westerners, Brits, yanks, a couple of Germans. We cleaned them out, kept them overnight then cable-tied them in a circle around a statue of the Cambodian prime minister for the cops to find the next morning. It was one of the times I had zero regrets about what I was doing, you know? Only truly bad people got hurt, we saved some kids and I didn't lose anyone I cared about.'

He heaved a sigh as his mind filled with the faces of so many dead people: comrades, friends, family, lovers and, at the front of the queue, his wife, simultaneously pregnant and cradling their baby.

Tara came to sit beside him on the sofa. She put her arm round his shoulders. His eyes pricked and he swallowed down a lump that had grown to the size of a grenade.

'You miss her so much, don't you, BB?' Tara asked softly.

He crumpled against her, sobs wracking his body.

'Oh, Jesus, Tar, it's like I've been gutshot,' he cried into her shoulder as she hugged him. 'The pain never leaves me. I just use work or action to numb it like a morphine injector.'

He recoiled from his own words. Why did his brain do this to him? Conjure up images that took him straight back to that dreadful, blood-soaked day on Scalpay? It was Eli who'd taken a round to the belly. Gabriel had raced back up the stairs with a fistful of morphine injectors to relieve her agony, only to find her dead. His mind had fled, taking his grip on reality with it, leaving him believing, for more than a day, that he'd been able to save her life.

'I don't know what to say, BB,' Tara said quietly. 'I've never had anyone in my life like you had Eli.'

He pulled himself upright and swiped a hand across his eyes.

'Never?'

She smiled, a little.

'I'm not a nun. But I never found anybody I could imagine sharing my life with. My future with. When you introduced me to Eli I could see it, though. Your life and hers intertwined until you grew old.'

'Maybe nobody in the Wolfe family gets to experience that,' he said ruefully. 'Mum and Dad didn't. I didn't. Sometimes I think we're cursed.'

She reared back.

'Cursed? What, you're some back-country peasant now? Listen to me! I grew up around those people in case you'd forgotten. Mummy Rita raised me in that little village out in the sticks and that's the kind of crap you used to hear all the time. But Mummy was a city lady, from Hong Kong. She told me once, "Wei Mei, luck and curses and gods and prophets, believe in it if you like. Me, I prefer to make my own luck. And if that fails, I've got a bloody big revolver in my knicker drawer".'

'So you think everything that's happened to me, was because of me? That was the luck I made?'

'No. Not the stuff that happened to you. The things that happened to the people you were *fighting* were because of you. But Eli? Britta? The others you lost along the way? You can't blame yourself.'

He sighed, stood.

'That's the trouble, Tar. I can't *stop* blaming myself. Eli wouldn't have been taken by Bakker if not for me. She wouldn't have ended up on that island if not for me. Britta wouldn't have been on that beach in Aldeburgh if not for me. Now they're both dead. And what about those boys I recruited and took over to Santa Rosa? Sparrow and Tiny are dead. They went because I asked them to and now they're *dead*.'

Tara's eyes flashed.

'No, you're wrong, BB. They *listened* because it was you asking. But they *went* because they wanted to. Them! Did you hold a gun to their head?'

'No. But—'

'Did you take hostages and threaten to kill them unless they helped you?'

'Tar, you know that's not what I mean.'

'*Did* you?'

He knew when he was beaten.

'No. I did not.'

And his sister knew when she'd won. She didn't pursue victory past the finishing line.

'Where are you going?' she asked as he shucked on a light jacket, the temperature in Paris several degrees cooler than down in Corsica.

'I need to see Marianne and Youssoo. Update them.'

'Try to give them hope. It's not over yet. Odette is still alive and if they're selling her, they'll want her to be healthy.'

Gabriel grimaced.

'I'll try to find a way to tell them that without making them think the worst.'

He left her in the apartment and headed north to the Eighteenth.

And a difficult conversation with a missing girl's mother.

40

Gabriel smelled Automat Cavally well before he arrived at its shop doorway. The soapy steam issuing from a vent and from the open door insinuated itself into his nostrils, reminding him of the lack of good news he had to impart.

He tried to imagine how it must feel, to be a parent and to know your child was alive and in such peril, and yet to be powerless to do anything about it.

He went inside, breaking into a sweat as the hot steamy air clung around him – *like a shroud*, an inner voice whispered.

A few women in colourful batik headdresses were folding clothes and talking animatedly. They fell silent when he walked in. Regarded him with suspicion. Did they think he was a cop? One of the Soltanis' men collecting protection money? Or merely a stranger, as out of place in the laundromat as a nun on a battlefield.

'I'm looking for Marianne,' he said to the nearest woman, her large body wrapped resplendently in a red, black and white dress of palm-leaf designs. 'Is she here?'

The woman kissed her teeth. Raised her chin.

'Who are you?'

'My name is Gabriel. I'm trying to find Odette for her and Youssoo.'

She nodded slowly, placing the sheet she was folding on the top of a pile in the pink plastic laundry basket on a chair in front of her.

'But you haven't found that little angel-child, have you?'

'No. I came close. That's why I need to speak with Marianne.'

Without taking her eyes off Gabriel, the woman called out.

'Hey! Rianne! A guy here called Gabriel is asking for you. It's about Odette.'

Marianne appeared from the door at the back of the shop. Her forehead shone with sweat. She forced a smile onto her face, but the grey-purple bags under her eyes told a simple story. A distraught mother, running on coffee and maybe a couple of hours of broken sleep each night. The rest spent in anxious tossing and turning, or maybe wandering the streets of Petite Afrique hoping to turn a corner and catch a glimpse of her daughter. Not missing after all, just lost, or maybe a head injury because, yes, that could cause amnesia. Or, and this any mother could cope with, a naughty child, running off to worry her parents: '*I hate you! I wish I'd never been born!*'

All these thoughts passed through Gabriel's mind in the time it took for Marianne to come up to him and hug him tightly.

Instead of being reassuring, the hug only intensified his guilt. What could he possibly say? We went down to Corsica, killed a few guys and still let them slip right out from under our noses? It wasn't my fault? They were expecting us? I let you down?

Marianne saved him the trouble.

She released him and stared up into his eyes.

'You did not find her.'

He shook his head.

'I'm sorry.'

'Is ... she alive?'

Gabriel reached for the right words. Something he could say that would give her hope without raising false expectations.

'I think so. We're not giving up, Marianne. Odette is alive. The Soltais have taken her but we still have time.'

She frowned. 'You said "we" before. Who is this "we"?'

'My sister, and a friend.'

'What are you going to do next? Do you have any leads?'

Gabriel was about to confess that right now he was flying blind, a thousand miles behind enemy lines with no map, no compass, not even the stars to navigate by. Except that wasn't quite true, was it? Because they did have a lead.

All of the men they'd encountered, all of the Soltanis' muscle, according to Jacko, were ex-French Foreign Legion. Surely they didn't just collect their papers, walk off-base and climb straight into a blacked-out SUV driven by Ali or Bashar? There had to be some sort of middleman. And he would know how to find them.

'One. And I think he's right here in Paris.'

41

Jacko reacted at once when Gabriel outlined his theory about a middleman helping the Soltanis recruit ex-legionnaires as their muscle. His eyes seemed unnaturally bright.

'I know him! I know the guy you're talking about. Well, a guy it could be, anyway. He was a recruiting officer for the Legion. I met him a couple of times when I joined. Real egomaniac. He was supposed to be interviewing me but he spent most of the time telling me about his military service. How many missions he'd been on, all his kills.'

Gabriel frowned. It was the question civilians always wanted answering. *Did you ever kill anyone?*

Everyone Gabriel knew always replied with a variation on the same answer. *I don't talk about that.*

Regular men didn't want to. Or not with outsiders, anyway. Only the psychopaths did. The army claimed it weeded them out. The men who joined up because they were fascinated by the idea of killing. Because they wanted to find out exactly what it felt like to extinguish another human being's life. But he'd met a couple. Supernaturally calm before a battle. Unconcerned about the idea that it might be them getting shot or blown to bits. Narcissists so convinced of their own godlike powers that it would never occur to them they could be the one crying for their mother, or their mates, as their guts spilled onto their boots.

'What's his name, this egomaniac?' Gabriel asked.

'Tom Gallou.'

Tara walked in and dumped a bag of groceries on the table.

'Who's Tom Gallou?'

Jacko ran through it all again.

Tara nodded and started putting the food away.

'We'll find him tonight.'

'How?' Jacko asked, incredulous. He waved an arm at the tall curtained window. 'France is a big country. Assuming he's even here.'

She shot him a disbelieving look.

'Ever hear of the internet, Jacko?'

Tara stabbed the screen of her MacBook.

'Tom Gallou. Former soldier in the French Army. Fifteen years with the Foreign Legion, including five as chief recruiting officer. Now holds a position as a deputy director of HR in the *Ministére des Armées* with special responsibility for the *Legion Étrangère*. Works out of a seventh-floor office at Hexagone Balard.' She grinned at Gabriel. 'Typical French. The Americans have the Pentagon, so the French have to go one better and give *their* defence HQ six sides.'

Jacko raised his eyebrows.

'Bit lax to put all that on their website.'

Tara shot him a look.

'You're joking, right? This isn't online. I'm looking at their internal directory.' She swivelled the MacBook round so Jacko and Gabriel could see.

The screen was busy with rows of names, job titles and contact details, plus a pop-up window illustrating an organisation chart.

'Kudos,' Jacko said, nodding. 'Good in a fight, beautiful *and* a hacker. What else do you do, shoot lasers out of your eyeballs?'

She ignored him, going back to the keyboard. But Gabriel glanced at Jacko, who was following every tap of Tara's fingernails. *Beautiful?* He hoped Jacko wasn't falling for Tara. That would complicate things. And it would only lead to disappointment.

But more important than any consideration of a romantic entanglement between Jacko and Tara was the fact that they now had a genuine lead. The very thing Marianne had asked for.

But how was Gabriel going to get Tom Gallou to talk?

Then an idea came to him. An idea that would mean a trip back to England.

42

BUCKINGHAMSHIRE, ENGLAND

Gabriel pulled the wrought iron rod screwed to the sun-warmed red brickwork. Somewhere beyond the oak door bound in black iron, a bell tolled.

He took a step back and waited. He felt unaccountably nervous. He'd known Don since he was a callow youth of nineteen and freshly recruited by the Parachute Regiment when Don had been the CO. But it had been a long time since he'd seen the old man, and he worried what he would find when the door opened.

Don lived deep in the Buckinghamshire countryside. His many enemies would have marvelled at how the architect of so much death and destruction could exist in such a rural paradise.

Birds filled the air with a cacophony of songs, from wheedling melodies to chirrups, chatters and swooping, fluting calls that imitated a mobile phone's ringtone. The cottage literally had roses growing around the door, their velvety pink blooms drenching the porch in the sweet scent of peaches.

The door opened and Gabriel mentally rehearsed his greeting. *Hi, Boss, I'm sorry to drop in unannounced, but I need help finding a missing girl.*

It would work, he had no doubt. Not an official mission, if such things even existed anymore. He'd heard on the grapevine that the Department and its successor had been wound up for the final time by the current government. But Don would do whatever he could to help.

The gap between the oak door and the red-brick wall widened, and Gabriel smiled.

'Hi, Boss, I'm—'

A young woman stood in the doorway. No makeup, her left eyebrow pierced by a tiny silver ring. Had Don sold the place? It was possible, Gabriel conceded. But the woman was only in her early twenties. Mid, at a pinch. How could she afford a place like this? Or was she living here with her parents, well-to-do bankers, perhaps?

She smiled. 'Can I help you?'

'I was hoping to see my former boss. Don Webster.'

'Of course! Come in.'

He followed her inside. Maybe she was a great-niece or something. As far as he knew, Don and his late wife Christine had never had children. Or a cleaner?

'The colonel's in the living room,' she said. 'My name's Holly, by the way.'

'Gabriel.'

At that, she turned and regarded him with a look of wonder.

'Not Wolfe?'

'Yes, why, has he mentioned me?'

'Mentioned you? You're "Old Sport" right? That's what he calls you.'

'Yes,' Gabriel said with a smile.

'I think it's fair to say he's mentioned you,' she said. 'Come on, but you might have to be quiet. He's watching one of his old films.'

Since Holly had opened the door, Gabriel had been struggling to understand what she might be doing in Don's house. But then, it fell into place. The way she talked about him solicitously, her desire not to have him disturbed.

'Forgive me if I've got this wrong,' he said, 'but are you Don's carer?'

'Yep. Live-in. Poor love has good days and bad ones, but on the whole more good than bad. He hired me a couple of years ago for physical therapy but I think he knew what was coming. Go in,' she said, pointing at the sitting room door. 'I'll put the kettle on.'

Trepidation making his heart beat faster, and wondering what he'd find – the old man in a wheelchair? Or hooked up to an oxygen bottle? – Gabriel went in.

The TV volume was loud. A young Charlie Sheen in fatigues carried an M16. *Platoon.* 'One of his old films'? Gabriel would have said *Platoon* was recent. Then he recalibrated. It had been made in the mid-1980s. Holly hadn't been born until after the new millennium. It might as well have been *Gone With the Wind*, or *The Magnificent Seven*. Jesus, *he* was getting old.

Gabriel took a few steps into the room and turned to take in the old man ensconced on a leather Chesterfield sofa.

The shock rendered Gabriel speechless for a few seconds. Don had always been such a physically imposing man. Not tall. But solid. A body honed in combat and kept in shape even after its owner had swapped a rifle for a desk. But the man sitting with a tartan blanket over his knees was thin. His cheeks were sunken and his eyes, once fox-sharp, were rheumy and red-rimmed as if suffering from a persistent infection.

He looked up. Smiled in a baffled way at Gabriel and flapped a hand towards the cushion next to him.

'Are you Holly's father? Anyway, have a seat. There's a good bit coming up.'

Gabriel sat. Struggling to process Don's appearance and his

failure to recognise him. He kicked himself for not having anticipated this. Dementia. Unless … couldn't certain drugs create confusion as a side-effect? Yes! Steroids did: he'd visited a vet in hospital in Paris who'd been convinced he was on a cruise ship. Or even a basic water infection?

He settled back, resolving to ask Holly what medication Don was on when she came back with the tea.

On screen, Charlie Sheen watched from a chopper as onrushing Viet Cong shot down a fleeing GI.

'Poor old Sergeant Elias,' Don said as the dying sergeant held his arms aloft as if in supplication to a God who'd forsaken him, before collapsing face-first into the mud.

Gabriel turned around and touched Don lightly on the forearm.

'Boss, it's me. Gabriel. Do you recognise me?'

Don shook his head, never taking his eyes off the screen.

'Poor old Elias,' he grunted. 'Hmm. Mm-hmmm. Never stood a chance. Force of numbers.'

Gabriel tried again. 'It's me, Boss. You remember me, don't you? Old Sport.'

Holly appeared bearing a Chinese lacquer tray with tea things. She set it down on a low table, out of the way of the TV. She shot Gabriel a sympathetic glance.

'His memory comes and goes. Keep trying.'

She sat and started pouring.

Don reached over the arm of the sofa and grabbed a remote. The picture froze, catching the hapless Sergeant Elias face-down in the mud. He twisted slowly around until he was facing Gabriel. The bewildered look in his eyes was heartbreaking. It said, '*I know I should recognise you, but I just don't*'.

'Boss?' Gabriel said, under Holly's encouraging gaze. 'It's me. Gabriel Wolfe. You used to call me Old Sport.'

He reached over and took Don's left hand in his and squeezed it.

It was as if someone had thrown a switch. Or maybe flicked off the safety on a pistol.

Don's eyes snapped into focus. He smiled. But this time it was in recognition not baffled welcome.

'Good grief! It's you, Old Sport. I thought you were living in Honduras.'

With a smile of relief splitting his face, and the anxiety receding from the place behind his heart, Gabriel nodded.

'I was, Boss. But I had to leave. I'm living in Paris now, with my sister.'

'Tara! That girl has spirit, Old Sport. More than her brother, I sometimes think. How is she?'

'She's fine.'

'Still in the triad game is she?' Don asked, in what he presumably thought was a conspiratorial whisper.

Holly's eyes widened fractionally, but she merely handed mugs to Don and then Gabriel, although as she passed Gabriel's tea to him she cocked her head on one side as if to say, '*Did I just hear him right?*'

Gabriel took the mug from her.

'Thanks,' he said, with a smile.

'Tara's between jobs at the moment. She had to sell her company.'

Don nodded. Blew across his tea and took a cautious sip.

'Good grief, Ivy, this tea's hot. What did you do, make it with boiling water?'

Holly smiled. Clearly this was an old joke. Gabriel thought he might even have heard Don make it to his secretary when he ran the Department out of an army base.

'Stop moaning, old man. What do you want me to do? Make it with cold? I can if you want?'

Don grunted and winked at Gabriel.

'It's fine. Just warn me next time.'

'Boss, I need your help,' Gabriel said. He glanced at Holly. 'Could we talk in private?'

Holly got up to leave but Don pointed imperiously at the chair she was sitting in.

'Permission denied, private.' He turned towards Gabriel.

'Anything you want to say to me, you can say in front of Ivy. Speak freely, Trooper Wolfe. I expect this is about a new mission, isn't it?'

Gabriel looked at the young carer. Could he really say anything in front of her? He supposed he could. After all, his days of running official ops covered by the Official Secrets Act were long gone. He'd never speak of them, but this was strictly a personal matter.

'It's all right,' she said. 'He spins me these crazy stories all the time. How he used to be in charge of some sort of black ops spy team. But I looked him up online. He was a colonel in the army. Actually spent his days in Whitehall behind a desk for the last ten years of his career.'

Gabriel spoke as much to Holly as Don. Explained about Odette. His search for her. And then the killer question.

'I need to get inside the Hexagon. I need a legend.'

Holly nodded approvingly. 'He loves playing along with stories. Keep going,' she whispered.

'Legend, eh?'

'I need to speak to a man called Tom Gallou. He's an HR director in the French Defence Ministry.' He handed Holly a slip of paper on which he'd written down everything Tara had found out about Gallou.

'What do you think, Boss?'

Don closed his eyes and nodded, murmuring, 'Hm, mm-hmm' to himself. Was he falling asleep?

His eyes snapped open.

'Meet me at my club in town tomorrow. Taylor's on Jermyn Street. Noon. I'll introduce you to someone who can help you.' He pressed play on the remote and faced the screen again. 'You'll stay for lunch?'

43

LONDON

The next day, Gabriel entered the vestibule of Taylor's at 11.45 a.m.

A bowler-hatted porter sat behind an antique desk, surfaced in gold-tooled green leather, scuffed from what looked like centuries of elbows. Gabriel introduced himself, figuring he'd have a few minutes to get settled before Don arrived. Holly had texted him that morning to explain she'd drop Don off at the club and collect him after their lunch. She'd occupy herself in the large branch of the Waterstone's bookshop on Piccadilly until Don was ready.

'Colonel Webster's already here, sir. If you'd like to follow me?'

Shaking his head at the notion he'd have been able to out-anticipate his old CO, Gabriel trailed the porter, who he now saw also wore a tailcoat, into the dining room.

The porter led him over to a quiet corner, where Don sat talking to a woman with a striking mop of silver hair. They were laughing loudly, and appeared to be halfway down a bottle of red wine.

After a discreet introduction, which, thankfully, seemed not to be needed, the tailcoated porter left them alone.

Don waved Gabriel to take the third chair and poured him a glass of wine.

'Gabriel, meet Louisa Harris. She's at Six. Helped me set up the Department back in the day.'

Gabriel took her outstretched hand, long, bony fingers, a slender wrist jingling with silver. Her grip was hard and as they shook she fixed him with a hawkish gaze. He felt his soul being weighed in the balance. And, apparently, found satisfactory.

'Don tells me you're something of a knight errant these days. Do you want to fill me in?'

She signalled a waiter, who brought over three menus bound in bottle-green leather, gold silk tassels swinging from the spines.

Gabriel repeated his story about Odette, and his remaining lead, the French civil servant who might be helping the Soltanis recruit former French Foreign Legionnaires as muscle.

When he finished, she nodded, then looked over his shoulder and raised her eyebrows. A waiter appeared a few seconds later.

'Lamb chops, pink, please. And I'd like chips instead of mashed potatoes. Don?'

'Hmm, dear?'

Gabriel looked at his old boss. Anxiety flickered in his gut. Don had a perplexed look on his face. He looked up at the waiter, then at Louisa and finally at Gabriel.

'What would you like to eat, Don?' Louisa asked.

'Oh, right, of course, of course. This is ... I mean, which meal are we? Lunch?'

'That's right. I'm having the lamb chops. With chips.'

Don paused for a ten-count as he scrutinised the menu. Gabriel's gut was squirming. He desperately wanted to intervene but on catching Louisa's eye, and the warning look in it, he held his tongue.

'That's sounds good. Me too, please,' Don said to the waiter.

'I'll have the same,' Gabriel said, wanting to support Don somehow and figuring that choosing the same food might reassure the old man.

Once the waiter had departed, Louisa laid her left hand over Don's right.

'A legend,' she said to Gabriel.

'Something that will get me in to see Gallou. I was thinking maybe a press pass, a fake magazine maybe. Something in the defence line. I can ask for an interview.'

She arched one silver eyebrow.

'He doesn't want much does he?' she asked Don.

'Who doesn't, dear?' Don responded.

Gabriel's heart clenched. Did Don think he was having lunch with his late wife? But Louisa appeared to be quite familiar with Don's memory lapses, or gaps, or whatever doctors would call this ... *thing* that had infiltrated Don's formerly razor-sharp mind.

'This rather adventurous young man having lunch with us.'

Don turned to regard Gabriel. Smiled. Extended a hand, the papery skin on its back laced with wriggling blue veins and painted with liver-spot camouflage.

'Don Webster. How do you do?'

Powerless, Gabriel took his old CO's hand and shook.

'Gabriel Wolfe. How do you do?'

'Hmm, mm-hmm. Wolfe, eh? I've a young lad of that name in my regiment. Stroppy little bugger, but brave as a lion. You have any brothers?'

Gabriel flashed on his last memory of Michael, his younger brother. Drowned, aged five. He swallowed, hard. Pasted a smile he wasn't feeling onto his face.

'Yes, sir. Michael.'

'Ah. There you go, then.'

When their food arrived, Gabriel discovered that dementia hadn't affected Don's appetite. The old man beamed as the waiter set down a plate of perfectly cooked lamb chops in front of him.

'I don't think we'll need to bother with a fake magazine,' Louisa said to Gabriel, cutting off a cube of pink meat and popping it between her lips. She chewed and swallowed. 'That really is rather good. We created our own journal some years back. Still running and rather well regarded in certain circles. *Papers in Asymmetric Military Strategy*. It was easier in the long run than constantly creating websites and all that tedious LinkedIn business. I still have some sway there and given your service for your country, I think we can extend certain temporary privileges to you. We'll set you up with National Union of Journalists credentials and a lightly massaged cv. And perhaps, anything you do learn about our French friends' military capabilities you might be kind enough to share with me in a debrief?'

Gabriel nodded, pleased at how cheaply he'd been able to procure what he needed.

'Of course.'

'How about a cover name?'

'I thought, Terry Fox.'

She pursed her lips.

'"Terry." Not trying to sound like a dinosaur, but that's a little too,' she tilted her hair to one side, setting her sleek bobbed hair swinging, '*new school* for PAMS. We've cultivated a certain image over the years. Terrence, though. We could work with that.'

Gabriel smiled. 'I'll have to practice introducing myself in the mirror, but I can live with Terrence.'

'Excellent,' she said with a grin in which a piratical gold tooth glinted.

* * *

Outside the club, once Holly had arrived and helped Don into a taxi, Gabriel turned to Louisa.

'Why are you helping me?'

'If Don asks, it's good enough. He and I go way back. Like he said, the Department was our baby.'

Gabriel looked down Jermyn Street, where the roof of Don and Holly's taxi was still visible.

'Is he all right?'

'Well, that bloody Alzheimer's isn't going to get any better, but he's in excellent hands. And it's early stages.'

'But what happens if it gets worse? He's got no family to watch out for him.'

She arched an eyebrow.

'No family? Gabriel, he has *us*. Not just you and me. We look after our own. There are places. Secure places where spooks with that dreadful disease can live out their days without worrying about breaching the Official Secrets Act. If and when the time comes, Don will be looked after.'

Doubt, and something darker, bloomed in Gabriel's imagination. '*Looked after.*' In the world they'd operated in, that seemingly compassionate phrase had an altogether more terminal meaning.

Louisa must have caught the thought's visible presence on his features. She laughed.

'Don't worry. I'm talking about mah-jong and bridge, well-tended grounds and hydrotherapy.'

He grinned, guiltily.

'Sorry. Old habits.'

'I can see that. So tell me, are you really going to spend the rest of your days wandering the earth righting wrongs on your own account?'

'Is that so bad?'

She shrugged.

'No. But you could do a lot more good if you were working within a more *strategic* framework.'

He smiled.

'You're not trying to recruit me, are you, Louisa? Last I heard, the Department was dead and buried.'

'Oh, it is. Embalmed, closed-casket, and locked in a lead-lined crypt.'

'Then, what?'

'You're interested?'

'No. Absolutely not.'

'In that case, nothing.'

Louisa raised a hand and a black cab swooped to a stop at the kerb. She gave the driver an address and stepped inside. Buzzed the window down.

She handed Gabriel a business card. Plain white. Her name and a landline. Nothing else.

'If you tire of playing Sir Galahad, give me a tinkle.'

Left alone in the street, Gabriel headed back towards Lower Regent Street. As he walked, he felt sadness descend over him like a veil. No great detective work needed to know why. Seeing his old CO like that, it was a shock. But as he covered the ground between Jermyn Street and the cobbled alley housing his hotel, he dug down to the truth. After his father, and Zhao Xi, Don was the third man to whom he'd looked for guidance. In some ways, it had been Don Webster who'd been the constant presence in his life. From eighteen until Gabriel's early forties, Don had been for Gabriel a true replacement for his father.

And now he was taking the first faltering steps out of Gabriel's life.

He reached his hotel a little after 4.00 p.m. And started making phone calls.

Early the next morning, he caught a flight back to Paris.

44

PARIS

For his interview with Tom Gallou, Gabriel donned the suit he'd bought a few days earlier. He paired it with a 1 Para regimental tie in burgundy silk with the winged parachute insignia embroidered in silver.

After a shave at a barber's on Rue Lincoln, Major Terrence Fox looked every inch the former soldier turned specialist journalist. He strode into the reception area of the *Ministère des Armées* projecting an aura of confidence bordering on arrogance, ignoring the uniformed and heavily armed guards.

The interview had been ridiculously easy to broker. It turned out French civil servants, even those in a glamorous office such as Gallou's, led such apparently dull lives that the promise of an interview with a respected British military journal was akin to Christmas, birthday and Bastille Day rolled into one.

'Good morning. Major Terrence Fox from *Papers in Asymmetric Military Strategy* to see Tom Gallou. He's expecting me,' Gabriel said to the receptionist, speaking a very proper form of Parisian French into which he let a trace of upper-class British bleed.

The young woman was immaculate in a grey jacket and sky-blue blouse, her hair swept up in a chignon, her hazel eyes masked by large glasses that gave her an air of an inquisitorial owl. She smiled, dispelling the image.

'One moment, please,' she replied in unaccented English. A typical Parisian ploy designed to keep foreigners in their place. It didn't matter how hard you tried. If you let on you were British, that's what you'd get in return. As if to say, '*It's lovely that you're trying, but it will be easier for both of us if I speak to you in your language rather than you continue mangling mine.*'

She consulted her screen, tapped a couple of keys and nodded. Instructed Gabriel to look into a webcam clipped to the top of her screen and printed him a visitor pass a few seconds later. She slid it into a plastic badge holder clipped to a red, white and blue lanyard and handed it over.

'Please take a seat. Tom will be down directly.'

'Directly' in French defence ministry time revealed itself to mean twenty minutes. A man with too much on his plate? A childish power play? Gabriel was turning over these possibilities when a man of fifty or fifty-five walked over. Six-five, at least eighteen stone, most of it muscle by the look of it. Grey hair brushing his collar, a silver polo neck jumper beneath a pale grey suit jacket. A direct, appraising stare. Even without Jacko's briefing, Gabriel would have had him pegged as a former soldier.

'Major Fox?'

Gabriel stood, offered his hand.

Gallou's grip was a bonecrusher. Gabriel squeezed back, to avoid having his knuckles ground inside the other man's meaty fist. And decided. Gallou was late by design. A small display of dominance. Fine. Gabriel wasn't here to win pissing contests.

'Thanks for seeing me at such short notice.'

Gallou shrugged and indicated Gabriel should follow him to a bank of lifts.

'Your article sounded very interesting. I may be a lowly pen-pusher now but I can still, just, remember when my life was about more, how shall we say it, *urgent* matters than compiling recruitment statistics for a minister who never got closer to combat than playing paintball in the Ardennes forest.'

Gabriel smiled.

'We have those kind of politicians in England, too. Very happy to pose in a tank turret, or holding a rifle, but the sharpest thing they've ever wielded is a paper knife.'

Gallou laughed, a guttural cough in which Gabriel detected a rampant high-tar habit.

They passed the lift journey in silence, surrounded by a group of young people Gabriel assumed had to be visiting students, or maybe interns. None looked out of their teens. Or were they regular civil servants in their twenties, and he was out of touch? He flashed on his first encounter with Holly, Don's carer, and the Old Man himself, here one minute, adrift the next.

The lift doors opened at the seventh floor and Gallou politely excused himself through the knot of whatever-they-were and led Gabriel to an office overlooking the traffic-choked *Boulevard de Général Martial Valin*.

'Coffee?'

'Please.'

Coffee ordered via an intercom, Gallou sat behind the desk and folded his hands on the blotter.

Gabriel lifted his chin towards the picture window.

'Beautiful location. Is it easy to get out here by public transport?'

'Not bad, but I drive. I have my own space and the Metro can be brutal in summer.'

'What do you drive? Anything interesting?'

Gallou smiled. 'You are a'—he slipped into English for a single word—'petrolhead?'

Gabriel grinned. 'I used to have a Jaguar F-Type. Totalled it, unfortunately.'

'I drive a black DS. You know it?'

'Of course! Best design Citroën ever came up with, in my opinion.'

'You know the play on words? When you say the initials aloud you get "Goddess".'

Gabriel nodded. '"F-Type" is rather more prosaic, I'm afraid.'

Gallou nodded towards Gabriel's tie.

'Paras?'

The conversation was moving towards the reason for Gabriel's visit. Good. The warm-up phase was over.

'Ten years. You?'

'Foreign Legion. Fifteen.'

'Tough gig.'

'It had its moments. I don't suppose you spent much time sitting on your arse playing "Call of Duty".'

Gabriel inclined his head.

'They kept us busy.'

A young man arrived with coffees, set one down in front of each man. His leaving seemed to signal they should get down to business. Gallou took a sip of his coffee, and nodded appreciatively.

'You said you wanted to talk about how the French military is responding to the changing nature of warfare, Terrence?'

'From a recruitment perspective, yes. I've spoken to your counterparts in Britain—'

'—obviously.'

Gabriel pretended a flash of irritation at being interrupted. If Gallou liked playing power games, he'd feel he'd scored a point.

'Indeed. And in Germany and Sweden so far.' He brought out his phone. 'Do you mind if I record our conversation?'

Gallou smiled. 'Actually I do.'

Gabriel imagined he was suffering from indigestion, let his mouth twist slightly.

'Old school it is then,' he said, retrieving a notebook and pencil from his briefcase.

'So tell me, Tom, where do you see the biggest threats to conventional thinking on war fighting?'

Gallou shrugged again and spread his hands wide.

'Radicalisation? Rogue states? Drones? Cyberwarfare? Take your pick.'

Gabriel made a note.

'And how is the Ministry responding to those challenges in terms of recruitment? I know you have special responsibility for the Legion.'

A guarded look came into Gallou's eyes.

'In the old days you wanted the same thing everybody did. Probably the same things Napoleon wanted. Or De Gaulle. Strength of character. Determination. Physical strength. Fitness, resilience. Calmness under pressure. The warrior spirit. And of course a willingness to fight, and to die, for your country.'

Gabriel nodded.

'"For blood shed".'

Gallou nodded.

'Exactly. A man who is prepared to bleed for France can expect to be loved by France.'

He sounded regretful. Gabriel could imagine him in uniform. A tough and unyielding commander. A harsh judge of those who fell short, but a fierce defender of those who passed his tests.

'And now?' Gabriel asked.

Gallou sighed heavily.

'Say you are engaging an enemy with drones. You need a man who can get up in the morning, kiss his wife, tousle his son's hair, then leave for work at a base in the countryside. Climb inside a container and control a Predator five thousand kilometres away. You select your targets, eliminate them. At the end of the day you clock out and go home to your family. Nod to your neighbour watering his lawn as you walk up to your front door.' Gallou raised a hand, pasted a cheesy grin onto his craggy features. 'He spent the day in meetings or selling software to bankers. You ended ten men's lives. Now, don't get me wrong, those ten men deserved to die. But you're basically a commuter. No camaraderie. No chance to decompress with your mates. Let off a little steam. That calls for a different set of skills.'

'I've spoken to people with PTSD,' Gabriel said. 'The closest they got to a battlefield was a widescreen monitor and a joystick. Could have been playing a videogame. Are you seeing that here?'

Gallou waggled his big right hand above the desk.

'Some. It's the big challenge right now. Selecting for a different kind of mental resilience. Back in the day, you lived like a warrior for six months or a year or whatever, then you got it out of your system in one go. Now, our guys have to do it at the end of every shift.'

Gabriel needed to move the conversation round to the Legion and what happened to the men who'd served after they were discharged.

'With that in mind, does the Legion offer any kind of aftercare for its former members?' Gabriel asked. 'Help them with counselling? Or to find employment?'

Gallou's eyes took on a hooded look. His lips tightened.

'Why are you asking about the Legion?'

Gabriel threw out a Gallic shrug.

'A friend served. Former Royal Marine Commando. I've always been interested.'

'We look after our own,' Gallou said shortly.

'Of course. As does the British Government. Though many veterans with PTSD might disagree.'

Gallou checked his watch. A military-style piece on an olive-drab webbing strap.

'I'm short of time, Terrence. Maybe we could stick to the matter at hand? Veterans' affairs fall outside my remit.'

But did they? Gabriel wondered. At this point he only had Jacko's recollections of Gallou to go on. But his deliberate prodding on a potential flashpoint had resulted in a pretty obvious tell from Gallou. The man clearly didn't want to talk about anything to do with the Foreign Legion.

'Of course.'

Gabriel asked a few more questions that had arrived in an email from Louisa while his plane was in the air on the way home from London. But after another ten minutes, Gallou stood abruptly and ended the interview.

'I have a meeting to go to. Excuse me.'

No handshake this time, and Gabriel took back the hand he'd offered.

Gallou escorted him down to the ground floor and there took his leave.

Gabriel handed his lanyard back to the receptionist and left the building.

But not for good.

45

After leaving Gallou, Gabriel returned to the apartment and changed into a set of drab, dark grey clothes, including a T-shirt and hoodie. He drove back out to the Defence Ministry and parked in a side street where he had an unobscured view of the carpark exit.

At 6.47 p.m., the red-and-white barrier pole lifted for the seventy-fifth time and a sleek, black car emerged from between the two steel pillars and took a right onto the street.

It was possible that two people employed by the Ministry drove a black Citroën DS, but Gabriel had already raised a pair of pocket binoculars to his eyes. No doubt about the identity of the driver. It was Gallou.

Gabriel had a moment or two in which to admire the swooping lines of the classic French car before he released the handbrake, engaged first gear and pulled out into the traffic four cars behind Gallou.

Gallou headed away from the city. Under the Périph and onto a main road heading southwest. Into the suburbs. Though as the scenery changed from urban to rural, Gabriel began to understand how the word 'banlieue' could have twin meanings.

This suburb, Fontenay-aux-Roses, was nothing like the rundown, graffiti-scarred estate where Marianne and Youssoo Diallo lived. Here were plenty of new or nearly-new BMWs, Mercedes and Audis. SUVs parked on private drives. Even the odd British marque – Land Rovers and Jaguars.

The car in front of Gabriel turned left, the one ahead of that turned right and suddenly he was cruising up to the rear bumper of Gallou's DS. He dropped back, but this only earned him an impatient blast from the horn of the car behind him. No option but to keep pace with Gallou and hope he didn't have acute enough eyesight to recognise Gabriel through two sets of auto glass.

Gabriel flipped down the sun visor and retrieved a cheap pair of sunglasses he kept under the fraying strip of elastic. Slid them on and reached for a baseball cap from the passenger seat. That should do it, especially since the last time Gallou had seen 'Terrence Fox' he'd had been wearing a sharp suit, shirt and tie.

The lights ahead were green, but as Gallou approached, they turned red. Gallou surged forwards, crossing the junction and leaving Gabriel stranded. He swore as a series of trucks, delivery vans and commuters streamed across in front of him.

'Come on, come on!' he muttered, before the lights finally turned green again.

The car behind him, which had hooted when he'd tried to slow down, did it again.

'All right!' Gabriel shouted, before accelerating across the junction fast enough to have the front tyres scrabbling for grip and sending the car into an unpleasant shimmy.

Gabriel craned his neck, straining to catch a glimpse of the black DS. Christ, it wasn't as if it didn't stand out among the cookie-cutter modern vehicles now suddenly clogging the road and preventing Gabriel from relocating Gallou.

In the end, after half a kilometre, and the looming disappointment of a wasted evening, he almost overshot his target. Gallou appeared in the doorway of a tobacconist's, lighting a cigarette and strolling back to the DS, which was parked in a slip road. Gabriel had no choice but to drive past and then pull in sharply to the side of the road. More tooting. A raised fist. A gaping mouth from which he could lipread French obscenities.

The DS pulled out and swept past him. He let two cars go past then floored the throttle and hurtled out in front of a Mercedes S-Class. This driver repeatedly hammered the horn and flashed his brights for good measure. Gabriel's knuckles were white on the steering wheel as he fought an overwhelming impulse to jam on the brakes and force a confrontation. It turned out it wasn't his to force.

With a muffled bellow from its high-performance, but thoroughly soundproofed engine, the S-Class overtook, swerving right across into the opposite lane, then came to a sudden stop in front of Gabriel. He swore, hit the brakes and came to rest a centimetre from the Merc's gleaming rear end, on which chrome letters declared it an S63, the hyper-tuned AMG performance version of what was normally a luxury saloon.

Gallou was getting away. But thankfully, the traffic on this stretch of the road had thinned and he was still visible. Not indicating, either. Maybe Gabriel could deal with Monsieur Road-Rage and still catch his quarry.

Gabriel had the forty-something man in an elegantly cut suit, snowy-white shirt and woven silk tie pegged from the moment he stepped out of the driver's door and placed one expensive-looking burgundy loafer onto the tarmac.

Banker.

Eyes blazing, he stormed over to Gabriel's window and, with a rolling motion of his index finger, demanded that Gabriel drop the glass.

A mistake.

Gabriel chose, instead, to leave the car. They were a similar height, but the banker was soft round the middle. Clearly used to getting his own way, though.

'What the fuck do you think you're playing at? That's a two-hundred-thousand-euro AMG S63 E Performance. You nearly wrote it off in this shit-heap.'

Normally, Gabriel would have negotiated. He shook his head. Normally? Make that before his life went to shit. When he had the mental resources to deal with entitled arseholes like the one currently making his second mistake by jabbing a pudgy finger in Gabriel's face.

Instead, Gabriel simply took hold of the banker's finger and applied pressure each side of the first knuckle, crushing the nerves there and bringing forth a squeal of agony from the banker's red, wet-looking lips.

He leaned closer.

'Get back in your car and drive on or I will tear your finger out by the root,' he said, while nodding and appearing, to all intents and purposes, to be meekly accepting a dressing-down from this master of the universe. 'Understand?'

'Yes, yes! Jesus, let go will you! It hurts!'

Gabriel released him, noting the faces of a couple of children pasted to the window of a passing SUV. He smiled at the boy. The boy waved.

The banker made his third mistake.

He launched himself at Gabriel, swinging a fist.

'You fuck! I do muay thai at the weekend. I'll fucking—'

His eyes rolled up in their sockets as Gabriel shifted his grip to a pressure point on the left side of his neck called the cervical plexus, and squeezed. His knees buckled, but Gabriel already had him in his grip.

Gabriel guided the temporarily paralysed banker back to his seat and lowered him into its fatly padded embrace. He closed the door, noting how some clever internal mechanism drew the door fully shut over the last few millimetres of travel.

Gabriel pulled around the becalmed S-Class and rejoined the stream of traffic. Behind him, the sounds of multiple horns beeping told him the impatient commuters of this leafy suburb had found a new target for their ire.

But where was Gallou?

He accelerated and shot down Boulevard General De Gaulle, straining to catch a glimpse of Gallou's big black shark of a car.

Nothing. Should he stay on the main drag or take a side-road and hope to pick Gallou up in the maze of residential streets?

'Shit!' he shouted, slamming the heel of his right hand down on the steering wheel.

He stayed on the Boulevard, right through town and out the other side into the countryside. The traffic thinned then disappeared and Gabriel took the little hatchback up to sixty. The road must have been built by the Romans: it was arrow-straight and without any intervening hills, he could see for at least a kilometre ahead. No sign of Gallou.

Decision-time. Gallou had to be back in Fontenay-aux-Roses. Gabriel executed a tyre-shredding U-turn and accelerated hard back towards the town.

He realised what he was going to have to do. Take each road in turn and pray that Gallou didn't keep his car in a garage. If he couldn't spot it on the street then the whole surveillance was a bust.

Quartering the southern quadrant of the town in this fashion took Gabriel two hours. He was about to give up and return to Paris when he caught a glimpse of gleaming black paintwork and chrome down a cobbled street. He reversed and took another look. It was the DS. Parked right there on the road.

He climbed out and walked down the narrow street. Keeping to the shadows, he observed the house outside which the big black classic was parked. The living room lights were on and then Gallou walked across the picture window as if on a movie screen, left to right, a cigarette in one hand, a tumbler of something golden in the other.

He paused at the window and looked straight at Gabriel. Had he spotted him? Gabriel maintained a statue-like immobility, frozen in place, not even blinking. Gallou leaned to his right, transferred the cigarette to his lips and began working a cord to lower a blind in front of the window. False alarm.

Breathing more easily, Gabriel walked across the street and circled around the back of Gallou's place, leaving the street for a lane that doglegged into an alley leading around a couple of corners to the small back yard of the house.

He opened the low wooden gate and, keeping to the lee of a fence dividing the property from its neighbour, approached the back door. Gabriel looked down. The paving slabs outside the door were littered with cigarette butts. He squatted down and took a closer look. One was still emitting faint curls of smoke. He straightened. On a glass-topped table an empty beer bottle sat beside its cap. Gallou's evening routine sketched out in two artefacts. Get home, come out into the back yard. Have a beer and the first cigarette of the evening.

Gabriel pulled a set of lock picks from an inside pocket. Then, reflexively, he tried the handle. And smiled with quiet satisfaction. Maybe Gallou had once been part of France's elite military forces. But time behind a desk on the seventh floor of the Hexagone had dulled his edge. The door was unlocked.

When it came to edged weapons, Gabriel had used them all, from sugar cane-knives to Cossack swords to tactical tomahawks. But for a job like this, he'd opted for something discreet. A simple flick-knife with a brass-riveted wooden handle. Well-worn, but with a razor edge, a snip at fifteen euros from a shabby little tool shop in the Eighteenth. He opened it, muffling the mechanism's *snick* with his palm.

He left the kitchen, walking on the balls of his feet, heart tripping along at a steady eighty-five.

And ran straight into Gallou, who was swinging a baseball bat at his head.

46

Gabriel ducked, felt the bat whistle over the crown of his head close enough to lift the hair from his scalp.

The fat end of the bat smashed into the door frame with a metallic clonk. '*Aluminium,*' his brain supplied helpfully. He drove a fist into Gallou's solar plexus, but the big man was already moving back, out of reach and Gabriel's knuckles only grazed the front of his shirt.

Gallou came at him a second time with the bat, this time jabbing the business end into Gabriel's face, forcing him to dance away or get his nose broken and, presumably shortly after that, his skull.

Feigning a trip, Gabriel staggered sideways.

With a bear-like bellow of triumph, Gallou raised the bat over his head and brought it swinging down. It scythed past Gabriel's left ear, but before he could congratulate himself for dodging the incoming hammer-blow, the bat slammed into his left forearm. The pain made him cry out, and the whole limb went numb, from fingertips to shoulder.

Gallou roared, stepped forwards and planted a fist in Gabriel's face. Blood spurted from his nose and he choked out a gout of the stuff as his throat filled.

The pain filled his eyes with tears, though the absence of a crack gave him hope his nose wasn't broken. He shot out his right foot and caught Gallou in the groin, eliciting a high-pitched cry. Gallou dropped the bat as he clutched his balls.

Gabriel shook his head, sending a spray of scarlet over the white-painted wall. He ducked another haymaker and slashed Gallou across the arm. The cotton of his shirt parted like a long wound, and the blade scored a line from elbow to wrist. Gallou's blood joined Gabriel's as a dozen tiny blood vessels let go.

Ordinarily, a knife against an unarmed man would be no contest. But Gabriel couldn't afford to kill Gallou. Not until he'd given up whatever he knew about the Soltanis.

Gallou stepped back, then turned and fled from the sitting room. Gabriel gave chase, only to run into a hail of metallic objects spearing across the neighbouring room, which was dominated by a highly polished dining table. Gold and silver flashed through the air. They were football trophies. Each miniature player caught in mid-kick, his leg arrowing in towards the ball, his arms out for balance. Plenty of sharp points to remove an eye or puncture an artery.

His arm windmilling, Gallou snatched up one trophy after another and hurled it across the table at Gabriel, who had to duck and weave like an amped-up boxer or risk taking one of the whirling metal missiles to the face.

Plates followed, once Gallou ran out of ammunition, smashing against the wall as Gabriel slid and ducked to avoid them, sharp fragments of pottery spinning through the air from the impacts.

He dived to the ground and scrambled, commando-style under the table towards Gallou's position. Gallou had no time to move before Gabriel raised his right fist and slammed it down onto Gallou's left foot, punching the blade through his shoe, his foot and into the floorboards beneath the carpet.

The scream set glasses on the dresser ringing. Blood rose from the surface of the shoe and pooled around the blade before overrunning the depression in the leather and pooling on the carpet.

Hammer blows from Gallou's fist rained down onto the tabletop above Gabriel's head. When those same hands appeared below the table, reaching down towards the knife's hilt, Gabriel grabbed them and yanked, down with all the force he could muster. Gallou's head met the thick wooden table with a loud clunk. A groan followed, and then he slumped sideways. He fell awkwardly, trapped between the table and a fireplace. His right foot, still pinned to the floor, twisted, releasing yet more blood. Gabriel yanked the knife out, closed and pocketed it.

Gabriel scrambled out from beneath the table. Gallou was out cold, a bruise already darkening his forehead. Gabriel swiped his sleeve across his nose, smearing a slimy mixture of blood and snot over his face. His left arm felt like someone had driven a truck over it but at least it was functioning.

He dragged Gallou out from the table, gritting his teeth with the effort. His left foot was bleeding profusely. No danger of death from loss of blood, but it would need treating. First things first.

He used the flick knife to cut the cord from the blinds shading the window and bound Gallou to a chair. So far, so amateur. Any special forces soldier worth his salt could escape that sort of rig given enough time. A second length went around his neck in a running noose and behind his back to his wrists, on down to his ankles. Now, any attempt to bring his arms or legs into play would result in self-strangulation.

Gallou regained consciousness ten minutes later. Gabriel was waiting, his nostrils stuffed with toilet paper. He'd also removed Gallou's left shoe and dressed the wound in his foot.

The big man stared at Gabriel with a mixture of hatred and contempt. He said nothing. No pleading to be released. No threats, which a surprisingly large number of people did on discovering they'd been bested in hand-to-hand combat and restrained. He just stared. Waiting.

'Where are the Soltanis?' Gabriel asked.

'Who?'

'The men you work for.'

'I work for the Chief Under-Secretary at the Ministry of the Armies. His name's Villeneuve.'

So Gallou wasn't going to make things easy. For Gabriel or for himself. Gabriel started again.

'You used to be a recruiting officer for the Foreign Legion. Correct?'

'If you say so.'

'And now I believe you work as a liaison between a pair of brothers who run an organised crime group and men leaving the Foreign Legion. The men are Syrians. Their names are Ali and Bashar Soltani. You provide them with muscle, don't you?'

Gallou did a decent job of hiding his surprise. But he had also only recently emerged from a spell of unconsciousness caused by a close encounter with a piece of solid, rustic-style French dining room furniture, and he would have to be in a certain amount of pain.

His eyes widened then narrowed as he fought not to let his emotions betray him. It was the confirmation Gabriel needed. Gallou could have denied it, stuck to his 'I'm just a lowly civil servant' line, and what would Gabriel have, really? The guess of a heroin-addicted veteran based on a single interview conducted years earlier. But by his facial expression and inability to figure out a response, Gallou had condemned himself.

When he finally replied, it was so pitiful Gabriel almost felt like coaching him.

'Fuck you.'

'Somehow you don't sound like an innocent civil servant anymore, Tom,' Gabriel said instead.

'You're a dead man. Ali told me someone was poking his nose into things that didn't concern him. You're fucked already, "Terrence Fox".'

Gallou spat blood at Gabriel, splotching the front of his T-shirt. He ignored it. Leaned closer to Gallou. No need to worry about biting, the cord digging into Gallou's neck would prevent even that most animalistic of counter-attacks.

'They kidnapped a child, Tom. A little girl. She's twelve years old. Her name is Odette Diallo. She's a French citizen and they're auctioning her off to some pervert. Nice line of business for a former soldier to be mixed up in. What's the Legion's motto again? Honour and Fidelity. That's it, isn't it? Nothing very honourable about selling a child is there?'

Gallou curled his lip.

'They're not real Frenchmen. Fucking immigrants. Swamping us. They breed like fucking rabbits, too.'

Gabriel slapped him across the face, hard. Gallou's head swung sideways and he winced as the thin blind-cord dug deeper into the soft flesh of his throat.

'I want to know where they've taken her, Tom,' Gabriel said, placing his hands on Gallou's shoulders and pushing down. 'I know about their house outside Paris. I followed them to their place in Bonifacio. It's a smoking ruin now. So they must have somewhere else. Where is it?'

Gallou looked up into Gabriel's face and grinned, revealing bloody teeth.

'You can torture me and you still won't know. The training I've had? Have at it. Knock yourself out.'

'Can I kill you then, Tom? If you're not going to talk to me? I mean, I can hardly let you go now, can I? Not after,' he swung an arm around to encompass the debris littering the dining room, 'all this.'

'You haven't got the balls.'

Gabriel drew back. Nodded.

'Hmm. That places us at something of a crossroads, then, doesn't it?'

Gabriel left Gallou tied to the chair and went upstairs. He found the master bedroom, a masculine space: everything squared away, grey and dark-green bed linen, militaria displayed on a chest of drawers. Photos of Gallou with his former comrades in camouflage, posing in front of a blown-up tank, grinning, their arms slung round each other's shoulders.

He opened the wardrobe and slid out a shallow drawer

divided into compartments. Ties in a range of blues, deep red and golds. Pushed it back in on its silent runners. Tried the one beneath it. Better. Belts. Leather mostly, some woven from elasticated cotton. He selected a buckled black number in soft, supple leather.

Downstairs again, he laid it across Gallou's lap.

'You're already choking me,' Gallou said. 'Don't you think that's a bit redundant?'

'It's not for your neck, Tom.'

Gabriel opened the flick knife and cut away Gallou's right shirt-sleeve. He pointed with the top to a spot on the inside of the forearm.

'The ulnar artery. And under here,' he relocated the point by a few centimetres, 'the radial artery. They're not the big gushers like the carotid and the femoral. The ones you and I were taught to target. But they'll get the job done. I want to give you one last chance. Tell me where the Soltanis have taken Odette and I'll leave you here, alive.'

Gallou's eyes were glued to the skin of his upper arm, where Gabriel was maintaining pressure on the knifepoint.

'I don't know, OK? I don't know. Look, this is cold-blooded murder. You can't. We both served our countries. That means something.'

'You're right, Tom, it does,' Gabriel said. 'Or it should. Because when you were serving France you were serving Odette and her parents. But now you're serving a couple of evil men who auction off young girls as sex slaves. And you seem to think that's an honourable thing to do.'

Gallou hitched in a breath and let it out in a piglike squeal as Gabriel pushed the knife point deep into the flesh of his forearm and punctured the ulna artery. Bright scarlet blood spurted across the room, catching Gabriel across the cheek before spattering the wall behind him, dripping off the wooden spokes of a sunray clock.

Gabriel sat back as the blood continued to spurt.

'I didn't sever it completely, Tom. If you do that the

perivascular sheath contracts around the artery and seals off the blood flow. It's called vasospasm, if you're interested. I had a mate in the Gurkhas. They're trained to twist their knife in the femoral artery to stop the process.'

Gallou's eyes were staring, the whites visible all the way round the irises.

'What the fuck, man? I'm going to bleed out!'

'Yes, you are. In somewhere between two and twenty minutes at this rate.' Gabriel leaned forwards, deliberately catching another hot jet of Gallou's arterial blood in the face. He held up the belt. 'I'll apply a tourniquet, if you want?'

'Yes! Yes, for fuck's sake, tie it off!'

'Of course.'

Gabriel looped the belt around Gallou's trembling bicep and threaded the free end through the buckle. And left it dangling there.

'Pull it tight!'

'Where are they taking her?'

'What?'

Gabriel slapped him again, rocking his head sideways so hard his tongue protruded between his teeth as the blind cord choked him.

'You helped send a twelve-year-old into the hands of torturers and sex-traffickers! Where,' – another slap – 'are,' – slap – 'the Soltanis?'

Gallou's eyes were rolling in their sockets. He wasn't in any pain. Or not from the cut to his arm, anyway. Adrenaline would be doing a great job of distancing him from the signals his nerves were shooting into his spinal cord. But the shock might be a problem. Gabriel needed an answer fast.

'Stop the bleeding and I'll tell you. I swear.'

Gabriel nodded and yanked tight on the belt. Gallou howled as the leather bit deep into his bicep. Gabriel braced the taut flesh with one hand and tugged the tourniquet tighter still before settling the buckle's prong into a hole. The damaged artery spurted once more then the blood flow slowed to a trickle.

'Now, Tom.'

'Martinique!'

'*Where* in Martinique?'

'OK, OK, I'm trying to think, Jesus. Yes! Rue Victor Hugo in Le Carbet. The big yellow house at the top of the hill. It's where they take the goods. I mean the people.'

Gabriel clenched his fist. Calling people 'goods'? It wasn't the first time he'd met someone who dehumanised his victims, but it never failed to anger him.

'Thanks,' he said tightly.

'OK, cool. We're good, yes? Now untie me and for God's sake call an ambulance.'

Gabriel stood. Closed and pocketed the knife. Then he bent over and pulled hard on the tourniquet. Gallou winced, but he managed to smile and nod.

'It's tight enough, man. It'll last until I get to the emergency room. I've survived worse.'

Gabriel leaned forward and murmured into Gallou's right ear.

'Tom, you work for a pair of sex traffickers and you tried to protect them, even after I told you they'd kidnapped a child. Do you understand what you're doing? You're sending children to hell.'

Gabriel had all he needed from Gallou. Maintaining tension on the belt, he pulled the free end back from the buckle until the prong slipped out of the hole punched through the leather.

He let the belt go.

Gallou's eyes popped wide open.

'What are you doing?' he yelled as Gabriel turned away. 'You can't leave me to die! Come back you nigger-loving fuck, come back!'

A jet of blood arced past Gabriel and splashed against the wall. But much of the force had gone and its successor barely made the skirting board.

Gabriel cleaned up in the bathroom then left the way he'd come.

He needed to book some plane tickets.

47

Gabriel stabbed a finger onto the map spread out on the cafe table. Three corners were held down by beer glasses. He, Tara and Jacko leaned in towards each other.

'Rue Victor Hugo is here,' he said. 'It leads uphill here.' A second tap. 'And the Soltanis' place is somewhere up here.' A third tap, harder than the first two. 'We have to assume they're keeping Odette there.'

'Think they'll have protection?' Jacko asked.

'Of course they will,' Tara snapped.

Gabriel looked at her. Had something happened between her and Jacko? Now wasn't the time.

'What do you think, Tara?' Gabriel asked. 'How many?'

'They're feeling safe. They think they left us behind in Corsica. They'd be expecting Gallou to tip them off if you came looking, but we know that's not going to happen. I'd say minimum of two, maximum of four. Why pay for guards you don't need?'

'They're going to be tooled up, though,' Jacko said. 'We need to get some guns.'

Gabriel shook his head.

'Too noisy. And the island's so small any shooting's going to attract the local law. Probably in the Soltanis' pay as well.'

'So, what are you saying? We're taking knives to a gunfight?'

Gabriel and Tara shared a look.

'Something like that,' Gabriel said. 'But first I want to scope out the place. Make sure they have Odette and she's unharmed. We confirm their numbers and firepower, then we make a plan.'

'We should just storm the place. Get the girl and exfil,' Jacko said. 'We have the element of surprise.'

'And they have Odette, Jacko,' Tara said, the impatience clear in her voice. 'If we go in all guns blazing—'

'But we won't have guns!'

'It was an expression! If we go in hot and heavy … is that better?' Chastened, Jacko nodded. 'Then they could just kill her.' Tara checked her phone. 'Oh, no!'

Gabriel looked up from the map. 'What?'

'The auction just started. They've set it for twenty-four hours.'

Jacko was half out of his chair, but Gabriel grabbed his elbow and pulled him back down again.

'Wait. If the auction's started, we know Odette's alive. And I'm guessing they've been looking after her, given what,' he swallowed the rising bile in his throat, 'what they're going to do with her.'

'We need to go and check it out,' Jacko persisted. 'Right now.'

'Yes, we do, but not dressed like this. We need to blend in.'

Jacko swung an arm around, scowling.

'Don't know if you've noticed, boss, but everyone else round here is Black. How do you suggest we blend in?'

It was a good question.

Gabriel looked around. The men he saw were dressed in short-sleeved shirts, shorts and sandals. And, as Jacko had said, they were all Black. The women were colourfully dressed in floaty cotton dresses, skirts and tops. Flattering, pretty, but hardly the stuff of disguises.

And then he saw a brown and white road sign. It listed two places of interest.

The first was Musée Paul Gauguin. Gabriel liked art but he had no interest in it today. But the second place listed on the sign had given him an idea.

He pointed it out to Tara.

'Think you could procure some camouflage for us?'

She followed his gaze, then looked back at him and smiled.

'Meet me back at the guest house.'

48

Tara was sweating by the time she reached the front gates of *Prieuré Sainte Marie des Anges*. She'd spent the journey uphill trying out, rejecting, selecting and refining an approach she thought might just work.

As she entered the manicured grounds of the Priory, she breathed a sigh of relief. Public opinion in France had largely turned against its colonial past, but the presence of a catholic monastic order in the northern tip of Martinique was a Godsend. Literally.

A group of nuns in white habits were walking around a gravel path, edged with fragrant lavender bushes buzzing with hundreds if not thousands of bees. The nuns were laughing and gesticulating. One was even smoking, a sight that took Tara aback.

She approached them, her hands clasped in front of her, glad that she'd packed a sober skirt suit, along with her charcoal grey ninja outfit, jungle camo and jeans.

She greeted the nuns in Parisian French.

'Good morning, sisters. A beautiful day we're having, no?'

The nuns, she now saw, were of mixed ages, the youngest in her early thirties, the oldest, with the strong-smelling cigarette held between her fingers, eighty if she was a day. They looked up at her greeting. Smiles mixed with, not suspicion exactly, but a kind of wondering. Tara knew she resembled neither a local nor a tourist.

'Good morning,' one of the young nuns said. 'Can we help you?'

'I would like to speak to the Mother Superior, please.'

'The Reverend Mother is extremely busy. And she certainly has no time for frivolous requests from influencers, or vloggers, or whatever you are,' the old nun said, before blowing a stream of smoke skywards.

Tara smiled, impressed with the old lady's grasp of contemporary social media trends.

'Apologies, sister, I am none of those things, and I share your distaste for them,' Tara said, with a genuine shudder. 'Treating the world as one gigantic backdrop for their egos and their narcissism. I have come from Paris to seek her help. I hope perhaps she will make an exception and see me. For a few minutes only.'

The elderly nun raised sparse white eyebrows.

'Paris?'

'Yes.'

'Help with what?'

'To save a little girl from the worst possible degradation one can imagine, and possibly death.'

She held her breath. It was the truth, the strategy Tara had decided upon as she climbed through the jungle-fringed curves of the road that led to the priory.

The nun stared at her for a few seconds, then dropped her cigarette into the gravel and stubbed it out with the toe of her shoe.

'Come with me.'

Tara followed her out of the garden into the cool of a white-painted cloister. Arches permitted a view of the central space, laid to a lush, thick lawn peppered with small pink, blue and yellow wild flowers. In the centre grew a palm tree, at the crown of which a workman, tethered to the scaly trunk by a webbing strap around his waist, was using a machete to cut away the dead lower leaves, which fell to the ground with a loud crackle.

They entered the priory through an ancient wooden door, sun-bleached to a silver grey and bound by blackened iron straps. Inside, the temperature dropped by at least ten degrees and Tara shivered as she followed the nun down a narrow corridor.

At the far end they doglegged left and right. Slit windows gave onto another courtyard at which a nun was conducting an outdoor lesson for a group of children, resplendent in old-fashioned school uniforms. Grey and burgundy, with white shirts under their blazers.

The nun stopped before a more modern door of varnished wood. A nameplate proclaimed it the domain of *Mère Supérieure Maggy Bonnard*.

She knocked, turned to look at Tara, then back at the nameplate.

'*Entrez vous!*' a bright voice called.

The nun opened the door and led Tara inside.

'Reverend Mother, I am sorry to interrupt your work, but this lady claims she must talk to you. She says it is about a young girl who is in danger. She has come from Paris specifically to speak to you.'

It was a slight exaggeration, but Tara was grateful for the way the nun had improved upon her original story.

The Mother Superior pushed her keyboard to one side and took off the glasses she was wearing.

'For reading,' she said with a smile. She looked past Tara, to the nun. 'Thank you, Sister Amelia.'

The nun bowed and left the office, closing the door behind her with a soft click from the latch.

'Please, sit down, Miss …?' the Mother Superior said with an inquiring arch to her eyebrows.

Tara had never been religious, but in the presence of the Mother Superior she felt compelled to tell the truth. As if to lie to a woman who was married to Christ would compromise the very thing she was trying to achieve, and for which she needed her help. Something about her reminded Tara of Mummy Rita, who'd raised her in that Chinese village a lifetime ago.

'Wolfe. But please, if you would call me Tara, I'd like that.'

'Then you must call me Maggy. We don't stand on ceremony here. I dare say the bishop wouldn't approve, but he is in Paris at the moment, so we can please ourselves, no? Now, tell me about this girl you have come all this way to save.'

In clear, unadorned language, Tara laid out the entire story from start to finish. About her and Gabriel's unorthodox backgrounds, and how they came to be involved in the search for Odette Diallo.

When she finished, Maggy said nothing for several seconds. Her lips were pursed and her gaze was fierce.

'Men,' she finally said. 'You know I try so hard not to be judgemental, after all, we are all God's children and created in His image. But I do believe there is something wrong with them. It must be in their DNA. They wage war, they rape, they kidnap, they torture. Our sisters in Africa, Nigeria, Congo, Mali, Senegal, they are threatened by gangs with machetes, with guns. The most terrible things are done to them.'

'My brother is a man. And he is a good man,' Tara said. 'So is our friend who has come to Martinique with us to help rescue Odette.'

'I am sorry, my child. It is a sin to judge all men against the failings of some. So how can I help you? I am afraid I have very little influence on the island.'

Tara explained.

When she'd finished, Maggy sat back.

'And that's all you need?'

'Just for a day or two. I can pay you for replacements.'

'Don't be silly. If they help you achieve your goal then the knowledge you have saved Odette will be more than sufficient payment.'

'Thank you, Maggy. From the bottom of my heart, thank you. When we reunite Odette with her parents, I will tell them of your help. I know they will want to recognise that in some way.'

Maggy nodded. 'I would do it anyway, but thank you. Tell me, though, Tara. Is it not a job for the police?'

'It should be, but sadly they are not interested.'

'And why are you and Gabriel? Interested, I mean.'

Tara thought for a while before she answered.

'If not us, who?'

49

Guard duty was as boring as fuck.

You stood around all day with a bloody Kalashnikov in this humidity, the sun boiling your brains, waiting for what? Three shit-for-brains vigilantes to do what, exactly? Drive a fucking tank up the hill and attack?

The image made him smile. He imagined emptying a mag into their heads, watching them explode like ripe melons. Or hacking them up with a half-metre-long machete. Like in the old days.

Something pattered onto his shoulder from an overhanging branch. He flicked at it and a large, hairy, black spider tinged with metallic turquoise dropped to the floor. A *Matoutou*, the local tarantula. Protected by those eco-fascists who ran everything in the Eastern Antilles these days.

He raised his foot and stamped the little creature into the mud. Its body burst with a dry pop and its guts squirted out from the cleated sole of his boot. He laughed.

'Not so fucking protected now, are you?'

'Hey! Mingo! Check these two out. The fucking God squad are on walkabout again. Better start praying your rosary.'

He looked over at his partner. Then followed the direction of his gun barrel. And grinned.

Fucking nuns. Fucking priests. He'd had his fill of them at the children's home: the nuns with their beatings, the priests in the small hours with their trembling fingers creeping down the front of his pyjama trousers and hot breath on the back of his neck.

And here came one of each, toiling up the hill in those ridiculous getups. Christ, the island was hot enough already. Trudging about the streets trying to convert people in all that gear. He was surprised they didn't all drop dead of heatstroke.

He waited for them to draw near then called out.

'Nice day for a walk, eh?'

They turned towards the sound of his voice. The nun's face hidden by her headdress, or whatever the fuck it was called. The priest looking like the Man from Delmonte with some crazy-ass straw hat tipped low over his eyes.

'Good morning, my son,' the nun said. 'Are you about to set off on a hunting trip? You certainly look equipped for it.'

He unshouldered his AK.

'What, this, you mean? Nah, this is for keeping vermin out.'

She nodded as if she understood. Silly bitch. Like a nun would know a pea shooter from a bazooka.

'You must have quite the problem. Is it rats?'

'Rats?' He laughed, starting to enjoy himself. This was actually fun. 'Yeah, rats. Fucking big ones.'

He enjoyed the way she flinched at the swear word. Good. Let her. There'd been one at the home. Sister Marguerite. He'd never forget her name if he lived to be eighty. Tall, stick-thin bitch with dry bushy hair the colour of a bullet casing. Fond of the strap. Used to say she'd whip the devil out of you as she lashed it across your bare buttocks, always managing to catch your ball sack if you hadn't tucked it away up front. Perverted cunt. When he'd left, and joined the militia, they'd paid a visit to the home. Hers was the first hand he took.

'Do you have any other unwelcome visitors, my son?' the priest asked, his head bent as if he daren't look up in case he caught God's eye. 'Is that why you and your friend carry those guns? We could ask the local police captain to send a patrol for you.'

'Oh, it's not just us, *padre*,' he said. 'Believe me, if trouble comes looking, there's four of us plus the owners. We don't need the cops to help us. We know how to take care of "unwelcome visitors".'

'Then we'll wish you good day. God bless you all,' the priest said, making the sign of the cross. 'And protect you from vermin.'

The guard winked at his partner. Levelled his AK at the priest and his pious little girlfriend and yanked back the charging lever with a loud crack that made them jump out of their skins.

'You, too, *padre*. And you, sister.'

As the two Bible-bashers hurried away, heads bent, no doubt shitting their hair-lined knickers, he burst out laughing.

A parrot squawked loudly from a tree across the road. Unable to contain himself any longer, he fired a burst and brought it down in an explosion of scarlet and yellow feathers that spiralled to earth.

* * *

The nun and the priest turned around and walked back down the hill away from the gun-toting pest controllers, their laughter ringing out until a burst from one of the guns drowned it out.

Neither flinched. But then, both were used to operating amid gunfire.

At the fork in the road, they doubled back on themselves, pausing only to divest themselves of the heavy cream robes. Beneath the clerical garb, they wore light cotton trousers and long-sleeved T-shirts in jungle camouflage. The trousers cuffs were bloused over high combat boots.

50

Cooler now she no longer wore the nun's habit, Tara daubed Gabriel's face with green and brown camo makeup from two small tins, and he returned the favour. They exchanged a nod, and left the road for the jungle that seemed intent on reclaiming what was manmade and returning it to nature. The hill climbed up and around the northern side of the plot of land on which the Soltanis' house stood.

Pushing through rather than cutting the vegetation, the better not to leave any identifiable signs of their presence, it took twenty-five minutes to reach a point at which they could surveil the rear of the property.

No fence, none needed. Once inside the chaotic jumble of soft-leaved plants, dripping with oversized, floppy-petalled blossoms in red, gold and yellow, a thick curtain of bamboo stood between the interlopers and the house. The stems were two inches thick and as strong as steel. Both Wolfe siblings had spent enough time in Hong Kong to have become accustomed to seeing the material used as scaffolding on construction projects.

'This is our way in,' Gabriel murmured.

Tara nodded, stretching out her right hand and giving a nearby bamboo stem an exploratory shake. It rattled softly – *clack-click-clack* – against its neighbours.

'They won't be expecting it.'

They settled back in the dense undergrowth and waited. Watching. A bird call pierced the chitter and buzz of the forest's insect life. A high-pitched musical whistle: short-long-short. Over and over again. Half an hour passed without any sign of human habitation. Gabriel forced himself to hope that Odette was alive and not mistreated, beyond being kidnapped and held prisoner by two sex traffickers planning to auction her off to some pervert from halfway across the world. He would save her. He had to. And then, once she was safe, he would mete out justice to the Soltanis.

'Because that always works out so well,' a quiet voice beside him whispered.

He resisted the urge to turn his head. He had no desire to come face-to-face with whichever of his ghosts was interfering with his thoughts.

The voice migrated to a spot between his ears and behind his eyes. A place he couldn't run from.

'Save one, lose one. That's pretty much the pattern isn't it?'

It wasn't a ghost. He knew that, really. It was his own doubting voice he heard. The wounded part of his soul that suffered each loss and stored the memories of the person who'd been taken from him. Michael. Smudge. His parents. Britta. Master Zhao. Eli. Their unborn child. And Don? Was the Old Man becoming lost to Gabriel? He was losing *himself*, that much was clear. However much Gabriel tried to do the right thing, to protect the innocent, rescue the kidnapped, defeat the warmongers, the corrupt, the immoral, the plain evil, it was always those he held dearest who paid the ultimate price, while he, Gabriel Wolfe, survived each encounter with the dark side of humanity. His injuries could be bound, his broken bones set; bullets could be dug out of him, knife wounds stitched closed, burns salved: but everywhere he went, everywhere he fought, everywhere he tried to do the right thing, he left a trail of bodies behind him in which the innocent lay alongside the guilty.

And yet, despite all he had experienced, all he knew about his past, here he was again. Who would he lose this time? Tara? Jacko? Odette herself? What was the point in killing evil men if those he cared about died too? It was as if God, or the Universe, or some other unseen, unknowable force were playing a zero-sum game. Telling him, *You take a bad life, I'll take a good one. Stability and balance are maintained.*

He sighed. What choice did he have? If he did nothing, Odette Diallo would truly enter hell. The Soltanis would go on plying their evil trade. And Tara might die anyway.

Gabriel turned to look at her. She was unaware of his gaze, concentrating entirely on the house just visible through the thick bamboo stems. As he watched, he became aware of a musical hum. A strangely pure tone with a rasp hidden somewhere inside it.

A two-centimetre-long wasp with black and plum-red wings and long yellow antennae alighted on Tara's bare forearm. Gabriel hissed at Tara. She turned her head and the wasp stung her then flew off.

Her eyes bugged out as she tried to suppress a scream. She clamped her hand over the puncture wound and he watched, powerless, as tears leaked from the corner of her eyes. She squeezed them shut and curled into a ball. He shuffled closer and laid an arm around her shoulders. She was trembling with the effort of keeping quiet. And there was nothing he could do about it. Slowly, she released a shuddering breath, and as the last of the air left her lungs, she permitted herself a long, low growl of agony, followed by a stream of gutter-Chinese so filthy he had to smile, despite her obvious pain.

'Let me see,' he murmured, once the shuddering had subsided and she'd raised her head from between her knees.

She took her hand away from her forearm.

A red lump the size of half a cherry had swollen on her skin.

At its centre the dark hole where the wasp's stinger had pierced the skin was clearly visible, surrounded by a smaller spot of white skin.

'Fuuuuuck,' she hissed out. 'I've had bullet wounds that hurt less than that. Mother*fucker*, what was it?'

'A wasp, I think.'

Her eyes bulged again.

'A wasp? Are you kidding me?'

'No, but it's given me an idea.' Gabriel got to his feet. 'Are you OK to keep watch?'

'It's about all I *am* good for right now. Why? Where are you going?'

'To see if I can find its nest.'

Gabriel climbed away from Tara, leaving her nursing her injured arm and maintaining a steady stream of inventive Chinese cursing under her breath.

It took twenty minutes of searching, turning his head and closing his eyes each time he heard that distinctive musical hum, but eventually he saw another of the black-and-plum-red wasps.

It was flying about two metres over the ground and he followed it as it zig-zagged through the plants before finally zooming towards a dead tree. Dangling from a slender stem was a pear-shaped papery mass about fifty centimetres from top to bottom. The exterior of the nest was the exact same shade of tawny-gold as the bark. As he watched, the wasp flew straight into a hole in its underside. Seconds later, another flew out. Gabriel retreated, anxious not to suffer the same fate as Tara.

He rejoined her.

'Any sign of more guards?' he asked.

She shook her head.

'Nothing.'

'Is the pain easing off?'

'Maybe a little. It felt like I'd been shot. Now it only feels like someone's holding a red-hot branding iron to it.'

'Hang in there, sis.'

She punched his shoulder with her good arm.

'*You* hang in there! You're not the one who got his arm deep-fried.'

'I thought you said it was like a branding iron.'

'I'll brand *you* in a minute!'

But she managed a grin.

51

The dress felt stupid on her.

Like something you'd wear for your first communion. White cotton trimmed with these totally lame lacy frills.

But that was when Odette was seven. A little kid. She was twelve now, already getting her periods. Boobs, too, which the boys were always commenting on, trying to get a feel in the corridor at school.

Arseholes. The last one who'd tried that got a kick in the crotch that left him squealing like a baby, rolling on the floor and clutching his balls. Odette and her girls had practically pissed themselves laughing. Loser. Nobody had tried it since then.

She tried to smile. Remembering how she and Nadia, Pierette, Mariem, Denise and Kénéline would cut loose after school, running round the neighbourhood or playing soccer in the hardcourt. But the smile faltered as she flashed on that awful moment when this Arab guy asked her for directions, and before she knew what was happening, something greasy smelling had been clamped over her mouth and nose and she'd blacked out.

She was in deep shit, she knew that. They'd told her what was going to happen to her. Seemed to be really pleased. An auction, like she was a pair of jeans on Depop or something.

Shit, she had to get out of here. Time was running short. No way was she going to let some middle-aged pervert take her virginity. Maybe back in Mum and Dad's countries that kind of thing happened. Arranged marriages, militias raping kids, girls getting married off to men old enough to be their granddads. But in France? No way. That was not going to happen.

Except, the men who'd kidnapped her, Ali and Bashar, they were careful. Always keeping her locked in a room. Bars on the window. They brought her meals to her room. And when they'd had to move her, first to Corsica, then here to Martinique, they'd drugged her.

Only they'd made a mistake this time. And she was working on it for all she was worth.

Under the mattress was an old wooden bedframe. Reinforced with these metal strips bolted to the planks. But one had been loose. Ever since she'd found it, she'd spent every moment she could wiggling it and digging at the wood around the bolts with her fingernails. They were torn and ragged now and they bled all the time, but little by little she'd got most of the wood out from around one of the metal slats. A bit more work and she'd get it free altogether. Then she could lever it out at the other end, and *then* she'd have a weapon. And that was going to change everything.

Those bastards thought they'd got some innocent little flower, but they'd soon find out the truth. Odette Diallo was a virgin all right, and she intended to stay that way until she was at least sixteen, but one thing she wasn't was innocent. You learned early how to take care of yourself in the Eighteenth.

The lock scraped and clicked. Heart in her mouth, she flopped the mattress back into place and sat on the bed like they'd instructed her to.

The door opened.

It was one of the guards. Really tall. Dad was one-seventy-five and this guy was even taller. His name was Jean. She'd wheedled that out of him on the first morning they'd been here. Stupid man. She could see the look in his eyes, like one of the neighbourhood dogs when there was a bitch in heat around, waggling her arse.

'Maybe I'll give you a road-test,' he'd said that first day, his lips moist, his eyes ranging lazily over her body.

'Maybe I'll scream and Ali will cut your dick off and make you eat it,' she'd retorted smartly.

'Bitch,' he'd snarled.

She drew in a breath, opened her mouth and threw her head back.

'No!' he hissed. 'The fuck? Don't do that.'

'Say sorry, then.'

'What?'

'I said, say sorry. Say, "I'm sorry Odette, for calling you a bitch".'

Eyes dark, he'd repeated the apology. And before he'd gone she'd asked for, and got, his name.

Jean stood there, a green plastic plate on a tray beside a pink plastic beaker and a squat little paper tub with a clear plastic lid. He was leering at her. And there was something else in his eyes. Kind of like the look a boy would get after winning a fight. Triumphant. Her belly flipped over.

'Got your lunch, Odette,' he said, putting the tray down. 'Something nice today. Blackened fish, plantain chips, corn. Ice cream for afters. Orangina.'

'Why not the usual shit?' she couldn't help but ask.

His grin widened, revealing cruddy-looking teeth.

'Oh, of course, you wouldn't have heard. The auction finishes at midnight.'

He left, slamming the door behind him. The familiar scrape of the key in the lock followed. He whistled loudly as he walked away. 'La Vie en Rose.' Mum had told her she'd walked down the aisle to that. Some old French lady used to sing it apparently, although all the grownups in the Eighteenth seemed to know it, wherever they came from.

She looked at the food. Turned aside and vomited.

And then she went back to work.

52

Back at the guesthouse, Gabriel changed into shorts and a loose white cotton shirt and rejoined the others in the kitchen. The guesthouse they'd hired was simple, but clean, and the other guests, who scuttled, pattered and buzzed around its three-room layout, were inoffensive.

He brushed the table free of a couple of large iridescent blue beetles, which took to the air with a loud whirring. Spread out a sheet of paper on which he sketched the layout of the Soltanis' compound.

The road curved gently around the front, up and over the crest of the hill. He marked the position of the two guards with Xs. Thick cross-hatching indicated the protective bamboo palisade at the rear of the property.

Gabriel tapped the paper with the tip of his pencil.

'No fence. They're over-confident.'

'So we go in that way, yes?' Jacko asked.

'You and I do, yes.'

'What about Tara?'

'I'm going to cause a distraction at the front gate,' Tara said. 'I got the taste for the religious life.'

ANDY MASLEN

'What do you mean?' Jacko asked.

'Well, they've seen me now so they'll recognise me. They'll be less wary. Basic psychology. I'll say I'm collecting for the orphanage.'

Jacko frowned. 'What orphanage?'

'There's always an orphanage, Jacko! And if they challenge me, I'll say we're building one. While I'm occupying the two gate guards, you and Gabriel get in and take care of the other two. Then it's just the Soltanis to deal with and we free Odette.'

'Pretty bold move, Tara,' Jacko said, rubbing his bristly chin. 'Maybe it would be better if we all went in the back way.'

She shook her head.

'They won't suspect me. I'll have the element of surprise *and* shock. When they're down I'll give the signal.'

'The signal's a short-long-short blast on a whistle,' Gabriel said.

'Whistle?' Jacko echoed.

Tara produced a length of bamboo, barely five centimetres as long as the width of her index finger. It had a notch cut through the surface, one centimetre from the end that she now placed between her lips. She blew. It emitted a piercing, high note.

Jacko grinned.

'Nice. Where did you learn to make those?'

'The village where I grew up. If we wanted toys, we had to make our own.'

Jacko nodded his appreciation. 'Better than all that plastic shit, anyway. Speaking of toys, I got my contribution while you two were playing dress-up on the hill.'

He rose from the table and left the room, coming back a few moments later with a roll of canvas tied with tapes. He loosened the bow and unrolled the thick, unbleached fabric.

Gabriel stood to get a better look at Jacko's 'toys'. Three sugarcane knives with riveted wooden handles, from which foot-long blades flared to an end about three and a half inches wide. At the tip, on the upper edge, each knife bore a hooked point. Gabriel had used them in Honduras. Mostly for cutting cane, using the hook to pulled the chopped plants free of those not cut yet. Once to castrate a rapist in a cage fight. He picked one up and hefted it. Decent balance for a machete-type weapon, given they were always point-heavy.

He nodded at Jacko. 'Not bad.'

'The edge is OK, but I bought a whetstone, too. Thought we could put a proper edge on them, boss,' he said, winking at Gabriel.

Tara had unfolded a flap of canvas and was holding a smaller knife. It had a four-inch blade, the edge curving up to a wicked point. The handle was a swirling wood-grain, dyed indigo but burnished back to let some of the wood's natural pale glow show through.

She smiled at Jacko.

'This is beautiful.' She depressed a switch on the stainless steel spine of the knife and folder the blade away.

'It's a Laguiole. There's a shop in town. Apparently you get all these French tourists wanting to play at Robinson Crusoe out here. They were a hundred and thirty euros each but I got a deal because I bought three plus the cane knives. I got him down to a hundred apiece.'

She opened the blade again. The spring mechanism emitted a solid, satisfying metallic click as the blade locked into place.

'What's the wood?'

'Birch. They use this special dyeing process. I got a bit lost, to be honest.'

Gabriel selected a blade of his own. Tara was right. It was beautiful. He hoped the mechanism would survive being soaked in blood. It was a hunting knife, after all.

'He sold guns, too, rifles, shotguns,' Jacko said, his eyes suddenly doubtful. 'Don't you think we'd be better off going in tooled-up?'

Gabriel shook his head.

'The Soltanis are bound to have bought the local police. At the first sound of shooting, they'll be up there in force. We're not killing any cops.'

'Not even corrupt ones?'

'We'd never get off the island. They'd close the airport. No. We do this silently. We kill the guards, then the Soltanis, rescue Odette and get out of Martinique on the next available flight.'

Jacko picked up one of the cane knives, stepped back and gave it an experimental swing.

'Sounds like a plan. When do we go in? The old way, 3.00 a.m.?'

'I considered it. But everyone'll be inside. Daylight means at least two guards will be on duty, if not all four. Easier to deal with them separately.'

'And there's a frightened little girl to think of,' Tara said. 'I don't want her in there with them one minute longer than necessary.'

'So when, then?' Jacko asked.

Gabriel picked up a second cane knife.

'Get changed.'

53

The metal strap was almost free. Odette dug deeper into the wood, ignoring the throbbing pain in her fingers, which were bleeding again.

Then a splinter slid under her nail.

The pain was like a bright, white light spearing into her brain. She bit her lip trying not to scream but it was coming anyway. She threw herself down on the bed and buried her face in the pillow while the howl burst free of her lips. Mother*fucker*, it was bad. And it kept on coming, like some mad seamstress had Odette's finger under her sewing machine foot and was stitching her nail down.

She had to look.

A long black line led from the ragged edge for about seven millimetres down into the nail bed. Darkish blood was welling around the entry point and running down each side. The tip of the splinter, a pale chestnut brown against the blood, poked out by a millimetre. At home, her mum would take it out with tweezers from her manicure set. Tears leaked from Odette's eyes, whether from the pain of the splinter or from being so far from her mum, she didn't know.

No! She was tougher than this. Tougher than some pathetic

piece of wood. There was nothing in the room she could use. They were careful not to leave her with anything she could turn into a weapon. Even plastic cutlery had been banned after she stuck one of the guards with a broken fork, leaving him with a pretty little gash in his cheek.

She brought the throbbing finger to her mouth and sucked the blood away. Copper, iron, salt. Took another look. The end of the splinter was sticking out just enough. She put her finger to her lips again and stuck out her tongue. Located the vicious little spur with the tip of her tongue and then closed her incisors around it.

Even that little bit of pressure caused a jolt of electric pain to shoot from her nail all the way up her forearm. *No going back, Odette, you need to get it out.* She nipped the little stub between her teeth and started pulling, ever so gently. The pain brought fresh tears to her eyes. But she didn't let up. The splinter slipped between her teeth. Blood welled. She poked her tongue onto the sharp little spur and tried again. Moaned under her breath as the pain jolted again.

It was coming, Holy Mother of God, it was coming. The pain was like a dark eel, sliding into her stomach and making her queasy. With a mixture of agony and relief, it came free.

She spat it into her palm. A miniature dagger, not even a centimetre long, streaked with her blood. She flicked it onto the floor and tore a strip off the sheet for a bandage, which she wound tight around her damaged finger.

She had no time to waste feeling sorry for herself. The metal strap had almost come free until the splinter went up her nail. She dug a finger under the end and pulled back. There was just enough space to get another finger under there. She hauled back, wiggling the metal. With a loud snap, the bolt at the loose end came free of the wooden bedframe. The strap bent out at an angle and she fell on her bottom as the resistance ceased.

Now she could get a proper grip on it. Both fists clamped tight around it. She started working it methodically against the second and final bolt. Up, down, in, out, left, right. The metal beside the bolt changed colour, going from a dark grey to this weird pale, streaky look. Almost like the bubbles on top of Dad's morning *café noir*. She bent it forwards and back, harder, faster. The area of discoloured, almost frothy-looking metal expanded. And then, with a snap, the whole thing broke off just behind the bolt.

'Oh, thank you, Jesus,' she breathed.

She had a weapon. A proper one. Steel, or iron or whatever. Fifty centimetres long. A round end with a nut and bolt through it. That could be the handle. And a broken end, like a sloppy capital letter W, three needle-sharp points where the metal had broken off.

She tested the sides, but they were flat. Pity. It would have been perfect as a sword. Michel at school had brought this Samurai sword down to the playground. Said it was his dad's. Said *his* dad had taken it off this dead Japanese soldier in the Second World War.

Odette had done the maths. Looked up the dates on Wikipedia. It was bullshit! Michel's granddad was born in 1977, 32 years after the war ended. Odette's theory was, Michel's dad had got it at Biron Market off one of those stalls which sold army shit to saddos to make up for them being office workers or Deliveroo guys or whatever.

So, no sword, Samurai or other. But as she hefted it in her hand and tried a couple of experimental jabs followed by swings, she reckoned it was good enough to knock someone out or maybe slash them across the eyes. She started tearing more strips off her sheet and winding them around the bolt-end. By the time she was finished, she had a very nice-looking weapon. Cloth-bound handle long enough for both fists. The remaining thirty centimetres a solid chunk of metal with that wicked-looking triple point. She slid it under the mattress and dragged the sheet down to cover the evidence of her handiwork.

Her finger was still hurting but now she found she could ignore it. The next person to feel pain in this room wasn't going to be her.

They'd made her sit in that stupid dress in front of a video camera for the auction. Told her if she didn't simper and smile they'd beat her.

She'd said it wouldn't look so good for the customer, would it, and then Ali had punched her right in the stomach. He'd laughed afterwards, told her he knew thirty-one different places he could hurt her where it wouldn't show. Not on the outside anyway.

But the reason Odette was feeling happier now than at any time in the last week was because they'd not given her any more sedatives. Ali said they couldn't have her looking all droopy eyed on camera like some sad little cartoon dog.

So now she was feeling sharp again. Like her old self. Like when she and her posse would be strutting through the neighbourhood giving the finger to anyone who kissed their teeth at them or asked why they weren't at school. Kénéline was her bestie, though. Had the quickest mind and the sharpest tongue. Some of the old ladies' faces when Kéké let rip! Talk about horrified.

'I'll tell your mothers you speak like that!'

'I'll tell your husband you pay for your groceries on your back!'

She tried to not to feel fear. Fear kills your mind, so fuck the fear and do it anyway. It wasn't the exact quote: they'd changed it to make it their own. They all loved that film, *Dune*. Zendaya was so cool in it. And she was Nigerian. OK, *half*-Nigerian. But still. And she had righteous combat skills.

Odette used to practise her moves at home or out on the streets. Not actually fighting, not unless it was really necessary. But the moves, man. Close to dancing. Close to ballet. Just beautiful.

She felt sparkly with electricity. Like she was powered by some huge fuckoff battery, or plugged into her own charger. Every hair on her skin tingled with a little wire. Her muscles were tight. Even her senses felt amped up.

She heard the footsteps coming down the corridor. The acidic stink of where she'd been sick was pungent in her nostrils. It didn't matter. She'd be out of here soon. Then run down the hill, find the police station and tell them what had happened. They'd call the French cops, the first time ever in her life she'd be glad to see a *flic*!

Or maybe it would be the Americans, seeing how close they were to the USA. The real feds! So cool. She'd say she was feeling shivery, score one of those cool blue bombers with the yellow capitals on the back. F.B.I.

She stood behind the door, her sword gripped tight in both fists, feet apart, trying to stop herself from breathing too fast. No point going all Samurai on Jean's ass if she fucking fainted.

The footsteps came to a halt right outside the door. Just like always. She raised the length of steel over her head. Pictured Jean's shaved head, with the white scar over his right ear. That's where she'd hit him.

The key scraped in the lock. Her heartbeat tripled. She cocked the sword over her shoulder. It seemed to vibrate in her grip. She imagined it powered by the same current that fizzed along every nerve in her body. Glowing blue-white like a light sabre. Another cool film. Specially the one with Rey in it. Daisy Ridley was English, so not as cool as Zendaya, obviously, but still. They were role models. You could be a girl and do anything. Like right now, Odette intended to stove Jean's skull in with a bit of old bed.

The door swung inwards. Jean stepped in. Odette screamed out a war cry – 'Die, you fucker!' – and swung the sword with all her might.

54

Beneath the nun's habit, Tara was sweating. It was only the heat that was doing it. Fighting had stopped making her sweat back when she'd been undergoing ruthless training by the Crane and the Bull, back at the special school on the mainland where the Chinese State Security Bureau transformed street kids into cold-hearted assassins. What little empathy for her victims the spooks had left intact, Fang Jian had eradicated when he took her back to Hong Kong to act as one of his personal bodyguards.

Her two latest victims stood before her now, smirking. One with his thumb hooked into a belt loop so the finger dangled suggestively near his crotch, the other giving her an insolent stare as he caressed the barrel of his AK. She could have told them the overall effect was less frightening and more like an outtake from a one-star Chop-Socky movie with them in the roles of "guards 7 and 8". Especially as she was playing the role of the undercover martial arts expert about to take out the entire gang of drug dealers.

'You want to ask *who* for *what?*' Barrel-stroker asked, turning to his friend and jerking his head back at Tara.

'Whoever owns this lovely house for a donation towards the

orphanage. Those poor children have nothing but a few clothes and their Bibles.'

'Listen, sister, our bosses are busy men. They don't have no time to be listening to no sob-stories from a f—, I mean from a nun, OK? Now, do us a favour and try someone else, yes?'

Tara shifted from foot to foot, as if he were making her anxious. Playing the role for all it was worth.

If he'd been paying attention, he might have noticed that this small action placed her at an angle to him. She now presented less of a target, and had gone into a balanced stance, the better to launch an attack from. But then, if he'd been paying attention, he'd also have noticed the way the right side of her habit was pushed out from her leg. Almost as if she had something gripped in her fist.

'Please, my son,' she said, injecting a wheedling note into her voice. 'If you could just allow me to see them, perhaps I could convince them. We are doing God's work. I'm sure your bosses are Godfearing men.'

The other one snorted.

'Well, they're Muslims, but I guess that means they love Allah or whatever.'

'So that's a yes? You'll take me to them?'

He smiled.

'Of course.' He glanced at Barrel-Stroker, whose was looking at him, mouth agape. Shook his head. 'See that shed over there?' He pointed to a broken-down wooden shack in a corner of the yard.

'Yes.'

'They're in there. Come on, we'll take you to meet them right now.'

His game was so obvious he might as well have been carrying a hand-painted placard. *'We're gonna rape you in the shed.'*

Tara offered him a smile of the purest gratitude. It was entirely genuine. She was thanking him for letting her inside. She waited while he unhooked a bunch of keys from his belt and fiddled around before finding the one that unlocked the gate. He swung it inwards and made an over-the-top beckoning gesture. He all but said, '*Entrez!*'

She did enter, and as she did, she swept her habit back and brought the sugar cane knife up. With a backward swing, she sent the heavy end of the cane cutting tool into Barrel-stroker's right bicep. He shrieked as the muscles and sinews parted around the razor-sharp edge. She bent back and kicked him in the face with the side of her right foot. He collapsed sideways, getting tangled in the sling of his Kalashnikov.

Crotch-grabber's eyes were out on stalks before arterial spray from the shrieking guard's arm caught him in the face and made him flinch. It meant that he didn't see Tara's second strike coming. Her left hand came up from her hip holding the hunting knife. She struck him hard in the belly and unzipped him from navel to neck, the blade shearing through his shirt, undershirt and skin as if they were tissue paper. He clutched his abdomen in a futile attempt to stop his guts from spilling onto the dusty ground, crying out in pain and shock.

Her third strike took him in the throat, cutting him off mid-scream. All four major blood vessels were severed in an instant, the carotid arteries loosing sprays and gouts of blood high into the air, the jugular veins releasing torrents of blood that sheeted down over his neck and chest. He died with bright scarlet froth bubbling from his lips, the only sound a dying hiss as his lungs gave up their last breath.

She whirled round. Barrel-stroker was stumbling to his feet, having untangled himself from the sling of his rifle. But he was limited to using his left arm. The right was a bloody mess: she'd hit him so hard with the sugar cane knife, she'd exposed an inch or so of bone.

He lifted the Kalashnikov to waist height, trying to get his finger seated round the trigger. She stepped inside the reach of the barrel, rendering the rifle useless. Grabbed him by the hair and yanked his head back. He dropped the AK and started punching her with his left fist. Hard blows into her stomach that made her gasp. She had to act fast before he tripped her. He was twice her size and the nun's habit, whilst a great disguise, was severely limiting her movements. Holding her hunting knife in a stabbing grip, she drove it into the side of his neck, then dragged it downwards, opening a gaping wound from ear to collar bone. She pushed him backwards and he tumbled to the ground, arcs of scarlet spurting high into the air. The sight of his own blood raining down on him would be his last.

She flipped her habit back and sheathed her sugar cane knife through a loop of cord she'd fashioned back at the guesthouse. But she kept the hunting knife out. Easier to conceal with a turn of the body. Then she looked down at herself. *A nun? Really, Tara? Which order, the Blessed Sisters of the Blood Spatter?* She shucked off the habit and dumped it by the shed where the two guards had intended to rape her.

She moved towards the house. A Jeep was parked round the side. She ran to it and leaned into the driver's side. Reached under the steering wheel and cut the wires leading from the ignition.

From a pocket, she retrieved the little bamboo whistle, brought it to her lips and blew the arranged signal: short-long-short. A reasonable facsimile of the fluting bird call she and Gabriel had heard while they were surveiling the rear of the house.

55

He couldn't deny it.

It felt good to be on a lurk. Improvised camo gear from a beachfront boutique. Green and brown jungle warpaint smeared over his face. Tooled up. Not with a rifle.

He was still, just, convinced they were better off keeping noise to a minimum. With the only means of extraction being regular commercial flights, drawing the attention of the local cops wouldn't play out well. Especially if, as the boss suspected, they were in the Soltanis' pockets.

But as Jacko glanced sideways at Gabriel, he felt an old, familiar and deeply troubling sensation building inside him.

It began, as it always did, with an indefinable sense of dread centred just behind his heart. But soon it developed sticky, slimy tentacles that spread like blood in water, uncoiling, lengthening, wrapping themselves around his nerves, blood vessels, intestines … cramping his guts, making him shiver despite the heat, before squeezing his muscles, driving poisonous spines in-between the fibres … bringing that special variety of pain that no analgesic could touch.

Except one. The big one. The one he'd surrendered to shortly after losing that last gig on the door of possibly the shittiest strip club in Paris. One of the other guys on the door had a friend who dealt. He made the introduction. And after that first blissful hit, when all the anger, the grief and the pain just dissolved in that golden light, he knew he was home.

Only now home was a million miles away.

The stuff he'd bought from a deckhand on a yacht in the marina in Fort-de-France was all gone.

He wrapped his arms around himself, trying to find a position to wait in that would stop his limbs from trembling. But dear God Almighty it was hard. He was terrified Gabriel would notice. And then what. Stand him down? No. Of course not. Stand him down to where? Return him to unit? What unit? It wasn't about punishment. It was about honour.

Gabriel would see that Jacko had fucked up. That Jacko was a liability. You couldn't lead an assault on an enemy position when a third of your force was Jonesing for a fix.

An involuntary groan escaped his lips.

* * *

At the sound, Gabriel turned to check Jacko. He was wincing. Like he'd eaten too many unripe plums. And hugging himself. A muscle below his right eye was flickering. The sun caught it an oblique angle, making a crescent-shaped shadow dance on his cheekbone.

'Everything OK?' he asked.

Everything OK? Of course it wasn't. Gabriel could see perfectly well that Jacko had a problem. And whatever he'd been taking to alleviate it had run out. The man was an addict. Christ, why had he brought him out here?

'I'm good, boss. Just the old combat adrenaline kicking in.'

Jacko thumped his chest. It was a decent stab at the old-soldier act, and maybe it would have fooled a wet-behind-the-ears lieutenant straight out of Sandhurst. But not a combat-hardened SAS commander who'd spent his post-army days in tricky situations from Iranian nuclear weapons facilities to Brazilian suicide-cult compounds.

Gabriel twisted round, holding onto one of the wrist-thick bamboo stems and eyeballing Jacko.

'Tell me the truth, Jacko. I know you're an addict. How bad is it?'

Jacko's face twisted and he groaned and clamped a hand to his belly.

''Scuse me, boss. Gotta go.'

He backed out hurriedly. Presently, Gabriel heard the rasp of a zip and the rustle of clothing. Then the unmistakeable sounds of diarrhoea. The smell hit him seconds later. A fruity, putrid stink. Flies buzzed in, whizzing past his ears as they homed in on this new source of sustenance.

Jacko appeared after a couple more minutes. His shamefaced expression bore its own eloquent testimony.

'Must have been something I ate.'

'Cut the crap, Jacko. I asked you a question. Your withdrawal. How bad? Can you fight?'

Jacko nodded. Pulled out his hunting knife and opened the blade. Held it out in front of him. The point wavered, the amplitude of the vibrating tip growing larger and larger. Jacko stared at it. Gabriel could feel the effort it was costing him to steady the blade. But eventually the point stilled. Jacko grimaced. More pain. After a moment, Gabriel realised he was trying to smile.

'I'm good, boss,' he said finally.

Gabriel wasn't convinced. Every soldier knew the tactic beloved by insurgents of every stripe. Shoot to wound and you brought two soldiers down. One with the injury, one to stay and help him. Taking Jacko into the fray would be doing the Soltanis' job for them.

'You can stay here. Cover my back if anyone tries to get behind me.'

'Not a chance. I'm in this for Odette. I'll manage.'

'You're sure?'

'I'm sure.'

Gabriel nodded. What could he do? Jacko didn't report to him. He could order him to stay behind and Jacko could ignore him anyway. Better to let him follow his heart. Maybe when the real adrenaline kicked in it would overmaster the evil effects of the heroin withdrawal.

He faced front again, only marginally distracted by the full-body shudder that wracked Jacko seconds later.

A shrill whistling call – short-long-short – put all concerns about Jacko into the background. Tara was inside the compound and the two gate guards were dead.

He turned to Jacko and pointed towards the rear of the house. *In we go.*

Gabriel braced his back against one of the thinner bamboo stems and used his feet to push another away to create a V-shaped gap. Jacko slipped through, then held two massive stems wide like Samson between the pillars of the temple while Gabriel clambered inside. He let them go and they sprang upright again, *clock*-ing together like a demented percussion instrument.

In unison, the two former troopers drew their sugar-cane knives. Held them in their right hands, hunting knives in their left.

Jacko hefted the heavy, machete-like weapon.

'Feels good to have a golok in my hand again,' he grunted.

Gabriel offered him an encouraging smile. Maybe it was going to be OK. Whatever happened after they freed Odette could be handled. He just needed Jacko to hold it together for another thirty minutes. By then either Odette would be theirs or they'd probably all be dead.

The yard was quiet. Gabriel pushed down on the handle of the door at the back of the house. It opened silently. And he was inside, Jacko at his back, *golok* held aloft.

Male voices erupted in what sounded like good-natured argument. The sound was coming from a ground-floor room at the front of the house. He signalled for Jacko to go left. He went right. Gabriel pointed to his own eyes. *No fighting yet, just observe and report back.* Jacko nodded and slid away towards the other side of the house.

Gabriel padded towards a door through which he could see pots and pans stacked on a wooden bench. The kitchen. The men's voices grew louder but when he peered round the corner of the door frame, the kitchen was empty. An acoustic quirk of the house's design, then.

He turned. Three more rooms at least to check before they could climb the staircase.

Jacko yelled out. Glass shattered. Men bellowed. And then the shooting started. Three incredibly loud percussive bangs as someone fire a large-calibre sidearm in a hard-walled room that acted like a gigantic echo chamber.

Swearing, Gabriel sprinted towards the southwest corner of the house. Two more shots rang out, deafening him.

He saw them through the open door to a living room. Jacko and a tall, dark-skinned man were wrestling, Jacko's right arm gripped around the elbow, rendering the golok useless. His left hand was clamped around his assailant's right wrist, in which a big, blued-steel revolver waved dangerously.

A second man was dancing around the two wrestlers, a pistol in his hand, trying to get a clear shot at Jacko.

He was yelling out to his partner in French.

'*Dégage du putain de chemin!*' Get out of the fucking way!

He had no shot, and clearly didn't want to get within range of Jacko's fearsome golok, even if it was currently waving impotently in the air. Then the man grappling with Jacko swung him around and let go of his arm, sending him wide of their embrace like a clumsy dance partner.

The guy with the pistol had a line of sight now. Gabriel had to act fast before he shot Jacko.

'Hey! Arsehole!' Gabriel shouted.

The second man turned, gun up but pointing wide, only to find himself being rushed by Gabriel, his own, unimpeded golok already completing its backswing.

The guard brought his arm round and started firing. Gabriel

penetrated the field of red-hot bullets spitting out from the pistol's muzzle in a cloud of red-hot gases and brought his golok down on the guy's right arm. The knife's designers were reckoning with tough sugar cane stems, easily a match for human bones. The heavy steel blade sheared straight through radius and ulna without slowing. The disembodied hand, still clutching the pistol flopped to the ground, as its owner screamed, holding the spurting stump aloft and painting great looping scrawls of scarlet over the whitewashed ceiling.

His scream ended in an abrupt cough as Gabriel swung the golok in a fast, backhand swipe aimed at his neck.

The blade juddered in Gabriel's fist as it bit into muscle and tendons.

He felt the crack as it severed the spine before it continued on its deadly journey, its speed unabated, emerging on the other side in a welter of blood and gore.

The guard's head spun, eyes wide yet unseeing, his lips forming a rounded O at the precise moment Gabriel decapitated him. It hit a coffee table, smashing the glass top and falling through the empty frame before coming to rest staring sightlessly at the ceiling, blood pooling beneath it.

56

Odette swung the improvised sword as hard as she could, aiming up so the business end would connect with Jean's thick skull right over that white scar above his left ear.

But the blade whistled through empty air before rebounding off the door jamb with a resounding clunk that sent an electric pulse shooting up and down her arm.

It wasn't Jean. It was Ali. And the shortarsed little bastard had cheated death by virtue of his lack of height. He whirled round, eyes wide, as somewhere else in the house shots rang out.

'What the fuck?'

Odette swung again, aiming lower this time, hoping desperately to hit him somewhere important. But she'd lost the element of surprise and Ali jumped back, out of range.

Did he have his gun? He'd shown it to her that first day when they'd stowed her in the boot of their car. A big semi-auto. A Glock maybe? It looked bigger and badder than the pieces the neighbourhood guys carried. More like a cop gun. But she wasn't going to wait around while he pulled it out the back of his waistband.

She shifted the grip of her left hand, moving it halfway up the bare metal blade. Using it more like a stabbing weapon, she lunged towards Ali's midsection. But he was on the move. Backing up and yelling. She jabbed at his face and the W-shaped tip caught in his right cheek, opening a big, bloody flap of flesh that flopped down over his jaw, exposing blood-streaked teeth inside his face. Shit, it looked ugly.

Ali screamed and clapped a hand over the rent in his cheek. It gave her another chance. She swung at him and as he dodged the incoming blow, which would surely have taken a good-sized chunk out of what remained of his face, he stumbled and tripped over the little table they'd given her to eat off.

His head hit the tiled floor with a big old clonk and his eye rolled upwards in its socket for a second. In the cartoons she and Kéké liked to watch on a Saturday morning, passing a joint between them as they giggled, blue birds would be circling Ali's head as his eye boinged around trying to get focused.

Odette raised the sword high over her head, holding the cloth-wrapped hilt in both hands and brought it down, fast, aiming for the centre of Ali's forehead.

At the last moment, he rolled sideways with a groan and the sword banged off the tiles, cracking one into a crazy star shape, sending sharp little fragments of clay spinning up. One caught her in the mouth. She tasted blood. Spat.

He was lying on his side, reaching behind him. The gun! It was there but it had snagged in his trousers. The more he yanked, the tighter it got. It was caught in a belt loop. She couldn't let him draw it. That'd be game over. For sure. She took a huge step towards him, preparing a backswing as she went, and then, like a champion golfer, swung down and through the ball.

The sound as the sword bashed his skull in made her retch. A wet crunch with a sort of soggy bit in the middle. Like when she dropped Mum's tagine full of lamb and apricot stew. Ali made this funny sort of sound. Like half crying and half-choking. She hit him again. Now stuff came out that looked quite a lot like her mum's special stew. Ali lay still, blood coming out of his head like a waterfall and spreading in a giant pool all over the floor. Litres of it!

No time to marvel over it. She had to escape. But first she wanted that shooter. She bent down and almost sicked up again as the stink of all the blood and brains went up her nose. She breathed through her mouth and pulled hard on the butt of the pistol. The belt loop gave with a brief ripping sound and now she held the gun in her hand. It was heavier than she expected. Almost as heavy as her sword.

Gun in her right hand, sword in her left, she turned to go.

And ran straight into Bashar.

Too surprised to move, Odette stood rooted to the spot.

Bashar backhanded her across the mouth with such force it loosened a tooth. She spat it out, along with a spray of blood. Before she had even time to think, he twisted her right wrist over, forcing her to go with it or have it broken. The gun fell from her hand and he kicked it into a corner. She tried to swing the sword but it had no power and banged harmlessly off his thigh.

Bashar grabbed the sword and yanked it out of her hand. He flung it away from him, sending it flying through the air before embedding itself, point-first into the wall.

That's when he saw Ali, face up in a pool of gore, half his face plastered to his chin with his own blood.

He grabbed her by the chin and twisted her face up to meet his.

'You killed my brother, you little bitch. You'll pay for that.'

Terror had her by the throat and was squeezing her lungs so even breathing was an effort. But she still had a spark of her old defiance left.

'W-won't your customer be angry about that?'

He slapped her, hard, rattling her remaining teeth, and dragged her away.

'He'll still get what he paid for.'

Odette kicked out at Bashar as he dragged her out a side door towards a waiting Jeep. She caught him on the inside of his knee. A pretty good shot. But the violence of his response shocked her.

He turned, grabbed a handful of hair and pulled her head back so hard she felt something go wrong inside her throat. He drew a knife and pressed it hard against her neck. She felt the edge prickle on her skin. Tried not to imagine the skin getting sliced open and all her arteries getting cut through.

He pushed his face into hers. She smelled aniseed on his breath.

'One more move and I'll cut your head off. The buyer can fuck your corpse for all I care.'

He meant it, she could see that. Her bravado left her and all of a sudden she felt very small, and very helpless.

'I'm sorry,' she whimpered.

He released her hair and resumed towing her towards the Jeep. She looked behind her. Two men lay on the ground in massive puddles of blood. They were dead. But who killed them?

A flicker of movement over by the side of the house. A woman appeared. Dark hair tied back. Combat gear. Proper street. A machete in her hand. One of Bashar's crew? Hardly. She'd heard the way Ali and Bashar talked about women. What they were good for. What you could do to them. How you dealt with them when you had no more use for them.

The woman raised a finger to her lips.

57

After decapitating the first guard, Gabriel whirled round, ready to help Jacko.

He was face to face with the remaining guard, their teeth bared like feral animals locked in a fight to the death. The revolver was trapped between their bodies, which twisted and turned in grotesque parody of a dance.

Gabriel raised his hunting knife and timed his strike for the next time the guard had his back to him. Two sharp stabs over his kidneys and a third high on the left side of his back, the blade turned sideways, the better to slip between two ribs and puncture his heart.

The bang as the revolver discharged the sixth and final round in its chamber was muffled by the pressure of the two men's bodies. A flesh and blood suppressor.

The guard grunted in surprise and fell backwards. Gabriel leapt back, yanking his knife free and dodging the jet of blood. In the dead guard's outflung right hand, the revolver emitted a curling wisp of smoke which eddied upwards and melted into the pungent blue-grey cloud already filling the room.

'Come on, Jacko,' he said, turning to go. 'We need to find Odette.'

He was halfway to the door when he became aware Jacko wasn't with him. Frowning, he turned, about to shout at Jacko to get his shit together.

Jacko was leaning against a sofa, his hands clasped over his belly. A patch of red was spreading out across his shirt from beneath the spot where his fingers were interlaced.

'Lucky last shot, boss,' he groaned. 'Like in those films where you always hope it's the bad guy who took the bullet. Only it's not.'

He toppled sideways, rolled over the arm of the sofa and ended up sprawled along the cushions, one leg hooked over the arm, the other dangling towards the floor. His hands came free and he moaned. The front of his shirt surged with more blood: the fabric shone wetly where the sun streaming in through the uncurtained window hit it.

Gabriel rushed back to him and knelt beside the sofa. He grabbed a decorative throw and wadded it into a fat square. Pushed it down over the wound and grabbed Jacko's hands.

'Press down on it, mate. Maintain as much pressure as you can bear. I'll see if they have a first aid kit.'

Jacko shook his head.

'Fuck that! I'm gutshot, boss. We both know what that means. Just find Odette, yes? I'm good here. I'll maintain the pressure, you find her. That's why we're here.'

Gabriel looked down. Stomach wounds were bad. But not fatal. Not always. If you got a decent trauma surgeon, and the bullet hadn't hit anything vital like one of the big internal arteries, there was always a chance. And Jacko was right, they had to find Odette. To be this close and then to let the Soltanis escape once more? It was unthinkable. But so was leaving a wounded comrade. That was drilled into you. No man left behind.

He had to decide. *Think, Wolfe, think!*

Tara ran into the room.

'BB! It's Bashar, he's got Odette. He's armed but I disabled the Jeep he's got her in. Come on!'

'Jacko took a bullet.'

'I'm fine!' Jacko said. He spoke over the top of Gabriel's head. Addressing Tara directly. 'Tell him, Tara. Get Odette. It's all that matters.'

Tara took three quick steps to the sofa and laid a hand on Gabriel's shoulder.

'He's right. Odette needs us now. Leave him.' Then, to Jacko. 'Hold on. We'll come back once we have Odette.'

Then she grabbed Gabriel's arm and lifted him bodily to his feet. Gabriel made his choice.

'Come on, then.'

They left Jacko and ran out of the house.

Gabriel readied his knives. They had to be in time to save Odette or it had all been for nothing.

58

What had the woman meant by putting her finger to her lips?

Was she there to rescue Odette? Why else? She didn't look like she was local. In fact, she didn't look like anyone Odette had ever seen before. Like, maybe she was a quarter-Chinese or something.

Bashar had his gun in his lap, pointing right at her. She knew better than to try anything. She'd just offed his brother. No way was he going to go easy on her if she tried anything.

Ali was a bully and she'd met his kind before. Yes, he enjoyed dishing out punishment, but he was basically your ten-for-a-euro thug. But Bashar? He was a different animal. There was a coldness in his eyes. Like when he looked at you, he wasn't seeing a person, just an object.

And right now, it was only her status as a valuable object that was keeping her from taking a bullet to the belly. He'd dump her in the forest and let the wild animals dispose of her body like spoiled meat.

But as he jammed the key in the ignition and twisted it violently, she got an inkling of what the woman had meant with that shushing gesture.

'Come on, you sonofabitch!' he said, switching the key off and then twisting it even harder.

The engine up front made this coughing, whining sound, like a moaning grumble on repeat. *I can't star-ar-ar-art! I can't star-ar-ar-art! Why you keep hurtin' me like that, man? Can't you see I ain't gonna star-ar-ar-ar-art?'*

Odette got it, then. The woman had fucked with the starter, or the fuel pipe, or taken out the spark plugs. She herself had never learned how, but Kéké knew all about cars. How to hotwire them. How to fiddle with them so they'd never start. How to break into them and boost the stereo or whatever goods some wealthy dipshit had left on the passenger seat.

It took Bashar longer to realise. But finally he slammed the heel of his hand down on the steering wheel.

'Fuck!' He grabbed her left wrist and dragged her bodily across the transmission hump and out of his door, scraping her hip painfully across the rough-edged metal. 'Come on. And don't mess me about or I'll take you into the jungle and do what your buyer should be doing to you. Then I'll gut you and leave you for the ants.'

Odette winced as her knees dragged over the door sill and she found herself scrambling for balance behind Bashar as he ran for a shed at the back of the yard.

He threw her inside and for a terrifying moment she thought he'd decided to rape her after all. But he ripped a grey tarpaulin off a dark shape. A motorbike.

Odette wasn't into bikes, but Kéké's brother Soufi had one of these. A Yamaha Ténéré with that cool blue and yellow paintjob. Built for the Paris-Dakar rally. Knobbly tyres, raised suspension, bash plate under the engine and a little plastic windscreen. Probably brilliant for tooling around the island, going off-road in the jungle, or racing along the beach at night.

For a moment she forgot her predicament: thinking of how much fun it would be to 'borrow' Soufi's Yamaha and for her and Kéké to fly around the Paris streets at three in the morning.

Maybe do a circuit of the Périph, or down the Left Bank once all the tourists had gone back to their hotels.

Her fleeting daydream was interrupted. Bashar lifted her bodily and dumped her astride the bike so her groin banged painfully against the petrol tank. He swung a leg over the saddle behind her, turned the key and thumbed the start button. No whiny protest from this engine. It coughed into life and settled into a steady burbling idle. He kicked the gear lever down and twisted the throttle. The bike leapt forwards. It would have wheelied but for Odette's weight over the tank.

They burst out into the yard straight into the path of the woman and a man she'd never seen before. Both in camo, both carrying these fuckoff machetes, had to be forty centimetres long at least. The man shouted something at the woman and they split up, the machetes cocked. Bashar leaned the bike over and opened the throttle wide, sticking his left foot down and sending the bike into a sliding doughnut that threw up a massive cloud of grit and dust into their faces.

He roared off again, heading for the gates. Odette had just enough time to glance down at one of the dead guards, lying face-down in a blackening lake of blood buzzing with hundreds of flies. She caught a whiff of it as they blew past, this sort of disgusting, metallic stink that was like licking rust.

Then they were through the gates and onto the road. Bashar accelerated hard, changing up through the gears. Odette's eyes filled with water as the wind scoured her eyeballs. She squeezed them shut but that made her feel sick, so she squinted through half-closed lids.

Where the fuck was he taking her?

59

Tara snatched up one of the guards' AKs and brought it to her shoulder.

Seeing her take aim at the fleeing bike, Gabriel yelled at her.

'Don't! He's got Odette. Shit! Where's he taking her?'

'He's going to try to get her off the island. A boat maybe?'

'Christ, I don't know, Tar.'

He turned round, surveyed the scene of their incursion. Two dead bodies. Spent shell casings littering the ground. A Jeep. Thank Christ! He pointed.

'We'll take that. Follow them. I don't care how many cops they've bought off. We can stop them.'

Tara looked stricken.

'Not in that, BB. I disabled it. It's why Bashar left on the bike.'

Panic gripped Gabriel then. They'd got within shouting distance of Odette and now Bashar had her again and they had no idea where he was taking her and no way to follow him. Unless.

He ran back to the house and in through the front door. The smell of blood and burnt propellant was everywhere. That old, old stink of battlefields since the Boer War.

Jacko was lying on the sofa. His eyes were closed, but his hands were still clamped over his belly. Gabriel checked his pulse. It was weak, and thready, but it was there.

He turned away and knelt beside the guard he'd stabbed. Rolled him onto his front and dug two fingers into the soft place under his jaw. He, too, had a pulse. Gabriel slapped him hard across the face. Again. Again.

He bent over him and yelled into his face.

'Hey! Wake up, you bastard, I need you. Wake up!'

Nothing.

Gabriel grabbed his shoulders and raised his torso off the ground. Shook him hard like a rag doll.

'I said, wake the fuck UP!'

The guard's eyelids fluttered open. His eyes rolled around in their sockets. He managed to focus on Gabriel.

Gabriel laid him down again, gently this time.

'Help me … please,' the guard whispered.

'I will. But you have to tell me where Bashar has taken the girl.'

The guard swallowed, wincing with the effort. He ran his tongue over his cracked lips.

'There's a landing strip about a kilometre from here. Head up the road all the way,' he paused, coughed, spraying a fine mist of blood into Gabriel's face, 'to the end. That's the strip. They've got a plane up there.'

'We need wheels. Is there anything apart from the Jeep and the bike Bashar took?'

The guard coughed again. More blood. Nodded.

'The shed. Another … bike. Ali and … Bashar like to go … off-roading.'

Gabriel stood. Looked around. Saw an old-fashioned telephone, green with the separate handpiece and base unit connected by a curly wire.

He strode across the smashed-up sitting room and lifted the receiver, placed it against his ear. He heard the steady burr of a working line.

Dialled the emergency number: 112. It was answered on the first ring. Either they were well-staffed or they didn't get many emergencies.

'*Urgence. De quel service avez-vous besoin?*'

The standard question from Martinique to Manhattan, Manchester to Montmartre. 'Emergency. Which service do you require?' Gabriel rattled off the bare essentials in rapid-fire French.

'Ambulance. Two casualties. One shot, one stabbed. Both bleeding heavily. The big yellow house at the top of Rue Victor Hugo. They don't have much time. Please hurry.'

He hung up as the operator was telling him to stay on the line.

He turned but Tara had already gone. He rushed out of the house and over to the shed. She was inside, a crumpled tarp lying on the floor beside another, already astride a Honda Africa Twin, its tall front forks signalling its status as an off-roader.

'Get on,' she shouted.

He climbed up behind her and she immediately released the clutch, screeched out of the shed and through the gates. She leaned the bike hard over into the turn, sticking her left foot down and barely slowing before opening up the throttle and sending the big bike hurtling along the road after Bashar Soltani.

The wind set the sugar cane knife flapping in its crude sling, banging against Gabriel's thigh, hopping about like a thing possessed. It had done so much damage already today maybe it had got a taste for blood. The last thing he wanted was to arrive at the landing strip bleeding from his femoral artery. He took one hand off the seat rail to steady it.

Tara took a left-hand bend at speed, throwing the bike over and almost unseating Gabriel. Keeping his hand on the knife was unbalancing him. He switched his other hand from the seat rail to Tara's waist, leaning forward and resting his forehead against her back. That was better. Now they were acting in concert, a single centre of gravity rather than two moving independently of each other.

The bend snaked into another and Tara expertly threaded the

big bike through them, taking a line that minimised the need to throw it left and right. Eventually the road straightened and she changed up through the gears again.

The speedo was nudging ninety, wind blasting past Gabriel's ears. He felt, rather than heard, Tara's sharply indrawn breath. Over her shoulder he saw a cat-sized animal ambling across the road in front of them. *Rat* was his initial thought. The creature had brownish grey fur, a long pointed snout, huge, black ears like a bat's and a brushy tail like a fox's. As it detected the sound of the onrushing bike and stopped dead, turning to regard them with cross-looking black eyes.

'Oh, shiiiit!' Tara screamed as she flicked the bike left. Gabriel prayed the—*manicou*, his brain supplied—would have the good sense to remain perfectly still. He caught a blur of tiger-striped tawny fur on its left flank as Tara blew past at eighty-five.

Surely they couldn't be far from the landing strip now? The guard had said a kilometre and at the speed Tara was riding it ought to be upon them any second now.

They crested a rise and Tara jammed the brakes on. The bike roared off the roughly tarmacked road and onto a rumbling patch of dried grass. A small, white plane was standing at the far end of the landing strip. Gabriel estimated the distance at around seven hundred metres. The wind was behind the plane. Not ideal for a take-off, but in the position Bashar found himself, beggars couldn't be choosers.

The sound of the plane's single engine floated across the landing strip towards him. As Gabriel dismounted, the note increased in pitch. He squinted against the sun. The plane was growing larger in his vision. Bashar was taking off. How long did a light plane need to get airborne? There were rules about clearing obstacles, too. Time was, Gabriel had them memorised for half a dozen of the most common scenarios. But that was then. This was now.

What options did they have? They could ride straight at the plane, force Bashar to turn aside and career into the thick jungle that fringed the landing strip.

But he doubted Bashar had lost a game of chicken in his life. In his shoes, Gabriel would just open the throttle wide, brace his elbows and grit his teeth. Relying on the fact very few people, if any, would willingly ride a motorbike into the whirling propeller of an oncoming plane. Not unless they'd always harboured a secret desire to experience life – briefly – as a hamburger.

Could Tara race past the plane, U-turn and ride alongside while Gabriel leapt from bike to plane? Clamber along the wing and break into the cockpit using his golok? He dismissed it instantly. *Great a grip, man. This is real life not a* Mission Impossible *film!*

Then what? He tried to clear his head. Time was running short. The plane was looming larger. The engine note was louder. Gaining strength and still rising in pitch. He could just make out the shape in the cockpit. Bashar Soltani. Not his features, but Gabriel knew he'd be grinning triumphantly.

His hand went to the hilt of the golok. Wishing it was just him and Bashar alone on this short-cropped improvised airfield in the middle of the jungle. And then he saw it. The only thing that would work.

'Ride straight for him!' he screamed into Tara's ear. 'When I thump your shoulder, drop the bike.'

She didn't question him. Just nodded, dropped the clutch, and roared off down the landing strip towards the plane.

Four hundred metres. The noise of the plane's engine was a steady drone now, fighting to compete with the bike's screaming engine and bellowing exhausts.

Three fifty. Gabriel loosed the golok from its cord sling and gripped it tight.

Three. He whacked Tara's left shoulder with his free hand. She slammed the brakes on, favouring the rear. At the same time she leaned the bike over and sent the back wheel past the gripping point. The bike slid over, dumping Gabriel onto his arse. He straightened his back and braced, sliding to a stop just two hundred metres from the plane, which was gathering speed.

Tara brought the sliding bike to a controlled stop, still astride the juddering red beast, which she finally let go and stepped clear of.

He could see the flaps working as Bashar prepared to get airborne. A factor in take-off calculations floated back to him out of the noise and stink of burnt aviation fuel drifting towards him.

Time to clear a fifty-foot high obstacle?

In contrast to a tree, low building or communications mast, Gabriel stood five feet ten in his bare feet. Bashar could pull back on the stick and clear him at almost any time.

Gabriel jumped to his feet and turned at an angle to the plane. He could see Bashar clearly now, through the blurred white circle of the propeller. He wasn't grinning at all. His mouth was a grim line.

Gabriel hefted the golok and brought it back over his shoulder.

The plane was a hundred metres away now. The noise from the engine was deafening.

Gabriel started running towards the plane.

Bashar's mouth opened wide. He was shouting.

Fifty metres.

Forty.

Bashar was screaming and leaning back. Pulling back on the stick with every sinew. Desperate to take off and clear the obstacle standing between him and freedom. Mowing Gabriel down might take him out of the equation, but the collision would damage the prop and at the very least, necessitate a second take-off attempt.

Twenty.

Gabriel stopped, cocked his arm and hurled the golok straight at the plane.

He flung himself to the ground as the heavy bladed knife flew end over end before smashing into the spinning propeller with a sound like a spanner falling into a waste disposal.

A loud bang split the air. Razor-edged shards of metal whirred overhead. Metallic screeching deafened him and then the rear right-hand wheel crushed the grass just a hand's breadth from Gabriel's head. The plane slewed violently left, then right, and then swung over in a hopping motion that drove the right wing tip hard into the ground. The plane catapulted skywards turning over and over before landing on its tripod of wheels again, one wing hanging broken towards the ground like a bird that had collided with a window.

Gabriel was on his feet in seconds, sprinting towards the plane. Odette was in there. Was she harmed? Was she *alive*?

60

Gabriel wrenched the cockpit door open.

Bashar Soltani had vanished. The control column was smeared with blood. A half-metre-long shard of propeller was stuck through the pilot's seat. But it was clean. No blood on the grimy white leather either.

And no sign of Odette.

She had to be in the back.

He clambered in and hauled himself through the narrow gap between the two seats up front.

And stopped dead.

Bashar Soltani, his lip split and spilling blood down through his black beard was leering at him from behind a terrified-looking young girl.

He'd found Odette.

But she wasn't out of danger yet.

His left hand clamped around Odette's forehead, Bashar held a narrow-bladed knife in his right hand and he was pressing its razor edge into the skin of her neck.

'That's far enough,' Bashar said.

Gabriel heard a bubbling sound beneath the threatening tone.

He hoped Bashar had broken a rib in the crash. Envisioned a sharp-ended spur of bone puncturing a lung. Broken and torn capillaries filling the little pink air sacs, one by one, drowning him in his own blood.

'I just want the girl,' Gabriel said.

'You can have her. But I'm leaving.'

'Not in this, you're not.'

Bashar scowled. Heaved in a breath and winced.

'Obviously not!'

Gabriel shifted his position, trying to get within reach of Odette, who was staring at him with pleading eyes, tears streaking down through the grime and blood on her face. Nothing serious, but she'd sustained a laceration to her forehead that would need stitching.

Bashar pulled Odette's head back, exposing her throat. He lifted his right elbow and tightened his grip on the knife.

'Not another millimetre,' he husked, the bubbling reduced to a whisper. 'Try anything and I'll slice her open. You'll try to save her and you'll fail. Did you really follow us all the way from the Eighteenth to Martinique to leave with nothing but a blood-soaked shirt to show for it?'

Gabriel held his hands up.

'I just want the girl. That's all. You can disappear. I won't come after you. I promise.'

Bashar sneered.

'You promise? I wonder if you can imagine how many times I've had men and women promise me things. "I promise I'll tell you everything. Just don't hurt my child." "I promise I'll keep my mouth shut. Just let me go." "I promise I'll give you names, if you'll just stop." And you know what? They were right. They *did* tell me everything. They *did* keep their mouths shut. They *did* give me names. But not because they promised. Because I *made* them. Just like I'm going to make you now. Get out.'

'What?'

'Get out of the plane. Stand where I can see you through the windscreen. I'll take the girl to the edge of the jungle and then I'll release her.'

It was a cunning ploy. Gabriel was out of options. He knew the kind of man he was facing. He knew the kind of job he'd done in Syria before going into business with Ali. But he had to keep negotiating.

'What's to stop you killing her and disappearing anyway?'

'There are two of you. You have my brother's bike whereas I'll be on foot.' He frowned. 'In fact, I have another condition. Get out of the plane, stand where I can see you and disable the bike. Slash the tyres, cut the fuel lines. Then we go back to Plan A.'

'Please,' the girl whimpered, wriggling a little in his grasp and stretching her right hand down by her side. 'I just want to go home to my mama and papa.'

Bashar sneered again.

'You see. Little Odette here wants to go home. You have the power to make that happen. You can even tell her parents their daughter still has her cherry intact. Though how long that will last, well, who knows. I mean, it's not as if—'

His eyes bulged and his mouth stretched wide. He screamed: an unnaturally high-pitched animalistic sound. Odette elbowed him in the face and sprang out of his grasp, over the seats and past Gabriel, leaping from the cockpit.

Gabriel looked down at the front of Bashar's trousers, following the man's own eyeline. A thin, white strip of metal edged in silver protruded from his crotch. Blood darkened the fabric then breached the surface and began running down his legs. Still howling that unearthly animal sound, Bashar looked down, horror etched across his features, at the fragment of shattered propeller Odette had just stabbed down into his genitals.

Gabriel whipped round to his right and dragged the larger shard of metal from the seat back beside him. He gripped it in both hands, ignoring the pain as the sharp edges dug into his palms, and drove it down into the centre of Bashar's chest.

Bashar's eyes widened until the whites were visible all the way round those ink-dark irises. His lips stretched over his teeth and then blood surged from his mouth, overrunning his lower lip. It was bright red and frothy. He died with a long bubbling exhale, hands flailing at the deadly length of metal that had pierced his heart.

Gabriel climbed out of the cockpit.

Tara was comforting Odette, who was curled inside her arms and sobbing uncontrollably. In the few seconds it had taken Gabriel to leave the aircraft, Odette Diallo had transformed from a courageous, resourceful prisoner back into the condition she should never have been forced to leave.

A young girl from a beautiful if tough neighbourhood, enjoying life on her own terms, before being snatched from the streets she knew so well and turned into something to be bought and sold by evil men.

'Take her back to the guesthouse,' Gabriel said. 'I'll walk.'

Tara lifted her chin to indicate the wreckage of the plane.

'What about all this? And the mess at their house?'

'The police can take care of it. Now their paymasters are dead they'll have to act like real cops for a change.'

'We need to check on Jacko, too.'

Gabriel nodded. Hoped their friend was OK. How realistic was it, though? A heroin addict with a gunshot wound to the belly?'

'Just be ready for bad news, that's all.'

Tara mounted the bike and Gabriel helped Odette clamber up behind her. Without being told she wrapped her arms tightly around Tara's midriff and laid her cheek flat against Tara's back.

Tara started the bike and toed it into first.

Odette looked at Gabriel.

'*Merci.*'

Tara twisted the throttle and gentled the bike back up the landing strip towards the road.

61

They reunited at the guesthouse and got cleaned up and changed. Odette was tall for her age and Tara found her some clothes from her suitcase that fitted.

'Can I call my mum?' she asked once she'd reappeared, wearing loose linen trousers and a simple white top.

'Of course, my love!' Tara said. 'Here, use my phone.'

Gabriel watched as Odette tapped in a number and held the phone to her ear. They locked eyes and she smiled nervously, biting her lower lip. He could make out the ringing at the other end of the line.

Then Odette's eyes widened and her smile transformed into one of genuine joy.

'Mum! It's me! I'm safe.'

She nodded and grinned, before tears sprang from her eyes.

Gabriel smiled at her as he listened to the screams of joy emanating from Tara's phone.

They talked for ten minutes, Odette reassuring her mother that she was unharmed, and that, in coded language Gabriel still understood, the Soltanis hadn't violated her. Eventually, after a protracted and tearful goodbye, she handed the phone back to Tara with an eyeroll.

'Mum's such a drama queen!'

* * *

Tara wanted to keep Odette at the guesthouse while Gabriel drove down to Fort de France to ask about Jacko, but Odette had insisted they stick together. She sat next to Tara in the back seat of the hire car, holding her hand and eventually, when the adrenaline had dissipated, falling asleep in her lap while Tara stroked her cheek.

The three of them made their way to the ER at University Hospital of Martinique. They entered the busy department reception. Tara booked Odette in to have her cheek looked at. While Tara and Odette took seats in one of the rows, Gabriel approached the reception desk on his own.

'A friend of ours was brought in here a couple of hours ago. He was shot. His name is Jacko Blake. He's English. He,' Gabriel hesitated, 'he may not have given that name. He's been living on the streets for a while. In Paris.'

If the unusual story fazed the nurse on duty, she was too professional to give any sign of her confusion. She smiled up at Gabriel from behind the desk and then bent to her keyboard.

'Yes,' she said, in English. 'Two men were admitted ninety minutes ago. Neither was conscious. Both very badly injured. We have them down as Patient A and Patient B. I'll call for a doctor to come and talk to you. Please, take a seat.'

Gabriel returned to Tara and Odette.

'Is he …' Tara began. She glanced down at Odette who was hugging her tightly, her head buried against Tara's chest, '… alive?' she whispered.

'I think so. They're paging a doctor.'

Ten minutes passed, during which Gabriel stared fixedly out of the window at a distant hill and tried to ignore the three people sitting together at the end of a row of seats. A redhead with freckles spattering the bridge of her nose and a copy of the Swedish newspaper *Aftonbladet* open on her lap; a black man in SAS dress uniform, his sand-coloured beret smoothed down rakishly over his right eye; and the woman who he'd recognise in the pitch-dark of a starless night just by her smell: lemon and sandalwood.

Footsteps close by.

'You are here about the Englishman?'

He turned.

A young female doctor in green scrubs, her head covered by a sweat-darkened scrub-cap printed with Lisa Simpson, came to a stop in front of him.

'That's right. His name's Jacko Blake.'

Gabriel didn't know why he told her that. It seemed important somehow to make sure they knew Jacko's name. 'Patient A' seemed more like a short step away from a toe-tag and a final resting place in a stainless steel fridge.

The doctor's eyes fell. And in that split-second movement, Gabriel knew. Jacko wouldn't be coming home with them. He'd given his life, or what was left of it, to help save a young girl he didn't even know from a degrading fate.

She raised her eyes and met Gabriel's pleading gaze.

'I am very sorry. Your friend passed fifteen minutes ago without regaining consciousness. He lost too much blood from his wound.'

Gabriel reached out a hand to support himself on a chairback. Tara placed her own over his and squeezed. The noise of the ER faded, replaced by a high-pitched whistle. He glanced over at the spot where Britta, Smudge and Eli were sitting. A fourth form flickered and sputtered in outline at the end of the row of seats. Fading in and out of view. His face was obscured by the oversized khaki greatcoat but it was all the information Gabriel needed to identify its wearer.

The doctor was still talking.

'Sir? Sir? Are you all right?'

'Sorry, doctor. It's just a lot to process, that's all.'

She nodded, her eyes sad.

'I understand, and I am sorry for your loss. I was saying, we did manage to save the Frenchman. Although he also lost a lot of blood he *did* regain consciousness. Did you want to see him?'

Gabriel frowned. Frenchman? The goon he'd spared in return for telling him where Bashar had taken Odette was definitely a local.

'You mean the Martinican?'

Her mouth quirked to one side.

'He is not from the island. He speaks very correct French. Actually he has a Parisian accent.'

Gabriel's pulse started racing.

'Can you take me to him, please?'

She nodded. 'This way, please. He is on a mild sedative and some strong painkillers, but he is conscious.'

* * *

The doctor left Gabriel at the door of the private room and he took a deep breath before pushing the handle down and entering. The guard he'd knifed had spoken fluent French, of course, like all Martinicans. But his accent was one hundred percent local. No way would an educated doctor, or for that matter, a cane cutter with minimal schooling, mistake him for a Parisian.

He flicked his eyes towards the bed, ready to be proved wrong. To see the dark-skinned guard lying there.

It was Jacko.

Gabriel's heart leapt. He grinned and stepped up to the bedside. Leaned over. Jacko's face was pale, and he had a nasal tube taped in place.

'Hey, Jacko, it's me. Gabriel. Can you hear me?'

Gabriel couldn't stop smiling. Of course the doctor would have taken Jacko for a Frenchman. His service in the French Foreign Legion and then years of living in Paris, ending up on the streets at that, had given him two things: a fluent command of the language and a Parisian accent. Given that assumption on the doctor's part, the only logical conclusion she could draw was that the dead guard was Gabriel's friend.

Jacko's eyes opened. He smiled dreamily up at Gabriel and opened his mouth. When he spoke, it was in French.

'Oh, hey, boss. Looks like I made it.'

'Looks like you did. You must be as tough as old boots in there, mate.'

'The bullet clipped my liver, but that's it. The rest's soft tissue damage.' He raised his eyes to the ceiling. 'I guess someone up there likes me. Did you find Odette?'

'We did. She's in the waiting room with Tara.'

'Good. Bashar?'

'Dead.'

'Also good.'

Jacko's eyes fluttered, then closed. Anxiously, Gabriel checked the monitor he was hooked up to. But Jacko's pulse was a steady seventy-five and the neon-green trace was spiking reassuringly across the little black screen. Blood pressure was high, but stable. He was going to be fine.

Gabriel left the room, closing the door softly behind him and went to find the doctor.

'Thank you for saving his life,' he said. 'It must have been a tricky operation.'

She nodded.

'In some ways, yes, it was miraculous. But the bullet went all the way through him. Our surgical team is one of the best in the Caribbean, too.'

'Well, please pass on my thanks to them.'

She frowned.

'But he is not your friend, no? You were enquiring about the Englishman?'

Gabriel started to explain and then changed his mind. The next few days were going to be complicated enough as it was.

'I'm just pleased you were able to save one of them.'

He turned to go but she stopped him with a hand laid gently on his elbow.

'The law requires us to notify the police of any injuries caused through violence. A stabbing? A gunshot wound? I'd say they qualified, wouldn't you?'

'Could it have been some kind of bizarre accident? They said they were going out hunting.'

She raised an eyebrow.

'Hunting? With a handgun? And what do you think they were hunting? The largest land mammals on Martinique are manicous. Not very good eating. Or perhaps they were after a matoutou? Do either of your friends suffer from arachnophobia?'

Gabriel knew when he was beaten. And the doctor fixing him with her gimlet gaze was savouring victory. Time to come clean. He took a breath.

'The girl we came in with? She's twelve years old. Her name is Odette Diallo. She was trafficked here by two Syrians. They were auctioning her off online. I don't need to tell you why do I?' The doctor shook her head. 'I came here with my … friends … to save her. There was a certain amount of fighting. Of force employed in self-defence. We won't leave the hospital. Call the police if you have to.'

She'd watched him closely as he outlined the reasons for their visit to Martinique. And for a long while she said nothing.

Finally she checked the notes she had on a clipboard.

'We do have to report these incidents. But this is a busy hospital. We are the largest French- and English-speaking university hospital in the Caribbean. We have sixteen hundred beds, over seven thousand staff, tens of thousands of patients. We are accredited by the Ministry of Health in Paris,' she said, with obvious pride. Then she nodded, as if confirming something she already knew, but was only now sharing with Gabriel. 'What I am trying to say is that means we must deal with a mountain of paperwork. And sadly, records – of admissions, for example – sometimes go astray. It can take days to find them. Sometimes longer. I am sure we will find the documents we need to report these two cases to the police. But as for when?' She held her hands wide and, with a conspiratorial look, and a tremendous Gallic shrug, said, 'Who can say?'

He looked into her eyes for a few seconds.

'Thank you.'

62

THREE DAYS LATER

The hospital buzzed with activity, but it lacked the hectic frazzled air of most hospitals Gabriel had been in. Nurses looked relaxed as they passed him in the corridors, doctors stood in huddles, chatting, orderlies and cleaners smiled at him with cheerful 'Good afternoon's.

He pressed the buzzer at the entrance to Jacko's ward and once admitted, went into the main area, nodded at a couple of the nurses he'd got to know and went into the side room where Jacko was sitting up, reading a French magazine.

'Hey, Jacko, how're you feeling? Have they said when you'll be well enough to travel?'

Jacko put the magazine down. He hauled himself upright in the bed, wincing slightly. But otherwise looking well.

'The doctors say I must be blessed,' he said with a smile. 'A centimetre to the left and it would have clipped the hepatic portal vein. Game over. I've never been religious, boss, but it's seriously got me thinking.'

Gabriel sat at the end of the bed.

'How about the withdrawal?' he murmured. 'Are you going to need help with that?'

Jacko shook his head. 'I told them everything. Like I said, I have this feeling I was given a second chance. They're helping me with that, too.'

'So should I book our flights back to Paris?'

Jacko looked away, out of the window, towards the distant hills, covered in dense green jungle.

'Yes. Three.'

'Three?'

'I'm not coming back. What's waiting for me in Paris? Rough sleeping, or a hostel where when you do sleep it's with one eye open? Back on the smack? Begging? Petty crime? I'll last a couple of years tops before they fish me out of the Seine.'

'So what are you going to do instead? Go to America? Back to the UK?'

Jacko smiled. Switched to French.

'*Je vais rester ici.*'

Gabriel thought about it. Martinique was French-speaking. Jacko spoke it fluently. Certainly well enough to fool a doctor. And plenty of islanders spoke English, too, thanks to the tourist trade.

'And you're a French citizen.'

Jacko nodded. Grinned.

'*Pour le sang versé.*'

Gabriel laughed.

'Well you certainly shed plenty of blood in Her service. I think the least She can do is permit a move to Martinique. What will you do for work?'

Jacko shrugged.

'I was thinking of applying for a job here. They always need people. I can cook, after a fashion. I can clean. I could wheel patients around, tend the gardens. Whatever they need.'

Gabriel nodded. It was a good plan. Maybe, like all plans, it would have to change once it made contact with reality, but Jacko was a resourceful guy. He'd be fine.

'I have to go. I need to get these flights sorted. We'll come back and say goodbye before we leave.'

'Nice one.'

* * *

Gabriel was back an hour later.

On hearing the news, Odette had insisted on being brought to the hospital to thank Jacko for helping free her. She'd been gaining in confidence day by day and had assumed a little of that Parisian cool that seemed to envelop the city's inhabitants from birth.

But when they went into Jacko's room, she reverted to a childlike innocence, climbing onto the bed and hugging Jacko fiercely.

'Thank you, Jacko. You saved me. I will never forget you. You'll be in my prayers.' She kissed him on the cheek then pulled a face. 'Ugh. Prickly. You need a shave!'

Tara said goodbye next, hugging Jacko, if not as tightly as Odette, then kissed him on the lips. A surprisingly long and, to Gabriel's eyes, passionate embrace.

'That's to keep you going until you find a nice Martinican woman to take care of you.'

Gabriel went last.

'I hope life here brings you peace, mate. Peace and good health. And yes,' he added, with a wink, 'the love of a good woman, too.'

A lump formed in his throat, then, and he had to look away.

63

From Orly Airport, they went directly to the Diallos' apartment.

Odette was bouncing around so much in the taxi's back seat, the driver scolded her over his shoulder.

'Blow me!' she said, but she was smiling, and he caught the look in her eye in the rear-view mirror and grinned back.

'Bit young for that kind of talk, aren't you?'

Gabriel caught Tara's eye. If the driver only knew how close Odette had come to the fate the Soltanis had arranged for her, he'd not be smiling. He paid the driver, added a tip in cash and all three got out into the stifling heat. Paris was hotter than Martinique and without the solace of a sea breeze to cool its heat-weary inhabitants.

Odette ran into the apartment building and was haring up the stairs before Gabriel and Tara had even reached the front door. They emerged onto the Diallos' floor to the sounds of a joyful family reunion. Marianne and Youssoo were standing in the

347

hallway, hugging Odette between them, and bestowing kisses on her cheeks and the top of her head. All three were crying and Gabriel signalled to Tara that they should hold back, just for a few more moments.

Eventually, the trio of Diallos broke apart and Marianne turned to Gabriel.

'You did it, Gabriel. You brought my baby home to me. And you, miss. Who are you?'

'Tara. I'm Gabriel's sister.'

Marianne hugged her tightly, kissing her three times on the cheeks, left-right-left.

'Then thank you, too. With all my heart, thank you.'

'There was another of us, too. A friend. Jacko.'

Marianne looked around.

'Then where is he? We need to thank him as well.'

Tara smiled.

'He's in Martinique. He's staying there.'

'Oh, my God, this is too much to take in. Come inside, come, come. We've prepared some food.'

Youssoo led them all inside the flat where the aroma of baked meats and a spicy pepper stew filled the air.

Over the next two hours, they consumed everything Marianne and Youssoo brought to the table, as Odette told the story of her capture and imprisonment. She glanced at Gabriel or Tara from time to time as she skated over what Gabriel could tell were unpleasant details. But she was unsparing for the most part and made sure her parents got the full picture of the climactic fight and chase that led to Ali and Bashar Soltanis' deaths and her own, eventual rescue.

Finally, it was time to leave.

Gabriel accepted Marianne's farewell embrace and a stern injunction to bring all his laundry to Automat Cavally, where she would provide her top-level service for free, forever.

Outside, Tara looked over at a car parked on the far side of the street. Her lips tightened, just for a second.

'Everything all right?' Gabriel asked.

'Absolutely!' she said with a bright smile. 'Let's get home, though. I'm tired. You drive.'

* * *

Tara opened some wine when they got back to the apartment. She sank into the embrace of a squashy leather sofa. Held her wine glass up.

'To us, BB. We did it.'

'To us.'

Gabriel drank. The wine hit his stomach and spread its warmth throughout his belly. For the first time since Sandrine had held Jacko's Fairbairn-Sykes to his throat he felt completely relaxed. They had done something good. No shades of grey. He, Tara and Jacko had achieved a one hundred percent, unalloyed win for the right team.

No innocents had lost their lives. No shady government type had popped up to inform him, slyly, that the mission he'd thought he was conducting was all a blind, and he was merely a useful idiot who'd removed a troublesome piece from the board in a game he only half-understood. They'd even helped Jacko find peace on a Caribbean island, far from the rough-edged life he'd been living in Paris. One that would surely have killed him within a few more years.

'I could get used to this, Tar,' he said.

'It's nice isn't it? Bloody should be for the price that wine merchant on Rue du Boccador charges,' she said with a grin. 'Lucky I can afford it.'

'Not the wine, though it's delicious, I agree. I meant helping people. Bringing Odette back to her mum and dad? That felt good.'

She sat up straighter, careful to keep her wine glass level, and looked right at him.

'It should, Gabriel! You did something unselfish. Nobody ordered you to. Nobody paid you to. You just did it because you knew it was the right thing.'

He frowned.

'Earlier, outside the Diallos' block, there was a car. You looked worried for a second. What was that? And don't tell me it was nothing. It's me, remember? BB. I know you. Maybe not as well as I ought to, as I'd like to. But well enough. We're flesh and blood, Tar. What's up?'

Tara sighed and placed her wine glass on the coffee table.

'The gossip is there's a new department in the state security apparatus.'

No need to identify the state. Gabriel knew she didn't mean the French. What had she been keeping from him?

'Go on.'

'It's called, you're going to love this, the Office for Family Reunification.'

'Nice.'

'Yeah. Really not. They're picking up ex-triad members all over the world and taking them back to China.'

'Jesus, Tar, why didn't you say anything?'

'You had enough on your plate, BB, that's why! You've been rebuilding *your* life, too. Working at the gym, making friends. I didn't want to worry you. And, you know, because you lost Britta and then Eli. I knew it would screw with your head if you were worried about losing me, too.'

'You think they're onto you?'

'I don't see how they can be. I mean look at me! I look completely different. No facial recognition software on the planet would match me to their records.'

'They won't just be relying on FRS, though, will they? They'll have intel, too. Informants, agents, media contacts, moles inside every government department from here to bloody Martinique.'

She went for a cockeyed, 'Dopey old me!' grin. 'Anyway, it's probably nothing. I'm just being paranoid.'

He grimaced. 'What's the old joke? "Just because I'm paranoid, doesn't mean they're not out to get me."'

She reached out for the bottle and refilled both their glasses.

'Forget it. I've got tripwires in place. If they seriously come looking, I'll have enough warning to bug out. Let's just enjoy the evening and,' she smiled brightly, 'this delicious if eye-wateringly expensive burgundy.'

Gabriel drank. Regarded his sister over the rim of his glass. Smiled at her.

Tara was right. Her layers of protection made the Soltanis' security arrangements look like kids guarding a treehouse.

He lay his head back against the cushions and started planning a lazy weekend.

He'd earned it.

EPILOGUE

Gabriel woke early the next morning.

He showered, shaved carefully, and dressed in a white T-shirt, navy chinos and trainers. Then he began the day he had planned with a short walk to buy fresh croissants.

The sun was shining, and the air smelled clean. The muggy heat that had blanketed Paris was gone. Displaced in the night by a cool, sweet-smelling breeze.

Gabriel stepped into the rush-hour bustle of Paris on a weekday morning. Avenue Montaigne was coming alive. The sales ladies opening the Dior boutique made minute adjustments to their coiffures. The equally sharply dressed men at the Ferrari dealership checked the time on ostentatious timepieces.

Parisians with the luxury of not needing to crowd onto the Metro to get to work thronged the streets. Some clutched paper bags from which the golden noses of baguettes poked, or drew pleasurably on pungent French cigarettes.

Others stopped to chat while their tiny dogs deposited their tiny turds onto the street.

Nodding 'Bonjour' to the few people he recognised, he strolled down the avenue to his favourite *boulangerie*, nestled shyly between a luxury leather goods boutique and a perfume shop. The queue was twenty deep, everyone enjoying, and commenting on, the change in climate.

He took his place behind a fortyish woman who was passing the time reading a paperback. *Crime and Punishment.*

'Good morning,' he said.

'Hi,' she said brightly. 'Going to be at least a ten-minute wait.'

'The croissants are worth it, though.'

She nodded. 'Totally.' Then she tilted her head on one side. 'You're British, right?'

'Is my accent that bad?'

Laughing, she switched to English.

'Not at all. Is mine? I go to conversation classes, but it's a work in progress.'

'American?'

'Yep.'

'Chicago?'

Her eyes widened.

'Milwaukee. But that's amazing. You pegged me as a Midwesterner from, what, ten words?'

He shrugged. 'I'm good with languages.'

'You must be.' She stuck out her hand. 'I'm Harper. Seabright.'

'Gabriel Wolfe,' he replied, shaking her hand, which was cool despite the heat. 'Your parents were fans of *To Kill a Mockingbird*?'

She rolled her eyes.

'I know, right? All my friends had popular-girl names, you know? Madison, Jessica, Ashley, Heather, stuff like that. I got Harper,' she added, pulling a goofy face that made Gabriel smile.

'It's a good name. I like it.' He gestured at her book. 'That's my favourite. I wore out my first copy. It literally fell to pieces in my hands one day.'

She laughed. And the sound, or maybe it was the fresher air and the bright sunlight bouncing off the shop windows, shifted something inside him. A lightening of his spirits. After everything that had happened over the past week, there was something refreshingly ordinary about standing in a bakery queue chatting to a stranger.

They continued talking, until it was Gabriel's turn to order at the counter. Presiding over the genial chaos from behind the patisserie-filled glass case was a briskly efficient woman in a white apron. Flanking her, two younger, prettier assistants a cynic would say had been hired to charm grumbling customers into just a *soupçon* more patience. All three women were red-faced and sweating. He bought his croissants and a couple of the thin baguettes Tara loved to slice lengthways and stuff with Bayonne ham and plenty of *Moutarde de Dijon*.

He stepped out of the shop to find Harper waiting for him on the queue-free side of the door.

'I don't suppose you'd like to grab a coffee some time and chat books?' Harper asked shyly. 'My friends don't really have time, and Parisian book groups are so snobby I refuse to join one.'

Gabriel hesitated. She was undeniably attractive. Auburn hair caught up in a messy bun. Large, dark eyes that sparkled with intelligence. Full, wide lips. But he'd been on his own since Eli. Yes, he'd slept with Pera that one time before leaving Honduras for good. But that seemed almost like a dream now. Could he start seeing somebody new? Wasn't that a betrayal?

A voice whispered between his ears. *It's not a* betrayal, *my honey. It's just coffee.*

He inhaled. Squashed down the flicker of anxiety in his belly.

'Sure. I'd like that.'

'Great! I thought for a moment you were going to turn me down. It's hard to make friends in this city although you seem to have managed,' she said, gesturing at the bulging paper bag of croissants and baguettes. 'Or are you going to eat those all by yourself?'

If she was fishing, it was elegantly done.

'I probably could, but some are for my sister, though she's probably still asleep. We share an apartment.'

'Lucky her. Sadly for *moi*, there's nobody at home waiting for me to bring them croissants.' She checked her watch, a real one, with hands, and frowned. 'Lord, I am *seriously* going to be late for my class. I'm sorry, Gabriel. How about tomorrow morning, though. Say ten?'

'That would be great. Where?'

'Do you know Gisèle's on Boulevard du Montparnasse?'

'Is that the one with all the plastic flowers inside and a unicorn's head in the window?'

'That's the one. Although I'm pretty sure the horn's made of straw.'

'Shame. But yes, I know it.'

'Cool. Hey! Give me your number. Just in case one of us is running late.'

They exchanged numbers and then Harper flicked him a wave and darted across the street, dodging a couple of vans, a food delivery rider and a flock of mopeds, laughing at the chorus of outraged shouts and horn-blasts her daring provoked.

Gabriel watched her disappear round a corner then started for home. He'd tell Tara about his coffee date with Harper. He could just imagine her face. Happy her big brother was even willing to spend half an hour in the company of a single woman.

He'd be sure to set her straight, though, if she started leaping to conclusions. It was no more than a chance encounter in the bakery queue. Maybe the start of a book club, that was all.

Five minutes later, he opened the door to the apartment and walked in.

'Tar? I have croissants from *Boulangerie Arlidge*. Come and get them while they're warm. Baguettes too. Your favourite: *ficelles*.'

Silence. He rolled his eyes. When Tara slept in, she really slept in.

He went into the sitting room. Glass crunched underfoot. He looked down, frowning. Hadn't they cleared away their wine glasses last night?

Shards of blue-green and red glass streaked with scarlet littered the carpet. This was no wine glass. It was the Murano fish from the bookshelf.

A tiny, ice-cold flame of anxiety flickered into life in his belly.

He put the bag of croissants down and looked around the room. A large oil painting hung askew above the fireplace, an L-shaped tear in the canvas in the upper-right corner. A chair lay on its side, one leg snapped clean off just beneath the seat, the exposed wood bright against the dark-brown varnish. His pulse picked up. He ignored it.

'Tar?' he called out. 'Tar? If you're playing a game it's not funny.'

The apartment was silent. He grabbed a butcher knife from the block in the kitchen and ran to her bedroom.

Her door was closed. He knocked loudly. No answer. He opened it and went in, knife held in front of him, ready to strike the assailant he felt sure was waiting there, yet still, some small, hopeful part of him was trying desperately to believe he would wake Tara and get an earful for his troubles.

The covers were on the floor by the wall. Too far from the bed. This was no sleeper roused from the depths by an urgent need to pee, kicking off the duvet in their hurry. This was the act of an interloper exposing their sleeping victim before striking. The bedside lamp lay on its side on the floor, the bulb broken.

Oh, Christ, what had happened here? Why even ask? he scolded himself. He knew. She'd been taken. And the awful, gut-freezing truth came at him like a guard dog off the leash. The Office for Family Reunification. A bland, faintly uplifting name that promised the complete opposite of what it delivered.

Tara had said she had tripwires in place. But clearly the OFR were adept at stepping over them.

He sat on the bed and pulled out his phone. Called her, heart hammering in his chest, mouth dry.

'Hi, this is Tara. Leave a message.'

He didn't bother. Tara was gone.

And he would have to find her.

READ ON FOR AN EXTRACT FROM
PURITY KILLS…

…the story of Gabriel's sister.

1

**1998 | A SMALL VILLAGE IN GUANGDONG
PROVINCE, CHINA**

The fish was a giant: Wei Mei had first seen it when her gang had been swimming in the river. An expanse of silver scales that flashed in the sun as it rolled over a few centimetres below the surface and dived for the bottom.

She planned to catch it and then sell it at the market. Think what she could do with the money someone would pay for it.

'You're twelve, Mei,' her best friend, Ping, had said when she'd shared her plan. 'You can't have a stall. The authorities won't permit it.'

'Who cares about the authorities? I'll do it anyway,' she said, folding her arms. 'By the time they find out, it'll be too late.'

Squatting by the edge of the slow-moving water, she pictured the fish snaking along the bottom looking for something tasty to eat.

'Come along, beast,' she murmured, eyes fixed on the softly rippling surface of the river. 'Come and get your dinner.'

So engrossed was she in the hunt that she failed to notice the older boy creeping up on her through the reeds and broad-leaved plants that thronged the bank.

Tan Hu was fifteen. A good head and shoulders taller than Mei and all of her friends except Beanpole. But Beanpole was too skinny to defend himself against the village bully.

Because that's what Tan Hu was. Actually, Wei Mei thought 'bully' wasn't strong enough to describe the kind of boy who would beat up little kids for fun. Throw sharp-edged stones at them when they were playing quietly in the dirt. Or steal their snacks right out of their hands and run off laughing as they cried.

Mei kept the line nice and taut against the current. Behind her, Tan Hu grinned as he manoeuvred into position. Keeping low, he slid a knife from a nylon sheath on his belt. As he watched her, he pressed the palm of his left hand against his groin, enjoying the hot, fluttering sensation it produced in the pit of his belly.

Mei blinked as a flash of sunlight bounced off the water. When she looked again, the tip of her fishing pole was dipping sharply.

With a cry of triumph – 'Got you!' – she jerked the rod up to set the hook in the beast's great bony-lipped mouth. Immediately the rod seemed to fight back, almost pulling free of her hands.

'Oh, no you don't!'

She heaved back and felt the fish resisting her, a surge of power like when you tried to lead a mule with a rope and it didn't feel like coming with you.

Straining every muscle, she levered the rod upright and was rewarded with a flash of silver as the fish broke the surface, rolling and thrashing in the dull green water.

She leaned backwards, and the combined strength of her arms, the bamboo pole and the heavy fishing line brought the beast curving and bucking towards the bank.

Leaning over and trying to avoid the gaping mouth with its double row of ugly, needle-pointed teeth, she stuck her thumb and fingers into its gill slits and clamped down hard. It was cold in there and slippery, but she squeezed tighter and readied herself to yank it out of the water.

She could already imagine what she'd shout at the weekly market.

'Come on, ladies and gents! Who wants this beautiful fish? One-hundred-and-fifty yuan and it's yours.'

She knew she'd have to haggle, but even a hundred would be a fortune.

Then another hand gripped the rod and pulled the giant fish closer. She whirled round, ready to thank whoever was helping her land the beast. And a cold tremor flashed through her.

Still holding the rod, Tan Hu swept his knife out in a wide arc and cut the line.

The fish folded itself double then disappeared back into the green-dark depths, showering the two children with water from its scimitar-like tail fin.

'What did you do that for, you idiot?' Mei shouted.

She punched Tan Hu in the face, drawing blood from his lower lip.

In response, he brought the knife up where she could see it.

'Do what I say or I'll cut you open like a fish belly,' he said. 'Take your clothes off.'

'No!'

He grinned; an oddly disjointed expression as if his lips had forgotten to tell his eyes something was funny.

'My friend here says you will.'

The knife was small, but the blade looked sharp. If she tried to take it off him, he'd probably stab her or give her a good cut. Mei wanted neither. Instead, she meekly said, 'OK, Hu.'

His eyes widened. 'Really?'

'Yes, really. Just turn around.'

'You'll run.'

'No I won't. Anyway, you can run faster than me, you know that,' she said, holding her hands wide. 'So what would be the point?'

He nodded. And, like the stupid brute he was, he did just that.

Mei launched herself at him, grabbed a handful of his thick, shaggy hair and pulled back hard. His head snapped back and he howled with pain. Then she dug her fingers into his throat, choking off the sound.

'Try that again and I'll come to your house at night and castrate you with your own knife. I mean it,' she muttered into his ear.

Then she shoved him, hard between the shoulder blades. With a cry, he pitched forwards into the swirling green water of the river they all called Little Mekong, even though the real one was way, way, *way* over to the west.

But as Tan Hu toppled in, Mei's foot slid in a patch of clay where the weeds had been torn away in the scuffle. She went in straight after him.

His head broke the surface a few seconds later. Ten metres downstream from where she was treading water.

'I'll kill you!' he screamed, spraying river water from his mouth.

'Try it!' Mei yelled back. 'Next time maybe I'll slit your belly open.'

He opened his mouth to shout something back but swallowed river water instead. Coughing, he went under again, only to reappear another twenty metres downstream, now facing in the direction of the current and striking out towards an overhanging tree branch.

Mei reached the bank easily: she was a strong swimmer. She hauled herself out and clambered to her feet, careful not to slide straight back in on the slippery red mud.

Laughing, she ran back the way she'd come, through bamboo and the pink-berried plants with long, sharp-pointed leaves that had earned them their nickname: Devil's Tongue.

Halfway back to the village she looked over her shoulder, just to check Tan Hu wasn't after her. Maybe he'd try it on again later, but she'd be ready for him this time. Probably she ought to take a knife from the kitchen just in case.

She looked forward again and crashed into Ping, who was running the other way.

Mei jarred her ribs as she tripped and fell onto the hard-packed red earth of the track. Ping stumbled, but stayed upright. Hurriedly, she pulled on Mei's wrists, dragging her to her feet.

'What is it?' Mei asked her friend as she rubbed her elbow. 'You look like a demon's chasing you.'

Ping's eyes were wide. 'There's a man at your house. He's got a gun! He was pointing it at your mum and shouting.'

Mei's heart was thumping in her chest. She'd forgotten all about the pain from the collision.

'What about? What was he shouting? Tell me!'

'You!'

'What do you mean, me?'

'He said she had to tell him where you were. He said he was taking you away. And he's wearing a suit!'

This was bad. Nobody from round here wore suits. The only people who had guns *and* suits were Party officials. Mei had seen them now and again when Mummy had taken her into Shenzhen. Mummy would delight in pointing them out.

'See those two over there? They're Party. Secret police, most likely. If they don't like you, you just disappear. Turn up three weeks later in a ditch outside the city limits with a bullet in your brain.'

At the time, Mei thought Mummy Rita was doing a poor job of frightening her. But one was actually here, in the village. And looking for her.

Mei took Ping by her narrow, bony shoulders.

'Listen, Ping. Listen to me really carefully,' she said. 'Go back to the village. Just act normal. If he asks you, say you haven't seen me.'

'Why? What are you going to do?'

'I'm going to get a better look at this guy without him seeing me.'

Ping's eyes widened.

'That's a really bad idea. What if he spots you?'

Mei grinned.

'He won't!'

With Ping gone, Mei turned off the track. She knew the woods round the village like her own skin. Every animal track, every fallen tree, every patch of boggy ground that would swallow you whole if you fell in.

She started working her way back to the village using every bit of her skill. She'd come out in a stand of bamboo just behind the house. Dense enough to hide in, but with enough light coming in between the thick green stems to spy on the house.

She wanted to get a good look at whoever was threatening her mum. Eventually he'd leave and then Mei would have a think about what to do afterwards. But, for now, she just needed to see him.

Reaching the house meant pushing through some dense patches of spiny shrubs. They had inch-long thorns hidden amongst gaudy orange flowers with black centres. It didn't seem fair that such pretty flowers concealed those evil little spikes.

By the time she reached the stand of bamboo, her arms, legs and face were scratched and bleeding. But that was fine. Scratches healed.

She peered through. At first she couldn't see either Mummy Rita or the Party man. Then she heard him. A deep, boomy voice riding over the top of Mummy's higher one.

'Where is she?'

'I told you already, Jian! I don't know. She's a naughty girl. Always running off. Never in school when she should be,' Mummy said, repeating the complaints she usually threw in Mei's direction. 'She spends every day by the river or in the forest. Why don't you look there?'

'Oh, I will. Maybe for now I'll just sit here. Bring me some jasmine tea.'

Mei frowned. Not at his rudeness. In her experience, men were usually rude to women. Party men, especially. But because Mummy Rita had called the man by his name. Jian.

That was weird. As far as Mei knew, the village headman was

the only Party official Mummy knew. And this wasn't him. And why did she sound cross with him and not frightened?

She decided it didn't matter. She'd ask Mummy later. What mattered was making sure the fat Party man with the gun didn't catch her.

And anyway, she had no idea what she might have done to attract the attention of the Party in the first place.

Sure, like Mummy said, she skipped school most days. But honestly, what was she going to do with all that stuff about fractions and minerals and the history of the People's Republic of China?

The stuff she really needed to know? How to fight off boys like Tan Hu? How to snap a chicken's neck? How to milk a goat or tell which berries in the forest were OK to eat? Those, she either knew already or could ask real people in the village, like the blacksmith or one of the farmers.

She took one last look at the man with his shiny silver gun and his slicked-back hair. *See you later, Mr Party Man!*

Something crackled in the dry grass behind her. Maybe a rat. Too loud for a mouse or one of the big purplish-black beetles that trundled around the place pushing balls of cow dung. She prepared to go.

The pincers that suddenly clamped on the back of her neck made her scream. A giant stag beetle had got her! She felt herself rising to a standing position without using her legs.

'Got you!' a man said from behind her.

With his fingers still digging into the soft flesh at the sides of her neck, the man marched Mei over to her house.

The fat man got to his feet, a broad smile on his face revealing flashing gold teeth. He put the gun away in a leather holster inside his suit jacket.

Mei was terrified. She started gabbling.

'Look, I don't know what I've done, OK? But I'm sorry. I love the Party. I love Chairman Mao. And all the ones in charge now. I know I've skipped school, but I can explain. Just, please don't hurt

1

my mum. I'm a disobedient girl. I never do what she says, it drives her mad, she can't control me. I'm—'

The torrent of phrases, most of which had come originally from Mummy Rita's own lips, dried as the fat man burst out laughing.

'Wait! You think I'm with the *Party*?'

He laughed harder, only stopping when a fit of coughing seized him. Bending double, hands flat on his wide thighs, he shook his head until the coughing stopped.

He pulled a red handkerchief from a pocket and wiped his streaming eyes.

'You hear that?' he said to the man gripping Mei's neck, 'She thinks we're with the Party!'

'Fat chance,' the man said, chuckling deep in his chest.

The first man cleared his throat and sighed out a big breath.

'Listen, Mei, I'm about as far from being a Party man as you can ever imagine,' he said. 'You won't remember me, but I've known you since you were a baby. I'm here to take you back to Hong Kong.'

'What?'

Mei couldn't believe what he was saying. Hong Kong? Why? And if he wasn't a Party man, what was he?

'Hong Kong,' he said. 'A place of opportunity, still, despite the handover.'

Mei had no idea what he was talking about. What handover? But she did know there was no way she was going to Hong Kong with him. She wasn't going *anywhere* with him.

She slapped at the man's hands around her neck.

'Get off me.'

Mei watched the fat man signal something with his eyes over her head. The other man let go of her neck.

'Do you need to get some things before we leave?' the fat man asked.

'I need to pee. Your bully-boy frightened me,' she said.

Fat man laughed again. 'Fine. But don't even think of running off. We'll only catch you.'

Mei shrugged. 'Who said I was going to run? Hong Kong sounds fun. And I hate it here anyway.'

Mummy Rita reappeared just as she said this. Mei watched her face crumple. Her lips trembled as she handed the small china cup of tea to the man she'd called Jian. Mei felt guilt wash through her. But she couldn't explain she'd only said it to get the fat man to relax.

'Fine,' he said. 'But be quick. We've got a long journey ahead of us.'

Mei nodded. She walked off around the side of the house. As soon as she was out of sight, she ran. She ran as fast as she'd ever run in her life.

She found Ping playing down by the stream that fed the Little Mekong.

'Ping!' she hissed. 'I have to go.'

'What? Where?'

'Shenzhen. That guy's not from the Party. I don't who he is, and I don't care. But he's not taking me to Hong Kong.'

Ping's lower lip trembled.

'You're coming back, though, right? When they've gone, I mean.'

Mei smiled. 'Of course, silly.' She had an idea. 'Look, if you really, really need to find me, leave a message somewhere only we know about.'

'But where?' Ping asked, crying properly now.

Mei looked up. Where would be a good place for a secret message? Mummy always took her to the big city on the bus. Yes! That was it.

'The bus station,' she said. 'Where the bus from here pulls in. Queue number seven. There's a stand selling *People's Daily*. All decorated with red-and-yellow banners. The hammer and sickle.'

Ping smiled tearily, wiping her snotty nose with the back of her hand.

'I know it. We went to Shenzhen last year. Dad bought a copy off the sales lady.'

'Put your message inside an empty drinks can and squash it

flat,' Mei said, 'then leave it at the back of the stand. I'll check every week.'

Ping nodded, gave an almighty sniff, then turned and ran back towards the village. Just before she disappeared out of sight, she turned and raised a hand in a farewell wave.

* * *

Three months passed. As did Mei's thirteenth birthday. Every week for her first month in Shenzhen, she checked round the back of the *People's Daily* stand at the bus station.

But soon after arriving, she fell in with a group of street kids and found she enjoyed the life. Stealing food from stalls, and wallets from head-swivelling tourists. Running from the cops if a daring raid caused too much commotion. Sleeping on the top floor of an unused carpark, warm in the humid night air of high summer.

Little by little, her memories of the village faded as the thrills of city living took hold of her.

2

With her practised thief's eye, Wei Mei spots the three rich kids
before Binyan does.

She picks out her mark. The one on the left, nearest the road.
She can hit him, snag his wallet, chuck an apology over her
shoulder – '*Sorry, mate, wasn't looking where I was going!*' – then escape
through the traffic.

He won't follow. His threads look too new, too fancy, too
damned expensive. No way he's going to risk a chase across nine
lanes of traffic. He might fall down and get his wuvvly wittle
blazer dirty and then what would Mummy and Daddy say?

She snorts. Who is she kidding? They'd probably buy him two
more to replace it. His mates'll cluster round him, when any fool
knows you leave the fallen man and go after the attacker.

Has Binyan even noticed? Probably not. He's probably
daydreaming about setting his next fire. It's how he got his
nickname.

Spark just about sums him up. Show a normal kid an empty

car or an abandoned building and they look for stuff they can sell on. Spark starts looking for matches.

Weirdo! But she likes him, just the same. They hang out together every day. Binyan calls her Juice.

'Because you've got the juice. You know, the rush, the swagger,' he exclaims, when she presses him for an explanation. 'The juice!'

But Mei knows better. She heard him once, talking to another member of their gang. 'Plum juice, man. It's my favourite.'

Her name means Beautiful Plum. Spark's in love with her. Or so he thinks. That's OK. He never tries anything. Good job, too, 'cause he'd have to learn to piss like a girl if he did.

She nudges him.

'I spy dinner,' she murmurs.

Spark nods. 'I got your back,' he mutters.

It's a tried and tested routine. She goes in for the kill, Spark lingers, ready to trip a pursuer or generally get in the way: whichever'll give Mei time to get away with the loot. Then they find somewhere quiet to divvy up the spoils.

The snazzily-dressed trio are about five metres away now. They've got that look. Not just the money. The confidence.

It comes from knowing they're protected. Not by bodyguards, nothing so obvious. Though she and Spark aren't averse to rolling the odd executive or tourist dogged by some shaven-headed goon with a bulge on his belt.

No. These kids have *protection*. The only kind that really matters. Their parents are high-ups in the Party. You fuck with them, the Party fucks you straight back. But, like, a thousand times worse.

Last year a girl – who they called Panda, on account of her striking black and white hairdo – pulled a knife on a Party kid and took his wallet.

'Total result,' she crowed later, round the fire on the top of an abandoned building as she showed them the genuine dollar bills the kid'd been carrying around.

Panda turned up dead three days after that. Slung onto a pile of stinking rubbish behind a cafe. Eyes crudely gouged out. Fingers removed. A Party pin hit so hard into the skin of her forehead it had lodged in the bone beneath. Her mouth stuffed with a crumpled sheet of glossy, coloured paper that, when they hooked it out, depicted a smiling Chairman Mao.

In blood-red writing, someone had added an unofficial slogan:

THIEVES NEVER LAUGH FOR LONG

Poor Panda. Mei had stretched out a hand and stroked her cheek. The dried blood gave her skin a sandpapery feel. They couldn't bury her. It wasn't their style, in any case. They just left her and moved on. You had to.

The Party kids are only a couple of metres away now.

Mei's heart is racing. It's mostly excitement. She's never been caught and doesn't intend to start now. Mostly excitement, sure. Maybe a little jag of fear running through the middle of it all like a guitar string vibrating.

'Ready?' she hisses.

'Ready,' Spark hisses back.

Mei takes a step to her left and then, as the Party kids draw level, stumbles sideways and gives the nearest one a hefty bump on the shoulder.

'Hey! What the fuck?'

He spins round. Shiny, well-fed face a mask of righteous indignation. *Where do they learn that expression?* she has time to wonder.

'Sorry, man,' she says holding him by the shoulder with her left hand, while her right snakes inside his Burberry bomber jacket. This style has the inside pocket on the right. 'I tripped. Are you all right? Did I hurt you?'

He sneers. Behind him, his two friends are watching with smirks on their faces.

'Yes, Ren,' one says sarcastically, 'did the street rat hurt you? Shall we call a private ambulance? Shall we get her friend here to fetch you a glass of water?'

'Piss off, Ching!' he snaps. He glares at Mei. 'Of course you didn't hurt me, you little street whore. Now fuck off.'

Which Mei is happy to do, his fat leather wallet nestling inside her own jacket. She and Spark are halfway across the road when a shout goes up.

'Hey! The little bitch stole my wallet!'

'Get her!' the one called Ching shouts.

Without turning her head, Mei shouts, 'Run!'

It's force of habit: Spark doesn't need telling. Together they dart through the traffic, zig-zagging between cars, motorbikes, vans and trucks.

Ignoring the parps and toots from the drivers' horns, Mei streaks for the pavement on the far side of Shennan Avenue, almost bumping into a drably-dressed woman fiddling with oversized sunglasses.

Mei's grinning. The Party kids won't dare chase them into the stinking, smoking traffic; once she and Spark are safe on the other side, they can dodge into an alley and make their way home via the back streets.

There's a loud bang. And a scream. A boy's scream.

Spark's scream.

She looks back, just for a second. Through a gap in the traffic she sees her friend lying in the road. Something's happened to his neck. His head's at completely the wrong angle.

Beyond him, she sees the three rich boys charging towards her. The leading boy, the one she rolled, actually leaps over Spark. His teeth are bared.

'Come here, whore!' he yells.

Tears streaming down her cheeks, Mei sprints away. Poor Spark. She hopes he's just injured. That some kind person will gather him up and take him to hospital.

Yes. That's what will happen. And once he's better, he'll discharge himself and come and find her. But for now, she needs to put some serious distance between her and the rich kids.

Mei reaches the safety of the pavement, although it's choked with people and keeping ahead of the rich kids is proving hard.

Now she can feel it. Fear. She doesn't want to end up like Panda.

She weaves through the oncoming shoppers like a snake, twisting and turning her body while keeping her balance as she races down the street. She's got a destination in mind. A place where she knows every square centimetre: every climbable fence, every blind alley, every elevated walkway, every nook, cranny and hidey-hole.

She reaches the side street that leads to the building site and – *Oh, thank you, thank you!* – it's almost deserted. Just a couple in drab, much-washed, old-people clothes gumming their way through coconut cakes they're eating out of a paper bag.

She skips round them and hurtles through the gates into the deserted site. The workers have all been redeployed to another city project. It's why she and Spark like to hang out here.

She risks a look over her shoulder.

Shit! The lead boy is only twenty metres away.

A lump of concrete the size of a mango whizzes past Wei Mei's head and bounces harmlessly off a corrugated-iron sheet with a loud clang.

'Come back here, bitch!' he screams after her. 'I order you!'

Yeah, like she'd follow *his* orders.

Mei runs on, deeper into the huge building site.

A fire is burning in a blue-painted oil drum. Three peasants from the countryside are gathered round it. They're passing a bottle from one brown hand to another.

They look over, mouths agape. Like they've never seen a sixteen-year-old girl fleeing three Party kids for her life before. Idiots!

Another lump of concrete flies past her head and strikes the oil drum with a boom like the world's most out-of-tune gong. She laughs. He might be rich, he might be protected, but he's got a shit right hand.

Mei streaks around a huge red-and-yellow crane and through the slit in the chain-link fencing she and Spark cut last month. This is the supply yard and it's the perfect place to lose them.

2

Huge piles of stone slabs, bricks and bamboo scaffolding poles everywhere.

She vaults a stack of wooden pallets and skids sharp-left down a narrow corridor between two temporary cabins the workers use.

Then her heart stops. One of the rich kids appears at the far end, turning the light to dark.

'Got you now, bitch,' he says with an evil smile.

Mei turns, intending to run back the other way. Then her hopes explode. Ching is standing at the other end. She's trapped.

3

They advance on her. Walking. More of that confidence they get spoon-fed from the moment they're born.

'I bet she's a virgin,' Ching calls out to his friend.

'Not for much longer!' he calls back.

Mei looks up. The cabins are about two and a half metres tall. Their sides are smooth.

She turns sideways onto the two boys, braces her back against one cabin and her left foot against the other. She's done this before, in the hills where she and Spark found a really cool cliff for practising being famous mountaineers.

With a grunt, she lifts her right foot off the ground and sticks it against the wall at her back.

Now she starts climbing. Push up, reposition left foot. Lift hands and stick the palms against the hot metal. Push up again. Reposition right foot.

The boys have reached the spot where she was standing a moment ago. The one called Ching stretches up a hand and manages to grab her dangling right sneaker. She jerks her knee up, pulling her foot free of his grasping hand, then kicks out and catches him a glancing blow across the face.

'Shit! You broke my cheekbone, bitch. You're going to pay for that,' he screams up at her.

What is he *talking* about? She's wearing knockoff Nike Air Jordans. How the fuck does he think she broke his bone with a squishy lump of foam?

He's jumping up, but she's safely out of range. Another couple of pushes and she's on the roof of the cabin.

She runs to the far side and looks over the edge. It's a big drop to the ground, but there's a pile of empty sacks about two metres out from the cabin. In the distance, she sees the peasants still round their oil drum. The rising heat makes their faces wobble. One looks over, smiles and waves. She sighs. How do they ever think they're going to survive in the city, acting like dumb cows?

The boys are shouting. Calling out. The usual names. Bitch. Whore. Cunt. Mei grins. They're down there and she's up here.

She backs up a few paces, gets into a sprinter's crouch, then hurtles towards the edge, leads with her right foot and leaps, arms outstretched, sailing over the gap, over the hard concrete strewn with cigarette butts and broken glass, and lands with a perfect roll on the pile of sacks.

She rolls to the edge and stands…and comes face-to-face with the third boy. Who she totally forgot about.

He's holding a stave of wood. He swings, but he telegraphs the move with an exaggerated backswing and Mei ducks as the club whistles towards her face.

The wood glances off the side of her head, spinning it round. Her vision darkens and tiny red fireworks pop around the edge of her vision. She staggers, but then is on her feet and running.

'Come back here, you!' he shouts.

Now she hears two more sets of running footsteps. The side of her face is warm. She puts up her hand and her palm comes away covered in blood. It's fine. She's had worse.

Hoping to throw them off by a metre or two, she tips her hips to the right, then suddenly jinks left, scooting round the back of a cute yellow dumper-truck, its scoop full of red sand.

But she's miscalculated.

She's boxed herself in between tight-packed pallets of bricks. She leaps towards the first stack and starts climbing. The toe of her Air Jordan misses the lip where one brick stands proud of its fellows and drags her fingertips painfully out of the crack she's wedged them into.

Searing pain shoots up her left arm, all the way from her fingers to her shoulder. She looks. Two nails have torn down to the quicks.

Then a hand grabs her right shoulder and spins her round. The incoming blow knocks her over, her head narrowly missing the edge of a column of bricks. A kick to her midsection drives the wind from her and she curls into a little ball.

'I've got her,' her attacker shouts. 'Here! I've got the little bitch.'

Groaning with the effort of pulling air into her bruised chest, Mei levers herself into a sitting position, but he kicks her arm out from under her.

'You're going nowhere, cockroach,' he says with a triumphant smile.

Sweat sheens his round face, which is the bright red of a ripe tomato like the ones Mummy Rita used to grow back in the village.

For a second, Mei wishes she'd never left. That she was back there now, wandering the hard-packed red-dirt roads, singing to herself, or helping one of the farmers drive oxen to a new paddy.

The two other boys arrive, out of breath. Panting. Their sleek haircuts are properly mussed up now and they've got smudges on their soap-washed faces. As for the clothes, Mei reckons Mummy and Daddy might have a few sharp words on *that* score.

'You stole Dalei's wallet,' the boy says.

She's identified him as the leader. That makes him the most dangerous. But also it makes the other two vulnerable. They'll look to him for a steer on how it's going to go down. And they get their courage from him, too. So he's the one she needs to deal with first.

'He can get more money. I can't,' Mei spits back, pushing herself away from them with her hands and heels.

He puts his hands on his hips.

'Do you know who we are?'

She thinks of the famous clowns from the State Circus. 'Are you Piggy, Ducks and Uncle Sam?'

He scowls. 'Ha, ha. Our fathers are members of the Shenzhen People's Governing Committee. They're very powerful. You picked the wrong boys, men, I mean, to tangle with.'

The one called Ren looks at his leader. 'Come on, Dalei, I thought we were going to fuck her. I'm as horny as a goat.'

That's when she pulls her knees up to her chest in a lightning-fast crunch, braces her hands against the gritty concrete beneath her and shoots her right leg out. Her heel connects square-on with the front of his expensive American denims. He emits a high-pitched squeal, like a pig when the village butcher draws his long, sharp blade across its throat.

He falls sideways and Mei rolls onto her belly and is on her feet in a second. There's nowhere to escape to, and she's had it with running, anyway.

The one called Dalei looks panicked. His eyes are wide and Mei sees the fear in them. Good. He's not used to his victims fighting back.

He swings wildly at her. She doesn't even have to duck, the blow is so poor. She just leans back a little as his fist passes harmlessly in front of her face. Then she lunges and gives him a faceful of clawed fingers, aiming for the eyes, but content to hit him anywhere on that expanse of fat, pork-fed flesh.

She catches him across the nose and one fingertip slips, disgustingly, inside, but the real damage happens when her index finger, tipped with a torn and dirty nail, scrapes across his eyeball. He screams and his hands fly to his face. Mei shoves him hard and he trips over his own feet and tumbles to the ground.

She turns and meets Ching's incoming fist which chops her across the neck: a vicious blow that sends a spear of agony lancing across her chest and making her feel sick.

Staggering, she lets herself stumble sideways as if she's hurt worse than she is. She crashes against the nearest pallet of bricks, but the sound is mostly where she shoves them with her right hip. She straightens and swings her right hand across in a fast, tight arc.

When she connects with the side of Ching's head, he emits a short, grunting groan. His eyes roll up in their sockets. Mei drops the sharp-cornered brick to the ground. Blood is coursing down his face from the wound to his temple. He is still on his feet.

He groans again; an odd, disconnected sound as if it's coming out of his body and not his mouth. Then he falls sideways, slamming into the pile of bricks before coming to rest on the ground. A pool of dark-red blood the colour of ripe plums spreads out beneath his head.

A hand grabs her ankle. She looks down. Dalei, is it? The one whose eye is closed and weeping a slimy mixture streaked with red. He's trying to pull himself to his feet using her leg as a support.

'I'll kill you, you little whore,' he croaks.

'Not today,' she says.

She stamps hard on his other hand and hears a crackle like dry twigs snapping.

Yowling like an alley-cat, he lets go of her ankle. Mei turns to see Ren, still rolling around, both hands clutching his private parts. Funny. She'd have thought he'd be feeling better by now. But time slows down when you're fighting. She thinks about braining him with a brick, then shakes her head. They've learned their lesson.

She's about to go, then smiles. Taps her forehead. *Silly me!*

Bending, she relieves the other two boys of their wallets and sprints away from them. She stops briefly at the group of peasants round the improvised brazier. Hands them one of the wallets.

'Here. No need to go to work today,' she says with a grin, then runs off back towards the street.

She fails to notice the new arrival among the group, a woman dressed in a dowdy blue smock and loose matching pants. Perhaps

3

because the adrenaline is messing with her perception. Or maybe just because the woman seems so utterly insignificant, even among a boring group of country bumpkins.

© 2025 Sunfish Ltd

Published by Tyton Press, an imprint of Sunfish Ltd, PO Box 2107, Salisbury SP2 2BW.

The right of Andy Maslen to be identified as the author of this work has been asserted by him in accordance with the Copyright, Designs and Patents Act 1988.

Cover illustration copyright © Nick Castle

Author photograph © Kin Ho

Edited by Liz Ward

❧ Created with Vellum

ACKNOWLEDGMENTS

I want to thank you for buying this book. I hope you enjoyed it.

As an author is only part of the team of people who make a book the best it can be, this is my chance to thank the people on *my* team.

The serving and former soldiers whose advice helped me to keep the military details accurate: Giles Bassett, Mark Budden, Mike Dempsey and Dickie Gittins.

For his insightful first read and suggestions, my first reader and sternest critic, Simon Alphonso.

For her brilliant copy-editing and proofreading, Liz Ward.

For his super-cool cover, my designer, Nick Castle.

The members of my Facebook Group, The Wolfe Pack, who are an incredibly supportive and also helpful bunch of people. Thank you to them, also.

And for being an inspiration and source of love and laughter, and making it all worthwhile, my family: Jo, Rory and Jacob.

The responsibility for any and all mistakes in this book remains mine.

Andy Maslen
    Salisbury, 2025

ABOUT THE AUTHOR

Photo © 2020 Kin Ho

Andy Maslen was born in Nottingham, England. After leaving university with a degree in psychology, he worked in business for thirty years as a copywriter. In his spare time, he plays the guitar. He lives in Wiltshire.

Printed in Dunstable, United Kingdom

67292781R00228